ACROSS AMERICA—RAVES FOR
Bread Upon the Waters

"DECEPTIVELY SIMPLE . . . THIS DANGEROUS HIGH-WIRE ACT, THE BLENDING OF A FAST-PACED STORY WITH THOUGHTFUL INTROSPECTION, IS EXECUTED WITH SEEMING EFFORTLESSNESS. . . . [SHAW] FLESHES OUT EACH OF THE MAJOR CHARACTERS, GIVING THEM DIMENSION AND REALITY, WHILE DEVOTING AS MUCH CARE AND ATTENTION TO THE LARGE CAST OF SUPPORTING CHARACTERS WHO MOVE THROUGH HIS INTRICATE AND SURPRISING PLOT. . . . IRWIN SHAW IS A THOROUGH PROFESSIONAL, A WORD USED HERE WITH ADMIRATION AND RESPECT."
—Evan Hunter, *The New York Times Book Review*

"A BREAKTHROUGH—SURELY HIS BEST NOVEL. . . . ONE IS CAUGHT UP IN, MESMERIZED BY, THE INTER-PLAY OF CHANGING RELATIONSHIPS. . . . A GRIPPING STORY."   —Clifton Fadiman, *Book-of-the-Month Club News*

"SHAW'S BEST NOVEL IN YEARS. DEEPLY FELT, IT IS PART CINDERELLA STORY, PART UNABASHED MO-RALITY PLAY, AND ALL THE WORK OF A MASTERLY TELLER OF TALES. IT'S EASY TO READ, HARD TO FOR-GET."   —*The Plain Dealer* (Cleveland)

"AS AN ENTERTAINMENT, AS AN EXAMINATION OF HUMAN SORROW AND HAPPINESS AND AS A WEL-COME RETURN TO TOP FORM FOR SHAW, *BREAD UPON THE WATERS* IS BUOYANT."
—*Pittsburgh Post-Gazette*

BOOKS BY *IRWIN SHAW*

NOVELS

The Young Lions
The Troubled Air
Lucy Crown
Two Weeks in Another Town
Voices of a Summer Day
Rich Man, Poor Man
Evening in Byzantium
Nightwork
Beggarman, Thief
The Top of the Hill
Bread Upon the Waters

SHORT STORY COLLECTIONS

Sailor off the Bremen
Welcome to the City
Act of Faith
Mixed Company
Tip on a Dead Jockey
Love on a Dark Street
God Was Here, but He Left Early
Five Decades

PLAYS

Bury the Dead
The Gentle People
Sons and Soldiers
The Assassin
Children from Their Games

NONFICTION

In the Company of Dolphins
Paris! Paris!

IRWIN SHAW

Bread Upon the Waters

A DELL BOOK

TO IRVING PAUL LAZAR

Published by
Dell Publishing Co., Inc.
1 Dag Hammarskjold Plaza
New York, New York 10017

Dell ® TM 681510, Dell Publishing Co., Inc.
ISBN: 0-440-10845-4
Reprinted by arrangement with Delacorte Press
Printed in the United States of America
First Dell printing—July 1982

PART ONE

*"Cast thy bread upon the waters,
for thou shalt find it after many days."*

ECCLESIASTES 11:1

1

He was in a strange bed. There was murmuring around him. An impression of white. Machinery. The sound of the distant breaking of the sea against the shore. Or perhaps the liquid surf of his blood, pulsing against interior walls. He was floating—somewhere. It was difficult for him to open his eyes, the lids were heavy. There was a man walking in spring sunshine. He had the impression he had met the man before. Finally, he realized, it was himself. . . .

Attired in mismatched flapping clothes, Allen Strand strode into the fragrant green hush of Central Park, the rumble of Fifth Avenue diminishing behind him. He walked slowly, his weekend pace. On work days he loped, his tall, lean figure crowned by a long narrow head, his nose, a sharp, inherited bowsprit, leaning into a private oceanic wind. His wing of straight, iron-gray hair flashed in the up and down sea motion of his stride. His daughter Eleanor, after meeting him once by accident on the street, had said she almost expected to see a bow wave curling around his prow as he sailed through the currents of city traffic.

The thought that he was going to see Eleanor that evening pleased him. She had a sharp eye and sharp tongue, and her observations were not always benign, but the glint of weapons she brought to the family dinner table made him look forward, as he strolled along the bench-bordered path, to what otherwise might have been a dutiful weekly ritual.

It had been gray and windy that morning, and he had thought it would be a good afternoon to get on a bus and go down to the Museum of Modern Art, of which he was a member—one of his few extravagances—and see a movie before dinner. That afternoon they were showing *Fort Apache*. It was a delicious retelling of a naive and heroic American myth, an antidote to doubt. He had seen it several times before, but he was attached to it, like a child who insists upon hearing the same story read to him each night before sleep. But the wind had died down by noon and the sky had cleared and he had decided to forgo the film for one of his favorite walks, several miles west toward home from the high school in which he taught.

This Friday it was warm and summery, the gift of May, the grass redolent of simpler country, the leaves of the trees a pale lime in the late afternoon sunshine. He dawdled, stopped to chuckle at a poodle running bravely after a pigeon, watched boys play an inning of softball, admired a handsome young man and his pretty girl, smiling dreamily, conspiratorially, their faces glowing with the promise of the weekend's sensuality as they approached along the path, oblivious of him.

The flesh of May, he thought. Praise God for spring and Friday. He was an indifferent Christian but the afternoon called for gratitude and belief.

He was unencumbered. He had corrected the week's test papers, the aftermath of the Civil War, and left Appomattox and the Reconstruction in his desk. For two days the children he had taught and graded were not his responsibility; at the moment they were hooting at games in playgrounds or experimenting with sex on tenement rooftops or hidden in hallways smoking marijuana or filling syringes with heroin bought, it was said, from the fat man in a baseball cap who stationed himself regularly at a street corner near the school. His hands free, Strand bent and picked up a small round stone and carried it with him for a while, linked to glaciers, enjoying the feel of the smooth ungiving curved surface, warmed by the day's sun.

Dinner would be late tonight, with the whole family assembled, and he went out of his way a bit to pass by the park tennis courts, where he knew his younger daughter,

Caroline, would be playing. She was a dedicated athlete. No marijuana or heroin for her, he thought complacently, generously pitying less fortunate parents. The holiday weather invited generosity and complacency.

Even at a distance from the court he recognized Caroline from the way she moved. She had a bouncy determined style of running for the ball and an almost boyish mannerism of running her fingers through her short blond hair between points.

The young man she was playing with seemed frail in comparison to Caroline, who, although slender, was tall for her age, full-bosomed and broad-shouldered, with long, well-shaped legs, legs that were admirably public under the brief tennis shorts and which Strand could see were being appreciated by the male passersby.

No marijuana or heroin, Strand thought, but what about sex? These days, a girl seventeen years old. . . . He shook his head. What had he been doing when he was seventeen—earlier even—and how old had the girls been with whom he had done it? Better not to remember. Anyway, sex was Caroline's mother's department and he was sure it had been satisfactorily taken care of, if something like that ever could be satisfactorily taken care of. He, himself, had done the necessary with his son and he had detected no later signs of revulsion or fear or undue fascination with the subject in the boy.

Although the young man on the other side of the court seemed stringy and undernourished to Strand, he hit the ball hard and the exchanges were sharp and equal. Strand waited for Caroline to hit a hard overhead smash and then called out "Bravo." She turned and waved her racquet at him and came over to the fence behind which he was standing and blew him a kiss. Her face was red and her hair was wet with perspiration, but Strand thought she looked delightful, even though the exercise had drawn the lines of her face tight, which made her nose, unfortunately shaped like a smaller model of his own, stand out more than it did when her plumpish face was at rest.

"Hi, Daddy," she said. "He's killing me—Stevie. Hey, Stevie," she called, "come and say hello to my father."

"I don't want to interrupt your game," Strand said.

"It gives me a chance to breathe," Caroline said. "I can use it."

Stevie came along the fence, brushing at the hair at the back of his head.

"I'm glad to meet you, sir," Stevie said politely. "Caroline tells me you were her first tennis teacher."

"She started to beat me when she was nine. Now I just watch," Strand said.

"She beats me, too," Stevie said, with a sad little smile.

"Only on days when you're in the depths of depression," Caroline said.

"I wish you wouldn't say things like that, Caroline," Stevie said crossly. "I sometimes find it difficult to concentrate, that's all. That isn't depression."

"Come on, now," Caroline said, with a comradely push of her hand against the boy's shoulder, "I wasn't suggesting anything *extreme*—like you going home and crying yourself to sleep when you lose a set or anything like that. I was joking."

"I just don't want people to get the wrong idea," the boy repeated stubbornly.

"Don't be so sensitive. Or be sensitive on your own time," Caroline said. "He's not usually like this, Daddy. He doesn't like people watching him play."

"I can understand that," Strand said diplomatically. "I'd still be playing tennis if I could figure out a way to do it in utter darkness. I'll be getting along, anyway."

"Very glad to have met you, sir," the boy said and went back to the other side of the net, pushing at the hair at the back of his neck.

"Forgive him, Daddy," Caroline said. "He had a *ghastly* childhood."

"It doesn't seem to have affected his tennis game," Strand said. "How has your ghastly childhood affected yours?"

"Oh, Daddy"—Caroline waved her racquet at him—"don't tease."

"See you at home. Don't be too late." He watched two more points, marveling at how swift the two young people were as their metal racquets made gleaming slashes in the air. Even when he had been their age he had not been quick. Fast reader, he thought as he started toward home again, and slow, deliberate runner. A choice of talents. No matter. He had bred a surrogate for speed.

The superintendent of the building, Alexander, was leaning against the wall to one side of the glass front door, smoking a cigar, scowling. He was a light tan man of indeterminate age with a close-cropped cap of gray hair and he was not one to smile easily. Given the neighborhood, which was on the thin edge of respectability with Columbus Avenue at the far end of the street and the howl of police sirens a frequent melody, one could understand why he was not often caught smiling.

"Evening, Alexander," Strand said.

"Evening, Mr. Strand." Alexander did not take the cigar out of his mouth. He was one of the last remaining men in New York who still wore a World War II combat jacket, as though for him the war had just entered into a different phase.

"Fine day, wasn't it?" Strand liked the man and appreciated the way he worried the old 1910 apartment building into passable condition.

"Okay," Alexander said, grudgingly. "We had it coming after the bitch of a winter. It won't last long, though. They say it's rain tomorrow." Optimism, like geniality, was not Alexander's strong point. "Your missus is home," he volunteered. "And your boy." He made a point of knowing who came in and out of his building. He liked orderly and recorded exits and entrances. It reduced unpleasant surprises.

"Thanks," Strand said. He had given Alexander twenty-five dollars and a bottle of Wild Turkey at Easter. His wife had protested at the magnitude of Strand's largesse, but Strand had told her, "We owe it to him. He is the sentinel who protects us from chaos." Alexander had thanked Strand briefly—but his attitude had not changed noticeably.

When Strand opened the door to his apartment, he

heard two kinds of music—the piano in the living room and the plaintive faint twanging of an electric guitar. There was also a delicious smell of cooking coming from the kitchen. He smiled at the combination of stimuli with which he had been greeted. The sound of the piano was from a lesson his wife, Leslie, was giving. She had gone to Juilliard with the intention of becoming a concert pianist, but while she played well she did not play well enough for that. Now the piano lessons and the music appreciation courses she taught three days a week at the private preparatory school not far from where they lived helped out considerably with the family budget as well as supplying an education tuition-free to Caroline. Without Leslie's help, in the face of ever-rising rents, they could never have kept the old rambling apartment, with its spacious, other-age rooms and high ceilings.

The tentative cadence of the guitar, considerately muffled by closed doors, was that of his son, Jimmy, who had inherited his mother's talent if not her taste in the composers he preferred.

Strand did not disturb either of the artists at their labors, but went into the dining room, where he couldn't hear the guitar, but could hear first the student, then Leslie, easily distinguishable from each other, going over a passage he recognized as from a Chopin étude. Because of it he knew who the student was: a television scriptwriter with a passion for Chopin. He had been told by his analyst that playing the piano would lessen tension. His tension might be lessened. Strand thought as he listened, but Chopin would never be in his debt.

Leslie had a mixed bag of students—among them a policeman with a good ear and harsh fingers who practiced all his off-time; a thirteen year old whose parents thought she was a genius, an opinion not shared by Leslie; a lawyer who said he would gladly play the piano in a brothel rather than appear in court; and several music teachers who wanted help in preparing their courses. All of whom gave Leslie a lively and interesting profession in her own home.

Strand loved music and when he could afford it took Leslie to the opera, and although from time to time he winced at some of the sounds that emanated from the living room and his son's bedroom, he liked the idea of the apartment being almost continually filled with melody. When he worked at home there was a desk in the big master bedroom where he could read or write in silence.

Strand hummed softly with the passage his wife was playing for the benefit of the neurotic TV writer. Seated at the round, battered oak table in the dining room, whose walls were decorated with the landscapes his wife painted in her spare time, he glanced at the copy of *The New York Times* lying on the table. Doom, he thought as he reached for an apple from the bowl of fruit that was in the middle of the table. As he ate he scanned the headlines of the paper that Leslie always left for him because he never had time to finish it in the morning. He was half through with the apple when the sound of the piano stopped and the sliding doors between the dining and living rooms were thrown open. Strand stood up as Leslie entered, followed by the television writer. "Oh, you're home," Leslie said, kissing him on the cheek. "I didn't hear you come in."

"I was enjoying the concert," Strand said. His wife smelled fresh and appetizing. Her long blond hair, tied up on top of her head now, was in disarray because of her habit of nodding vigorously when she played. What a nice woman to come home to, he thought. She had been a student of his in her senior year, and the first day he had seen her sitting demurely in the front row of his classroom he had decided that she was the girl he was going to marry. Schools in New York were different then. Girls wore dresses and combed their hair and did not think it outlandish to look demure. He had waited until she was graduated, had taken careful note of her address, had called on her and to the dismay of her parents, who considered his choice of teaching in a public school a mark of predestined lifelong failure, he had married her after her first year at Juilliard. The parents had changed their minds a little by the time Eleanor was born, but not much. Anyway, they now lived in Palm Springs, and he did not read the letters they wrote to Leslie.

"I hope the noise didn't bother you," the television writer said.

"Not at all," Strand said. "You're coming along nicely, I must say, Mr. Crowell."

"You must have been listening while your wife was at the piano," Crowell said gloomily. His tension did not seem to have lessened noticeably since a week ago Friday.

Strand laughed. "I can tell the difference, Mr. Crowell."

"I bet you can," Crowell said.

"Mr. Crowell and I are going to have a cup of tea, Allen," Leslie said. "Will you join us?"

"Love to."

"I'll just be a minute," Leslie said. "The kettle's on." As she went into the kitchen Strand admired her slender figure, the curve of her neck, the blue skirt and white, schoolgirlish blouse she wore, her firm legs, her fair, soft resemblance to his eldest daughter.

"Marvelous woman, that," Crowell said. "The patience of an angel."

"Are you married, Mr. Crowell?"

"Twice," Crowell said darkly. "And I'm working on a third. I'm up to my ears in alimony." He had a pudgy, tormented face, like a blighted peeled potato. Leslie had told Strand that the man wrote gags for situation comedies. From Crowell's face, it seemed a harrowing profession. He paid twenty dollars a half hour for his lessons, twice a week, so the pain must have been well rewarded, especially since he went to an analyst five times a week. Modern American economy, Strand thought. One-liners, the couch, and alimony.

"Some day," Crowell was saying, "we must have a drink together and you can tell me how a man can stay married in this day and age."

"I haven't the faintest idea," Strand said lightly. "Luck. Sloth. A conservative distaste for change."

"Yeah," Crowell said disbelievingly, pulling at the fingers of his pudgy hands. He glanced at the newspaper spread out on the table. "You can still stand to read the newspapers?" he said.

"A vice," Strand said.

"They drive me up the wall."

"Sit down, sit down," Leslie said, coming in from the kitchen carrying the tea things and a plate of cookies on a tray. She poured, her hand firm, a slight housewifely smile on her face, and passed the cookies. Crowell shook his head sadly. "On a diet," he said. "Cholesterol, pressure. The lot."

Strand helped himself to a handful. He didn't drink much and never had smoked but he had a sweet tooth. He hadn't gained a pound since he was twenty and he noticed Crowell staring glumly at the small mound of biscuits on his saucer. Crowell would have liked milk with his tea but when he asked if it was skim milk and was told by Leslie that it wasn't, drank his tea as it was, without sugar.

Leslie, acting like a hostess, asked Crowell if he wouldn't like to abandon Chopin for a while and try a little Mozart, but Crowell said he'd rather not, Mozart was too damn sure of himself for his taste.

"He had a tragic end," Leslie reminded him. "Very young."

"Tragic end or no tragic end," Crowell said, "he always knew just where he was going. Chopin at least was melancholy."

Leslie sighed. "As you say, Mr. Crowell," she said. "We'll go on to the Waltz in E Flat Major next Tuesday."

"In my head," Crowell volunteered, "I hear just the way it should come out. Only it never comes out that way."

"Practice," Leslie said tactfully. She had a low, musical voice, like a soft minor chord on the piano. "It will come."

"Do you mean that, Mrs. Strand?" Crowell asked accusingly.

Leslie hesitated. "No," she said, then laughed.

Strand laughed, too, chewing on a cookie, and finally Crowell laughed, too.

When he had gone, Strand helped Leslie carry the tea things into the kitchen. He embraced her from behind while she was tying on an apron and kissed the back of her neck and put his hand on her breast. "You know what I'd like to do now?" he said.

"Ssh," Leslie said. "Jimmy's in the house and he never knocks on doors."

"I didn't say I'd *do* it. I just said I'd *like* to do it."

"There must be some reason you think you ought to flatter me today," Leslie said, smiling. "Or else you've had an especially pleasant afternoon."

"A nice walk through the park. The sap is rising everywhere." Strand released her. "I saw Caroline playing tennis."

"That girl," Leslie said. "She'll develop legs like a weight lifter."

"There doesn't seem to be any danger so far."

"Who was Caroline playing with?" Leslie stirred a sauce that was simmering in a pan on the stove.

"A new one," Strand said. "Plays a nice game. But from what I could tell—well—a little too fine for my taste."

"I hope you didn't give him your old-fashioned father-of-a-virgin stare."

"Whatever are you talking about?" Strand said, although he knew well enough. After more than twenty-three years of marriage they had yet to agree on standards of proper behavior, especially for the young. Leslie was invincibly open-minded and said of her husband, sometimes with amusement, sometimes without, that although there was only a seven-year difference in their ages, they were three generations apart.

"You know what I'm talking about," Leslie said. "I've seen what you did with one look to some of Eleanor's poor young men when she started having beaux. You turned them into stalagmites before they had a chance to say hello."

"They ought to have thanked me," Strand said, enjoying the little argument. "I fitted them for the trials of their later lives. Do you remember the climate in *your* house when I first came around?"

Leslie chuckled. "Polar," she said. "One of the things I admired about you was that you didn't seem to notice it at all. But then you were a grown man."

"Your father helped make me a grown man."

"Well," Leslie said, "he did a good job of it."

"Thank you, my dear." Strand bowed ironically.

"Anyway, if Caroline wants to play tennis with somebody who can give her a decent game, who cares what he does when he's not on the court? I think I know him. Did Caroline introduce him?"

"Name of Stevie. She didn't think it worthwhile to tell me his last name."

"Stevie. That's it. He's been here once or twice in the afternoon. A very nice boy."

Strand sighed. "If you had to battle with the kids I see five days a week, you might change your attitude a bit about the innocent young."

"You ought to ask for a transfer to a more civilized school," Leslie said. "I've told you a thousand times."

"Tell that to the Board of Education," Strand said, picking up another cookie. "As far as they're concerned, there are no civilized schools. Anyway I like the challenge. Anybody can teach history at Saint Paul or Exeter." He wasn't quite sure that this was true, but it sounded convincing.

"You let everybody take advantage of you," Leslie said, stirring vigorously.

Strand sighed again. This was an old story between them. "I bet," he said, "the Duke of Wellington's wife thought he let everybody take advantage of him."

Leslie laughed. "When you begin to throw historical figures at me," she said, "I know I've lost the argument. Get out of my kitchen. I have to concentrate on dinner."

"It smells heavenly. What're we having?"

"Piccata of veal, pizzaiola. Leave me alone now. I have to think Italian."

As he went out the door, back into the dining room, Strand said, "The least we could do is prevail upon Jimmy not to open doors without knocking. Especially on weekends."

"He's your son," Leslie said. "Prevail." She waved him away.

Well, he thought as he sat down at the table and picked

up the newspaper again, one thing is sure—we find plenty of things to talk about.

He was reading when Jimmy sauntered in, barefooted, in jeans and sweatshirt, his thick curly black hair, a genetic throwback in the blond family, chopped off low on the nape of his neck. The nose, though, was undoubtedly his father's. "Hi, Pops," Jimmy said, collapsing into a chair, "how're they treating you?"

"I'm still standing," Strand said. Jimmy was the only one of his children who called him Pops. He squinted a little at his son. "Which is more than I can say for you. Have you looked into a mirror recently?"

"I'm above small vanities like that, Pops," Jimmy said easily.

"You look positively gaunt. People will think we never feed you. Have you eaten anything today?"

"I only got up a couple of hours ago. I'll do justice to Mom's dinner."

"What time did you get in this morning?"

Jimmy shrugged. "What difference does it make? Four, five. Who keeps track?"

"Sometime, Jimmy," Strand said, a touch of irony in his voice, "you must tell your old man what you find to do till five o'clock in the morning."

"I'm searching for the new sound, Pops," Jimmy said. "I play or I listen to music."

"I understand they stop the music at Carnegie Hall well before five o'clock in the morning."

Jimmy laughed, scratched under the sweatshirt. "Carnegie Hall isn't where it's at this year. Haven't you heard?"

"You have purple rings under your eyes down to your shoulders."

"The girls love it," Jimmy said complacently. "It makes me look like a haunted genius, one of them told me. Don't you want me to look like a haunted genius?"

"Not particularly."

Jimmy took a wrinkled pack of cigarettes from his jeans pocket and lit up. Strand watched disapprovingly as Jimmy inhaled and blew the smoke out of his nostrils. He was the only one in the family who smoked.

"Jimmy," Strand asked, "do you ever read what scientists say about the relation between smoking and cancer?"

"Do you ever read what the scientists say about atomic pollution?"

Strand sighed, the third time since he'd come home that evening. "Okay," he said resignedly. "You're old enough to make your own decisions." Jimmy was eighteen and made enough money at odd jobs he never explained so that he never had to ask Strand for any. He had finished high school, not disgracefully, a year ago, and had laughed when Strand had suggested college.

"Tell me, Jimmy," Strand said, "I'm curious—just what is this new sound you keep talking about?"

"If I knew, Pops, I wouldn't be searching for it," Jimmy said airily.

"Will you tell me when you find it?"

"The sarcasm's getting pretty heavy around here, isn't it," Jimmy said, but without rancor. "Okay, I'll tell you. If and when."

Strand stood up. "I'm going to shower and change for dinner," he said. "How about you?"

"Oh, it's Friday," Jimmy said, standing. "Thanks for reminding me. Don't worry, Pops." He put his arm affectionately around Strand's shoulder. "I'll shine myself up." He sniffed. "I see Mom's still in her Italian period. I'd hang around here if it was only for the food."

"May I suggest a shave while you're at it?"

"Suggestion noted." He squeezed Strand's shoulder lightly. "I have a great idea—why don't you go on my rounds with me some night? I'll introduce you as one of the New Orleans pioneers of boogie-woogie. The girls'll fall all over you."

Strand laughed, warmed by his son's touch on his shoulder. "They'd never let you in again."

"Now," Jimmy said seriously, "let me ask *you* a question. Do *you* ever look in a mirror?"

"Occasionally."

"Does it occur to you from time to time that you don't look so good yourself?" His face was earnest now. "You look awfully tired, Pops."

"I feel all right," Strand said shortly.

"I have a few bucks I've saved," Jimmy said. "After school's over, what if I stake you and Mom to a couple of weeks on the beach somewhere?"

"Thanks, Jimmy," Strand said. "Hold on to your money. You'll undoubtedly need it—and soon. Anyway, I like the city in the summertime."

"Okay." Jimmy shrugged. "Have it your way. But if you change your mind . . ."

"I won't change my mind."

"You're a stubborn old dude." Jimmy shook his head and dropped his arm from Strand's shoulders and stubbed out his cigarette. "Have it your own way. And if you happen to find the new sound, come on in with it. The door's always open for you." He started toward the kitchen. "I've got to see just where that drooly smell is coming from."

When he went into the bathroom to take his shower Strand looked at himself in the mirror. Jimmy was right. He *did* look tired. There were bags under his eyes and the eyes themselves and the skin of his face looked faded. He fought the temptation to lie down and take a nap. If Leslie came in and found him dozing on the bed, she'd worry and ask him if he wasn't feeling well, because he never napped in the afternoon. He didn't want her telling him that he was overworked and ought to see a doctor. He stayed in the shower a long time and turned it on ice-cold at the end. As he started dressing for dinner he felt better even if the mirror didn't show him *looking* any better. Fifty is no age to feel old, he told himself, even after a week's work.

When he went back to the dining room, Eleanor was setting the table. "Hi, baby," he said, and kissed her. "How're things?"

"I'm rising like a rocket in the office hierarchy," she said, putting napkins in place. "My boss says he expects me to be the first woman vice president of the company in ten years. He says that when we work together he forgets I'm a pretty girl. What do you think of that?"

"I think he's making a pass at you."

"Of course," she said complacently. "With no luck. But I think he's off by a couple of years. On the high side."

She worked as a computer systems analyst for a big conglomerate concern on Park Avenue. She had been a mathematics major and had taken computer courses in college and she was quick and had a confident and no-nonsense manner. She had been with the concern for only two years but was already entrusted to set up computer programs for all sorts of businesses and institutions in and out of New York. Her passion for her work was very much like Leslie's devotion to music. Eleanor had tried to explain it to her father, who was fearful of the fate of ordinary humanity in an increasingly computerized and impersonal world. "It's like producing order out of chaos by stretching your imagination and your talent to its limits. You go into a hospital, say, and you see duplications of work, human error, time being wasted that might cost lives —honest but faulty diagnoses that a machine can correct in a matter of seconds, doctors mired down hunting through records when they could be relieving pain—and presto, you set up a system and you have the pleasure of seeing everything fall into place, everything working, and you know it's your doing. And it's the same thing in a business. By the simplest of means you free poor, haunted clerks from thousands of hours of boredom. Contrary to what you believe, Dad, it makes humanity more human—not less."

Strand admired her eloquence and dedication but remained unconvinced, although he was happy that she was not content to be merely a pretty girl. She had gone away to college, working at summer jobs and tutoring during the school year to pay her way, and she now lived alone in a small apartment in the East Seventies. It had been a sad moment for Strand when she announced, the day she received her degree, that she no longer wanted to share the room in the family apartment with her kid sister. Neither Strand nor Leslie had objected; as they told each other, Eleanor was a capable, level-headed girl and could take care of herself and it was only normal for young people to strike out on their own. And as Eleanor had said, "It isn't as though I'm going off to Lapland or Peru. I'll be just across the park and when I'm in trouble I'll scream so loud you'll hear me right across the reservoir." Until now, she hadn't screamed. When she got her job and told her father what her salary was, he congratulated her, a little ruefully, since, fresh out of college, she was making more than he was after twenty-seven years in the public school system.

"I'm getting a three-week vacation this summer," Eleanor said, starting to put a corkscrew into one of the two bottles of Chianti on the sideboard, "two weeks paid and one week unpaid and I want to go to someplace new. Have you any ideas, Dad?"

"Ummn." Strand pulled reflectively at his ear. "That depends. Are you going alone?"

The cork came out with a pop and Eleanor put the bottle on the table. She turned and looked squarely at her father. "No," she said flatly.

"A young man, no doubt."

"No doubt." She smiled.

"What does he want to do?"

"He's not quite sure. He's making noises about going to a Greek island and just lying on the beach and swimming."

"That doesn't sound too bad," Strand said.

"He promises there won't be any computers or even a typewriter on the island. He says I'll come back to my job with renewed zest." Eleanor touched up a small bunch of flowers she had brought with her and put into a bowl in the middle of the table. "He's been there before." She smiled. "With another lady."

"He told you that?" Strand asked, trying to keep the tone of censure out of his voice.

"He tells me everything," she said. "He's one of those."

"Different times," Strand said, trying to make his voice light, "different whatever it is. In my time . . ." He stopped and grinned. "In my time, nothing. Do you tell him everything?"

"Selected everything." Eleanor laughed.

"Why don't you bring him around some evening?"

"He's not big on families, he says. Anyway, I'm not sure about him. Yet. We'll see if he passes the three-week test. Then maybe I'll expose him to the elements."

"Well," Strand said, "send me a postcard. I wouldn't mind a Greek island myself. And not only for three weeks, either. Maybe when I retire . . ."

Eleanor came over to him and put her arms around him and looked seriously up at him. She was shorter than her sister and more slender and she had inherited her pretty straight nose and deep blue eyes from her mother. "It seems awfully unfair, doesn't it?" she said softly. "My being able to go off like that for three weeks after working just about two years and you . . ."

Strand patted her back gently. "We're not suffering. We opted for a family. You don't have a family . . . yet."

"Hallelujah," Eleanor said.

Leslie came in from the kitchen, taking off her apron. "Dinner's just about ready," she said. "Mrs. Curtis is all set to serve." Mrs. Curtis was Alexander's wife, and she helped out three times a week. "Are we all here?"

"Caroline's not in yet," Eleanor said, breaking away from her father.

"That's strange," Leslie said. "It's been dark for fifteen minutes. She can't still be playing tennis. And she knows what time we eat."

"She probably stopped for a soda or something," Strand said. "Give us time for a drink. Leslie, Eleanor?" He went over to the sideboard and opened the cupboard where there was a bottle of whiskey and a bottle of sherry.

"Nothing for me, thanks," Eleanor said. Strand had never seen her drink except for a little wine, and he wondered if she was as abstinent when she dined with the young man who told her everything or only reserved her sobriety for her parents. Selected everything, as she had just said.

"I'll take a glass of sherry," Leslie said.

As Strand poured the sherry and a Scotch and water for himself, Jimmy came in, showered and clean, smelling of soap. "Hi, Eleanor," he said. "How's the beauty of the family?"

"Working her fingers to the bone," Eleanor said. "My, you look shiny tonight."

"In your honor," Jimmy said. "When you grace the family board with your presence the least I can do is shave."

"You know, you actually look handsome," Eleanor said, "when you pull yourself together. A little bit like a Corsican bandit cleaned up for Mass."

Jimmy grinned. "I have my fans. In modest numbers."

"Jimmy," Strand said. "We're having a drink, your mother and I. Want to join us?"

Jimmy shook his head. "Have to keep in training for the Olympics."

"Olympics?" Eleanor asked incredulously. "What Olympics?"

"1966," Jimmy said, grinning again. "I expect to take the gold medal for instant gratification."

"My money's on you, brother," Eleanor said.

They were competitive with each other and Eleanor didn't hide her disapproval of Jimmy's mode of life and choice of companions. Jimmy, who had a high opinion of his sister's intelligence, in his turn was contemptuous of Eleanor's wasting her life, as he put it, wallowing in what he called the brainless, computerized, bourgeois water bed. There was an unformed and unaimed leftishness in Jimmy's occasional outbursts that was troubling to Strand, with his ordered, pragmatic view of the society they were saddled with, but he didn't attempt to argue with the boy. The inevitable throes of youth, he told himself when Jimmy sounded off. He knew Jimmy and Eleanor were genuinely fond of each other, but sometimes their exchanges became unpleasantly wounding.

He cleared his throat loudly and raised his glass. "To . . . well . . ." He turned toward Eleanor. "To Greece."

Leslie looked puzzled. "What about Greece?"

"I'll tell you later, Mother," Eleanor said. "Girly talk."

"The poor cook misses everything in the kitchen. All the gossip," Leslie said, sipping at her sherry. "Well, if Caroline doesn't turn up in the next five minutes we'll just have to sit down without her. Did she say she'd be late when you saw her, Allen?"

"No." The Scotch was his first drink of the week and he was rolling it around in his mouth appreciatively before swallowing it when the doorbell rang.

"That must be Caroline," Leslie said, "but she has her key . . ."

The bell didn't stop ringing, a long, loud, constant clamor.

"Good Lord," Leslie said. "She knows we aren't deaf."

Jimmy glanced quickly at his father. Strand could see the look of alarm on his son's face and had the feeling it reflected the expression on his own.

"I'll get it," Jimmy said and hurried out of the dining room. Strand put his glass down and followed him, trying to seem casual. Jimmy was just opening the door when Strand reached the hallway. Stumbling, half-falling, Caroline lurched through the doorway. She was supporting a man, whose head was lolling on his chest, and they were both covered with blood.

2

"He's exactly your age," he heard a voice saying, or re-membered he'd heard a voice say. A familiar voice...

Jimmy sprang forward and tried to put his arms around both his sister and the man she was holding and Strand lunged to help him. The man groaned.

"I'm all right," Caroline said, gasping. "Hold on to *him*. It's his blood, not mine." She was still holding her tennis racquet in her free hand. The sweater and jeans she had put on over her tennis clothes were stained. She released her grip on the man as Strand held him up with his arms around the man's waist. He was a big man and heavy, a nasty swollen cut across his completely bald head and alongside his temple and left cheek. The leather wind-jacket he wore was slashed in a dozen places. He struggled to raise his head and stand erect. "I'm all right," he mum-bled. "Please don't bother, sir. I'll just sit down for a moment and . . ." He slumped again in Strand's arms.

"What's happening here?" Strand heard his wife's voice behind him. "Oh, my God."

"Nothing serious, my dear lady," the man mumbled, trying to smile. "Really."

"Eleanor," Leslie said, "go call Dr. Prinz and tell him he must come over immediately."

"No need, really," the man said, his voice growing clear-er. With an effort he stood up straight. "My own doctor will take care of it presently. I don't want to trouble . . ."

"Take him into the living room," Leslie said crisply, "and put him down on the couch. Eleanor, just don't stand there. Caroline, what about you?"

"Nothing to worry about, Mother," Caroline said. "I'm just spattered, that's all. Let go of me, Jimmy. I don't need any stretcher-bearers." Her voice sounded hard and angry, a new note that Strand had never heard before from her.

"If you'll just let me try to manipulate by myself, sir," the man said, "you'll see that . . ."

Gingerly, still ready to catch the man, Strand stepped back. He noticed that the sleeve of his own jacket was stained from a gash across the knuckles of the man's hand and then was ashamed of himself for noticing it. The man took a respectable step forward. "You see?" he said, with the dignity of a drunk passing an alcohol test before a policeman. He touched his cheek, looked calmly at the blood on his hand. "A minor bruise, I assure you."

Slowly they all went into the living room. The man seated himself firmly on a wooden chair. "It's very kind of you, but you shouldn't take all this trouble." He was a man, Strand guessed, of about his own age and almost as tall. If he was suffering, there was no sign of it on his slashed, discolored face.

"Jimmy," Leslie said. "Go and get some warm water and a washcloth." She looked at the blood-covered face. The blood was still dripping onto the living room carpet. "A towel. Two towels. You'll find some bandages and adhesive tape in the medicine chest. And bring in the ice bucket."

"No need to bother," the man said. "It's hardly more than a scratch."

"Caroline," Leslie said, "you look as though you've been through a war. Are you sure there's nothing the matter with you? Don't be foolishly brave now."

"I told you," Caroline said, her voice suddenly trembling. "I'm fine." She was still holding the tennis racquet, as though she would need it for some new and important game in the next few seconds. The steel frame of the racquet, Strand saw, was bloody, too.

"What happened?" he asked. He had been standing to one side, feeling awkward. He had never seen that much blood before and it made him squeamish.

"He was mugged and . . ." Caroline began.

Eleanor came in. "Dr. Prinz isn't in. His answering service said he'd call back within the hour."

Leslie groaned.

Eleanor put her arms around Caroline and cradled her. "Baby," she said, "it's all right now, it's all right. Are you sure you're not hurt?"

Caroline began to sob, her shoulders quivering. "I'm ff—ff—fine," she cried. "I just have to wash my face and change my clothes, that's all. Oh, I'm so glad everybody's home."

Jimmy came in with the bowl of hot water and the towels and bandages and the ice bucket. As Leslie soaked a towel and began gently to clean the wound on the man's scalp, he said, "You're all too kind. I apologize for making such a mess and being so much trouble." His voice was surprisingly calm now, as though he were excusing himself for ringing the wrong doorbell by mistake. His speech had the accent of good Eastern schools. He didn't move or wince as Leslie wiped the blood away, then worked on the raw flesh of the wounded hand, the towel becoming a sullen rusty iron color. She worked swiftly, without fuss, as though caring for damaged strangers were a commonplace event in her home. "I'm afraid there will have to be some stitches," she said matter-of-factly, "when the doctor comes. I hope I'm not hurting you."

"Not at all," the man said. "I trust my appearance doesn't shock you. Things always look worse than they actually are." He managed a smile, meant to reassure her.

"Caroline," Strand said, "how did all this happen?"

"If I may," the man said, "I'd like to explain. My dear young lady," he said to Caroline, "I'm sure you want to get out of those gory clothes."

"Eleanor," Leslie said, "take her into the bathroom and put her under a warm shower." Leslie was a firm believer in the efficacy of warm showers in all emergencies. "And tell Mrs. Curtis to hold dinner."

"Oh, dear," the man said, "I'm spoiling your dinner. Do forgive me. I really can get up and go home, you know." He made a move to stand.

"Sit still," Leslie said briskly, as Eleanor led Caroline, still gripping her racquet, toward the bathroom. Leslie began wrapping lengths of bandage around the man's head, her hands moving deftly and efficiently.

"Allen," she said, "put a lot of ice in the clean towel and make a compress of it."

As Strand followed her instructions she said to the man, "There's going to be some swelling on your cheek. Hold the ice to it and press. It'll help keep it down."

Docilely, the man put the towel-wrapped ice to his cheek. To Strand he looked absurdly like a small boy who had been in a fight and now was allowing his mother to repair the damages.

Jimmy peered curiously at the man. "Somebody gave you an awfully good whack, mister," he said.

"It's not the first time," the man said. "It could have been worse. Much worse. If it hadn't been for the young lady charging to my rescue. The avenging angel." He laughed softly. "Quite the reverse of the usual situation."

"Where did it . . . ?" Strand asked.

"In the park. I was a little later than usual this evening. Pressure of business. The old trap." Leslie had gotten most of the blood off him by now and he looked sedate and confident of himself, slightly florid, but with a strong, well-formed face that reminded Strand of the portraits of Spanish conquistadors, confident and used to giving orders. "I was on my usual daily spin around the park, the advice of my doctor—you know how fussy they are about men approaching middle age who lead sedentary lives in offices . . ."

Leslie stepped back to examine her handiwork. "That's about the best I can do for the moment for the upper works," she said. "It doesn't look too bad. Now for the hand." She began to wrap bandages across the knuckles and under the palms, tearing strips of adhesive tape with a ripping noise.

"I lost my hat somewhere," the man said. "I imagine that would help my appearance."

"What were you hit with?" Strand said. "Maybe you need a tetanus shot."

"The . . . the instrument," the man said dryly, "looked immaculate to me, although I wasn't in the position to make certain at the time. I'm sure my doctor will do whatever is necessary."

"What instrument?" Jimmy asked curiously.

"From my reading," the man said, "I would expect it would be a piece of lead pipe. Oh, I've been remiss. Let me introduce myself. I'm Russell Hazen." He said the name as though he expected it to be recognized, but as far as he knew, Strand had never heard it before.

"Allen Strand," Strand said. "And this is my wife, Leslie. And my son, James."

"I'm honored." Hazen made a small, sitting-down bow. "I hope we meet again under more auspicious circumstances."

Bloody or not, Strand thought, he had the vocabulary of a lawyer. *My honorable colleague, who has just hit me over the head with a lead pipe . . .*

"You don't have to talk, you know," Leslie said, "if you don't really feel up to it."

"I want you to know," Hazen said, ignoring Leslie's invitation to silence, "that you have an extraordinarily courageous daughter . . ."

"What did she do?" Jimmy asked. He sounded disbelieving, as though of all the virtues he might think his sister might possess, physical courage was not one that would immediately come to his mind.

"As I was saying, I was making my daily spin around the park . . ."

"Spin?" Jimmy asked. "What kind of spin?"

For the young, Strand thought, wishing Jimmy would shut up, the facts came first and compassion after, if at all. Jimmy sounded suspicious, as though if the truth were finally to come out, his sister's condition, the blood on her clothes and the hysterical sobbing in Eleanor's arms, were at bottom Hazen's fault.

"On my bicycle," Hazen said. "Excellent exercise. One does not need a team or a partner and especially on a fine spring day like today one can enjoy the bounty of nature."

He must have learned how to speak in the eighteenth

century, Strand thought, without changing his expression as he listened to the man.

"I stopped for a little breather," Hazen continued. "I went off the path a little and leaned against a tree and I smoked a cigarette, I'm afraid. My doctor would undoubtedly say I was undoing all the good the exercise had done me. Still, a lifetime habit, comforting at certain moments. . . . I was thinking about a problem that had kept me at my office a little later than ordinary and I thought that perhaps five minutes or so of reflection . . ."

"Then they jumped you?" Jimmy was not one for reflection, his or anyone else's.

"It was dusk," Hazen went on evenly. "I was enjoying looking at the lights in the buildings on Central Park West in the calm air." He stopped, touched the wound on his cheek lightly. "Then, as you say, James, they jumped me."

"The bastards," Jimmy said.

"Young, deprived people, with ugly racial memories," Hazen said, shrugging. "Lawlessness the order of the day, property a flaunting of unearned privilege . . ."

Speech for the Defense, Strand thought. *Your Honor, let me introduce certain extenuating circumstances . . .*

"You mean they were black?" Jimmy said harshly.

Hazen nodded soberly. "I have been warned by my friends from time to time. Especially after dark."

"Damnit," Jimmy said to his parents, "how many times have I told you Caroline should stay out of that goddamn park?"

"How many times, Jimmy," Strand said, "have I told you you ought to stop smoking and you ought to get to sleep before five o'clock in the morning?"

"Stop wrangling, you two," Leslie said sharply. Then to Hazen, "How did my daughter get involved in this?"

"She appeared out of nowhere," Hazen said. "Through the bushes, I imagine. The three men—boys, actually, no more than fifteen, sixteen, I imagine—had crept up behind me. The first I knew I was hit on the head, I was staggering a bit, but holding firmly on to my bicycle, which was the object of the assault. My hat flew off, they hit me again along the cheek and one of them pulled out a knife and began to slash my jacket . . ." He looked down, fingered the tattered leather. "I doubt they actually wished to stab me, merely to frighten me into letting go of my machine, the cut on my head came at this moment. . . . I was shouting, although it was with some difficulty, as one of them had his arm around my throat. Amazingly strong, a boy that age."

"And you held on to that bicycle all that time?" Jimmy asked incredulously.

"It was my property, James," Hazen said mildly.

"Christ," Jimmy said. "For a bicycle. How much did it cost? A hundred? A hundred and fifty?"

"Slightly more than that," Hazen said. "It is a French machine. Ten gears. But the money was not the point. As I said, it was my property, not theirs."

"And you were willing to take the chance that they'd kill you for a lousy bicycle?"

"The principle is not open to question," Hazen said with dignity.

"You were willing to get killed?" Jimmy repeated.

"I didn't reason it out calmly at the moment," Hazen said. "But I imagine the thought must have crossed my mind. Luckily, your sister appeared, completely surprising the young rascals. She screamed before she struck and the noise froze them for a moment. In that moment—it all went so fast I couldn't follow it—she laid about her with her tennis racquet. With the side. It must be quite a weapon. Sharp edged and all that. She smashed the hand of the boy with the knife with her first blow and he cried out and dropped the knife. With her second blow she opened the face and I'm afraid did grave damage to the eyes of the boy with the lead pipe and he dropped the pipe and bent over and staggered away, with his hands to his eyes. Then she struck the boy who had the knife across the face twice and he fell to the ground. You never think of a tennis racquet as a weapon, do you? The third boy merely ran away. All this time, your sister was screaming —wordlessly, I must say—although no one seemed to hear it, or if they did, paid no attention to it. She said, 'Hold on to me,' and she seized the handlebars of the bicycle and we ran—I believe we ran—out of the park. And here I am." Hazen smiled up at Leslie and Strand.

God, Strand thought, that little girl! "I'm glad now," he said, "I gave in when Caroline asked me to buy her a steel racquet." He had to make the little lame joke to keep from showing the emotion he felt, the fear that had swept through him for his daughter as Hazen told his story.

"I, too," Hazen said gravely. "More than glad. It is not perhaps too much of an exaggeration to say that I owe my life to your daughter. Tell her, if there is any way I can show my gratitude . . ."

"I'm sure she's happy you're safe and sound," Leslie said. "Comparatively speaking." She permitted herself a little smile. "That's reward enough." She looked at Strand, her eyes wet. "What do you know about our baby girl?" she whispered.

"More than I knew twenty minutes ago," Strand said. He put his arm around his wife's shoulders. Someone was trembling, but he didn't know whether it was Leslie or himself.

"Did you call the police?" Jimmy demanded.

Hazen laughed flatly. "The police? In this city? I'm a lawyer, James. What could they do?"

I guessed right, Strand thought. Lawyer.

Hazen started to push himself up from the chair. "I've kept you from your dinner long enough. Now, I'd better be getting ho—" He staggered and sat down, hard, a puzzled look on his face. "Perhaps another few minutes of rest," he said in a choked voice.

"You stay right here," Leslie said, "until the doctor comes."

"Perhaps," Hazen said weakly, "it might be advisable. If you don't mind."

"Do you want me to call your home," Strand asked, "and tell them where you are and that you'll be home later?"

"No matter," Hazen said. "Nobody's expecting me. I'm alone for the weekend." His voice sounded cold and distant as he spoke.

He had trouble at home, Strand thought, as well as in

the park. "I was just having a drink before dinner when
you came in," he said. "I think you could use a drink,
too."

"Thank you. That *would* be useful."

"Straight? Or with water? All we have is Scotch." He
didn't mention the sherry. After what Hazen had been
through, Strand doubted that sherry would do much good.

"Straight, please," Hazen said, leaning his head against
the back of the chair and closing his eyes.

"Better pour a whiskey for me, too," Leslie said as
Strand started toward the dining room.

The phone rang in the hallway as he was pouring the
drinks. He left the glasses on the sideboard to answer it.
It was Dr. Prinz, irritated. He stopped sounding irritated
when Strand told him briefly what had happened and he
said he'd come over as soon as he could, he was with a
patient who had just had a heart attack and it might take
some time.

When Strand came back with the drinks Leslie said,
"Jimmy's gone downstairs to get Alexander to lock the
bicycle in the cellar for the night." Strand nodded. It
would be foolish to have it stolen now.

Hazen was still sitting with his head back and his eyes
closed. "Here we are," Strand said, hoping his voice
sounded cheerful. "A little bit of Highland sunlight."

"Thank you, sir." Hazen opened his eyes and took the
glass in his good hand. Nobody offered a toast and Hazen
finished his drink in two gulps. Leslie drank hers quickly,
too, and then sat down as if she suddenly had realized
how tired she was.

"I feel the stirrings of life," Hazen said wanly.

"Another?" Strand said.

"Thank you, no. This was all that was needed."

Mrs. Curtis came in, looking pecky, as Leslie described
her mood when things were not going her way. "I'm sorry,
ma'am," she said, looking sternly at the bandaged man in
the wooden armchair, "the soup's on and everything'll be
ruined if . . ."

"We're waiting for the doctor, Mrs. Curtis," Leslie said.
"I'll tell you when . . ."

"If you don't mind having a scarecrow at the table while you eat," Hazen said. "I would appreciate it if you'd let me sit with you while you . . ."

"I think it would be wiser if . . ." Leslie started.

"Maybe Mr. Hazen's hungry," Strand said. He himself was hungry and he had been looking forward to dinner ever since he had come home and smelled the aroma from the kitchen.

"Come to think of it, I *am* hungry," Hazen said. "I had just a sandwich at my desk for lunch. I certainly would enjoy a bowl of soup, if it's not too much trouble."

"All right, Mrs. Curtis," Leslie said, "put on another place. We'll be right in."

Mrs. Curtis gave one more accusing look to Hazen, destroyer of dinners, and went back to the kitchen.

"Well, talk of the silver lining," Hazen said, with an attempt at heartiness. "And I thought I was going to have to dine alone tonight."

Although Hazen had spoken without any trace of self-pity, Strand had the feeling that, despite the cost, the prospect of not being alone that night was a welcome one for him.

Hazen looked around the big living room, taking in the grand piano, the stacks of sheet music, the orderly shelves of records, Leslie's landscapes. "What a nice room," Hazen said. "I take it yours is a musical family . . ."

"We all *listen*," Strand said. "My wife and son are the only ones you might call musicians."

"My mother used to play the piano for me," Hazen said, with a funny little dismissing gesture. "Ages ago. Does your son play the piano?"

"My wife," Strand said. "Jimmy plays the electric guitar. Country rock, I think it's called."

"And the landscapes?" Hazen said. "I don't recognize the artist."

"My wife," Strand said.

Hazen nodded, but didn't say anything.

Eleanor and Caroline came into the room. Caroline was in clean slacks and sweater, her face scrubbed from the shower, no signs that she had vanquished three hoodlums

in solitary battle barely an hour ago and had broken into
hysterical weeping in her sister's arms. Finally, she had
left the racquet behind her. She was smiling and looked
gay and younger than her seventeen years. "How's the
patient?" she asked.

"More or less in good repair," Hazen said. "Thanks to
your mother. And you, Miss Caroline, how do you feel?"

"Oh." Caroline threw up her arms airily. "Triumphant.
I have new faith in my powers." She giggled. "I don't
know if I'd do it again, though, if I had any time to think."

"How was it you were alone?" Strand asked. "Where
was that boy you were playing with?"

"He lives on the East Side," Caroline said.

"Will you ever be able to use that racquet again?" Hazen
asked.

"I'm afraid not," Caroline said. "It *is* a little bent. If
they'd only let me hit my opponents instead of the ball I
bet I'd sweep through tournaments." She giggled again.

"Weren't you afraid?" Hazen asked.

"Only later," Caroline said. "And that doesn't count,
does it?"

Jimmy came in and said, "The bicycle's locked in the
cellar. You can send somebody around for it whenever
you want, Mr. Hazen. It *is* a beauty."

"I'll have one of my secretaries pick it up in the morning," said Hazen. "I don't believe I'll be using it much for
the next few days. Unless Miss Caroline volunteers to act
as my bodyguard."

"I think I'll quit while I'm ahead." Caroline giggled
again.

Mrs. Curtis appeared at the doorway to the dining room
and glared.

"Oh, dear," Leslie said, "I think we'd better be sitting
down."

Strand made a move to help Hazen as he stood up, but
Hazen ignored the outstretched arm and took a step, without wobbling, toward the dining room as Leslie led the
way.

"What a pretty table," Hazen said as Leslie seated him
on her right. His speech was a little muffled, as he held

the iced towel to his cheek with his bandaged hand. "I hope I'm not intruding on an important family conference."

"We have a rule," Strand said, feeling the pangs of hunger, "that the only important thing we talk about on Friday nights is food." That wasn't true and he said it only to be polite. Last Friday there had been a discussion about politics that had ended in shouting and Eleanor's describing her father's attitude as Early Louis XIV. They had all enjoyed the evening. He picked up the bottle of Chianti. "Wine?" he asked.

"Thank you," Hazen said. "I'm terribly thirsty suddenly."

"Loss of blood," Caroline said gaily.

"Terror, my dear," Hazen smiled at her. "Pure terror."

"What do you think those three boys are thinking about now?" Caroline said, dipping into her soup.

"They're planning where they can steal three tennis racquets—no, four—" Hazen said, laughing crookedly because of his jaw, "and wondering where they can get a girl to help them in their next nefarious project."

Caroline giggled again. "Oh, I'm a dangerous tennis-person," she said.

Strand shook his head wonderingly. This must be what the atmosphere must be like in a football locker room, he thought, after a particularly rough victory.

Hazen spooned his soup clumsily with his left hand. His mouth was beginning to swell noticeably, but his eyes were bright and he seemed to be enjoying himself. "Excellent," he said, "excellent. May I pay my compliments to the cook?"

"That's Mother," Caroline said. She was obviously proud of her family this evening, as well as being proud of herself.

"An accomplished tribe," Hazen said gallantly. He turned toward Jimmy. "And you, young man, what do you do?"

Jimmy looked around the table. "According to my sister, I bring dishonor on the family name," he said. "I frequent stews and dives."

"Jimmy," Leslie said, protesting, "what a thing to say."
Jimmy grinned at her. "It's a private phrase of affection
between us. She's not serious. Are you, Eleanor?"

"Only sometimes, honey." Eleanor smiled back at him.

Hazen looked at Jimmy curiously, then turned his attention to Eleanor. "And you, my dear?"

"I slave and strive for promotion," Eleanor said shortly.
She had been unusually silent for her. Strand sensed that
for some reason, like Jimmy, she did not approve of Hazen
and he made a mental note to ask them both why after
Hazen had left.

Eleanor stood up to help clear away the soup bowls as
Mrs. Curtis came in with the platter of the main dish and
put it in front of Leslie to serve. "I'm afraid the soup is
all I can manage," Hazen said as Leslie reached for his
plate. "Although it does look and smell delicious." He
took a sip of his wine.

"What day of the week is it, Mr. Hazen?" Jimmy asked.

"What sort of a question is that?" Leslie looked at her
son suspiciously.

"I want to see if he has a concussion," Jimmy said. "If
he has a concussion he ought to lie down in a dark room
and close his eyes."

"Friday," Hazen said, smiling. "I believe it's still Friday.
I may not be able to chew at the moment, but I don't believe I have a concussion, thank you."

It occurred to Strand that Jimmy was more interested
in getting Hazen out of the room than in the state of his
health, but when he looked over at his son, Jimmy stared
innocently across the table at him.

"And you, Mr. Strand, if I may inquire," Hazen said,
"what is your profession?"

Pretrial investigation, Strand thought. *Your lawyer must
have the facts as you see them so that he can handle your
case efficiently.* No, not a lawyer, Strand corrected himself,
a little annoyed with the man. More like a general reviewing the troops, asking homely little questions to prove
that despite the stars on his shoulder he was at heart a
true democrat. "My profession—" He cleared his throat.
"I struggle with the bloodthirsty instincts of the younger

generation," Strand said, purposely vague. He had decided that Hazen was an important man, more from his manner than from anything he had said, and that he would have much the same estimate of him Leslie's father had if Strand said he merely taught in a high school.

"He teaches at River High." Leslie had sensed her husband's hesitation and spoke almost pugnaciously. "He's the head of the history department."

"Ah." Hazen sounded impressed. "When I was young I wanted to be a teacher. A useful life. More useful than the law, I told my father. He was not of my opinion. I took my law degree." He laughed deprecatingly. "The arguments were short in my father's house."

"They're not short here," Strand said. "I'll say that for them."

"Refreshing." Hazen turned to Caroline. "And you, young lady? Are you in college?"

Caroline, who had been eating as though she were starving, laughed. "If I'm lucky, in the fall. I graduate from prep school next month. With my marks . . ." She shook her head sorrowfully.

"You don't go to River?" Hazen asked.

"It's across town," Leslie said hastily.

"Daddy says it's too dangerous. I told him if it wasn't too dangerous for him it wasn't too dangerous for me." She giggled. She was not a girl who was ordinarily given to giggling, but Strand forgave her this evening. "That was *one* short argument. I lost. I go to school ten blocks from here."

"I read about it, of course," Hazen said, "about the violence in the public schools, muggings, children stealing from other children, weapons. I've always taken it with a grain of salt. Mr. Strand, have you found . . . ?" He stopped.

"Well," Strand said, "it's not like Sunday school in Vermont, say. There are incidents. Yes, there certainly are incidents."

"Have you been involved?" Hazen leaned forward, interested.

"Once or twice," Strand said. "Last term a boy threat-

ened me with a knife if I didn't pass him. He had cut
one-half the classes and on the final examination he got a
grade of 32 out of a possible hundred."

"Did you pass him?"

Strand laughed. "Of course. If he wanted a passing grade
badly enough to threaten to kill me, I thought he deserved
it. At least he didn't try to take my bicycle."

Hazen touched the bandage on his head ruefully. "Perhaps you're more intelligent than I," he said. "Among the
ruffians, do you see any gleams of hope?"

Strand shrugged. "Of course. Though most of them are
doomed to be snuffed out, I'm afraid, in very quick order.
In my senior class, for example—there's an undersized
Puerto Rican boy who seems to have been reading history
since he was a child. I just read a paper of his this afternoon. About the Civil War. He has some ideas of his own
on the subject."

"For example . . . ?" Hazen said. He seemed genuinely
interested.

"For example, he wrote that the Civil War was a great
mistake." As he spoke about the boy, Strand remembered
the round dark face with white teeth bared in what could
be a sneer or an insolent smile. "He wrote that the South
should have been allowed to go its own way, that in a
short time they'd have had to free the slaves anyway, and
a million lives would have been saved. By now, he wrote,
the South and the North would have been united in some
way, even in a loose confederation, and all of us, black
and white, would have been spared a century of misery.
That, of course, is not what he's been taught and I must
warn him that if he answers questions in that way on his
Regents, he'll fail."

"How do you think he'll react to *that?*"

"He'll laugh. Passing the Regents doesn't mean much
to him. He can't go to college, he'll have to be looking for
a job as a dishwasher or hustling on the streets from this
summer on, what does he care about the Regents?"

"It's a pity, isn't it?" Hazen said thoughtfully.

"It's today," Strand said.

"What mark did you give him for his essay?"

"A," Strand said.

"You must be an unusual teacher."

"He's an unusual boy. In another paper he argued that the way he was taught history was bunk. His word. Bunk. He wrote that cause and effect in historical movements are just designed to make it easy for historians to package our past into neat little phony parcels. He's done some reading in science—physics—and he's latched on to the theory of randomness—you've read something about that, I suppose?"

"A little." Hazen nodded.

"He takes it to mean that nothing is or was inevitable —everything springs from accident—the random collisions of particles, in politics and economics, as well as in nature and the laboratory. Given that theory, he says, the Industrial Revolution might just as well never have come about if ten people happened never to be born, World War II not occurred if Hitler had been killed on the Western front in 1917, the Civil War avoided if Lincoln had decided he wanted to continue in Springfield as a lawyer . . ."

"And what mark did you give him for that rather unorthodox bit of philosophizing?" Hazen asked.

"A." Strand laughed. "Maybe because it was so different from all the other papers. He can also spell."

"Do you think he's interested in going to college if he could?"

"No. He's confided in me that education is bunk, too. Still, a boy like that once in a while makes you feel it's all worthwhile."

"I can understand," Hazen said. He took the cold compress away from his cheek for a moment, looked at it consideringly, then put it back. "I suppose education has changed since my day—all education."

"Where were you educated?" Strand asked. As the head of the family, he couldn't allow Hazen to ask all the questions.

"The usual," Hazen said offhandedly. "Yale, Harvard Law School. In the footsteps of my sainted father. He hadn't heard about randomness."

"The ruling class," Jimmy said. "The cradle of our government. The grave of America."

"Jimmy," Leslie said sharply. "Don't be rude just to shock people."

"Jimmy may be more accurate than he sounds, Mrs. Strand," Hazen said.

He's not as sure of himself as he thinks, Strand thought. Come to think of it, he doesn't look like a man who sleeps well at night. And it isn't just because of the bandage around his head, either.

The doorbell rang and Jimmy got up to answer it.

"That must be Dr. Prinz," Leslie said.

"You must have an exceptional doctor," Hazen said. "Making house calls these days, especially at the hour of dinner."

"He's an old classmate of mine from City College," Strand said.

"I have several old classmates who have become doctors," Hazen said. "When I'm ill I go to their offices or they send me to a hospital."

Dr. Prinz came bustling in. He was a small, thin man with thick glasses and a harassed look. He played the violin, not too badly, and three or four times a year there were musical evenings at his apartment, at which he and Leslie performed in a trio with another musical doctor. "Hello, Allen, Leslie," he said. "What've you been up to now?"

"Mr. Hazen here has been mugged," Strand said. "Leslie has supplied first aid."

"New York." Prinz made a small, snuffing, disapproving sound. "Mr. Hazen, could you come with me into the bathroom? I think I'll need a strong light."

"Of course," Hazen said.

Prinz watched closely as Hazen stood up, then nodded, satisfied, as Hazen showed no signs of tottering.

"If you need any help . . ." Leslie said.

"I'll call if I need you, Leslie," Prinz said. He took Hazen's arm gently and led him out of the room.

"I hope Jerry remembered to bring some anesthetic," Leslie said.

"I'm sure he did," Strand said. "I told him over the phone I thought there'd have to be some stitches."

"He's pretty brave, Mr. Hazen," Caroline said. "If it'd been me, I'd have been hollering all over the place."

"He sure likes the sound of his own voice, doesn't he?" Jimmy said.

"Sssh," Leslie said. "He's just in the bathroom."

"A hundred thousand dollars a year, at least," Eleanor said. "I see them around the office. Once you get up around there, the sound of your own voice is the music of the spheres."

"Whatever he makes," Strand said, "I admire the way he's taking it."

"One thing," Caroline whispered, giggling, "I'm sure glad *I'm* not bald. I didn't know what hair was really for until tonight."

"He sure was lucky you came along when you did," Jimmy said to Caroline. "The least he could do would be to offer you a new racquet."

"You're all hopeless," Leslie said. "We don't need any favors. Everybody ready for dessert?"

They were finishing their coffee in the living room when Hazen and the doctor came in, Hazen with a new bandage around his head like a turban, and a thick white pad plastered onto one side of his face with adhesive tape. He was pale and Strand was sure that the operation in the bathroom had not been pleasant, but he was smiling, as though to reassure his hosts that all was well.

"All mended," Prinz said. "For the time being. You'll have a headache, though. It might be a good idea to have your doctor take some X rays of your skull tomorrow. Make sure you have plenty of aspirin in the house. Take a sleeping pill, too. You'll need it. And"—Prinz smiled grimly—"don't look in the mirror in the morning."

"Would you like a cup of coffee, Jerry?" Leslie asked.

Prinz shook his head. "No time. My heart attack's in the hospital by now and I have to look in on him."

"Anybody we know?" Strand asked.

"No." He peered coldly through his thick glasses at

Strand. "But he's exactly your age. When're you coming in for a checkup?"

"The next time I feel absolutely marvelous." Strand laughed. "I'd rather not be told what I have if I don't know it's there in the first place."

"Have it your own way," Prinz growled. "I'm too busy as it is. Good night, all."

Strand walked with him to the door. "He's all right, isn't he? Hazen?"

"He's damned lucky," Prinz said as he put on a black felt hat with a wide brim that made him look like a rabbi. "He told me about Caroline. Idiot. Maybe she ought to join the police force. See if you can get her to take a sleeping pill, too. And don't let her go out tonight. She has a funny look in her eye."

"She says she didn't get hurt."

"Not anyplace where a doctor could find it, maybe." Prinz said enigmatically. "Give her the sleeping pill."

Strand held the door open for him and the doctor went out, on the way to his heart attack, a man exactly Strand's age.

Strand went back into the living room, where Jimmy was pouring another straight Scotch for Hazen. Hazen was holding the glass steadily in his hand. "To help me face the night," he said to Strand. "Thank you for Dr. Prinz. He has a very clever pair of hands."

"How many stitches?" Jimmy asked.

"Five or six," Hazen said carelessly. "The good doctor said he'll send the bill to you. If you have a pen handy, I'll write my address down and you can send it on to me."

Jimmy took a pen and a scrap of paper out of his jacket pocket, and Hazen wrote swiftly on it and handed it to Strand. The writing was steady and even, Strand noticed as he put the paper in his pocket.

"It's just off the corner of 82nd Street and Fifth Avenue," Hazen said. "Right across from the museum. Very handy." He finished his drink and stood up, carefully putting the empty glass on an ashtray, so that it wouldn't stain the end table next to his chair. "The next time you go to the museum perhaps you could come and visit me.

I have quite a lot of hospitality to repay. Now I must go. I've bothered you fine people enough for one evening."

"I don't think you ought to go alone," Strand said. "I'll go with you. We can get a taxi on the corner."

"Oh, there's no need, I assure you," Hazen protested.

"Do you have anyone to take care of you?" Leslie asked, looking worried. "If not, you could stay here. Jimmy wouldn't mind sleeping on the couch for one night."

"I'll be perfectly all right," Hazen said. Strand noticed that he hadn't said whether there would be anyone in his apartment. "Dr. Prinz gave me his telephone number if anything comes up. But I'm sure I won't need it."

"I'll take the taxi with Mr. Hazen," Eleanor said. "I have a date on the East Side anyway."

"That's very kind of you," Hazen said.

"Anyway," Strand said, "I'll go down with you and see you safely into the taxi. I wouldn't want you to get another crack on the head between here and Central Park West."

"As you say," Hazen said. "Although, really, I hardly feel like an invalid." As Eleanor went to get her bag and coat, Hazen said, "Good night, Miss Savior," to Caroline, smiling, and bowed a little as he shook Leslie's hand and said, "I won't begin to try to tell you how grateful I am to you—to all of you. . . . I hope we can meet again—under more—ah—normal circumstances." He patted the turban on his head and looked down ruefully at his slashed leather windjacket. "My houseman is going to go into shock when he sees me."

Downstairs, Strand and Hazen and Eleanor walked toward Central Park West. Strand could see that the man was peering at him intently.

"It seems to me, Mr. Strand," he said, "that I've seen you someplace before tonight."

"No," Strand said, "I don't believe we've ever met."

"I didn't say we've met," Hazen said, with a touch of impatience. "I remember people I've met. It's just that your face is somehow familiar."

Strand shook his head. "Sorry, I can't help you."

"I don't blame you for not recognizing me." Hazen

laughed. "My own mother wouldn't recognize me, the way I look tonight. Ah—" He shrugged. "Eventually it will come to me!"

They walked in silence for a moment. Then Hazen touched Strand's arm and said, with the utmost seriousness, "I must tell you something that perhaps I shouldn't say— I envy you your family, sir. Beyond all measure." He dropped his arm and they walked in silence. Then, as they reached a corner and saw a vacant taxi bearing down on them, he took a deep breath. "What a lovely night," he said. "I have a very peculiar thing to tell you. I've enjoyed it, every minute of it."

Strand lay in the big bed in the silent dark room, Leslie's head cradled against his shoulder, her long hair soft against his skin. His delight in the beauty of his wife's body and the exquisite use she made of it had never lessened from the first day of his marriage and as they had made love tonight, he had whispered, "I adore you." What had been a long-desired pleasure had become, with the passage of the years, a passionate and overwhelming need. The peace he felt now, he knew as he lay in the silence, listening to her gentle breathing, would be deliciously brokn once more by morning. Weekend.

He sighed contentedly.

"You awake?" Leslie asked drowsily.

"Just."

"What did you and Eleanor mean when you said something about Greece?"

"That?" Strand said, barely remembering. "She told me she might go to a Greek island on her vacation. With a young man."

"Oh," Leslie said. "I suppose that's what she meant when she told me it was girly talk."

"I suppose so."

Leslie was silent for a moment. Then she said, "Did she say who the young man might be?"

"No. She said he'd been to the island before." Strand hesitated. "With another lady."

"He said that?" Leslie sounded incredulous and moved away a little from him.

"He tells her everything, she says."

Leslie shook her head slightly against Strand's shoulder. "That's a bad sign," she said. "Especially if she believes it."

"I wouldn't worry too much about that."

"Why doesn't she bring him around so that we can get a look at him?" Leslie asked, a little annoyed.

"She's not sure of him yet, she says."

Leslie was silent again for a moment. "Do you think she's in bed with him now—like us?"

"Not like us, surely."

"She scares me a little," Leslie said. "She's too sure of herself."

"Like Mozart."

"What?" Leslie sounded puzzled.

"That's what Mr. Crowell said was wrong with Mozart, don't you remember?"

"And I said Mozart came to a tragic end."

"Eleanor has always known how to take care of herself."

"I'm not so sure. She's had everything pretty much her own way so far. If something suddenly went wrong—I don't know—she might not be as strong as she thinks she is. Then there'd be no telling how she'd react. Maybe I ought to investigate the young man a little."

"I wouldn't do that."

"Why not?"

"You might find out things that will disturb you—unnecessarily."

Leslie sighed. "I guess you're right. We can't be armor for our children. We can only be supporting troops."

Strand laughed. "You sound as though you've been browsing in my library."

"Oh, I do a lot of things I don't make reports about," Leslie said lightly. "Sleepy?"

"More or less."

"Good night, dear." She snuggled closer to him. But after a few seconds she spoke again. "She didn't seem to cotton to our visitor, did she?"

"Not particularly."

"Nor did Jimmy. Did you notice?"

"Yes."

"He seemed most gentlemanly."

"Maybe that's why the kids were standoffish," Strand said. "Gentlemanliness is suspect these days with the kids. They equate it with hypocrisy. Hazen said he thought he'd seen me before."

"Did he say where?"

"He couldn't remember."

"Do you?"

"Not a clue," said Strand.

"You know what Jimmy said about him when you were downstairs getting a cab?"

"What?"

"That he sounded exactly like the men they kept putting into jail after Watergate. He says Mr. Hazen has a porous vocabulary, whatever that means."

"Half the time these days," Strand said, "I don't know what Jimmy means when he talks to me, either."

"He's a good boy," Leslie said defensively.

"I didn't say he wasn't a good boy. He's just using another dictionary from the one I'm used to."

"Don't you think our fathers felt very much the same thing about us when we were Jimmy's age?"

"Tell me about the generations, mother," Strand said, teasing her, "about how they come and they go."

"You can make fun of me if you like. Still . . ." Leslie left the thought unspoken. "All in all, I thought it was an interesting evening."

"Downstairs," Strand said, "Hazen said he enjoyed it, every minute of it."

"Poor man," Leslie said. She kissed Strand's throat. "Now let's *really* go to sleep."

3

"I envy you your family, sir," a voice had said, sometime in the past. Years ago? Last night? *"Beyond all measure."* Who had said it? To whom had it been addressed? What family?

Strand was reading in the bedroom. Saturday morning was a busy time for Leslie, with children coming in for lessons every half hour from eight to one, and Strand locked himself away, so he wouldn't hear the artless matinal tinkling. He read idly. He kept two books on his bedside table that he liked to dip into at odd moments—Prescott's *Conquest of Mexico* and *Conquest of Peru*. Himself an armchair historian, whose farthest trips afield for material were occasional visits to the reading room of the 42nd Street public library, he especially treasured the eloquent accounts written by the blind scholar immured in Cambridge, of desperate deeds performed in far-off places by indomitable men who had changed the face of the planet with a handful of swords and a meager troop of horse, with never a thought of the verdict of history that would be brought in centuries later by the inhabitants of the continent of guilt they left behind them.

For other reasons he also admired the works of Samuel Eliot Morison, who had fought in naval wars, sailed the ocean routes of Columbus and Magellan and written about primitive voyages and bloody battles in such vigorous, manly prose. If he had been ambitious he might have aspired to be a Prescott. The life of a man like Morison, he admitted sadly to himself, would have been beyond him.

When he was young he had hoped to make his name as a historian, but when his father died during Strand's last year in college, leaving behind him a derelict electric appliance repair shop and an ailing wife and a pitifully small amount of insurance, Strand had to give up whatever plans he had had for continuing in graduate school. The next best thing, he had made himself believe, was to get a license to teach history in high school, where he would at least be working in a field he was devoted to and could make a living for himself and his mother at the same time. By the time his mother died he was already married and Eleanor had been born, so now he read history and taught it but did not write it. If he had his moments of regret, he had his compensating moments of contentment. Rereading a well-loved book on a quiet Saturday morning was just such a moment.

He had had breakfast early with Leslie and Caroline, half-listening to their chatter as he scanned the *Times* over his coffee. Caroline reported that she had heard Jimmy come in about three. Jimmy's door was still closed and Caroline guessed that her brother would make an appearance around noon. Caroline seemed none the worse for her experience of the night before. She had been dressed for tennis at the breakfast table, and had gone off to play with an old wooden racquet and had promised to come home before dark.

On Saturday mornings Mrs. Curtis came to clean and answer the doorbell and let the children in as they arrived for their lessons. Occasionally, Leslie would ask Strand to come into the living room and listen to a little boy or girl who had suddenly become a pianist. But this morning he had not been invited to one of these impromptu concerts, so Strand understood that no particular talent was on display and that Leslie would be edgy by lunchtime.

He was reading, for the fifteenth time, the account of Cortez's battle on the causeway leading to the city of Mexico when the telephone rang. He went down the hallway and picked it up. It was Eleanor. "How's Caroline?" she asked.

"No visible damage," Strand said.

"I've been doing some homework," Eleanor said. "On Mr. Russell Wrenn Hazen. I looked in *Who's Who.* Caroline brought home a whale last night."

"What do you mean, a whale?"

"A big one," said Eleanor. "He's the head man of one of the largest law firms in Wall Street, founded by his father, now dead. He's on the boards of about a dozen giant corporations, starting with oil and going down to agrobusiness and chemicals, he's a trustee of his old school, he has one of the biggest collections of Impressionist and modern art in America, begun by his father and added to by sonny boy, he is mentioned for his connections with museums and the opera and is noted for his philanthropic interests. He played hockey for Yale back in the dark ages, is on the National Olympic Committee and belongs to a lot of clubs, including the Racquet and Century and Union Club. Married to a Social Register lady, née Katherine Woodbine. Three children, grown, two daughters and a son. Want any more?"

"That will do," Strand said.

"*Who's Who* doesn't mention his bicycle riding," Eleanor said. "I suppose that'll be in the next edition. At dinner I thought he wasn't just one of the run-of-the-mill Central Park exercise nuts."

"I gathered he was a man of some importance," Strand said. "Still, to his credit, he didn't advertise."

"He doesn't have to. Do you know anybody else in *Who's Who?*"

"Not offhand," Strand said. "Well, there's an old professor of your mother's at Juilliard. . . . That's about it. Did he say anything to you in the taxi?"

"He wanted to know why I said I slaved when he was putting us all through the third degree."

"What did you tell him?"

"I said it was just a figure of speech. He said he hoped to see more of us. He struck me as being a lonely man, although after reading about him it doesn't seem possible."

"I had the impression," Strand said, "that you didn't like him very much."

"It wasn't that, exactly," Eleanor said. She sounded uncertain, as though she still hadn't made up her mind about Hazen. "I just sensed a gap between him and us. No, not a gap. An abyss. Didn't you?"

Strand laughed. "I'm not really an abyss man," he said. "No. Are we going to see you over the weekend?"

"Sorry. I'm off to Connecticut for a spot of rural luxury. I'll call on Monday."

"Have a good time," Strand said, as he hung up. He wondered where Eleanor had found a copy of *Who's Who*. She hadn't sounded as though she was in a library and he knew she didn't have one in her apartment. Probably she had been calling from her young man's place. He tried not to think of what she had been doing the night before, after she had dropped Hazen. He shook his head. Her life.

As he went back to the bedroom and picked up Prescott again he wondered, without envy, how a man could divide himself into as many parts as Hazen, by Eleanor's report, must manage, and why he did so.

He started reading again, but there was a knock on the door. It was Mrs. Curtis. "The man who had dinner here last night is here," she said. "He looks something awful, all the colors of the rainbow, but he has some flowers for Mrs. Strand and he said if you weren't busy he'd like to see you for a minute. He wants his bicycle but Alexander's not around this morning."

"When will Alexander be back?" Strand asked, as he put on a worn old tweed jacket, his Saturday costume, and slipped his feet into moccasins.

"Not for an hour. He had to go downtown for a piece for the boiler."

Strand went along the long dark hallway past Jimmy's closed door to the foyer. There were some prints on the walls, and some old posters for one-man shows, as well as a flower piece of Leslie's. Not mentioned in *Who's Who*, Strand thought. Hazen was standing holding a big bouquet of flowers wrapped in paper. Another long paper-wrapped package was lying on the table in the foyer.

"Good morning, sir," Hazen said. "I hope I'm not disturbing you."

"Good morning," Strand said as they shook hands. "Nobody disturbs me on Saturday morning. It's my time for doing nothing." Hazen *did* look awful, as Mrs. Curtis had said. He had a wool ski hat pulled over the bandage on his head, making his head look grotesquely large, and his face was swollen and misshapen, the skin below the pad of bandage on his cheek a sickly mixture of yellow, purple and green. His eyes, though, were clear and bright and he was neatly dressed in a beautifully fitting dark gray suit, his shoes glittering in a mahogany shine.

"How did the night go?" Strand asked.

"It passed." Hazen shrugged. "And your daughter?"

"Off playing tennis. She was gay as a bird at breakfast."

"The resilience of youth," Hazen said.

He says the most banal things, Strand thought, as though they are pearly-new gems of observation.

"I bought a few flowers for your wife," Hazen said, moving the bouquet with a little rustling of paper. "For her kind ministrations."

"She's busy now with a lesson," Strand said.

"I hear," Hazen said. He made no comment on the quality of what he heard.

"She'll be most pleased. Mrs. Curtis," Strand said, "would you please put Mr. Hazen's flowers in water."

Mrs. Curtis took the bouquet from Hazen and went back into the kitchen.

"I have something for Caroline." Hazen indicated the paper-wrapped package on the table. "A new racquet. Made by the Head people. I noticed that the racquet she demolished in my defense was a Head."

"It wasn't necessary," Strand said, "but I'm sure she'll be delighted."

"The gut is in the package," Hazen said. "I wasn't sure just how tight she would like it strung. All she has to do is take it into the tennis shop at Saks and they'll do it for her."

"You've had a busy morning, Mr. Hazen," Strand said.

"It's not yet eleven o'clock and you've already been to Saks and the florist's."

"I'm an early riser," Hazen said. "Another thing I inherited from my father."

"I know something about your father," Strand said.

"Oh, you do," said Hazen, flatly. "I'm not surprised."

"My daughter, Eleanor, just called. She looked you up in *Who's Who.*"

"Oh, she did? I didn't think she was that interested in me."

"She said there wasn't anything in it about your bicycle riding."

Hazen smiled. "We'll keep that part of my biography to ourselves, shall we? I'm not particularly proud of last night."

"I don't see anything much that you could have done about it," Strand said.

"I could have stayed home," Hazen said. "I was foolish, considering the lateness of the hour. Still . . ." His face brightened. "It gave me the opportunity of meeting you and your charming family. I really am taking too much of your time. I had just planned to leave the racquet and the flowers here in the hall and pick up my bicycle. But the superintendent's door didn't answer and I . . ."

"He's away," Strand said. "If you wait here for a moment I'll ask Mrs. Curtis where the key for the cellar is."

"Thank you," Hazen said, "if it's not too much trouble."

Mrs. Curtis was putting the bouquet into a big vase in the kitchen.

"Pretty, aren't they?" Strand said. He had only the vaguest notion about flowers. He was sure about roses and chrysanthemums but after that he was usually at a loss for floral identification.

"For what they cost," Mrs. Curtis said, jabbing harshly at the blossoms, "you could feed your family for a week."

"Mr. Hazen would like to get his bicycle out of the cellar," Strand said, ignoring Mrs. Curtis's comment on the household's economic situation. "Do you know where Alexander keeps the key?"

"You go into the boiler room," Mrs. Curtis said, "it's

open and there's a shelf on the right-hand side, high up. At the near corner you'll find the key. That man going to ride his machine through the park in his state?"

"I imagine so."

"He'll scare the animals in the zoo right out of their cages." Mrs. Curtis jabbed again at the flowers. "Mind, put the key back when you're finished with it."

"I will," Strand said. He went back into the foyer, where Hazen was still standing, a small frown on his face as he listened to a scale that was being played with considerable inaccuracy in the living room. Strand smiled. "Usually, it's better than that," he said. "That obviously is not one of Leslie's star pupils."

"Still, it must be rewarding," Hazen said, correcting his frown. "All those young people . . ." His voice trailed off.

"I know where the key is in the cellar," Strand said. "I'll take you down . . ."

"No need," Hazen said. "I've bothered you enough. I have my man downstairs. If you'll just tell me where the key is . . ."

"I was just going down to take a little walk, anyway," Strand said, although the idea hadn't occurred to him until that moment. He opened the door and followed Hazen to the elevator. On the ground floor, there was a tall man of about thirty-five dressed in corduroy pants and a sweater. Hazen introduced him as one of his secretaries, Mr. Conroy. He was an unathletic-looking man, with a gray complexion, the color, Strand thought, of ashes leeched by years of acid rain. The clothes he was wearing seemed incongruously informal on him. Strand wondered what Hazen's other secretaries looked like and how many he had and whether they made up in beauty and charm for Conroy's depressing appearance.

They went down the steps to the boiler room and Strand found the key. He opened the cellar door and Conroy, with quick, efficient movements, took hold of the bicycle. Strand offered to help get it up the stairs, but Hazen said, impatiently, "Conroy can handle it himself, can't you, Conroy?"

"Of course, sir," Conroy said.

Strand locked the door and put the key back in the boiler room. Conroy was waiting for the two men when they came out of the building into the sunlight.

"Just leave it with the doorman," Hazen said.

"Yes, sir," Conroy said and mounted the bicycle.

"Until Monday morning," Hazen said.

"Yes, sir," Conroy said. "If you need me over the weekend, my answering service will get me."

"If I need you," Hazen said.

He and Strand watched the man ride off. "I don't imagine he belongs to any union," Strand said, "your Mr. Conroy. On tap for work on the weekends."

"Able fellow," Hazen said. "He's paid enough to put in an extra hour here and there. And he's not married. That helps." He chuckled. "If you don't mind, perhaps we could go a little way on your walk together."

"Which way would you like to go?" Strand asked. "Into the park?"

Hazen shook his head, smiling. "Not just yet, please. The memories are still rather fresh. Perhaps toward Lincoln Center . . . ?"

"Fine," Strand said, as they began to walk. "I always like to look at it. It gives me some hope that in the long run the city will not be totally destroyed."

They walked comfortably in silence for a while. "I've been wondering about your name," Strand said.

"Why?"

"There's a William Hazen whose name is a footnote to American military history."

"Really?" Hazen sounded interested. "What did he do?"

"He went to West Point, then fought the Indians and during the Civil War he was a colonel under Sherman in Georgia at the head of a regiment of Ohio volunteers and captured Fort McAllister."

"Good Lord, man," Hazen said, "how do you know all that?"

"A history teacher is a mine of useless information."

"What else did he do? If he was important enough, maybe I'll claim him."

"He became a general and started the Signal Corps."

Hazen laughed. "The Signal Corps. I have an old friend who was an infantryman in World War Two and he wasn't very fond of the Signal Corps. According to him, in the infantry they said, 'Take the star out of the window, Mother, your son's in the Signal Corps.' I guess I won't claim him after all. Anyway, my family came to New York in 1706 and never got to Ohio. What about *your* ancestors?"

"I don't know much about them," Strand said, sorry he had brought the subject up. "My parents came to New York in 1920, from Lancashire. My father had been gassed on the Somme and he said he'd had enough of England. When I asked him about his and my mother's family, he said they weren't worth talking about." He shrugged. "I took his word for it."

Now the silence between them was a little strained and when Hazen spoke again, it was on a different subject. "I've been thinking about something you said last night," he said. "About that Puerto Rican boy in your history class."

"His name is Romero, Jesus Romero."

"You know," Hazen went on, "scholarships are quite easily arranged for promising young people these days. Especially for those in minority groups. In the best colleges. Do you think the boy would be interested?"

Strand considered for a moment. "I'm afraid on the basis of his marks, he wouldn't be considered promising. I understand from other teachers that he's practically useless in their classes. I doubt that he'll pass enough subjects even to graduate."

"Too bad," Hazen said. "Do you think he's intelligent enough so that if he applied himself for a year or so he could pull up his grades?"

"Not in River High School, no. It's not an atmosphere conducive to application."

"What if he could get a scholarship for a year, even two—one of the good preparatory schools—where the— ah—influences are healthier? Could he be improved to a point where a college would be ready to give him a chance?"

Strand shrugged. "That would depend upon his attitude, of course. Right now, except for the fact that he's done a surprising amount of reading on his own—more often than not in fields that have very little relation to the courses he's taking—he's just about like the other students in the school. That is to say he's scornful of authority, immune to discipline, suspicious of the intentions of his teachers . . ."

"*Your* intentions, too?"

"I'm afraid so," Strand said. "He delights in provoking me. When I lecture, following the curriculum, as I have to do, he often just gets up and walks out of the room."

Hazen shook his head sadly. "All that money, all that effort, all that good will going into our schools," he said, "and what do we get for it?"

"Rebellion," Strand said. "Sometimes concealed, very often open."

"I can imagine the difficulties," Hazen said. He shook his head. "Still, we can't just wash our hands of the whole thing, can we?"

Strand wasn't sure just which "we" Hazen meant and by what process he, Allen Strand, might be included in the plural.

Hazen stared soberly ahead of him as he walked, seemingly oblivious of the curious stares of the passersby at his ski cap and battered face. "We can't just abandon a whole generation or a good part of a whole generation to nihilism—that's the only word for it—nihilism," Hazen said, an oratorical gravity in his voice. "The best of them have to be saved—and I don't care where they come from, the slums, farms, great estates, ghettos, anywhere. This country is in for some terrible times and if our leaders are going to be ignorant, uneducated, we are heading for catastrophe."

Strand wondered if Hazen was voicing long-held beliefs or had suddenly seen some handwriting on the wall that had been hidden from him before his scalp had been opened by a piece of pipe. He himself, involved in the daily struggle with the young, found it more comfortable not to look far ahead, and he felt that the present state of the nation could hardly be worsened, regardless of the education or lack of it of its leaders.

"Ah, well." Hazen spoke in his normal tone. "We'll do what little we can. If you think it would be of use to talk to the boy, do so. And let me know what he says."

"I'll give it a try."

Almost as though he knew what Strand was thinking as they walked side by side, Hazen said, "Have you ever thought of getting out of the public school system? It must be dispiriting, to say the least—year after year. Perhaps teaching somewhere out of the city, in a small private school where the rewards, anyway intellectually, would be more commensurate with the effort you put in?"

"My wife talks about it from time to time," Strand said. "I've thought about it, yes. But I was born in New York, I like the city. I'm a little old to tear up roots."

"What degrees do you hold?"

"M.A.," Strand said. "I took it at night in New York University, while I was teaching during the day."

"Any writing in the field?"

"Not really," Strand said. "I'm more of a reader than a writer."

"You know," Hazen said, "if I were a trained historian some of the things you were talking about last night— the theory of randomness, especially—would tempt me to examine various periods in that perspective. It could lead to some amusing speculation on how differently great events could have turned out with just the smallest alteration of the elements involved . . ."

"For want of a nail, the shoe was lost," Strand said, "for want of a shoe, the horse was lost, for want of a horse, the kingdom was lost. That sort of thing?"

"More or less. Although perhaps not quite so primitively."

"I'll suggest it to Romero," Strand said lightly, "and give you the credit for the inspiration."

"No, seriously," Hazen said, "I think the reconsideration of American history, especially along those lines, would make a good deal of sense. I'm not an expert, of course, but it seems to me that America—the United States—blundered into greatness; there was nothing fore-ordained about it. And we're blundering into decline, back toward Europe, terrorism, factionalism, cynicism in private and public life, and I hope there's nothing fore-ordained about *that*, either."

"You're a pessimistic man, aren't you, Mr. Hazen?"

"Perhaps less so than I sound. I've been disappointed. Some hopes have been dashed. Institutions I have worked for have not lived up to expectations. People I thought I loved have not turned out as they might have. Characters have been stunted, careers unrealized. But no, I am not pessimistic to the point of surrender. I believe in struggle, intelligence, essential moral values. A night like last night—your daughter's instant coming to the aid of a stranger in trouble at considerable peril to herself, your family's unhesitating solicitude, the easy affection I felt flowing from one to the other around the table, the sense of unity without constraint, the absence of any signs of that mortal disease, loneliness—I don't want to make too much of it, but a night like that in this day and age is a strong remedy for pessimism."

"I'm afraid you're laying a very heavy burden of meaning on a simple family dinner," Strand said, uneasy with all that praise. "You're going to make me self-conscious each time I take out my key to unlock my front door."

"I'm talking too much," Hazen said. "A lawyer's vice. Never leave well enough alone." He laughed. "The flowers and the racquet should have been enough. I see I've made you uncomfortable. Forgive me. I'm not used to modest men. Oh, that reminds me." He reached into an inner pocket of his jacket and brought out a small envelope. "I have a pair of tickets for the Philharmonic tonight. They're doing a concert version of Berlioz's *Damnation of Faust*. Would you and your wife like to go?"

"There's no need . . ." Strand protested.

"I can walk along the street looking as I do," Hazen said, "but can you imagine the stir at the Philharmonic if I showed up like this? Please take them if you can use them." He pushed the envelope toward Strand. "They'll just go to waste, otherwise."

"But you were taking somebody," Strand said. "You have two tickets."

"My guest for the evening decided she had other plans," Hazen said. "You and your wife do like the Philharmonic, don't you?"

"Very much."

"Then take these tickets, man," Hazen said decisively. "You're not the sort of person who hates Berlioz, are you?"

"Not at all."

"Some other evening, when I'm more presentable, we can all go together."

"Thank you," Strand said, putting the tickets in his pocket. "Leslie will be overjoyed."

"I consider myself more than compensated," Hazen said.

They were in front of Lincoln Center now. Hazen squinted at it. "Somehow," he said wearily, "we have lost the knack for harmonious public building. Still, it's a useful place." He looked at his watch. "Well, I must be getting back to the office."

"You work on Saturday afternoon?"

"It's my favorite time of the week. The office is empty and quiet, the telephone doesn't ring, there's a neat pile of papers waiting for me on my desk, I buy a sandwich and a bottle of beer and take my coat off and loosen my collar and I feel like a boy studying for an exam he knows he's going to pass. What do *you* do on Saturday afternoons?"

"Well," Strand said, "in the springtime, like now, I'm afraid I indulge in my secret vice. I watch ball games on the little portable TV set in the bedroom, while Leslie gives her lessons in the living room." The TV set had been a present from Eleanor, although Strand didn't feel he had to tell Hazen that. "I love to watch the Yankees play. I was a dud at sports when I was young and I suppose that when I see Reggie Jackson striding to the plate, all power and purpose, I somehow feel that I know what it's like to be dangerous and gifted and knowing that millions of people are cheering you or hating you." He laughed. "Leslie rations me. Only two games a week."

Strand felt that this man, whose idea of pleasure was to pore over a pile of legal papers in a deserted office, was looking at him curiously, as though he had come upon a species that was new and unfamiliar to him.

"Do you get up to the Stadium often?"

"Rarely."

"I have a standing invitation to use the owner's box there. Maybe on a nice Saturday afternoon I'll forget my office and we could sneak up and watch a game. Would you like that?"

"I certainly would."

"Maybe when Boston comes to town. I'll look at the schedule. How about the winter?"

"What?"

"I mean what do you do on Saturdays in the winter?"

"Well," Strand said, "when they're showing an old movie I like at the Modern Museum, I try to get in."

Hazen smacked his fist into the palm of his other hand. "That's it. The Modern Museum. That's where I've seen you. The Buster Keaton picture."

"You like Buster Keaton?" Strand asked, a little incredulously.

"I mark his pictures on the schedule they send me and if it's at all possible I sneak off and see it." Hazen grinned, which made the various colors of his battered face take on new patterns. "Anybody who doesn't appreciate Buster Keaton," he said with mock gravity, "should be denied the vote. However," he added, "I try to see all the Garbo pictures. She reminds me of how the times have deteriorated. We used to have a goddess as our ideal and now what have we got? Carhops. Doris Day, that Fawcett woman." He looked at his watch again. "I like to keep to my schedule. I arrive every Saturday at the office at one o'clock sharp. If I'm two minutes late, the watchman downstairs who checks me in will call the police. We'll talk about the beauties of the past some other time. I hope. And if you want to see a Yankee game, let me know."

They shook hands.

"I've enjoyed our walk," Hazen said. "Perhaps, if we're both in town next Saturday morning, we can do it again."

"I'll be in town," Strand said.

"I'll call you. Enjoy Berlioz."

Strand watched as Hazen got spryly into a cab, his big form filling the doorway.

Buster Keaton, for God's sake. As the cab sped away Strand took the envelope out of his pocket and looked at the tickets. They were for fifth row orchestra. The glorious uses of money, he thought. He put the tickets back into his pocket with a tingle of pleasure and started toward home.

4

Berlioz. A roaring flood of dark sound. Unfairly treated by posterity.

A cool, woman's hand on his forehead. "I need you," someone had said. He tried to open his eyes to see whose hand it was on his forehead, but the effort was too great. Whoever . . .

"I don't get it," the boy was saying in Strand's little office. Strand had told Romero that he would like to see him for a moment after classes were over and had been a little surprised when the boy actually appeared.

"I explained to you," Strand said, "that I mentioned you to a . . . a friend of mine, a new friend, who happens to be an influential man, and he said that if you were interested in continuing your education he would try to get you a scholarship . . ."

"Yeah, yeah," Romero said impatiently. "I heard all that. I mean, man, why's he picking on me?"

"I said you were promising," Strand said.

"I'm not making any promises," Romero said sullenly.

"I wasn't using the word in that sense," said Strand. He found it difficult, after the long day, to keep his patience with the short, ragged boy, his face hard and suspicious under his tangled hair. Dressed in shapeless blue jeans, dirty sneakers, and a faded football jersey that was much too large for him and had probably been stolen from some locker room seasons ago, Romero lounged carelessly against the desk, impudently fingering an unlit cigarette. The number on the jersey was 17. The boy wore it to school every day, and sometimes in Strand's dreams the number 17 crossed against a confused cloudy background. "What I meant was that of all the students in my classes who might not otherwise go on to college, on their own, that is, you showed the most original intelligence."

"You're kidding, ain't you, Professor?" Romero said, smirking. "What'd you really say—that you got a kid in your class who proves that Puerto Ricans're all some kind of nuts? What's the game?"

"It isn't any game," Strand said shortly, regretting that he had ever said anything to Hazen about the boy. "And leave the Puerto Ricans out of it, please. My friend is interested in education, he has useful connections, he feels that out-of-the-ordinary students should be given a chance . . ."

"I still don't get it, Professor," Romero said stubbornly.

"Don't call me Professor. I'm not a professor."

"Okay—Mr. Strand—I mean, like what's in it for him? Some guy I don't even know."

"There's nothing in it for him," Strand said. "Except perhaps some personal satisfaction if you do well and embark on a successful career later on."

"What do I have to do—sign a contract or something giving him half of what I make for ten years?" Romero took a battered Zippo lighter out of his pocket, then thought better of it and put it back.

Strand shook his head sorrowfully. The boy obviously did not confine his reading to books on history and science. The gossip columns about Hollywood and show business and agents clearly had not been neglected in his choice of reading matter. "Romero," he said, "did you ever hear of charity?"

"Charity." The boy laughed, meanly. "I sure have heard of charity. My old lady's on welfare."

"This has nothing to do with welfare. I'm not going to sit here and argue with you all day. If you want to devote a year or two of your life to really studying—hard—there's a good possibility you can get a scholarship for a college. I think you can make it, if that means anything to you. I suggest you go home and talk it over with your mother and father."

"My father." The boy laughed again, his teeth gleaming white in the dark, smudged face. "That man's long gone. I ain't seen him since I was nine years old."

"Your mother, then."

"She won't believe me. She'll beat the shit out of me for making up stories."

"Then consult with yourself, Romero," Strand said angrily. He stood up. "If you decide you want to make something of yourself, come and tell me. If you want to be a bum all your life, forget it." He collected some papers and stuffed them into his briefcase. "I've got a lot of work to do at home. I have to leave. I'm sure you have many important things to do yourself this afternoon," he said sardonically, "and I won't keep you any longer."

Romero looked at him, smiling, as though making the teacher angry gave him some points in a secret competition with his classmates.

"Get out of here, get out of here," Strand said and then was ashamed because he had spoken so loudly.

"Whatever you say, Professor," Romero said and went to the door. He stopped there and turned. "I can take care of myself, understand?" he said harshly. "Nobody has to lose any sleep about Jesus Romero."

Strand went over to the door and closed it, hard. Then he went to his desk and sat down and put his head in his hands.

As he loped down the steps of the school building Strand overtook Judith Quinlan, of the English department. He had overheard some of the students calling her Miss Quinine, although as far as he knew not to her face.

"Good afternoon, Judith," Strand said, slowing down. She was a small woman and when they walked to the bus together, as they did frequently, there was no way for her to keep up with his usual pace unless she trotted along beside him. She had a delicate but nicely rounded body and a sad little indoor face, and she used no makeup. Her favorite color, at least for school, was a dun brown. Her reputation as a teacher was good and he liked her and they occasionally lunched or had a cup of coffee together. He never could make up his mind how old she was—somewhere between thirty and forty, he thought.

"Oh, Allen," she said as they reached the sidewalk and she automatically began to walk faster, "how nice to see you." She glanced sidewise at him. "You look as though they've been grinding you today."

"I didn't know it showed. It was only the usual." Strand slowed down even more. "Thirty lashes."

She laughed. She had a nice laugh, low and unforced. She wasn't really pretty, but she had pale gray direct eyes that squinted a little as though in an effort to find out exactly what he was saying to her. "I know what you mean. I was going to stop for a coffee. Would you like to join me?"

"I feel as though I could use a bottle of Scotch," Strand said, "but I'll make do with coffee."

They passed the fat man with the baseball cap at the corner.

"I've heard he sells heroin to the kids," Strand said.

"I've heard he sells numbers tickets to them," Judith said.

"Probably both. Or maybe he's just a simple child molester."

"There're some children in my classes I'd gladly have him molest." She glanced at Strand again. "You look as though you're about to come to a slow boil. Has it ever occurred to you that you're not really cut out to be a teacher?"

"I'd have to consider that," Strand said thoughtfully.

"I shouldn't have asked that question."

"Why not? Recently I've been asking it myself." He didn't tell quite how recently it had been—since Saturday morning. "I'm of two minds. *There's* an answer for you."

She smiled. "Wouldn't it be nice," she said, "if we actually did have two minds—one to go off and work, the other to sit at home and ponder."

"Well, there are certain things we can safely say in favor of our profession," Strand said. "It is underpaid, arduous, unappreciated, dangerous from time to time, and we have long holidays. We can also go on strike, just like the garbage collectors."

In the coffee shop, over their steaming mugs, Judith said, "All this term, I've been trying to decide whether or not to come back next year."

"What do you mean by that?" Strand poured sugar into his mug.

"Aren't you afraid of diabetes or getting fat or anything like that?" Judith asked, shaking her head as Strand offered her the sugar dispenser.

"I glory in my health," Strand said. "It's the one thing I'm comparatively sure of. Now—are you serious about what you just said?"

"Yes." Judith nodded slowly, her neatly bobbed black hair, a few streaks of white showing in it, moving gently around her face.

"What would you do if you didn't come back?"

Judith shrugged and took the coffee mug up to her mouth with both hands, making her look momentarily childish. "Become a veterinarian, maybe," she said. "Handling wild animals would come easy after what I've been going through. Or become a nun. I'm a lapsed Catholic, but for the peace of a convent maybe I could unlapse."

"Did you ever think of marriage?"

Judith blushed and Strand was sorry he had asked the question.

"Of course," Judith said. "But the offers haven't been —well—brilliant."

"You're an attractive woman." As he said it, Strand realized that he almost believed it.

"I've been waiting, as the girls say, for Mr. Right to come along. So far," she said, sounding defiant, "Mr. Wrong has shown up. Several times. I'm a simple woman, but I'm not simple enough to believe that marriage would solve any of my problems. Has it solved any of yours?" she asked challengingly.

"Some," Strand said. "And created others," he added, to keep from sounding smug. "Children . . ." He was about to say "money" but refrained. Instead he said,

"There are a lot of places in this world I'd like to see. But on a teacher's salary you don't do an awful lot of traveling. I encourage it in my offspring and tell them to bring back photographs. One of my daughters is thinking of going to Greece this summer." He didn't know why he had brought that into the conversation.

"I made a tour of the Lake District last summer," Judith said. "The English teacher's dream."

"How was it?"

"Dreary." Judith laughed sourly. "It rained all the time and I was with a group of English teachers from the Middle West. We discussed Wordsworth for one day and spent the rest of the time on how to present *Hamlet* to teenage children. I didn't say much. It's hard to explain that most of the children I have anything to do with have seen murders—real murders—on their own blocks and would gladly kill their uncles, and their mothers and fathers, too, if they had the chance."

"I must go to Vienna some day with a group of history teachers," Strand said, "and tell them about the difficulties I have in explaining the position of Metternich at the Congress of Vienna to my classes."

They both laughed. "Ah," Judith said, "we'll both come back next year, won't we?"

"Doomed," Strand said. "Obsessed. Though we have our triumphs, don't we?" He thought of Jesus Romero that afternoon. "Some of them pretty hard to bear."

"A girl I taught some time back and told she could be a writer had a short story in *Penthouse* last month," Judith said. "Pretty damned sexy. I hid the magazine from my mother when she came to visit me."

"Tomorrow will be a better day," Strand said, finishing his coffee and standing.

"Don't bet on it," Judith Quinlan said, as she stood, too.

There was nobody in the apartment when Strand got there, and he took advantage of Leslie's absence to take a nap. He felt exhausted and it was delicious to fall asleep.

He awoke with the feeling that someone else was home.

It couldn't have been Leslie or she would have come into the bedroom. He smoothed the bedcover so that she wouldn't see that he had been napping and put on his shoes and went into the hallway. He could hear dishes being rattled in the kitchen and went in there. Caroline was sitting at the table drinking a glass of milk and eating a piece of cake. He saw from the white cotton collar above her sweater that she had been playing tennis.

"Hi, Daddy," she said. "Join me?"

Strand looked at his watch. "I'll wait for dinner."

"I couldn't," she said. "I'd swoon with hunger." She put a big hunk of cake in her mouth. It had soft chocolate icing and she licked the smudges off her fingers. "Yummy," she said.

He sat opposite her, smiling, vicariously enjoying her appetite. "If people can have chocolate cake," she said, her mouth full, "I can't understand their going for cocaine. Oh, I met our friend again."

"Which friend?"

"Mr. Hazen. He came around to the courts. He sure looks a mess. Like a lopsided cantaloupe. That ski hat. It must have been knitted by a blind Norwegian troll."

"Be kindly, Caroline, please," Strand said.

"He's okay, though. Really. He said he came to make sure I got home safely. He said he didn't want me to get into any more incidents. That was some incident the other night. *Mother!* I'd still be playing, only he kept looking at his watch and fretting. We had a nice talk on the way home."

"Did you?" Strand said. Somehow, the thought that a busy man like Hazen would take the time to walk a seventeen-year-old girl across the park made him uneasy. He remembered what he had said to Judith Quinlan when they had passed the fat man in the baseball cap at the street corner—"Maybe he's just a simple child molester." It was just a joke, of course, but child molesting itself was no joke and older men in all walks of life were not immune from the disease. He himself had been deeply troubled by a lovely high school friend of Eleanor's who was constantly around the apartment. He had to make a conscious effort to keep from touching her and he had to hide what he felt when she kissed his cheek in greeting and he was tortured by the most realistic and explicit erotic dreams about her. He was not the sort of man to go beyond these involuntary excursions, but who knew what sort of man Hazen really was? People didn't go around wearing signs that read "Child molester." And he had to face the fact that Caroline was no longer a child but fast becoming an attractive young woman. He knew he couldn't say anything of this to Caroline, but if there were any developments that looked ominous he would speak to Leslie, whose instincts were more dependable than his. "What did you talk about?" he asked Caroline.

"A lot of things." Caroline took another chunk of cake and washed it down with the milk. "He watched me and he commented on the way I played. I was surprised. He knew what he was talking about."

"He was an athlete when he was young and he belongs to the Racquet Club."

"Is that so," said Caroline, unimpressed. "Anyway, he said I was pretty good and that I should try to get more spin on my second serve and hit my backhand flatter and I agree with him one hundred percent. He asked me if I wanted to go in for tennis seriously—you know, coaches and training and all that jazz—and I told him no, I wasn't good enough, I'd never make it and I'd just eat my heart out getting put out of tournaments in the first round. He said that was wise, we should recognize our limitations. On a tennis court," she said grimly, "it's no big deal recognizing your limitations I told him, and he laughed." She laughed. Then she became more serious. "What did I intend to do with my life, he asked. He doesn't mind asking questions, does he?"

"What did you tell him?"

Caroline gave him a sidelong, covert glance, hesitated, as though she were about to say something, then changed her mind.

He was conscious of a lie, a subterfuge. It was not like Caroline. She was not a secretive girl. She had gone through the usual choices as she was growing up—ballet dancer, actress, nurse—but that was only until she was about twelve. Since then she had been content, it seemed, merely to pass in school and play tennis when she could. He was surprised that she had spoken as openly as she had with Hazen. She was a shy girl who spoke very little and guardedly, except with the family; she had few friends, all of them girls, and he knew from Leslie and Eleanor that she thought boys were making fun of her when they made any advances and fled from them.

"What did you tell Mr. Hazen?" Allen repeated.

"I told him I intended to grow up," Caroline said, almost defiantly.

"Did he laugh?" Strand asked.

"He doesn't laugh much, Mr. Hazen," Caroline said. "He said he was very much impressed with Eleanor. Naturally." She spoke without a trace of jealousy, as though she accepted the fact that Eleanor was the star of the family. "He said if there were more young women like that there'd be no need for the Equal Rights Amendment or magazines like *Ms*. They must have had a real heart-to-heart conversation in the taxi. He didn't mention Jimmy." She scowled, as though she considered this a slight to her brother. "Has *he* got any children?"

"Three," Strand said. "A boy and two girls. Approximately the same age as you three."

"It's funny, he never said a word. Do you go around bragging about us?"

"Bragging isn't the word," Strand said. "I mourn your mother's fecundity."

"I bet," Caroline said, smiling. She got up from the table and leaned over and gave Strand a kiss. "Oops," she said, "chocolate on the foredeck." She took out a handkerchief and wiped the chocolate off, then put the remains of the cake in the refrigerator and tossed the empty milk carton into the trash basket. "He's going to call you tonight, he said."

"What for?"

"He wants to invite us all out to the country this weekend. He has a house on the beach in East Hampton with a pool and a tennis court and everything. It sounds super, doesn't it?"

"Super," Strand said.

"He says there are some good players I could have a game with and if anybody wanted to ride, there are horses nearby. He said he'd pick us up in his car Friday afternoon and get us back Sunday night."

"Your mother has lessons on Saturday morning."

"Once, just once," Caroline said, "she could let those brats play baseball or smoke pot or look at television on Saturday morning. Just once."

"We'll talk it over when your mother comes home."

"I'll tell you the one thing that's wrong with you and Mother," Caroline said. "You're too conscientious."

"Perhaps you're right. Now you'd better go in and take your shower before your mother gets home."

"Righto," Caroline said cheerily and started out of the kitchen. Suddenly she stopped. "Oh, one more thing."

"What's that?"

"Mr. Hazen said he talked to one of his partners at the office and his partner convinced him he ought to report the crime, that's what he called it, the crime, to the police. He's already done it, he said something about his civic duty, and that he wasn't thinking clearly the night it happened. He said that there'd probably be a detective around to ask me questions. How do you talk to a detective?"

"I'm not an authority on that," Strand said. "I've never talked to one that I know of."

"I hope he's a young one," Caroline said and started off again, but Strand stopped her.

"Caroline," he said, "don't tell your mother about the detective."

"Why not?"

"Because probably it'll never happen and it's no use reminding her of what Mr. Hazen calls the incident. She may not have looked it to you, but she was terribly upset about you Friday night and I know she's started to worry about your going into the park even during the day."

"Okay, Daddy," Caroline said. "She's your wife."

"By the way, Caroline, did you thank Mr. Hazen for the racquet?"

"Of course," Caroline said, with dignity. "I'm not a *complete* savage. Profusely." Humming, she went down the hall toward her shower. Strand rinsed off Caroline's plate and glass and knife and dried them, to hide the predinner malfeasance from Leslie. As he put them away he wondered if he ought to go to the nearest precinct house and tell whoever took charge of those things to please not send any detectives to the apartment, it had been too dark for his daughter to have recognized any of the boys involved and she was preparing for her final examinations and he'd prefer it if she weren't distracted for the time being. He had a hunch that with all the major problems the police had to cope with in the neighborhood they'd be only too glad to file the report and forget it.

He heard the phone ringing and went into the foyer to answer it. It was Eleanor.

"How was the weekend?" he asked.

"Green," she said. "I slept and the others drank most of the time. The people I was staying with know the Hazens. Correction on my first report about your friend. He *had* three children. The boy died. O.D.'d."

"What?"

"O.D.'d. Overdosed. Heroin. Five months ago. Everybody was away for the weekend and he left word with the help he didn't want to be disturbed. They didn't disturb him and when they finally broke the lock into his room it was all over."

"Oh, God."

"Chilling, isn't it? Maybe you ought to go into Jimmy's room and look for needles."

"Eleanor," Strand said firmly, "do you know anything about Jimmy that you haven't told us?"

"No. Only you can't be too careful. The places he hangs out—and the people . . ."

"I'm sure he isn't . . . isn't one of those."

"Maybe Mr. Hazen was sure, too. Why don't you ask him?"

"I'll do nothing of the kind."

"I suppose you're right," Eleanor said. "No use getting the wind up. It was a random thought. Forget it. I heard some more about the Hazen family, too. His wife is not well liked, it seems, spends most of her time in Europe. The daughters're not anyone's pets, either. One is living with a so-called New Film director in San Francisco, no visible means of support. The other is in Rome, occupation unknown. Both very pretty according to my friends. No wonder Mr. Hazen liked the idea of having dinner with us. Although he is reputed to have a mistress. Not such sizzling news toward the end of the twentieth century, is it?"

"No," Strand said.

"Kisses to everybody," Eleanor said. "See you on Friday night."

Strand hung up, stared at the telephone. O.D.'d. He shivered. The sense of guilt must be an impossible burden. Good reason for talking about the nihilism of the young, the responsibility toward the new generation, the offer to help Jesus Romero, the walk through the park with a healthy young athlete. All those clubs, all those board meetings, all that money and your son is left undisturbed for two days . . .

Strand went down the hallway, stopped at the door to Jimmy's room. He looked at it for a long time, then tried the handle. The door was unlocked and swung open a little. Strand hesitated, then closed it firmly.

At dinner, which they were eating in the kitchen, there were only Strand, Leslie and Caroline. Jimmy made sporadic appearances for the evening meal, but conscientiously told his mother if he was going to be absent. Strand hadn't told Leslie about Hazen's invitation and he could feel Caroline's imploring eyes on him. "Now," she finally said, in a stage whisper.

"Now what?" he asked, although he knew what she was talking about.

"You know. The weekend," Caroline said.

Leslie looked at him inquiringly. She had been busy with dinner since she got home and he had been working on the schedule for the final exams and aside from a kiss of welcome and a few words about their respective days, guarded and noncommittal on his part, with no mention of detectives or Jesus Romero or young men found having O.D.'d.

"What weekend?" Leslie asked.

"It seems that Mr. Hazen was passing by the tennis courts and walked Caroline home," Strand said.

"That was thoughtful of him."

"Very," Strand said. "It turns out that he has a house in East Hampton . . ."

"With a tennis court and a pool," Caroline put in. "Heated. The pool, I mean. And it's on the ocean."

"What in the world would people need a pool for with the whole Atlantic Ocean just in front of them?" Leslie asked sensibly.

"Oh, Mother," Caroline said. "For bad weather. And the ocean's *cold*."

"Well," Leslie said, "it's his money. Anyway, what's Mr. Hazen's house on the ocean got to do with us?"

"He invited us out for the weekend," Strand said, "via Caroline."

"*All* of us," Caroline said.

"That's carrying gratitude for a single bowl of soup pretty far," Leslie said. She looked at Strand. "What do you think?"

Strand shrugged. "What do *you* think?"

"He'll pick us up in his car on Friday afternoon," Caroline said, the words tumbling out of her mouth, "and drive us back on Sunday night."

"There're all those lessons on Saturday morning," Leslie said doubtfully.

"Those snooty juvenile delinquents," Caroline said. "They'd vote you Woman of the Year if you gave them one Saturday off."

"Sssh, Caroline," Leslie said. "I'm thinking."

"There's too much thinking going on in this house," Caroline said despairingly. "We'll think ourselves into absolute *inertia*."

"Will you keep quiet for a moment, Caroline," Strand said crossly.

"He's a lonely old man," Caroline persisted. "The least we could do would be to cheer him up a little. The house has sixteen bedrooms he told me. How would you like to be alone rattling around in sixteen bedrooms week after week? You and Mother're always telling me we should be considerate of the needs of others. Well, let me tell you, Mr. Hazen is an other."

"Miss lawyer," Leslie said crisply, "if you'll stop for a minute, maybe we can discuss this."

"There's nothing to discuss," Caroline said.

Leslie touched her hand gently.

"All right," Caroline said, sitting back, resigned and folding her arms. "My lips're sealed."

"Are you sure he included us all?" Leslie asked. "Jimmy and Eleanor, too?"

"Sure," Caroline said.

"Did he say as much?" Strand said.

"Not in so many words," Caroline admitted. "But it was certainly implied."

"Allen," Leslie said, "you look as though a little sea air wouldn't do you any harm."

"Now," Caroline said triumphantly, "we're beginning to talk some sense around here."

"I imagine I could postpone the lessons," Leslie said thoughtfully. "Some way. And I'd have to talk to Eleanor and Jimmy, see what they want to do . . ."

"If they *deprive* me," Caroline said, "for their own selfish reasons, I'll never speak to either one of them again."

"Don't talk like a baby," Leslie said. "I said we'd discuss it."

Then the phone rang and Strand stood up from the table. "I'll get it," he said. "It's probably the lonesome lawyer, himself."

It was Hazen on the phone. "I'm not interrupting your dinner, I hope," he said.

"No," Strand said. "We were just finishing."

"Did you enjoy the Berlioz?"

"It was superb," Strand said. "Thank you again."

"Not at all. Any time you want to go, just let me know. They send me tickets for just about everything and very often I find I'm not free on a particular evening."

"Caroline told me you walked her home," Strand said, thinking, What must it be like to be sent tickets to just about everything? "It was very thoughtful of you."

"She's a lovely child," Hazen said. "And bright, along with everything else. Did she tell you about our enjoyable little conversation?"

"She did," Strand said. He couldn't help thinking about how Hazen would describe whatever conversations he had had with his son before they broke the lock on the door. "I had a little conversation myself with a young person this afternoon," Strand said. "The boy I told you about—Romero. Not exactly enjoyable."

"What did he say?"

"He'll think about it."

"Would it help if I talked to him?" Hazen asked.

"I doubt it."

"Well, you know best. Did Caroline ask you about coming out to the Island this weekend?"

"Indeed she did," Strand said. "She's been bludgeoning her mother and me all through dinner about it."

"You *are* coming, aren't you?" Hazen sounded anxious. Sixteen bedrooms to rattle around in and a heated pool to swim in by himself. "We're still trying to see if we can work it out," Strand said.

"Your other daughter and your son are invited, too, of course."

"So Caroline implied. I don't know what their plans are. Can I call you on Wednesday or Thursday?"

"Anytime," Hazen said quickly. "Have you got a pencil handy? I'll give you my office telephone number."

"Right here," Strand said and jotted down the number Hazen gave him over the phone. "By the way, Caroline tells me you still look a bit the worse for wear."

"It's nothing," Hazen said quickly. "If I don't look in the mirror or infants don't scream in their carriages at the sight of me, I forget anything ever happened."

"Caroline also mentioned something about the police,"

Strand said, lowering his voice, so it wouldn't carry into the kitchen.

"Yes. A useless formality, I'm afraid. But one of my partners is on the Mayor's Juvenile Crime Commission and he says assembling accurate statistics is one of the hardest parts of the job and more to please him than for anything else, I . . . You don't mind, do you?"

"I suppose not," Strand said, but he knew he sounded reluctant.

"Well, I hope you can make it this weekend," Hazen said. "I'll await your call."

They said their good-byes and Strand hung up. He went back into the kitchen.

"Well?" Caroline asked anxiously.

"It must be tough, filling those bedrooms," Strand said, sitting down.

"You didn't answer me," Caroline wailed.

"I said I'd let him know later in the week," Strand said. "Now let me eat my dessert."

5

Forget them, forget the men falling . . .

It was Conroy who came to pick them up on Friday afternoon, in a long Mercedes limousine with jump seats. Mr. Hazen sent his apologies, Conroy said, he was unexpectedly detained at the office, but would come down later in the evening. Strand sat in the front seat beside Conroy. Leslie, Eleanor, Caroline and Jimmy sat in the back. Strand had been a little surprised when Eleanor had said that she'd like to go. She loved the Hamptons, especially out of season, she said, and had a lot of friends there she'd like to see. That was another thing he hadn't known about Eleanor, Strand thought, as he put down the phone —that she was familiar with the Hamptons and had many friends there. He wondered what other revelations she had in store for him and for that matter what information Leslie, Jimmy and Caroline, now all chattering briskly in the back of the car, would divulge to him when they thought it convenient to do so.

"By the way," Conroy said, "there's a station wagon in the garage you can use if you want to get around."

"I don't drive," Strand said, "and neither does my wife. But Eleanor has a license." She had owned a beat-up old Ford the last two years in college. He turned and said, "Eleanor, did you hear what Mr. Conroy said? There's a station wagon in the garage you can use."

"Does that go for me, too?" Jimmy asked.

"Of course," Conroy said.

"I didn't know you had a license, Jimmy," Strand said.

"A friend loaned me his car for a few afternoons," Jimmy said, "and I tootled around and took the test."

Strand shook his head. Something else he hadn't been told about his family.

Conroy asked if they wanted him to turn the radio on and get some music, but Leslie vetoed the idea. "We never can agree on what we want to hear," she said, "and I don't want my ride to be spoiled for Jimmy and Caroline and Eleanor nor theirs for mine."

Strand enjoyed the trip. It was a balmy evening, the sun still shining. Conroy drove well and after they got out of Queens the traffic was light and the big Mercedes smoothly ate up the miles through the lines of trees of the Parkway. In a way Strand was glad that Hazen had been detained at his office. If he'd been along Hazen would have kept the conversation going and Strand preferred to ride in silence. Conroy didn't speak and Strand felt no need to listen to the holiday babble going on behind him. He was glad they had all decided the weekend would be a treat and he looked forward to seeing the inside of Hazen's house. You could tell a great deal about a man from seeing the way he lived. Hazen was a new breed of animal for Strand and he was growing more and more curious about the lawyer. Strand was by nature cautious about quick impressions of people and had not yet made up his mind about what he really thought about Hazen. The circumstances under which they had met had been bizarre and with all his talking, Strand realized as he thought about it, Hazen had managed to find out a great deal about the family without telling anything much about himself except that his family had arrived in New York in 1706 and had never gone to Ohio. His absolute silence about his own immediate family, for example, was well beyond the bounds of ordinary discretion and except for confessing that he was a lawyer and went to symphony concerts, he had confined himself almost entirely to impersonal abstractions. From *Who's Who* Strand knew a considerable amount about the public man; the private one was still concealed.

While waiting for the car to come to pick them up Eleanor had said of Hazen, "That man wants something."

"Why do you say that?" Strand had asked.

"A man like that always wants something," Eleanor had said, and he had been annoyed at her cynicism. In Strand's code you didn't accept hospitality, especially of this lavishness, from somebody about whom you had misgivings, even if they were only as vague as his daughter's.

Leslie, who had a proprietary interest in the man whose wounds she had tended and admired the stoical way he had behaved when he was in pain, had snapped, uncharacteristically, at Eleanor, "If you feel like that, why don't you just go someplace else for the weekend?"

"Sorry," Eleanor had said. "I thought we were in America. Freedom of speech. Guaranteed by the Constitution, and all that."

"Hush, everybody," Strand had said. "This is a holiday."

Jimmy had just grinned, pleased that for once Eleanor and not he was on the receiving end of a rebuke. Caroline had paid no attention to what was going on, but had sat dreamily humming to herself, cradling her racquet in its new case.

Looking out at the swiftly passing spring countryside, Strand thought about the exchange between his wife and his daughter and wondered if what Eleanor had said had some truth in it, then decided it was just idle spite, born of Eleanor's jealousy or distaste for some of her superiors under whose orders she chafed on her job and whom, rightly or wrongly, she identified with Hazen. For himself, Strand decided that he would accept Hazen at face value. The face so far, he had to admit, was somewhat obscure, but he had detected no signs of malice or desire for advantage. Quite the opposite. If anything, after the news about the son, Strand pitied the man and sympathized with him. If Hazen was using the family to alleviate his loneliness, that hardly could be called manipulation. Strand remembered his fleeting suspicion of Hazen's intentions about Caroline and smiled. Hazen would hardly have asked them out to his house *en masse* if he was plotting to satisfy his lust for the seventeen-year-old daughter of the family.

He dozed, the steady motion of the big car lulling him, and awoke only as the car slowed down and turned into a private road leading from a stone gate through a long alley of high trees toward the sea, whose rumble could now be heard.

Conroy stopped the car in a raked gravel courtyard and tooted the horn. "Here we are," he said and they got out of the car. An enormous rambling white clapboard house loomed up against the clear twilight sky.

"Man," Jimmy said, whistling, "that's some hunk of architecture."

"It was built by Mr. Hazen's grandfather," Conroy said. "They thought big in those days."

The old American doom, Strand thought, from shirtsleeves to shirtsleeves in three generations, obviously didn't apply to the Hazens. The grandfather could be proud of the grandson.

Conroy touched the horn again, and in answer to the signal a man and a woman came hurrying from the house.

"Mr. and Mrs. Ketley," Conroy said. "They take care of the house. They'll bring up your bags." He introduced them to the servants. The man wore black trousers and a starched white cotton jacket. His wife was dressed in a black uniform, with a white apron. They were both middle-aged, pleasant-appearing people who looked as though they had worked hard all their lives.

"I'll be saying good-bye to you now," Conroy said. "I have to go back to town to pick up Mr. Hazen at the office and bring him back here."

"You're going to make this whole trip all over again?" Leslie asked.

"It's nothing," Conroy said. "We should be here by eleven."

"If we'd known, we could have waited until Mr. Hazen was ready to leave," Leslie said. "It seems like such an imposition."

"Mr. Hazen wouldn't have heard of it," Conroy said. "Make yourself at home, he told me to tell you, and ask

the Ketleys if there's anything you want. Dinner is ordered for you." He got into the car, faithful servitor,
bicycle rider, anonymous, forever on duty, messenger in
neutral livery, man of many small useful talents. He
started the engine, made a sweeping turn in the courtyard
and the taillights of the Mercedes disappeared down the
alley of trees.

"This way, please," Mr. Ketley said, leading the family
toward the front door of the house, which was flanked by
two huge carriage lamps that snapped on as they walked
across the flagstones that bordered the entrance.

As they went into the front hall, from which a broad
staircase with a mahogany rail curved up to the next floor,
Mr. Ketley asked if they would like to be shown their
rooms or prefer to have a drink first to refresh themselves
after the journey.

Strand said he'd stay down for a while, but refused the
drink with thanks and strolled into the living room while
the Ketleys led the way upstairs for the others. The room
was large, with dark wood wainscotting on which hung
paintings by Pissarro, Vlaminck, Chagall and Dufy, as
well as some abstract oils by painters whose work Strand
could not identify. A grand piano stood in one corner,
closed. There were flowers everywhere in large bowls and
low, comfortable sofas and easy chairs of a nondescript,
unpretentious style that contrasted with what looked like
authentic Early American wooden chairs, tables and desk.
There was a big fireplace, with a fire laid but not lit. The
windows and a door along one side fronted on the ocean.
Hazen might complain that he had too many bedrooms
vacant for his psychic comfort, but his creature wants
were certainly handsomely taken care of. Still, there was
little in the house, or at least in the living room, that spoke
of its owner. And except for the piano and the paintings
there was no indication of the particular interests of the
inhabitants. Through a half-open door, Strand glimpsed a
small library. He would examine the books at another
time. He didn't want Mr. or Mrs. Ketley to catch him
prying. The house had obviously been built at the turn of
the century, and its fixtures and furnishings looked as

though they had been supplied as needed by several generations with varying tastes.

Strand opened the door that led out to the terrace and the roar of the sea filled the room. He stepped out and looked across at the dark expanse of the Atlantic in the twilight. The sea itself was calm, but long rollers from far out swept in and crashed on the beach. Just below the terrace a fine mist rose from the surface of the swimming pool, reflecting the lights from the house.

Strand breathed deeply, luxuriating in the tonic salt air. Far off along the dunes there were other lights from houses that also faced the ocean, but there were no immediate neighbors. If the grandfather had wanted peace, he had chosen the site for his mansion shrewdly. Little more than a hundred miles from New York City, there was the feeling of limitless space, of a benevolent climate whose silence was broken only by the sound of the sea and the cries of gulls. Standing there, Strand thought, you could forget that your fellow citizens were struggling to breathe in the city, crowded inhumanly in fetid subway cars, assaulted by the clamor of traffic, forced to waste their days in mindless occupations. On the border of the sea, the air fragrant with the odor of salt and the scent of grass and flowers, for one evening at least, you could forget the wars that were at that moment being fought all over the earth; for one evening forget the men falling, the towns going up in flames, the bloody clash of races, tribes, ambitions.

Yes, Strand thought, as he went back into the house, closing out the rumble of the Atlantic as he shut the door, Leslie was right, a little sea air won't do me any harm.

There was a fire going in the dining room fireplace when they went in to dinner and candles on the table. Eleanor had changed into pale blue slacks and a cashmere sweater and Jimmy had taken off his necktie, which, Strand supposed, Jimmy believed made him appropriately dressed for a country weekend. Leslie, who rarely wore slacks, although she had fine legs, had put on a long, printed cotton skirt and a blouse that left her arms bare.

Caroline had scrubbed her face in the shower and looked, Strand said to himself, dotingly, new-minted. To Strand, sitting at the head of the table, his family presented a picture of decorous and attractive health and in the light from the fire and the candles Leslie looked like a beautiful, only slightly older sister to the two girls who sat on either side of him. "Believe it or not," she had whispered to him when she came down to dinner, "there's a Renoir drawing in our room. A nude. Imagine that. In a *bedroom*."

It was a splendid meal, clams and delicious bluefish, served by Mr. Ketley. He poured a white French wine and they all took some, even Caroline, who said, in explanation of her inaugural indulgence, "Well, this is the first time I've ever had dinner in front of a fireplace. Isn't it sexy?"

Jimmy raised his glass in a toast. "Here's to the rich," he said.

Caroline giggled, impolitely, Strand thought, as she sipped at her wine and Strand glanced surreptitiously at Mr. Ketley to see how the man was reacting to this tribute to his employer. But Mr. Ketley was wrapping a towel around a second bottle of wine and he seemed not to notice what was said at the table. Still, taking no chances, Strand raised his glass and said, "To the kind hospitality of our absent host."

By the wink that Jimmy flashed him he knew that Jimmy understood what his father was doing. He would have to speak to Jimmy later and remind him to look to his manners for the weekend.

After dinner Mr. Ketley came around with a box of cigars. Strand started to shake his head, then reached into the box and took one. As he used the clipper that Mr. Ketley gave him to cut the end of the cigar, Leslie looked at him doubtfully. "Are you sure want—" she said.

"If at her age Caroline decided that this was the night for her first glass of wine," Strand said, "I guess her father is old enough to try his first cigar." He puffed diligently as Mr. Ketley held a lighter for him. The smoke tasted surprisingly good.

"Mr. Ketley," Jimmy said, "I think I'd like one, too."

"Jimmy," Leslie said.

"I like the way it looks on Pops," Jimmy said. "Maybe it'll improve my appearance, too." He took a cigar from the box, examined it approvingly. "Havanas. Sneaked into the country under the guns of the Gringo Imperialists. I'm doing my bit for World Revolution."

Definitely, Strand thought, as Jimmy lit the cigar and clenched it between his teeth at a jaunty angle, definitely I'll have to have a little talk with him about what is and what isn't permissible to say in this house. He was pleased to see that after the first few puffs Jimmy waved the cigar around, twirling it in his fingers, and smoked it only enough to keep it alight. It was less than half smoked when Jimmy crushed it out in an ashtray as he and Eleanor said their good nights and went off in the station wagon to Bridgehampton, where, according to Eleanor, there was a cozy bar with a lot of nice people usually hanging around it and where the owner played a good jazz piano in the evenings.

Caroline said she wanted to watch television and settled herself in front of the set in the small library, and Strand and Leslie decided to take a walk on the beach. Dressed warmly against the evening chill and holding hands they strolled on the hard sand left by an ebbing tide, occasionally feeling a little sting of salt on their faces from the waves foaming onto the beach. The moon was up in a clear sky and there was a brisk wind and on the horizon they could see the lights of a ship going east.

Leslie squeezed her husband's hand. "Only perfect," she murmured.

Strand sat in one of the easy chairs in front of the dwindling fire in the living room. The house was quiet and he was alone. Leslie was upstairs preparing for bed and she liked solitude for the ritual of creaming her face and brushing her hair. Eleanor and Jimmy had not yet come back and the Ketleys had long ago gone to their room at the rear of the house. Strand sighed contentedly as he

watched the dancing patterns of the fire. Then he heard
the sound of a car driving up to the house and stopping.

A moment later Hazen and Conroy came into the living
room and Strand stood up to greet his host. "Good eve—"
he said, then stopped. There was something wrong with
Hazen. Under the dark felt hat that sat squarely on his
head his eyes stared straight ahead, unseeingly, and he
walked slowly and stiffly, with great care, as if he would
stagger if he went any faster. At his side, Conroy looked
haggard, his hands out, ready to catch his employer if he
started to fall. As Hazen came closer, without seeming to
notice Strand standing in front of him, there was a strong
smell of whiskey. He was very drunk. Conroy made a
little apologetic grimace at Strand as Hazen sprawled, still
with his hat on, into a deep easy chair.

"Conroy," Hazen said, speaking very slowly and deliberately, "I want a whiskey. And bring the soda bottle. I'll
pour the soda myself. I don't want you goddamn drowning
the Scotch."

"Yes, sir," Conroy said and went over to the sideboard
that served as a bar.

"Excellent secretary, Conroy," Hazen said, still not looking at Strand. "Excellent chauffeur. But unde—undepend-
able when it comes to drink. Strand," he said, without
turning his head, "you're a lucky man. You do not have
to deal with thieves. I, on the other hand, deal almost ex-
clusively with thieves, week in, week out. Week in, week
out. It isn't love that makes the world go round, Strand,
as they say, it is greed, naked, over—overpowering, criminal greed. I tell you, Strand, if the laws of the land were
ever enforced, three-quarters of our most re—respected
citizens would be in our country's jails. For Christ's sake,
Conroy, am I going to have to wait all the fucking night
for my drink?"

"Coming, sir." Conroy, cupbearer, among other things,
hurried over with the glass and the small bottle of soda.

Without looking up, Hazen put out his hand and Conroy put the glass into it. "Now, pour the soda," Hazen
said. "Gently, gently. Enough!" Conroy, dose-dealer, had
barely put a thimbleful of soda into the whiskey. "Conroy

does not drink and does not approve of others drinking."
Hazen glared up at his secretary. "Am I being accurate,
sir?"

"More or less, sir," Conroy said, bowing a little.

"More or less." Hazen nodded solemnly. "Conroy is a
more or less man. A teetotaler, he tolls the drunkards'
knell. An anal type. Beware of teetotalers, Strand, they will
have their total revenge." He laughed hoarsely, then carefully, stiffly, like an automaton, raised the glass to his lips
and drank. "For this relief," he said, "much thanks." He
laughed hoarsely again. "Strand," he said, "I travel in the
country of despair. Do you believe in God?"

"Yes."

"Conroy," Hazen said, "get the hell to bed."

"I thought perhaps you might need me," Conroy, ashen
with fatigue but ever available, said nervously. "I'm not
tired, really."

"I'm tired," Hazen said. "You tire me. Get out of here.
I can go to bed by myself. I don't need you to assist in
my dreams. Get out of here, man. Go."

"Yes, sir," Conroy said. "Good night, sir. Good night,
Mr. Strand." He went out the front door, watchdog of
power, uneasy at dismissal.

"There's a room for him over the garage," Hazen said.
"Conroy. I don't like the idea of his sleeping in the same
house with me. Understandable, isn't it, Strand?"

"Well . . ." Strand mumbled, at a loss. "I don't know
him and . . ."

"Understandable. Did I ask you if you believed in
God?"

"Yes."

"And what did you answer?"

"I said I did."

"You are out of joint with the times, Strand. Do you
believe in the Ten Commandments?"

"I would say yes," Strand said, feeling foolish at this
drunken catechism in the middle of the night.

"One meeting with my col—colleagues," Hazen said,
"and your beliefs would change. Honor thy father and
thy mother. It's late, Strand. I like to sit here alone and

have a little nightcap in the waning hours and reflect. Reflect. I mentioned my admiration for Mr. Buster Keaton on our walk, did I not?"

"You did." Now what? Strand thought, regretting that he had not gone up with Leslie before Hazen arrived.

"He knows the whole thing is a cosmic joke. Our plans fail, our achievements are der-derisory, we are balked at every turn, we are doomed to slip on every banana peel, and he accepts it all stoically, with silent dignity, to the sound of divine laughter. A lesson for us all." Hazen laughed harshly, the sound like a cry of pain. "Reflect," he said. "I'm sure you would rather join your charming wife upstairs, the holy bonds of matrimony, as it were, than stay down here and be embarrassed by my re—reflec— flections on religion. I am perfectly well, sir." For the first time, he turned his head and looked at Strand. His face was desolate. "Despite some evidence to the contrary, I am not a drinking man. Thou shalt make no graven images. I am surrounded by graven images. Weep for the times, Strand, and sleep well. Good night, sir."

Strand hesitated. He was troubled. Under the drunken but magisterial calm of his host, in the alcoholic hours of the night what turmoil lay, what appeal for help? He shook his head. Better not to get involved. Sea air or no sea air. "Good night," he said and went out of the room, feeling profoundly inadequate. As he climbed the stairs he knew he wasn't going to tell Leslie about Hazen. If he were to describe the scene she'd rush downstairs and try to reason with Hazen and put him to bed and he knew that wouldn't do, it wouldn't do at all.

When he got into bed she reached for him, sleepy and warm. "I'm bushed," he said. It was the first time he hadn't responded to her. There always has to be a first time, he thought, as he tried to sleep.

When Strand came down the next morning, he saw Hazen sitting at the breakfast table, reading the *Times*. He was dressed for tennis and wearing an old sweater against the early chill. The scar on his bald head was still an ugly red, but Strand could see that the wound was closed and well on its way toward healing. Hazen's cheek was still slightly discolored, but his skin otherwise was a healthy pink. As Hazen rose and shook his hand, Strand saw that his eyes were clear and his hand steady. After that night, Strand thought.

"I hope you slept well," Hazen said, his voice calm and courteous. "Ketley brought another copy of the paper for you . . ." He pointed to the sideboard, where a fresh copy lay. "I dislike having my paper all fussed up and I imagine most fathers of a family are a bit like me in that respect, too."

"I must confess I am," Strand said as he seated himself opposite Hazen. If Hazen chose to ignore the events of the night before, to pretend that nothing had happened, no grief revealed, Strand certainly was not going to bring them up. "I'll read it later. But please don't let me interrupt you."

"I've read enough for the moment," Hazen said, folding the paper and putting it to one side. "The usual disasters. Was the dinner all right?"

"Perfect."

Hazen nodded. "They're an excellent couple, the Ketleys. What would you like for breakfast?" he said, as Mr. Ketley came in from the kitchen. "Juice, bacon and eggs?"

"That would be fine." At home he refused to allow Leslie to get up to make him breakfast and made do with a cup of coffee and a roll. He was always starving by noon.

"You heard what Mr. Strand wants?" Hazen said to Ketley.

"Yes, sir," Ketley said.

"Oh, by the way," Hazen said, "will you tell Ronny that if he wants to have a catch this morning, I'll be ready for him after my tennis match."

"I'm sure he'll be waiting for you," Ketley said and went back to the kitchen.

"Ronny's his grandson," Hazen said. "He's eleven. He pitches for his Little League team. I give him a target to throw at." He poured himself a cup of coffee. "I'm terribly sorry I had to let you shift for yourselves last night," he said, "but there was no getting away. Conroy is sleeping the sleep of the just. I had a refreshing nap in the car while he drove. I heard your children come in about two in the morning . . ."

"They didn't disturb you, I hope."

"Not at all. I just happened to hear the station wagon drive up. They were as quiet as could be."

"They went to a bar in Bridgehampton that Eleanor knows about."

"Amazing how young people can hang out in dingy bars for hours on end. Especially since, according to Ketley, they hardly drink at all."

As Ketley came in with a glass of orange juice and a fresh pot of coffee, Strand wondered what else the man had included in his report about the family.

"I trust Caroline wasn't with them on their nocturnal revels," Hazen said.

"No. She looked at television for a while and went to bed early."

"Good," Hazen said. "I've arranged for some young people to come over this morning for tennis. They're pretty sharp and she'll have to be at her best to keep up with them."

"I see you plan to play, too."

Hazen shrugged. "I may join in for a set or two. They're polite young people and they'll respect my age. They'll try to keep the ball within strolling distance when they hit it at me." He sipped at his coffee. "The arrangements are all right?" he asked.

"The arrangements?" Strand asked, puzzled.

"I mean, you're all comfortably installed and all that? No lumps in the bed or leaking plumbing or noisy pipes?"

"A lot better than comfortably," Strand said. Maybe, he thought, Hazen *had* actually forgotten the night. If so, so much the better. "Magnificently. It's a delightful house."

Hazen nodded absently. "It's a nice house. Made for hordes, of course. The families of our fathers. I often am tempted to sell it. Except on a shining morning like this." He waved toward the windows, flooded with sunlight, the ocean glinting. "If you want to swim later, the pool's heated."

"No, thank you," Strand said. His legs were skinny and he didn't like to be seen in bathing trunks. "I'll just laze around."

"Whatever you like," Hazen said. "There are no rules here."

What he means, Strand thought, is that the rules are so set that nobody notices them anymore.

Ketley came in with the eggs and bacon and toast and put them in front of Strand. "Sir," he said to Hazen, "there's a telephone call for you."

"I was afraid there would be," Hazen said. "Put it into the library for me, please." He stood up. "Excuse me," he said to Strand. "I'm afraid this is going to be a long one. Make yourself at home." He strode out of the dining room. Strand noticed that his legs were long and muscular and could have been those of a young man. All that bicycle riding.

He shook his head, marveling at the constitution, both physical and mental, of the man. He was glad Conroy wasn't at the table. There would be a touchy moment when they next met. Well, he decided, I'm not going to let it spoil my day. He ate his breakfast contentedly, spreading marmalade over his toast and drinking three cups of coffee while he read the *Times*. Hazen didn't come back to the table, and when he was finished, Strand went out on the terrace and lay back in a reclining chair, his eyes closed, his face turned to the morning sun.

The tennis court was off in the garden behind the house, protected from the wind by tall, neatly clipped hedges. Caroline and Hazen and two young men were starting to play when Strand reached the court. He had gone upstairs to see if Leslie would watch the game with him, but Leslie was still in bed, eating her breakfast off a tray that Mrs. Ketley had brought her. She told Strand that this was one Saturday morning in her life that she was just going to do *nothing*. "If the bliss becomes boring after a while," she said, "I may put on some clothes and come down to the court. But don't expect me. My feeling is I'm just going to luxuriate here until lunch." She said nothing about his unaccustomed refusal of the night before.

Strand settled himself in a canvas chair in the little shaded pavilion beside the court. It was a hot day and he could see that Hazen was already sweating, his white cotton sun hat wet just above the brim. The alcohol is coming to the surface, Strand thought. At least it shows he's human. Hazen and Caroline were partners and they seemed, to Strand's inexperienced eye, just about as good as the two young men, who had obviously been playing expertly coached tennis since childhood. Hazen had a cool, accurate game and hit the ball as hard as the others. He didn't run much, but always managed to be in the right place and made as many winning shots, it seemed to Strand, as Caroline, who did a great deal of bouncing about and dove in showy acrobatic leaps at the net. She was obviously enjoying herself and smiled smugly, Strand thought, when she scored an ace on a service or put away an overhead smash. The young men had started rather condescendingly by hitting balls at half speed and not going for the corners, but after Caroline and Hazen won the first two games, they began to slam the ball and flick it along the lines, showing no indulgence either for the age or sex of their opponents.

The set went seven–five and was won by the young men. By that time some other players, two more young men and a heavyset girl, had arrived and introduced themselves to Strand in a spate of names he could not remember. They were not the kind of names Strand read off the roster of his classes at school. They seated themselves alongside Strand in the shade of the pavilion to watch the end of the match, impartially calling out "Good shot" or saying "Wowee!" after an especially hard-fought point.

"That's it for me, ladies and gentlemen," Hazen said, when he hit the set point into the net. "Thank you very much. Caroline, excuse me for failing the team."

"I missed a couple of key ones," Caroline said politely. She took losing with the same lightness as winning, Strand noticed, approvingly. No competitor himself, he disliked people who were sullen when they were on the short end of the score. Hazen, of course, despite his apology, was as unruffled as ever. His wins and losses, Strand could see, were in other fields.

"I ought to be making the excuses," Caroline said to Hazen, as she came toward the pavilion. "Don't you want to play another set? I'd love to sit out and tell my father my secret troubles."

"No," Hazen said. "My old bones have had it for the day. Time for the younger generation." He came over to the pavilion, taking off his hat and mopping his forehead with a towel. He was a little redder than usual, but he wasn't breathing hard and if his bones felt old, it didn't show in the way he strode off the court.

There was a big pitcher of iced tea in the refrigerator at the back of the pavilion and Hazen poured some for Caroline and the two young men who had played with them, while the newcomers warmed up on the court.

"Hey," one of Caroline's opponents, the taller and better player of the two, whose name was Brad or Chad, said to her, "you've got quite a game there, lady. We could clean up in mixed doubles. You going to be out here all summer?"

"No," Caroline said.

"Pity. You'd be an ornament to the season." He was good-looking, in what Strand would describe as the standard American blond way, with an easy, self-assured manner. Maybe, Strand thought, I should have been more serious about my tennis when I was young.

"Caroline," Hazen said, putting down his glass of iced tea, "you can come out here, you know, whenever you want. You might enjoy playing in some of the local tournaments."

Caroline looked quickly at her father. "I'd love to," she said. "If I have the time."

Strand said nothing. After the scene with Hazen the night before, he wasn't sure he liked the idea of Caroline becoming a constant visitor to the house.

"Come on, Caroline," the tall young man whose name

was Brad or Chad said, "let's us be partners and *whomp* them."

As they went out onto the court together to play one of the new boys and the heavyset girl, Hazen said, "I'm going to take my shower now. Watching the kids play depresses me."

"I'll walk back with you," Strand said. "See what the rest of the family is up to." He waved to Caroline, who was running her fingers through her hair, brushing it back, preparing to receive service. He waited for Hazen to put on his sweater and the white hat and then started toward the house at his side.

"I enjoyed that game more than any I've played in months," Hazen said. "Thanks to your delightful daughter."

"You played very well, I thought," Strand said.

"I kept my end up, that's about all. The day I know I can't I'll donate my racquet to the Smithsonian Institution. Four, five years . . ." His voice trailed off, the onset of age in its tone. He was still sweating and he mopped at his face with the towel. "Those young men," he said, "are a little old for your daughter. At this season the boys her age are away in school or college and can't make it for the weekends. That fellow she's playing with now is twenty-four. He's in his father's firm in Wall Street, seems to take all the time off he wants. Very sure of himself with the ladies." Hazen glanced significantly at Strand. "Single and otherwise."

"He seemed gentlemanly enough to me."

Hazen laughed. "I wasn't suggesting that he goes around raping children. I just thought it might be a good idea to inform Caroline that he's much older than she. If you don't mind my saying so, she seems to have led a most sheltered life until now. Not like the run of young girls I see at the parties around here in the summertime, at all. You know, rich children of split homes, parents given to drink and promiscuity . . . well . . ."

"Her mother is very protective," Strand said, annoyed at the implicit warning. "The baby of the family and all that." Then he felt that he sounded as though he was blaming Leslie and added, hastily, "I'm sure Caroline knows how to take care of herself."

"It would be a pity if she didn't," Hazen said gravely. "She has the quality of innocence. It's too rare to be jeopardized. As for her tennis . . ." Hazen shrugged. "She has a surprisingly accurate notion about how good she really is."

"Not good enough," Strand said. "She told me she'd told you."

Hazen smiled. "For one so young to say something like that is rare, too. Has she ever said anything to you about what she wants to do after she finishes her schooling?"

"Not really," Strand said. "I guess she's like most young people her age these days who have no special talents—waiting to see what turns up."

"Didn't she tell you that she wants to go to an agricultural college out west?"

"Agricultural . . . ?" Strand repeated incredulously. Why in the name of God would she want to hide something like that from him? "This is the first I've heard of it. Why? Did she tell you?"

Hazen shook his head. "She just said she wanted to go someplace where life was simpler and she wasn't surrounded by concrete."

"It's true City College isn't surrounded by prairie," Strand said. "But it's a good enough school and it's cheap and she'd be living at home." He resolved to question his daughter when they were alone together.

"The money mightn't be all that much of a problem," Hazen said. "There's always the possibility of a scholarship."

"Not with her marks. Eleanor got one, but Caroline's no scholar, even if it's a father who says so."

"She told me something else that might be useful," Hazen said. "They're giving more and more athletic scholarships to women these days, and . . ."

"Her tennis may be all right for Central Park, but she knows herself she'd never get anywhere with it . . ."

"Not her tennis," Hazen said. "I agree with you. But I noticed how quick she is. She runs extraordinarily fast. I asked her if she'd ever raced and she said she'd won the hundred yard dash in her school field day last month."

"Yes," Strand said. "I remember. Still—field day at a small private school . . ."

"I asked her if she'd been timed and it turns out she did the hundred in ten-four. For a girl who's had no training and hasn't been coached that's most impressive. With good coaching she might get close to Olympic time. It's a pity that her school doesn't have any interscholastic program or a lot of good schools would be after her. I know the public relations man for an institution called Truscott College— that's in Arizona, which is west enough for anybody—and I believe if he mentioned that I'd seen a good prospect for their teams my friend could get their physical training department interested. And the school has a strong agricultural section."

"Did you mention any of this to Caroline?" Strand asked worriedly, sensing vast new family complications looming before him.

"No," Hazen said. "I thought it would be wiser to talk to you and her mother before I raised any hopes."

"Thank you," Strand said dryly, annoyed, despite himself, that his daughter had vouchsafed information about herself to an almost complete stranger, information that she had kept hidden from her parents. At home when they had people in, she answered questions in monosyllables and took the first opportunity to go to her room. "I'll have a little talk with that girl."

"Anyway," Hazen said, "I thought you and your wife should at least know what the possibilities are."

"We live in funny times," Strand said, smiling. "When a girl can run herself into an education. Maybe I'll buy a stopwatch and time my pupils instead of annoying them with examinations."

"If you decide you and Caroline want to explore the situation, I'd be glad to call my friend at the college."

"It's very kind of you to offer to help, but I imagine you have enough other things to think about, without worrying about how my daughter can learn to be a farmer three thousand miles away from home."

"I gathered she doesn't intend to go in for farming. She said she'd like to study to be a veterinary after and that would be a proper start."

"Veterinary . . ." Strand couldn't keep the dismay out of his voice. And he remembered his conversation with Judith Quinlan in which she had said, jokingly, that if she gave up teaching she would be a veterinarian. Was it some new female aberration taking hold suddenly in the heart of the city? "Veterinary," he repeated. "Why, we've never even had a cat or a dog in the house. Did she tell you what gave her that idea?"

"I asked her and she seemed shy—embarrassed, perhaps—about answering," Hazen said. "She just mumbled something about private reasons. So I didn't press her."

"What do *you* think about the idea?" Strand said, almost aggressively.

Hazen shrugged as they walked along. "I believe in this age it is the fashion to allow young people their own choice of careers. It's as good a policy as any, I suppose. It's my feeling—perhaps an illusion—that I would be a happier man today if my father had not dictated what I was to do with my life. Who knows?" He turned his head and peered curiously, his eyes narrowed, at Strand. "Supposing, all other things being equal, when you were your daughter's age, you could have made a choice—would you have chosen as you did?"

"Well," Strand said uncomfortably, "no. My dream was to be a historian, not to feed a few hand-me-down facts about the past to unruly children. If I could have gone to Harvard or to Oxford, spent a few leisurely years in Europe among the archives and libraries—" He laughed ruefully. "But I had to make a living. It was all I could do to find enough odd jobs to keep me going long enough to get my B.A. at City College. Perhaps if I had been stronger . . . Well, I wasn't stronger. Old ambitions." It was his turn to shrug. "I haven't thought about them for years."

"Supposing," Hazen said, "somehow, you had gone to Harvard, had the years in Europe, been able to become the man you had hoped to be, seen your name honored on the shelves of libraries, wouldn't you have been—well"—he searched for the word—"more satisfied, shall we say, than you are now?"

"Perhaps," Strand said. "Perhaps not. We'll never know."

"Do you want me to call the man at Truscott?" Hazen, Strand recognized, was gifted at putting witnesses in a corner, where the answer had to be yes or no.

Strand was silent for a moment, thinking of what the apartment would be like with Caroline gone for months at a time while she was at school, then permanently after that. He and Leslie, too, would then have to face up to the problems of vacant rooms. "I can't give you an answer now," Strand said. "I'll have to talk this over with my wife. Don't think I'm ungrateful for your interest, but . . ."

"Gratitude has nothing to do with it," Hazen said crisply. "Remember there's a lot I have to be grateful for. It's well within reason to believe that I wouldn't be standing here talking to you today—or anywhere, for that matter —if it hadn't been for Caroline's intervention in the park."

"She didn't even know what she was doing," Strand said. "Ask her. It was just a reflex action on her part."

"And all the more admirable for that," Hazen said. "There's no great rush. Speak to your wife and the girl and let me know what you decide. Lunch is at one. I've invited some friends, among them two men you might be interested in talking to—a history professor from Southampton College and an English instructor."

The perfect host, Strand thought. If his guest were a test pilot Hazen probably would have dug up two other test pilots to compare crashes with at lunch.

As they reached the house Strand saw a tall, very thin boy, standing in the driveway, holding a fielder's glove and a catcher's mitt. "There's the other half of the battery," Hazen said. "Would you mind umpiring?"

"I'll do my best," Strand said.

"Good morning, Ronny," Hazen said. "This is Mr. Strand. He'll call the balls and strikes."

"Good morning, sir." Ronny handed Hazen the catcher's mitt. Hazen punched at the pocket of the mitt as they walked across the driveway to the lawn that bordered it. He put his towel down as home plate and Ronny, his face very serious, paced off to his pitching distance. Hazen crouched behind the towel, bending easily, and Strand took his position behind him, trying not to smile.

"You get five warmup pitches," Hazen called to the boy, "and then it's play ball. The usual signals, Ronny. One finger for the fast ball. Two for the curve, three for the pitchout."

"Yes, sir," Ronny said. His windup was elaborate, with a succession of little jerking motions and a final turning of his body, so that his back was facing the plate before he turned and threw.

Strand recognized the style from watching the Yankees on television. The boy had obviously been impressed by Luis Tiant, the old Cuban pitcher who had the most spectacular pitching motions in baseball. Once again he had to mask his smile.

The ball came over the towel slowly. Strand guessed that the boy had intended a curve.

After the fifth pitch, Strand called, "Batter up."

"Right in there, baby," Hazen said. "Breeze it past 'em."

Ronny bent over to peer at the sign, very Tiant-like, lifted his left leg and threw.

"Ball one," Strand barked, getting into the spirit of the game Hazen was playing with the boy.

Hazen looked over his shoulder, glowering. "What's the matter, Ump, you blind? Aren't you going to give us the corners?"

"Play ball," Strand said loudly.

Hazen winked broadly and turned back to face the pitcher.

After fifteen minutes in which Strand generously had counted ten strikeouts against four walks, Hazen stood up and went out to Ronny and shook his hand, saying, "Good game, Ronny. In another ten years you'll be ready for the big leagues." He gave his mitt to the boy, who was smiling for the first time, and he and Strand went into the house.

"That was a nice thing to do," Strand said.

"He's a good kid," Hazen said carelessly. "He'll never amount to anything as a ballplayer, though. He's about a half second too slow and he'll never get there. The day he realizes it will be tough for him. I used to love the game and when the day came that I knew, in my bones, that I'd never hit the curve I could've cried. So I turned to hockey. I had the talents." He smiled unpleasantly. "Brutality and cunning. Thanks for the umpiring. See you at lunch. I'm ready for my shower now. You'd be surprised what work it is to bend your knees like that for ten minutes." He went toward his wing of the house.

Strand didn't go up to the bedroom where he supposed his wife was still enjoying the comfort of doing nothing on a Saturday morning. He wasn't ready to talk to Leslie just yet. Instead he went out to the pool where he found Eleanor and Jimmy sunbathing.

Eleanor was stretched out on a mat on her stomach, in a bikini, with Jimmy squatting beside her rubbing lotion on her back. She had undone the straps of her bra so that she wouldn't have any white lines across her eventual tan and her position, with her breasts almost showing, was, at least for Strand, decidedly erotic. Her body, with its slender waist, swelling haunches and satiny skin, reminded him disturbingly of her mother's, and after a first glance, as he sat down on the edge of a beach chair, Strand kept looking out to sea. Eleanor and Jimmy were playing a word game, one of them giving a letter and the other adding to it with the object of forcing the opponent into the letter that would make a word and thereby losing the point.

"E," said Eleanor. "Hi, Dad. How's Miss Wimbledon 1984 doing out there?"

"Making the boys run," Strand said, wishing she'd tie up her bra.

"V," Jimmy said.

"Obvious, Jimmy," Eleanor said. Then to Strand, "We ought to give the old terror of Central Park a unanimous vote of thanks for all this splendor she's introduced us to. I, Jimmy. I haven't seen our genial host yet. What's he planning for our entertainment?"

"Lunch," Strand said.

"Sorry about that," Eleanor said. "Will you make my excuses? I'm asked out to lunch. Man I happened to meet at Bobby's Bar's coming to pick me up for lunch with the lit'ry set. He writes poety. For the little magazines. Don't look so aghast, Dad." She laughed. "The poetry's pretty poor but he's got a regular job. I, Jimmy."

"Happened to meet," Jimmy said. "He was waiting for you last night, gasping. C."

"Astute of you, Jimmy." Strand didn't know whether she meant Jimmy was astute for saying C or for realizing that the meeting the night before had been prearranged. She sighed. "You're a clever fellow. I challenge you. What's the word."

"Evict," Jimmy said triumphantly.

"Got me," Eleanor said. "You have a tiresome way with words. He always beats me," she said to her father. "And I'm supposed to be the smart one in the family."

"You're done," Jimmy said, putting the cap on the bottle of lotion. "Want to play some more?"

"Not for the moment," Eleanor said. "The sun stuns me. I'll just bake until my cavalier comes to claim me."

"I'm going to take a few turns in the pool," Jimmy said, standing. He was tall and thin, like his father, with his ribs showing and his big fierce nose jutting below the same beetling full dark eyebrows. Without pleasure, Strand made the comparison between his son and the young men he had just been watching on the tennis court. Where they were lean and long-muscled, Jimmy was plain skinny and didn't look as though he could last even one set on the courts. Jimmy professed to find all forms of exercise sweaty and life-shortening. When he was teased by Caroline about his sedentary ways, he quoted Kipling's jibe about the gentleman athletes of Britain—"flannelled fools at the wicket . . . muddied oafs at the goals." At least there was no danger, Strand thought, that Hazen would attempt to send Jimmy off to school on an athletic scholarship.

Jimmy dove into the pool with a great splash and happily paddled about in a stroke that Strand would have been hard put to describe.

"Who's the cavalier, as you call him, who's coming to take you to lunch?" Strand asked.

"You don't know him," Eleanor said.

"Is he the one you told me about? The Greek island one?"

Eleanor hesitated for a moment. "The same," she said. "He thought it would be a good idea for us to meet on neutral ground. You don't have to see him if you don't want to."

"Of course I want to," Strand said.

"He's presentable, if you're worried," Eleanor said.

"I wasn't worried about that."

"Good old Dad."

"Do you think it's polite to go off like that without telling Mr. Hazen? After all, you haven't even seen him here yet and you've spent the night in his house."

"It's not my fault he didn't make dinner last night," Eleanor said. She sounded defensive. "Anyway, he's paying his debts to Caroline and you and Mother, and I'm sure that's enough for him."

Debts, Strand thought. An unpleasant way of putting it. "Will you be back for dinner?"

"If you want me to."

"I want you to."

Eleanor sighed. "I'll be back."

"Eleanor," Strand said, wishing she would sit up and tie her bra, "I'd like to ask you a question."

"What is it?" She sounded wary.

"It's about Caroline. Do you think she's old enough to go away to college?"

"I went at her age," Eleanor said. "Anyway, I thought she was going to City. That's not away. It's just uptown."

"Supposing we changed our mind about it?"

"What are you and Mother going to do about her tuition and board and all that? Take on other jobs? I don't think at your age . . ."

"What if we thought we could manage it?"

"How?"

"Somehow." He was afraid Eleanor would hoot at the idea of Caroline in a track suit.

Finally Eleanor tied the bra straps behind her back and sat up. "If you want the truth," she said, "I think she'd be better off at home. She's younger than I was at her age. By a long shot. For one thing, there never are any boys around the house or calling her on the telephone. Haven't you noticed that?"

"Not really," Strand admitted.

"When I was her age, the phone was ringing day and night."

"It certainly was."

"She thinks she's ugly," Eleanor said. "She thinks she turns boys off. That's why she likes to beat them on a tennis court. I at least confound men with my brains." She laughed complacently. "It's more dignified—and more permanent."

"Ugly?" Strand was shocked. "Caroline?"

"Parents," Eleanor said. "Do you think when I'm a parent I'll be blind, too?"

"But she's not ugly. Just now, Mr. Hazen went out of his way to tell me how delightful she was."

"Geriatric praise," Eleanor said. "Not worth one eighteen-year-old squeeze in a movie theater."

"What if I told you that I think that she's—well—if not exactly beautiful—a very pretty girl?"

"Geriatric fatherliness," Eleanor said curtly. "You asked me what I thought about my sister. Now, do you want me to humor you or do you want me to tell you what I think?"

"That's a loaded question," Strand protested.

"Loaded or not, what do you want?"

"There's only one answer to that," Strand said, trying to sound dignified.

"She thinks she's ugly because of her nose. It's as simple as that. Kids have been making fun of it since she was in the first grade. It's your nose and it's great on you and it's okay on Jimmy, he'll grow into it. But for her—with noses like Mother's and, let's face it, mine, in the family, it's the doomful curse of the Strands. Understand me, Dad," she said more gently, seeing the stricken expression on her father's face, "I'm not saying she's right to feel the way she does or that she isn't a marvelous little girl, but that's the way it is. If a girl feels she's not pretty and she's off on her own, away from the loving support of good old Mother and Dad and a nice safe bed to run home to every night, she's very likely to . . . oh, hell, to fall into the arms . . . into the *life* of the first boy or man who says she's pretty, no matter what his motives are and how good or bad he is for her. You asked for my advice? Keep her home with you until she grows up."

Jimmy was climbing out of the pool, shaking the water off his torso and pulling at his ears.

"Don't ask *him* any questions," Eleanor said. "That's more advice."

"Some day, Eleanor," Strand said, "I'm going to ask you what you think I ought to do with *my* life."

"Stay as you are." She got up and kissed his cheek. "I couldn't bear it if you changed."

Strand was alone on the terrace. Eleanor had gone up to dress for her lunch and Jimmy had wandered off along the beach. Strand was glad that Leslie hadn't come down. When he was worried, as he was now, she invariably sensed it and she would have pried out the reasons and her blissful lazy morning would have been ruined. One member of the family tormented by the problems of life in the twentieth century was enough for today.

Strand was considering going up and getting into bathing trunks and taking a swim in the pool. For the moment there was nobody around to notice the poverty of his legs or the resemblance of his gaunt frame to Jimmy's. Just as he was about to stand up Mr. Ketley came out of the house. "Mr. Strand," Mr. Ketley said, "there's a gentleman here for Miss Eleanor."

"Tell him to come out here, please," Strand said.

When the young man came onto the terrace Strand rose to greet him. "I'm Eleanor's father," he said, and they shook hands. "She'll only be a minute. She's getting dressed."

The young man nodded. "I'm Giuseppe Gianelli," he said. "Embarrassingly melodious." He laughed. Strand guessed that he was twenty-eight, twenty-nine. He had a deep easy voice and he was strikingly handsome, large green eyes that seemed to have golden flecks in them, a dark face and thick black curly hair. He was almost as tall as Strand and was dressed in white slacks, sandals and a blue polo shirt that left his muscular tanned arms bare, stretched tightly over his wide shoulders and was loose around the middle. Strand was thankful that he hadn't been caught in bathing trunks.

"Nice little place they have here," Gianelli said, looking around. "Somebody had thoughtful ancestors."

"My son said, 'That's some hunk of architecture,' when he saw it last night."

Gianelli chuckled. It was an easy, soft sound that went with his slow, slurred voice. "Good old Jimmy," he said. "He had quite a time for himself last night."

"What did he do," Strand asked, "get drunk?"

"Oh, no, nothing like that." Gianelli smiled. His face, which was almost sculpturally masculine in its bold lines of brow, nose and jaw, softened suddenly and surprisingly. "If he'd been drunk, naturally I wouldn't say anything about it to his father. No, he had only a beer or two. He gave a concert."

"On what?" Strand had prevailed upon Jimmy not to take his electric guitar along on the weekend, convincing Jimmy that there were limits even to a millionaire's hospitality.

"Some girl had a guitar lying around," Gianelli said. "She played a song or two. You know, one of those mournful, why am I alive, why is the world so mean to me sort of jingles. When she finished, Eleanor asked her if she'd lend her guitar to Jimmy and Jimmy went to town, along with the pianist. He really can play, you know, Mr. Strand."

"So far," Strand said, "I haven't educated myself enough in the new music to fully appreciate him."

"You should have been there last night," Gianelli said. "He must have played more than an hour. Didn't Eleanor tell you?"

"We had other things to discuss this morning," Strand said and knew that he must sound stuffy to the man. "Jimmy keeps saying he's looking for a new sound and I've taken it for granted that when he finds it he'll tell me the news."

"I don't know what he found last night," Gianelli said, "but he found *something*."

"In the future," Strand said, "perhaps I ought to accompany my children when they go out at night."

"You could do worse," Gianelli said affably. "Do you mind if I sit down?"

"Sorry," Strand said. "By all means."

They both sat.

"Eleanor said she'd just be a minute," Strand said. "You know what a woman's minute is when she's getting dressed to go out."

"Eleanor's pretty good about being on time," Gianelli said. "Five minutes here and there. I have no complaints on that score."

He talks as if he owns her, Strand thought resentfully. He was careful not to show his resentment. If she was prompt with Giuseppe Gianelli, she was behaving unusually. She was notorious in the family for her tardiness. You're in for some surprises later on, young man, Strand thought, meanly. If there is going to be a later on.

"Has Eleanor told you anything about me?" Gianelli asked, turning his deep green eyes on Strand, looking frank and candid, man-to-man. This lad has been around, Strand thought. "I mean, anything of any interest?"

"She said you wrote poetry," Strand said. "Then she told me not to look aghast, the poetry was poor and you had a regular job."

Gianelli chuckled. It was hard for Strand not to be warmed by the soft, agreeable sound. "She's something, isn't she?"

"Something," Strand agreed. "She didn't recite any of the poetry to me."

"This is your lucky day, Mr. Strand," Gianelli said.

"She didn't tell me what your job was, either." Good God, Strand thought, I'm sounding like an old-fashioned father inquiring into the qualifications of a suitor to his daughter's hand in marriage. "She knows a great variety of young men and they all seem to have peculiar occupations."

"Mine isn't so peculiar." Gianelli sighed. "I wish it was. I work for my father. He's a building contractor. I deal in cement, bricks, labor relations, trucks. I consider it a temporary aberration on my part. My father doesn't have a high regard for my poetry, either. He thinks I came under the influence of Communist faggots at the Wharton School of Economics." He laughed, dismissing his father.

The middle generation, Strand thought. Father in shirtsleeves, sonny in white slacks in the Hamptons. Gianelli. Contractor. Reader of newspapers, moviegoer who had seen *The Godfather*, Strand wondered about connections with the Mafia. Cosa Nostra. In the movie the son was a college graduate, too. Ashamed of himself for the thought, he switched the subject. "Eleanor did tell me you were thinking of going to a Greek island on her vacation this summer." He looked searchingly at Gianelli to see if there was any reaction. There was none.

"Spétsai," Gianelli said carelessly. "I have some friends there who have a house on the water. It's within invitation distance of Onassis's former place. Dead now. The idea came up late one night, the way ideas like that do."

The idea of spending three weeks on an island with a woman who was not his wife, within invitation distance of a Greek shipping tycoon, had never come up in Strand's life, at any hour of the day or night, but he didn't think it was necessary to tell Gianelli that. "By the way," he said, "where did you meet Eleanor?"

"Oh, it was just one of those evenings at Bobby's saloon," Gianelli said easily. "Last summer. We were at the bar and we fell to talking."

Fell to talking, Strand thought, remembering how he had carefully found out Leslie's address and telephone number, had waited a year before daring to call, had sweated under the glares of her father and mother when he had finally appeared in her family's living room to take her to dinner and the theater. Fell to talking and then an island in the Aegean and after that, what? This was a generation, he thought, discomforted by nothing. In principle, he approved. But he wasn't sure of what he felt sitting there in the sunshine waiting for the young man to take his daughter to a lit'ry lunch and then where?

"We found out we had interests in common," Gianelli was saying.

"Like what?" Strand asked.

"Nondrinking." Gianelli grinned. "Wallace Stevens. What we like about New York and what we hate about it."

"That should have kept the conversation going for a while," Strand said dryly.

"Till about three a.m."

"Aside from writing poetry, what would you want to do?"

"Do you really want to know?" Gianelli looked at him seriously.

"Of course."

"I was the editor of the newspaper at Brown. That's where I went to college. I liked that. Maybe it was just because I liked seeing my name in the newspaper. Vanity. But I think it was more than that. I'd hoped my father would finance me into a small-town newspaper somewhere. Where I'd live in a house with some grounds around it and be my own boss, small crusades and all that—putting the rascals in jail, keeping the unions honest, blowing the whistle on the deals, getting a decent congressman elected, cleaning up the library board and the zoning regulations, no more Vietnams or Watergates, little things like that. Romantic, idealistic, rich boy American dreams. Putting my imprint on the age, within my modest abilities. My father said, 'Be quixotic with your own money.' End of interview."

How willing the new generation was to talk—about themselves, Strand thought. But admirable in its way. "Have you told Eleanor any of this?"

"All."

"What does she think?"

"Thumbs down," Gianelli said. "You're on your own, baby! She's climbing to the seat of power over the prostrate bodies of graduates of the Harvard School of Business and the idea of putting on a green eyeshade and editing an article on a high school graduation in a little backwater town has no charms for her. Do you think I'm a fool, too?"

"Not necessarily." Gianelli's idea was more than a little attractive to Strand, but there were also the dreadful statistics of the annual bankruptcies of small businesses in America and the gobbling up of frail independent newspapers to be considered. "You won't have much time for Greece, though."

"There're better things than Greece," Gianelli said.

"Well, now you know the worst about me." He grinned again. "Should I leave now and let you tell Eleanor you kicked me out of the house?"

"Stay where you are." Strand stood up. "I'll see what's keeping her."

But as he was going toward the house, Eleanor came out, looking crisp and haughty, nose short and straight and in the air, a bright scarf tied around her head. "Hi," she said. "You're early."

"On time," Gianelli said, standing. "Never no mind. I filled in your father on my faults and virtues. Ready?"

"As ready as I'll ever be. Don't I look ready?"

"You look glorious," Gianelli said.

"That will have to do," Eleanor said. "See you later, Dad."

"Later when?" Strand asked.

"Just later." She smiled at him and took Gianelli's arm.

They went off. Together, Strand had to admit to himself, they *did* look glorious. Being a father had its ups and downs.

After they had gone, Leslie came on to the terrace, dressed for lunch in the long cotton skirt and her hair piled up on her head in the fashion that always gave Strand a sensation that was somewhere between adoration and anguish. "How do I look?" Leslie asked, uncertainly.

"Glorious," he said.

Strand didn't enjoy his lunch, although there were perfect cold lobsters and paté and cold wine and avocado salad on the buffet arranged on the terrace, now shaded with a huge awning. And the sea was blue and calm and the two teachers from Southampton College and their wives were amiable enough and moderately intelligent. He kept looking at Caroline, or, more accurately, at her nose. It certainly wasn't disfiguring, he thought, angry with Eleanor for having made such a fuss about it; in another age it might even have been considered handsome on a woman. But he couldn't help but notice that while the three young tennis players and two other girls who had been invited were all eating together in a high register of conversation and laughter, Caroline had chosen to eat off to one side with her mother and the wife of the history professor.

Goddamnit, he thought, Eleanor was right. Geriatric fatherliness. He wanted to go over to Caroline and take her in his arms and say, "My darling, you're beautiful," and weep into her soft blond hair.

Instead, he turned to the history professor beside him and said, "I'm sorry, sir, what was that you were saying?"

The professor, who looked a little like Einstein and knew it and had let his hair grow into a mane like the scientist's, stared at him queerly for a moment. "I was asking you how you treated the subject of Vietnam in your classes. In the public school system, I mean."

"We don't teach modern history."

"Vietnam isn't so modern," the professor said. "After all, *our* problem with it goes all the way back to World War II. History is a seamless web after all. Boys went directly from our halls into the armed forces. We had a crisis of conscience that nearly split our department in two."

Strand decided that the man was not to be taken seriously. "It was not included in our curriculum," Strand said, knowing he was being rude, knowing that it wasn't because of anything the man had said, but because of his conversations with Hazen and Eleanor that morning and seeing Caroline eating at her mother's side. His department hadn't been split and neither had he. He had deplored the war, had written his congressman, signed petitions at the risk of his job, had said at his dinner table, with Jimmy listening, that he approved of the boys who had fled to Sweden or had registered as conscientious objectors. But he couldn't say that over cold lobster and paté de foie gras in the sunny picnic atmosphere on the edge of the sea.

Luckily, at that moment, sparing further conversation with Einstein, Hazen came over. "Excuse me, Mr. Strand," he said, "may I talk to you for a moment?"

"Of course," Strand said and stood up. He followed Hazen into the house.

"I'm sorry to disturb you," Hazen said in a low voice in the empty living room, "but I have to leave for the city now. That telephone call at breakfast this morning. I'm just going to slip away. I don't want to break up the party with a lot of farewells and explanations. You understand, don't you?"

"Certainly."

"Make my apologies to your wife. Even though we've spent so little time together this weekend," Hazen said, "I've enjoyed having you all here. *All* of you," he said emphatically. "The next time I'll cut the telephone wires."

"It's been a memorable holiday already," Strand said. If Jimmy had been there, and had known what had happened the night before and had overheard the conversations of the morning, he would have said, "You can say that again, brother."

"You'll call me during the week, won't you?" Hazen said as the two men shook hands. Conroy was waiting in the hallway, patient charioteer, dressed in a dark business suit, and he and Hazen went quickly out the door to the waiting Mercedes.

6

*Your name honored on the shelves of libraries. . . . Did
he know his own name? There was this other man, using
his name, leading another life. Vigorous, not lying in a
strange bed, with the sound of surf or blood in his ears . . .*

"How was the weekend?" Judith Quinlan asked.

"Conspicuous consumption," Strand said. "In the best
sense."

Judith laughed. "I can guess what you mean." It was
a raw afternoon, with gusts of rain, and they were seated
by the streaked window of the coffee shop after school,
glad to be out of the weather for a quarter of an hour
with the day's work done. Strand had told Judith a little
about Hazen and, trying not to boast, had described Caroline's adventure in the park. He sipped his coffee gratefully. He was in no hurry to get home. He had had a trying night with Leslie on Sunday after Conroy had deposited them in front of their apartment building. The
traffic coming in from the Island had been bad and the
trip had taken a long time and his face was burning from
the two days of sun and he knew that Leslie had noticed
he was brooding about something and would get after him
about it as soon as they were home. He was not in the
habit of hiding things from her and had no practice at it
and he knew that he would sound either foolish or sullen
when she started on him.

And, for the first time in their married lives, when he
had tried to make love to her on Saturday night, he had
been impotent. Leslie had pretended that it was nothing
and had fallen peacefully asleep next to him, but he had

tossed uneasily all night and when he did sleep had vague, ominous dreams. And then, on Sunday, she had said she had a slight headache and had kept to her room all day. He had not wanted to have the whole thing out with her until he had decided what position he was going to take about Hazen's offer for Caroline, so his only refuge was silence. Since he was not ordinarily silent with Leslie, he sensed her growing disquietude and was aware of the searching looks she kept giving him in the car, although she didn't say anything with Jimmy and Caroline seated beside her.

Eleanor had driven into town with Gianelli. Leslie had been a little sharp with Eleanor, too, because although she had told Strand that she would be present for dinner Saturday, she had called at the last minute and said the gang (whoever that might be) had decided to go to Montauk for dinner. She hadn't come back by the time they had gone to bed and there was no telling what hour she had finally come in. Then on Sunday she had packed her bag in the morning and gone off with Gianelli, saying there was an all-day party on at a movie director's beach house in Westhampton and there wouldn't be any sense in coming all the way back just to ride in with them in the evening.

Jimmy, too, had found a girl in the bar in Bridgehampton and missed lunch and dinner to go to her place and had arrived at Hazen's house just in time to get into the car with them.

Only Caroline, who had played ten sets of tennis during the two days, and who now, exhausted, was sleeping with her head on her mother's shoulder, seemed to have enjoyed the weekend completely, saying, just before she dozed off, "What a dreamy way to live." Strand wondered if she would have been so content if she had heard what her sister had said about her in those few minutes at the pool. Finally, he knew, he would have to tell Leslie all the things that were bothering him, but he had to sort them out for himself first. Without asking Leslie if she wanted to listen to the radio, he had turned it on in the car

to make conversation difficult, and he knew Leslie was
going to ask him about *that,* too.

The memory of the night before made him frown as he
stirred his coffee and looked out at the rain beating at the
window.

"You don't look as though the weekend did you much
good," Judith said.

Strand touched his face, which was beginning to peel.
"I'm not used to the sun," he said.

"I don't mean that," Judith said. "Did anything bad
happen in school today?"

"No. Nothing happened. Neither good nor bad."

Romero had slouched into his office, surly, with the
familiar mocking grin on his face and said, "I consulted
with myself like you said I should and I decided, What the
hell, what have I got to lose, just carfare, I might as well
see the man and see what he's selling."

"He's not selling anything." Strand wrote Hazen's office
address on a piece of paper and gave it to Romero. "Write
him a letter saying you're interested. That way you won't
even be out carfare."

"Ain't you going to go there with me?" Romero sounded
almost frightened.

"I think Mr. Hazen would prefer to handle this just
between the two of you."

Romero looked at the address uncertainly, then squashed
the piece of paper into his jeans pocket. "Write a letter,
for Christ's sake," he said aggrievedly. "I ain't never written a letter in my life."

"I have one suggestion to make, Romero," Strand said.
"If you *do* write the letter, make it sound like the papers
you give me, not the way you talk."

Romero grinned. "I got dual nationality, don't I?" And
slouched out of the office.

Strand had not told Judith about Romero and now, in
the coffee shop, he was tempted to speak about him, perhaps get her to help tame the boy. But he knew Romero
had never been in any of her classes and it would be no

favor to her to expose her to that mocking smile, that impenetrable insolence.

"No, as Mondays go," Strand said, "it was even a little above average. But I do have a couple of problems."

"Animal, vegetable or mineral?"

Strand laughed. "All three. The weekend actually passed off quite well . . . quite well." This was technically almost true, if you did not consider the last weary hours of Sunday night, with the prospect of a week's labor looming darkly over the spirit.

Or if you didn't include Hazen's drunken tirade or the argument in the bedroom.

Strand and Leslie rarely argued. He had always told her she was a serene woman and that that was one of the things he loved most about her. But there was nothing serene about her as she sat on the edge of the bed, her mouth grim, her eyes scanning him like weapons, while he fiddled, hanging up his jacket, taking off his tie.

"What is it, Allen?"

"What is what?" he said.

"You know. You're hiding something from me. What is it?"

"Nothing. I'm tired." He yawned, almost convincingly. "I had a long talk with Hazen about the fate of Romero —that's the young boy who . . ."

"I know who he is," Leslie said shortly. "I also know that isn't what's bothering you."

"I'm tired," Strand said weakly. "I have a hard day ahead of me tomorrow. Why don't we just postpone it until . . . ?"

"I will not be left out of things. I'm your partner or I'm nothing."

"Of course you're my . . ."

"It has something to do with the family," Leslie said harshly. "Something you know and I don't. Is it that young man who came to pick up Eleanor? You talked to him. Did he worry you? I saw him from the window. He looked perfectly all right to me. It's not because he's Italian, is it?"

"You know me better than that. As far as I could tell, he's fine. Now, please, let's go to sleep."

"Did you have a fight with Eleanor?" Leslie persisted. "Another one of your medieval attacks?"

For a moment, Strand was tempted to tell his wife what his talk with Eleanor had really been about. The preposterous idea that Caroline thought she was ugly. The ludicrous discussion of Caroline's nose. And Hazen's troubling suggestion about sending Caroline off to a distant college. But he wasn't up to it yet. He felt bone-weary, badgered, uncertain. If he let it all out he'd be up the entire night struggling with Leslie. From the way her mouth was quivering he knew there would be tears. Her tears unmanned him at the best of times.

"I just have to go to sleep now," he said.

"Go to sleep," she said. She got off the bed and strode out of the bedroom. A moment later he heard her at the piano, all doors open, both things disastrous indications of storm at that hour of the night.

He sighed, put on his pajamas and went to bed.

He went to sleep almost immediately and when he woke in the middle of the night, Leslie was in bed, too, but on the other side, not touching him.

In the morning she pretended to be asleep when the alarm clock woke him and he left the apartment without going in and kissing her as he did on other mornings. She was a serene woman with a good temper and she did not like to fight, but when she was angry, the anger lasted for days, cold and distant and untouchable, making him feel he was an exile in his own house.

Strand looked across the table at Judith Quinlan, drinking her coffee with her two hands around the mug in that affecting, childish way she had, her soft pale eyes sympathetic and concerned. Suddenly he felt that he had to confide in this nice simple woman who was intelligent and understanding and not involved in his problems and who could be depended upon not to break into tears.

"Some things came up," he said. "Family things. Nothing tragic. Decisions to be made. After you've brought up two children you think you've learned the trick and can handle the third. Not true. They're all different. What went with one doesn't necessarily go with the others, at all. Maybe I worry too much, maybe I ought to let things just happen. . . . The way I was brought up . . ." He shrugged. He had been an only child, he had been lonely, his father had been much older than his mother, a sickly, failing man who had no time for a scholarly son and who used what energy he had left when he came home from work to argue with his wife about money. "My own family life . . ." Strand said, "well, there was no overflow of love." He chuckled dryly. "Maybe I developed a sentimental notion of what a family might be. Anyway, it made me feel that when I had children of my own I'd be responsible for them, protect them. And luckily, or maybe unluckily, my wife had always felt the same way. We're involved, maybe too involved, selfishly involved, in their lives. I don't know. As a man said to me over the weekend, I'm out of joint with the times. . . . It's hard to unlearn."

"Are they in trouble?" Judith asked, her eyes grave. He could see that in her mind she was running through all the possible troubles young people could get into in New York City these days and thinking how dire those troubles could be.

"Nothing gruesome." Strand smiled. "In fact, it's quite the opposite." Then he told her about Hazen's offer to send Caroline away to college and the reasons for it. He didn't tell her about Eleanor's reaction and what Eleanor's reasons were for believing that Caroline should be kept at home. That would have been too painful. . . . Even as he spoke he felt again the resentment against his older daughter that had risen in him when she had spoken to him and he was afraid the resentment would show. "My immediate reaction was to say no," he said. "I'm afraid my pride was hurt. That I was being left out of the decision-making process, that I wasn't capable of taking care of my own child—somehow Hazen, the whole weekend— made me feel like a loser. . . ."

"Nonsense," Judith said sharply. She had sat quietly,

playing with the coffee mug while he had talked, and now she impatiently pushed the mug away from her.

He patted her hand gently. "I'm touchier than I seem," he said.

"What does your wife think?" Judith asked.

"That's another thing. I haven't told her yet."

"Why not?" Judith looked surprised.

He shrugged. "I don't know. We were surrounded by strangers. In someone else's house. Then, at home, she sensed something and I . . . I didn't know what I really felt myself and I dissembled. I'm *awful* at dissembling. And we had a little argument. Which," he said, "I'm afraid will continue this evening. That's neither here nor there," he said, with false briskness. "It'll blow over. What do *you* think?"

"Of course," Judith said, "I don't know your daughter, but if she were mine, I'd grab the chance for her. Charity or no charity. Of course, I'm probably warped—the job I have here, the kind of school we're in—but to get her out of the city these years to a good college—I'd think it was a gift from heaven. Education in this city, why, it's just a continuation of war by other means."

Strand laughed. "Clausewitz couldn't have said it better. I have to tell that to my friend Hazen. Maybe we ought to have it engraved above the portals of every school in the system." He left a tip for the waitress. "I think we ought to go now."

"What are you going to do?" Judith asked, gravely.

Strand hesitated. "I don't know. I'll decide between now and the time I get home."

Outside, it was raining harder and it was impossible for the tall man and the tiny woman both to keep dry under her umbrella. "I'll splurge today," Strand said. "We'll take a taxi. I'm beginning to like the habits of the rich."

They were both quiet in the taxi for a long time.

"I hate to see you bothered like this," Judith said. "With all the other things you have to cope with. Why don't you just let Mr. Hazen talk to Caroline and let her make up her own mind?"

Strand nodded. "I suppose you're right. My wife might suppose differently, though. Very differently. As for me . . ." He sighed. "I'm struggling between selfishness and wisdom. Only I don't know which is which."

As the taxi drew up before Judith's building, which was only three blocks from Strand's, she said, "If you're not in a hurry, why don't you come upstairs with me and have a drink? A little whiskey may make things look clearer."

"That's a fine idea," Strand said, grateful for Judith's feminine concern, her appreciation of the uses of postponement.

He had never been in her apartment before. It was high up in an old building and had been designed as an artist's studio, with a big window facing north and a bedroom off it. The walls were lined with books, the furniture was brightly colored (he had expected dark brown) and everything was neat and crisply tidy. There were no signs that a man had ever been there before.

He sat in a corner of the big sofa watching her getting out ice from the refrigerator in the kitchenette that was separated from the main room by white-painted louver doors. She was so small that she had to stand on tiptoe to reach the whiskey bottle and two glasses from the cupboard on the side of the refrigerator. He noticed that the whiskey bottle was only half full and he wondered if Judith Quinlan sat alone at night and drank herself to sleep.

She poured the Scotch over the ice cubes, ran some water into the glasses from the tap and put them on a little tray with a saucer of salted almonds. She placed the tray on a low coffee table in front of the sofa and said, "There," and sat down beside him.

They took their glasses and as she lifted hers, Judith said, "Welcome to my house."

The whiskey tasted fine. "Imagine," Strand said, "drinking on a Monday afternoon. The very path to ruin."

They laughed comfortably together.

"What a nice place this is," Strand said. "So quiet. And it seems to be so far away from . . ." He stopped. It was hard to say what the room was far away from. "Well," he said, "just far away."

Judith put her glass down firmly. "Now," she said, "I'm going to do something I've been wanting to do for a long time." With a quick movement, she knelt on the couch beside him, her arms around him, and she kissed him.

Amazed, he sat rigidly, conscious of the glass in his hand, afraid that the whiskey would spill. But after the first moment, with her lips soft but determined on his, he relaxed, leaned back, pulling her down with him, not caring about the whiskey anymore. He put his free arm around her and kissed her, hard. He felt her hand fumbling with the buttons on his shirt. She opened the shirt and her hand, soft and light, caressed the skin of his chest, then down to his belly. Astonishing Miss Quinlan. She kissed his cheek, many small, tender touches, whispered into his ear, "I need you, I need you." He leaned back further, her hands like petals on his body, proving to him that the impotence of Saturday night had been merely temporary.

Suddenly she stopped, wriggled out of his encircling arm, jumped up and stood before him. Her hair was mussed, she was smiling, there was a look he had not seen before in her eyes, playful, mischievous. She looked beautiful, he thought, in the cold light of the big north window, and most desirable.

"Well," she said, "shall we?"

He stood up, saw that the whiskey hadn't spilled. "That was lovely," he said. "Surprising and lovely."

She laughed, lightly, gleefully. "I didn't ask for a description," she said. "I asked about an action."

He shook his head sadly. "I would love to," he said. "But I can't. Anyway, not now."

Her face grew grave. "You're not offended, are you?"

"God, no," he said. "I'm flattered. Delighted. But I can't."

"Will you think about it?" Her eyes were downcast now and it hurt him that he was hurting her.

"Of course I'll think about it," he said.

"You came up here to get away from your problems,"

she said, with a low, sorrowful laugh, "and now I've given you a new problem. I was clumsy. I have no talent for such things." She lifted her head, looked at him squarely. "Still, at least now you know. We both know."

"Yes," he said.

She came over to him and buttoned his shirt. He kissed the top of her head. "Now," she said, "let's finish our drinks."

As he walked slowly in the wet dusk toward his home, his feelings were mixed. He was elated and dissatisfied with himself at the same time, but he didn't feel like a loser this afternoon. Nothing like this had ever happened to him before and certainly not since his marriage. He had not considered himself attractive to any woman but his wife. And her attachment to him had been built, he was sure, on her appreciation of his intellectual and moral qualities rather than his physical attributes.

Hazen had asked him if he believed in the Ten Commandments and he had answered that he did. Believing in them and obeying them were not one and the same thing. Even if he had not committed adultery, from time to time he had coveted his neighbor's wife, which was natural and inevitable although contrary to the fiat from Mount Sinai. The messenger of the God of Israel in the desert, announcing the Law to a wandering tribe, could not have known what it would be like millennia later on the highways and byways of the City of New York.

Then he remembered the tone of Judith's voice when she said, "Now I'm going to do something I've been wanting to do for a long time." A long time, he thought. I'm fifty, he thought, there isn't all that amount of time to think about anything. On the corner of his own block he nearly turned to go back. But then he saw Alexander leaning against the front of the building and knew that Alexander had seen him. He walked briskly down the block and said, "Good evening, Alexander. Miserable weather, isn't it?"

"Miserable," Alexander said, huddling into his combat jacket and chewing on his cigar.

When he opened the door to his apartment, he heard Leslie playing. He stopped and listened for a moment. It was a Schubert sonata, in a minor key, low and haunting, fitting for a dark, wet afternoon. He took off his raincoat and hat and hung them up neatly in the foyer. Then he went into the living room. "Good evening," he said.

Abruptly Leslie broke off playing and stood up and faced him. "Good evening," she said coldly. She did not move to kiss him. No better than last night, he thought, or this morning. Still, the ritual of the homecoming kiss was as old as their marriage. He went over to her where she was standing before the piano bench and leaned over and kissed her cheek.

"You're late," she said. She sniffed. "And you've been drinking."

"I stopped in at a bar," he said. Not quite the truth, but easy to say—shamefully easy. "I got wet and chilled. One whiskey." He shrugged. "Is Caroline home?"

"No. She went to the library."

"Anybody call?" The words were the usual words after the day's absence, but the tone was not at all usual.

"No."

"I don't want to interrupt your playing. I'll go into . . ."

"You're not interrupting anything. I've played enough."

The telephone began to ring. "I'll get it," Strand said, grateful for an excuse to leave the room.

It was Hazen. "Sorry to have left you in the lurch at my place the way I did," Hazen said. "But the wires were burning in New York. I hope everything was all right."

"Couldn't be better," Strand said with false heartiness.

"Something has come up," Hazen said. "The police called my office this afternoon. They think they may have caught at least one of my attackers. At least, the boy was involved in the same sort of job they tried on me. They'd like Caroline and me to come to the twentieth precinct. It's near you—"

"I know where it is."

"At nine o'clock tomorrow morning to see whether we can identify him. Do you think Caroline would mind very much?" Hazen sounded anxious. "Of course, if she doesn't want to do it, they can't force her. But a single identification probably wouldn't hold up as conclusive in court and . . ."

"Caroline's not home yet," Strand said. "I'll ask her when she gets in."

"Good," Hazen said. "I'd like to see the rascal put away for a few months, although with the way the courts are these days, that's probably too much to hope for. You can call me back at the office. I'll be working late tonight. Oh, by the way, I've already talked to my friend at Truscott and he says he can arrange to have one of their alumni who does some scouting in New York for them take a look at Caroline."

"Good God, don't you have anything better to do with your Monday mornings?"

"It only took me five minutes."

When Strand went back into the living room, Leslie was standing at the window, looking out at the rainy street.

"That was Hazen," Strand said. "The police think they may have found one of the boys. They want Caroline and Hazen to come down tomorrow morning and identify him."

"What did you tell him?" Leslie still kept looking out the window.

"That I'd ask Caroline and call him back. I don't particularly relish the idea of Caroline getting mixed up in something like that."

Leslie nodded. "Neither do I. Still, she may have strong feelings about it."

"Leslie, darling, please sit down," Strand said gently. "I have some things to tell you. The things I didn't want to talk about last night."

Slowly, she turned away from the window and sat down facing him. "It was after Caroline had played tennis with Hazen," Strand said, "and he and I were walking back to the house . . ." Then he told her everything: Hazen's offer and his arguments for sending Caroline off, the possibility of the athletic scholarship, and as completely as he could remember, about his conversation with Eleanor.

Leslie listened quietly, her face showing no emotion, her hands folded in her lap. When Strand had finished, she said, "Eleanor is right, of course, about Caroline. She *does* think she's unattractive. She does hate her nose. She *is* painfully shy. She hides it from us, she's been hiding it from us since she was a child."

"You knew?" Strand asked, incredulously. "You knew all along and you didn't tell me?"

Leslie reached out and touched his hand. "What good would it have done?" Her tone was gentle now and loving. "Don't you have enough to worry about?"

"I feel like an absolute fool," Strand said.

"You're not a fool. Sometimes you're unobservant, that's all," she said. "Especially about your children. Now, the question is, what are we going to do about it?" She smiled. "Notice I said we."

"Hazen wants us to let him talk to Caroline."

"Tempt her with visions of perpetual western sunshine." Leslie smiled again. "Well, why not? A little perpetual sunshine would be a welcome change for us all."

"But to study to be a veterinary, for God's sake! How do you think she got an idea like that?"

"Don't know," Leslie said. "Maybe she read the Englishman's book—*All Creatures Great and Small*—and it seemed like an interesting profession—meeting different kinds of people, out in the open air and all that. If she's really got her mind set on it, I wouldn't stand in her way."

"Why didn't she ever say a word to either of us about it?" Strand knew he sounded aggrieved.

"Maybe she was just waiting for the right moment. Girls learn early not to blurt out everything to their parents."

"You'd be for letting her go away?"

Leslie nodded.

"Well," Strand said, "they'll probably be seeing each other tomorrow morning at the police station. They can talk there. It's an ideal place for temptation."

Leslie stood up and moved toward him and leaned over

and kissed him on the forehead. She touched his hair. "You need a haircut," she said.

When Caroline came in a little before dinner time, Strand told her about Hazen's call. Leslie was giving a lesson to her policeman pupil in the living room and they went into the kitchen to get away from the clanking chords that the representative of the law was clubbing out of the poor piano. "Mr. Hazen said he was going to go to the police station, but that if you didn't want to go, they couldn't force you."

Caroline's face grew very sober and she ran her hand through her hair. Strand hoped she would say she didn't want to go, but she said, "I'll go."

"You're sure now?"

"Positive. Those boys shouldn't be on the street. I can't forget what they were like—a pack of wild animals, grunting, stabbing, hitting, grabbing. I just hope they found the right one."

"All right." Strand sighed. "Your mother and I'll go along with you."

"There's no need. I'm not a baby."

"I said we'd go with you," Strand said.

Caroline sighed and started out of the kitchen, but Strand stopped her. "Sit down for a minute, Caroline. There's something I have to talk about with you."

Caroline looked at him suspiciously but seated herself in one of the chairs at the kitchen table. Strand sat facing her. "I understand from Mr. Hazen," he said, "that you talked about going out west to college."

"Oh," Caroline said, sounding on the thin edge of guilt, "he told you."

"Yes."

"I didn't say I was going," she said. "I just said that if I had my druthers that's where I'd like to go. I also told him I had no druthers."

"He told me that there was a chance you *could* have what you call your druthers."

"He did?" Caroline looked surprised. "He didn't tell *me*."

"He wanted to talk to me first."

"What else did he tell you?" Now she was wary.

"That you wanted to go to an agricultural college to prepare for a veterinary's degree."

"Is that a crime?" Her voice was hostile.

"Of course not," Strand said soothingly. "But your mother and I would like to know why you want to do it and why you didn't tell us long ago."

"I wasn't sure long ago. I didn't want to say anything while I was undecided. Besides, I was afraid you'd laugh at me and tell me I was a sentimental little girl. Well, now it's out. Laugh if you want," she said.

"Nobody's laughing, Caroline," Strand said gently.

"Anyway, it's pointless even talking about it." She made a gesture of dismissal with her hand. "Fairy tales for the young. It'd take money, a lot of money. We're rich in affection around here," she said ironically, "but when it comes to worldly goods . . ." She shrugged. "I'm not blind. When was the last time you bought a new suit?"

"Let's come to that later," Strand said. "Right now I'm interested in your reasons. What do you know about animals?"

"Nothing, yet. Well, I do know *something*. That they suffer and suffer horribly and deserve to find relief. Is it so weird to want to use your life to make this awful world just a little more human?" Her voice rose in anger, as though she felt she was being attacked.

"I don't think it's weird," Strand said. "In fact, I find it admirable. But people suffer, too. Yet you don't want to be a doctor."

"I don't want to be a doctor or a politician or a general or a social worker, because I'd be no good at any of those things. Eleanor could be anything she wanted but I can't. I may be stupid, but there's one thing I know and that's *me*. I don't get along easily with people and they'd scare me and I'd be clumsy and say all the wrong things and feel they were always laughing at me behind my back."

Oh, my poor dear daughter, Strand thought sorrowfully.

"Animals're better." Caroline went rushing on. "They don't talk. Or at least not so we can understand them.

They wouldn't embarrass me." Now she was on the brink of tears.

Strand leaned over the table and patted her hand. "All right," he said. "Now I know how you feel, although I think maybe you're too hard on yourself. As you grow older, I think you'll have a higher opinion of your value."

"If I have to stay in this city, fighting day and night to try to keep up with all the smart kids around me, I'll just be wiped out for good." She was wailing now.

"What if I were to tell you," Strand said, "that you've convinced me and that I think it *would* be better all around if you went away to school?" He paused. "And there may be a way we can swing it, worldly goods or no worldly goods."

Caroline looked at him disbelievingly. "What're you and Mummy going to do—get jobs at night to send me to Arizona?"

"Nothing as drastic as that." Strand laughed. "No, Mr. Hazen has come up with an idea."

"You're not thinking of asking him to lend you the money, are you? I wouldn't go if . . ."

"Not that, either," Strand interrupted her. Then he told her about Hazen's plan for an athletic scholarship. She listened, wide-eyed. "He's already talked to his friend at the school," Strand went on, "and they can arrange for an alumnus who ran on the team and who lives in New York to talk to you and time you. If you're really serious about the whole thing, I advise you to do a little practicing."

"I'm serious all right," she said. "Boy, am I serious."

"I'll talk to the head of the physical education department at your school and maybe they can give you a little coaching."

"It sounds bananas," Caroline said, shaking her head wonderingly. "I run one race in my whole life against girls who would take all week just to get around the block and for that some dopey school is going to pay my way for four years? I think Mr. Hazen was kidding you, Daddy."

"He's not the sort of man who goes in for kidding," Strand said. "Whom you were running against doesn't matter—it's the time that counts." Strand stood up. "By the way, the name of the school is Truscott. And Mr. Hazen said it has a strong agricultural department. If you're positive you want to give it a try, your mother and I will do all we can to help you. If it doesn't work out, we'll look for something else."

Caroline looked pensive, rubbing her nose. "Arizona," she said. "It sounds yummy. Positive! Hell, I'll run for my life."

"You can talk to Mr. Hazen about it," Strand said as he started out of the kitchen, "after you get through with the police tomorrow morning."

But Caroline didn't get a chance to talk to Hazen the next morning, because after she had pointed at the young boy with the livid scar fresh across his forehead and the bridge of his nose, and said, very calmly, "Yes, I am sure, that was the one with the knife," she began to scream, putting the heels of her hands into her eyes and bending over, weaving from side to side. She was still screaming when Strand carried her in his arms out of the station house with Leslie and Hazen hurrying beside him. Conroy was there with the Mercedes and they took her directly to Dr. Prinz's office and he gave her a shot and after a while she lay on the couch, silently, her eyes wide open, staring at the ceiling.

She stayed home from school for two more days, not going out of the apartment, quiet and subdued, her room gaudy with the flowers and littered with huge boxes of chocolates that Hazen sent her. Hazen called twice a day to find out how she was. During one of his calls he mentioned that his friend at Truscott was arranging to have someone in New York take a look at Caroline when she felt she was ready to perform. Hazen too wanted to see her but was understanding when Leslie told him that for the time being it was better if she were left alone.

Then, on Thursday morning, Caroline came into the kitchen, dressed to go out, as Strand was having breakfast. She was humming and the color had returned to her cheeks and she told Strand she was going to school. "Are you sure it's the right thing to do?" Strand said. "After all, it's only a couple of days. You can wait till Monday."

Caroline shook her head. "I don't want to hang around the house anymore. Don't worry, Daddy, I'm over the glooms. I don't know what came over me back there—in the police station—seeing that awful scar on that boy's head and knowing I did it. And he was so young, like a scared baby. And looking at me with a funny, puzzled look on his face, as though he couldn't understand why I was doing that to him. And the way that detective gripped his arm, like a handcuff, and he was going to be put behind bars just because a silly little white girl pointed at him. . . . I was so mixed up, Daddy," she said, trying to keep back tears, "all I could do was scream."

"Don't think about it. You did what you had to do. Now forget it."

Caroline nodded slowly. "I'll try. But I'm not going into the park anymore, I'll tell you that." While she was drinking her juice and boiling some eggs for herself, he went into the bedroom and awoke Leslie to ask her what she thought about allowing Caroline to leave the house. "She's digested it," Leslie said, after a moment's thought. "Or she's pretending she's digested it. Anyway, the best thing we can do is let her act normally, or what she thinks is normally." Still, Leslie dressed hurriedly and, making an excuse that she had some early shopping to do, walked to school with Caroline. Before she left, she told Strand that she was going to invite Hazen to dinner. She was sure, she said, that he would accept. Which he did. Immediately and with pleasure. "I get the impression he eats dinner alone every night of the week," Leslie said to Strand when he came home in the afternoon.

"Funny," Strand said. "I had the same feeling that first night."

"I also told him," Leslie said, "that we would be grateful if he could manage to get Caroline into that school."

"What did he say to that?"

"He said he wished all young people knew what sort of education they wanted and were as eager to get it as Caroline."

"He should have been a headmaster."

"I guess law pays better," Leslie said.

When Hazen came into the apartment that evening he was carrying a sports bag with a warmup suit in it and a pair of track shoes. Caroline blushed, somewhere between gratitude and embarrassment, at the gift. "I'll *fly* with these," she said.

"You just give me a week's notice," Hazen said, "as to when you think you'll be ready and I'll make sure everything is arranged correctly. There's a track on Randall's Island. I suggest you get some starting blocks and try out the shoes a few times."

During dinner they all carefully avoided talking about the scene in the police station. Hazen did most of the talking, telling them what the summers had been like in East Hampton when he was a boy and of the great tennis tournaments that had been held there on grass before the game became professionalized—when the best players were glad to come merely for the pleasure of playing and going to the parties and being put up for the week at the houses of the club members. For the first time he spoke of his family and Strand learned that he had a younger brother who taught philosophy at Stanford and a sister who was married to an oil man in Dallas and had her own private plane. He did not mention his own children or his wife. But he seemed relaxed and happy to talk, like a man who had spent too many silent evenings in his lifetime. He even told a joke on himself, with his father as the hero of it. "When my father died," he said, "*I* inherited his old secretary, among other things. A forbidding lady by the name of Miss Goodson. One day she was in my office while I was lighting a pipe, a habit, among others, I had picked up from him, as well as the practice of law. She looked at me sternly. 'If I may say so, Mr. Hazen,' she said, 'you remind me of your father.' Naturally, still a young man at the time, I was gratified at the remark. My father had been one of the most distinguished attorneys in the country and had served brilliantly on several important government committees and as president of the

New York Bar Association. 'Just exactly how do I remind you of my father, Miss Goodson?' I said, preening a little. 'You drop your lighted matches into the wastebasket and start fires just like him,' she said." Hazen laughed with the rest of them. They were having dessert by then and Hazen sighed contentedly as he put down his spoon. "My, what a delicious meal. I'm afraid," he said to Caroline, "you won't be able to eat like this when you get to Arizona."

"*If* I get to Arizona."

"If whoever is using the stopwatch is honest, I have every confidence you'll get there," Hazen said, making it sound like a judgment at the bar. "You won't have to give up your tennis. There'll be time for both. But I don't imagine you want to play in the park anymore."

"Never," Caroline said.

"In that case, we'll have to arrange something else, won't we?" he said, as he sipped at his coffee. "I'm a member of the Town and Country Tennis Club on East 58th Street. Would you like to play some doubles with me on Saturday morning?"

"That would be super," Caroline said.

"I'll introduce you around," Hazen said. "There are quite a few players there worthy of you and you can go whenever you want as my guest."

"Aren't you going out to the Island this weekend?" Strand asked. He didn't like the idea of Hazen piling up debts of gratitude.

"Not this weekend," Hazen said. "I have an appointment in town Saturday evening."

"I'm afraid you work too hard, Mr. Hazen," Leslie said.

"Russell, please," Hazen said. "I think it's about time we moved on to a first name basis. Leslie?"

"Of course."

"Thank you. Work." He paused reflectively. "It's my pleasure. I don't know what I'd do with myself if I didn't work. If possible, I plan to die before I have to retire." He chuckled, to take the sting out of his words. "Anyway, I'm the senior member of the firm so they can't push me out to pasture, no matter how gaga I get. Well," Hazen said, standing, "I must be getting on. I have some dull reading to do before I get to bed. Thank you for a most agreeable evening. Good night, Caroline, Leslie." He hesitated, then said, "Good night, Allen."

"I'll see you to the door," Strand said. He cleared his throat. "Russell." At the door, where they could hear the faint clink of dishes from the kitchen, where Leslie and Caroline were cleaning up, Strand said, "By the way, that Romero boy came into my office the other day. He said he was interested. I told him to write you a letter. To spare you his presence as long as possible."

Hazen laughed. "Is he as bad as that?"

"Worse."

"I'll look for the letter." Hazen stared gravely at his host. "You're not regretting it, your decision about Caroline, I mean, are you?"

"Not yet," Strand said.

"You won't," Hazen said. "I guarantee. Oh, by the way, the Yankees are playing Boston this Saturday. If the weather's fair, can you get away?"

"I'm sure I can."

"Good. I'll call you Saturday morning after I introduce Caroline at the club."

The two men shook hands and Hazen went out the door.

Later, in bed, Leslie said, "We have a very happy little girl in the house tonight."

"Yes," Strand said.

"*You're* not so happy, though, are you?"

"I'll get over it," Strand said. Then, bitterly, "Why the hell is she so anxious to get as far away from us as possible?"

7

He was floating through blurred whiteness. He moved. There were tubes attached to him. There were voices in the far distance, unrecognizable. Sleep, insensibility, were infinitely precious.

Saturday was a great success. The weather was warm and sunny, the Yankees won, the manager and the first base coach came over to the owner's box where they were sitting to shake Hazen's hand, which made Strand smile and say, "Come on, Russell, they all know you. What's that stuff about only taking in an occasional game?"

"Well, Allen," Hazen said, "I have to admit I do sneak out of the office when I can and it's a nice day. I never played hooky when I was a kid and I try to make up for it now and then." Dressed for sport in a loud checked jacket and wearing a tweed hat tilted down over his eyes to shut out the glare of the sun, he meticulously made entries on his scorecard of hits, runs, errors, strikeouts and substitutions. He ate three frankfurters during the course of the game and drank two beers, saying "I'm not going to weigh myself for a week."

When Jackson hit a home run he stood up and roared with the rest of the crowd and he groaned aloud when the Yankee shortstop made an error. He caught a foul ball with a one-handed lunge as the ball curved into the box and stood up and tipped his hat in mock gravity as the crowd applauded him.

There was a young boy wearing a Yankee cap sitting in the next box with his father. He had on a fielder's glove for just such eventualities as foul balls and had leaped to catch the ball that Hazen had caught and then had sunk back into his seat embarrassedly. Hazen leaned over and gave the ball to the boy. "Here you are, lad," he said. "This is for you." He smiled as the boy stared with wonder and disbelief at the treasure in his hand.

"You've made his week, sir," the boy's father said.

"May he have many more like it," Hazen said, with a little pull at the visor of the boy's cap. Watching him, Strand remembered Hazen's uncondescending and comradely relationship with the Ketleys' grandson while they were playing catch. The man had a gentle, affectionate way with children and Strand wondered how he could have gone so wrong with his own son and daughters.

The entire afternoon had shown a playful and youthfully attractive streak in Hazen for which his usual composed and judicial manner of speaking and behaving had not prepared Strand and for the first time he felt a warmth for the man that broke through the watchful reserve with which he had up to then regarded the lawyer. After this day, Strand thought, it will be easier to be his friend.

Conroy was waiting with the car at the gate when they left the stadium, a benevolent policeman disregarding the fact that the car was in a no-standing zone and touching the visor of his cap as Hazen and Strand approached. Strand felt a touch of what he knew was unworthy, elitist superiority as he got into the car, leaving the thousands of other spectators to herd their way toward the steps leading to the platform of the elevated tracks.

"A fine afternoon," Hazen said, with a sigh of contentment as he sank into the back seat of the Mercedes beside Strand. "We must do it again soon. You know, if the Yankees'd lost we'd be fretful and down and I'd be feeling the three frankfurters and complaining about heartburn. But they won and I'm looking forward to a big steak for dinner." He laughed. "Imagine a man my age depending upon the Yankees for his digestion. Well, we've got to be partisans about *something* and there's damn little else in this day and age that we can cheer about." He took a leather-encased flask with a silver top out of the pocket of the topcoat he had left in the car when they went into the ballpark. The top had another small cup inside it and he gave it to Strand and poured for both of them. "Bourbon," he said. "It's more American. Well, here's to Jackson."

They both drank. Strand felt that it was a fitting end to the afternoon.

When the car drove up in front of Strand's building, Hazen said, "I'm not sure about next weekend, but if I can make it, can you folks come out to the Island with me?"

"I'll see what Leslie's plans are," Strand said.

As he was getting out of the car, Hazen said, "I'll call you on Wednesday and you can tell me then."

It was three weeks before they went to East Hampton again. Hazen had called and told Strand that he had to go out of town to places like Washington, Los Angeles, Dallas, Tulsa, and Chicago, but that if the Strands would like to go to the beach for the weekends, the Ketleys would be alerted and Conroy would drive them down. Strand had declined, without discussing the matter with Leslie. The end of term work was piling up on him, he told Hazen, and he'd better stay in town.

"Well, then," Hazen said, "when I get back. That's definite, isn't it?"

"Definite," Strand promised.

"Another thing," Hazen said. "I've been in touch with the assistant district attorney and they're going to allow the kid to plead guilty to a reduced charge, so tell Caroline to stop worrying. She won't have to appear in court."

"That was thoughtful of you," Strand said, relieved.

"They'll probably release the kid on probation and he'll be stealing bikes the next afternoon. Oh, well, you have to pay a little for the pleasure of living in Fun City."

"Have you heard from Romero yet?" Strand asked. Since his last conversation with the boy, Romero had avoided him and had cut all his classes. Judith, too, had avoided him. Strand couldn't decide whether he was glad or sorry that there were no more drinks in her neat, feminine apartment, with the north light coming in through the big studio window.

"No word from your protégé. I expect he's finding it a difficult letter to write," Hazen said. "If you see him, tell him I look forward to talking to him."

"I'll tell him," Strand said.

"Has a man called Burnside gotten in touch with you yet?"

"No."

"He will soon. He's the alumnus of Truscott who was a track star there. I spoke to him on the phone and he sounded agreeable. He can watch Caroline next Thursday, if that's all right with her. Is she up to it yet?"

"She tells me she is," Strand said. "Her gym teacher found some starting blocks and they've been working out every afternoon together. And she's cut out desserts."

Hazen laughed. "I hope she's not fretting."

"Not noticeably. She's enchanted with your tennis club."

"Good," Hazen said. "I hear she's much in demand. It's amazing, the variety of friends you can make with a good forehand. It's too bad Eleanor doesn't play. There are a lot of important people at the club, in all kinds of businesses, and she could make some very useful contacts there."

"Eleanor," Strand said, "makes her own contacts."

"I've noticed that. Oh, I nearly forgot—I have some tickets for concerts and the ballet and the theater piling up that I won't be able to use. I'll send them over with a messenger."

"You're too generous by half," Strand said, but was pleased even as he said it, thinking of the nights ahead for himself and Leslie.

"Nonsense, Allen," Hazen said. "I'd feel guilty if they went to waste."

"Thank you, anyway."

"If anything comes up while I'm gone," Hazen said, "just call Conroy at the office."

Strand wondered if Conroy, who certainly looked in need of amusement, ever got a free pair of tickets from his boss.

"I'm sure nothing will come up," he said.

"Just in case," Hazen said. "Well, keep well and give my love to the family."

Love, Strand thought as he put down the phone. It was the first time he had heard Hazen use the word. A figure of speech. No more.

Hazen was in the Mercedes with Conroy at the wheel when they drove up in front of the apartment building precisely at four thirty. Strand, Leslie, Caroline and Jimmy were waiting for him. Eleanor was due to leave for Greece the next week and had so many things to do to get ready that she couldn't take the time off to go along with them.

Jimmy was bringing along his guitar. When Strand had protested, Jimmy said that when they were at Hazen's house the time before, over lunch, Hazen had told him he'd heard the young people talking enthusiastically about Jimmy's performance at the bar in Bridgehampton and said that he'd like to hear what Jimmy could do on the instrument. "All right. Take it with you. But for God's sake don't play it unless you're specifically asked."

Leslie had worried a little about canceling still another Saturday's lessons, but Caroline's delight at the prospect of the holiday was infectious and now Leslie greeted Hazen warmly as he got out of the big car with Conroy to help them stow their bags in the trunk. It was a warm, muggy afternoon and the radio had promised more of the same for the next two days and Jimmy had voiced what they all felt about getting away to the seashore when he said, "It couldn't have happened at a better time or to nicer people."

When they got to the house it was still light and still hot. "We have plenty of time before dinner," Hazen said. "I suggest we all take a dip in the ocean. Clear the city out of our souls."

Even Strand approved of the idea after the muggy day at work. His family knew what his legs looked like and by now Hazen must have guessed that he was not built like a fullback. When they assembled on the beach fifteen

minutes later Caroline and Jimmy went splashing into
the waves with wild whoops of joy. Hazen lunged at the
sea as though he intended to batter it into submission, and
Strand and Leslie watched him swimming strongly in an
impromptu race with Caroline, who had a deceptively
easy stroke that made her knife through the water at a
smart pace.

Leslie looked curvy and pleasantly buxom in a one-
piece black bathing suit, her fine legs firm and rosy in the
light of the westering sun. She was not as full-bodied as
the woman in the Renoir drawing that hung in their room,
but, Strand thought approvingly, if Renoir had been alive
today he would have been happy to use her as a model.
She went in sedately, but then plunged into a wave and
swam methodically toward where Jimmy was paddling
just beyond the line of the breakers. Strand went in gingerly, conscious of the way his bathing trunks flapped
around his skinny legs. But once he was in he felt light
and buoyant, his skin tingling deliciously in the cold water.
He had a thrashing stroke that Eleanor had once described
as the slowest Australian crawl in the history of swimming.

The sun was low on the horizon when they came out
and Strand shivered a little and noticed that Leslie was
shivering, too, as she toweled herself. They smiled at each
other. "I feel ten years younger," he said.

"What a luxury," she said, shaking the sea water out of
her hair, "to be shivering on a hot day like this."

When Strand came downstairs, leaving Leslie to get herself ready for dinner, Hazen was already in the living
room, a drink in his hand. He was wearing bright red
pants, an open shirt and a linen jacket. He had told them
that there was a little dinner party arranged for the evening and Strand had dressed carefully, with gray slacks
and a blue blazer that Leslie had had pressed for him, and
a necktie.

"Join me?" Hazen said, lifting his glass.

"Not for the moment, thanks," Strand said. "I feel too
good to drink."

"Lucky man," Hazen said. "The swim *was* bracing. The

ocean was innocent today. But it isn't always like that. A man drowned off this beach last summer. Tell the children to be careful." He sipped at his drink. Then, abruptly, "I want to ask you to forgive me for the drunken scene the last time you were here."

"I've forgotten it," Strand said.

"I'm sure you haven't, Allen." Hazen looked at him steadily. "I had had a trying day. Most trying. It won't happen again." He made a dismissing gesture with his hand, the night obliterated. "By the way, I bumped into Eleanor yesterday afternoon. Did she tell you we had a drink together?"

"No." So. No drinking at home, but a little bracer now and then to prepare for the evening. "She didn't say anything."

Hazen nodded. "She has more important things on her mind. There's a bar near my office where I sometimes drop in for a drink after work. It turns out it's near her office, too. There was a young man with her. A Mr. Gianelli." He paused as if to see what effect the name would have made on Strand.

Noncommittally, Strand said, "I've only met him once. Briefly. At your house, in fact."

"Oh, yes," Hazen said. "He told me how much he liked the house. They kindly insisted I join them at their table. Over drinks Eleanor told me a little about herself."

"At that age," Strand said, "that's likely to be the chief subject of a girl's conversation."

Hazen smiled. "A man's, too," he said. "Do you remember what you talked about mostly when you were twenty-two?"

"Not really. It was a long time ago. Nearly thirty years." He reflected, trying to remember. His closest friend then had been a young man by the name of O'Malley, who had been a classmate of his and who described himself as a Trotskyite. O'Malley had been disappointed with him, he remembered, because Strand, according to O'Malley, was interested only in getting ahead, fitting in meekly with what O'Malley called the system. For O'Malley, the system represented a gigantic fraud, a war won, and its prin-

ciples cynically betrayed, victory thrown away, Stalin
triumphant and bloodstained, McCarthy rampaging and
threatening America with fascism, bloody British imperial-
ism, the rape of Ireland. O'Malley was willing to fight on
all fronts and was looking for barricades to defend. Ancient history. Strand wondered what had ever become of
O'Malley and if he had ever found a suitable barricade.
"I think we talked a great deal about politics in those
days," Strand said.

Hazen nodded. "There's a subject. Were you ever in the
armed services? Korea?"

"No. When I took my physical, they discovered I had
a heart murmur. I never knew I had it and it's never
bothered me."

"I enlisted," Hazen said. "My father thought it was a
good idea. I was an ensign in the Navy. Sailing a desk in
Washington. Also my father's doing. Is your father still
alive?"

"No. He died a long time ago."

"There's much to be said for it," Hazen said. "Having
a dead father I mean. Wasted years." He sipped carefully
at his drink. Obviously there was going to be no drunken
scene tonight. "Your daughter, Eleanor, strikes me as
being a very clever girl."

"She is that."

"But dissatisfied." Again the steady, probing look.

"A common disease for youth," Strand said lightly.

"She says if she were a man she'd be getting twice what
she's getting now and be head of her department to boot,"
Hazen said.

Strand tried not to look surprised. She had always
sounded enthusiastic when talking about her work at the
office.

"Bright young people don't like systematic climbing,"
Hazen said. "They want to get promoted in leaps and
bounds. They're sure they could run the company ten
times better than some old fuddy-duddy who should be
working standing at a high desk and using a quill pen. I
imagine there are quite a few ambitious young people in
my office who say the same thing about *me*."

"That must have been a long drink," Strand said.

"Two, to be exact. The young man with her, Mr. Gianelli, seemed to have had several more. To be honest, he was somewhat under the weather, as though he had stopped at more than one bar during the afternoon. He became quite excited during the course of the discussion. He said to her that she kept saying she was fed up being bossed around by idiots but when she is offered a chance to get out and be her own boss she looks at him as though he's crazy."

"Did he say just what he was offering her?" Strand asked carefully.

"The implication, as far as I could figure it out, was marriage," Hazen said. He stared closely at Strand.

Strand managed to keep his face blank. "I did gather they were—well—fond—of each other."

"Mr. Gianelli then appealed to me," Hazen said. "It seems he feels that he's not cut out for the job with his father—he's the middle one of five sons in his father's business and understandably he feels somewhat constrained. He asked me, rather loudly, if *I* thought it was crazy to start a small newspaper somewhere, the two of them together as publishers and editors."

"What did you tell him?" Strand asked, thinking, There must be some aura of wisdom and power, some secret quality, that Hazen has for the young, that makes them bare their souls to him immediately. "Did you ask the young man where he expected to get the money for this noble project?"

"He said something about his brothers agreeing to chip in to help him if he finds a suitable spot. They quite obviously would not be displeased to see him gone. Five brothers in the same business. There are also two sisters and brothers-in-law. Italian families." He smiled indulgently at Mediterranean abundance. "I know something about the father. A client of mine deals with him. Hardheaded but fair, my client says. And quite successful. It is a group that has shown remarkable upward mobility in recent years. Except, of course, in Italy." He smiled bleakly at his witticism. "The father, I take it, with some justice, is not enthusiastic about the enterprise."

"Did *you* tell them anything?" Strand asked, almost accusingly.

"I said youth is the time for risks and I had to go home to dress for dinner." He paused. "How would you and your wife take it?"

"We try not to meddle," Strand said shortly.

"I'm constantly amazed," Hazen said, "about how you let your children go their own way." There was neither approval nor disapproval in the way he said it. "It was different in my own house. We were told very definitely what we were to do. My brother rebelled, of course. He didn't even come back from California for my father's funeral. We hardly communicate. I hear that he is happy. It may just be a rumor." He smiled ironically.

From upstairs came the sound of Jimmy's guitar, random chords, some dark and sad, others suddenly light, as though Jimmy were having a dialogue with himself on the instrument, one part of him gloomy, the other mischievous and mocking.

"If the noise bothers you," Strand said, "I'll go up and tell him to stop."

"Oh, no," Hazen said. "I like the sound of music in the house. I told him I'd like to hear him play."

"He said as much. I thought perhaps you were being polite."

"I'm not as polite as all that," Hazen said.

The two men listened for a while. Jimmy started a song that Strand had never heard before. Jimmy was singing, but Strand could not make out the words. It was not a dialogue anymore but a plaintive, sweet solo murmur, with sudden harsh interjections.

"My mother, as I believe I told you, used to play the piano for me," Hazen said. "Only when she was still young. She stopped. Several years later she died. She went in silence."

Went in silence, Strand thought. What a way to describe the death of your mother.

"I think I'm going to treat myself to one more drink,"

Hazen said, lifting himself from his easy chair. "Can I get one for you?"

"Not just yet, thank you."

While Hazen was at the sideboard mixing his drink, there was a bustle at the door and a tall woman with a scarf wrapped around her head like a turban came in. "Make one for me, Russell," she called as she came through the door. Her voice was high and vigorous and she smiled at Strand nicely as she entered the room. She was dressed in a skirt and sweater and she was wearing shoes with low heels. Forty years old, bony, not my type, Strand thought automatically.

"Oh, Linda," Hazen said from the sideboard, "I was afraid you were going to be late."

"The traffic was ferocious," the woman said, rolling the *r* to emphasize how ferocious. "Friday night. The march of the lemmings to the sea. Hello." She extended her hand to Strand. "I'm Linda Roberts. Russell can't do two things at the same time, like making drinks and introducing his guests."

"Good evening," Strand said. "I'm Allen Strand." Her hand was surprisingly callused. He guessed she was a golfer. She had large gray eyes, carefully made up, and a bold sweep of lipstick on what otherwise would have been a narrow mouth. She went over to Hazen and kissed his cheek, leaving a little scar of red. "The usual," she said.

Hazen had already begun to mix her a martini. She watched approvingly. "Martinis make everything worthwhile, don't they?" she said, smiling at Strand.

"So I've heard," Strand said.

"Russell, do I have to dress for dinner or can I sit at table in my traveling rags?"

"There'll just be a few friends," Hazen said, coming over to her with her martini.

"A blessing," she said, accepting the martini and sipping it. "A benediction on you, dear Russell. I *will* comb my hair, though." She sank into a chair, cradling the stemmed glass, frosty with cold.

"Linda is staying with us for the weekend, Allen," Hazen said, as he went to get his own drink.

"I'm the last-minute addition," Linda Roberts said to Strand. "I didn't think I could get away. I just got back from France to find out there was a mess at the gallery. A shipment of pictures arrived from our French branch and a half-dozen of them looked as though they had crossed the Atlantic in a canoe. I've been dreaming of this martini since the Triborough Bridge."

But Strand noticed that her drink was only half-finished before she started up to comb her hair. She halted at the doorway and frowned. "Good heavens," she said, "what is that funereal wail?"

Hazen laughed. "It's Allen's son, Jimmy. He's a guitarist."

"Oh, my." Mrs. Roberts put her hand up to her mouth in mock dismay. "You must forgive me, Mr. Strand. I'm absolutely stone-deaf. I was exposed to Wagner at an early age and have never gotten over it."

"That's all right," Strand said, amused. "At home we let him practice only behind locked doors. I'm afraid different generations have different notions of what constitutes music. I stop at Brahms myself."

"I like your friend, Russell," Mrs. Roberts said and went briskly out of the room, carrying her martini.

There was silence in the room for a few seconds as Hazen stirred the ice in his glass with his finger and Strand wondered if this was the reputed mistress. Offhand, he liked the woman, but he wouldn't have chosen her as his mistress. If someone had seen him going up to Judith Quinlan's apartment and then coming out with his hair mussed and a bemused expression on his face would Judith be known as his reputed mistress? Reputations are easily made.

"She visits here from time to time," Hazen said, as though he owed Strand an explanation. "Always on the spur of the moment. The house is so big . . ." He stopped. "She's the widow of one of my best friends. Forty-seven years old. Went off like . . ." He snapped his fingers. "Playing golf. Heart."

"She seems to be bearing up bravely," Strand said and Hazen gave him a peculiar sharp look.

"She wisely keeps herself busy. She's half-owner of an art gallery and is very clever at the business. It's associated with a gallery in France and it gives her an excuse to visit Europe several times a year. She sounds foolish at times, but I assure you she's no fool," Hazen said stiffly. "And she devotes herself extensively to charities."

"I hope that when I'm gone my widow will be able to devote herself extensively to charities, too."

"He was in Wall Street. Very shrewd," Hazen said, ignoring Strand's remark, which Strand now realized had been facetiously rude. "Boy wonder. Overwork. Did you read that postmen live longer than the executives of large corporations?"

"All that walking," Strand said, wishing that the others would come down before the level of conversation sank any lower.

"You can take off your tie, you know," Hazen said. "Probably nobody else will be wearing one. East Hampton has become proletarianized. Not like the old days. My father insisted that we dress for dinner almost every night. Now almost anything goes. See-through dresses, jeans, red pants like the goddamn things I'm wearing. I'm sure it all has the most somber sociological implications."

Strand undid his tie and stuffed it into his pocket. His neck was so thin that it was almost impossible to get shirts that were long enough in the sleeve for his arms and still snug around the neck. Hazen looked at him curiously. "I've observed that you eat very well . . ."

"Like a horse," Strand said.

"And yet you remain so thin."

"Meager."

"I wouldn't complain. If I ate like you they'd have to wheel me around in a barrow." He sipped at his whiskey. "But none of your family runs to fat."

"No. Eleanor sometimes goes on a crazy diet if she sees she's gained a few ounces."

"Ridiculous," Hazen snorted. "At her age, with her figure."

The doorbell rang. "My dinner guests," Hazen said. "I hope they don't bore you. Parties in the Hamptons can be stuffy."

At dinner, Hazen sat at the head of the table, with Leslie on his right, her hair swept up, and Caroline on his left. Next to Caroline was one of the young men she had played tennis with three weeks before. Strand noticed with some amusement that it wasn't the good-looking one, Brad or Chad, whom Hazen had warned him about. Next to him was a lady named Caldwell, who had one of the houses down the dunes and who had come with her husband and daughter. The daughter sat next to Jimmy and looked about Jimmy's age, although Strand was never sure about how old girls really were. In his classes he had girls he knew were sixteen who looked twenty-five. A big, jovial man by the name of Solomon, with long straight gray hair that made him look like George Washington, sat next to the girl. Then came Linda Roberts, on Strand's right, who was not dressed in her traveling rags, as she had described them, but in a long, flouncy mauve-colored gown that left her rather bony shoulders bare. Mrs. Solomon, a sharp-faced but pretty woman with a boyish haircut and a deep tan, sat on Strand's left and Caldwell, who had been introduced as Dr. Caldwell, a middle-aged man with the mournful diplomatic face of an ambassador who has just been ordered to deliver a nasty note to a volatile government, completed the table, sitting between Mrs. Solomon and Leslie. Conroy, Strand saw, although he lived on the grounds, was not on his employer's social list.

The conversation was lively and Strand was pleased to see that Leslie and Caroline were obviously enjoying themselves and that the Caldwell girl who had been invited for Jimmy seemed deeply interested in what Jimmy was telling her. But it was difficult for Strand to hear more than snatches of what people were saying because Linda Roberts kept talking to him in a high, piercing voice. "I'll be terrible company tonight," she had warned him as she sat down. "I'm exhausted. Jet lag." She had just come back from France, where, she said, besides the work at the gallery in Paris, there had been a wedding that she just couldn't avoid attending. "Four hundred guests," she said. "Luckily it didn't rain so the reception in the garden didn't turn into a marine disaster. I've been flooded out of one June wedding after another and you always feel that when a marriage starts with everybody cowering for shelter, there'll be a divorce in a year or two. Russell has told me all about you and your lovely family and how much you've done for him. You must be proud of your daughter. If it had been me I'd have just screamed and fallen into a dead faint. I don't know what's ever going to become of dear old New York. Nobody dares wear jewelry anymore. It's all in vaults in banks. The insurance." She sighed, heaving her bony shoulders. "Russell says you're a history teacher. What fun that must be. It was one of my best subjects in the University of Michigan, but I don't read the newspapers anymore—just the society page and the movie reviews—everything else is so *pessimistic*. You must forgive me. I can hardly speak, I'm so exhausted. Airports are hell, anyway. The worst is Fiumicino. I've almost stopped going to Rome because of it. Everybody travels so much these days, you see the strangest people in first class. My husband was on the verge of buying a Lear jet, but then he died. I always like to arrive at Nice. The airport's just along the sea and it's a little like the good old days when you could take one of those glorious plush ships to Europe, with bouillon served at eleven by those smart stewards going along the deck chairs. And now they've even taken those beautiful Italian boats out of service. Heavenly pasta. I don't like to sound like an old fuddy-duddy, but there's such a thing as carrying progress too far. They've ruined the Côte d'Azur, of course, it might just as well be Miami Beach, but I just rush from the airport to my little nest, it's in the hills above Mougins and never put my foot out of it except to walk around my garden. You know Mougins, don't you, Mr. Strand?"

"Allen," Strand said gallantly, wondering how fast and how long Mrs. Roberts could talk when she wasn't suffering from jet lag.

"Allen," she said. "I had a beau by that name. Lovely

young man. Divine looking. People were always asking
him if he wanted to go into the movies. But he was a
serious horseman. He absolutely wilted when I married
my husband and he immediately married a woman who'd
been divorced four times. Stupendous alimony. He came
with his wife to visit me and my husband, and Allen
sulked for three days and we had to pretend we were
packing to go to Ischia to get them out of the house.
Vulgar little thing, the wife, I mean, she sunbathes with
her breasts bare. She was inordinately proud of them, her
breasts, I mean. She came up from being a cheerleader at
the University of Texas and her first husband played football and beat her all the time. I couldn't find it in my
heart to blame him. You and your beautiful wife—my
heavens, she is stunning—must come and visit me in
Mougins. Do you get to France often?"

"No," Strand said, trying to pay attention to the delicious rare slice of lamb on his plate. "Not often."

"You'd love Mougins. It's a haven of peace tucked
away in the hills. My husband bought it for me as a
wedding present. He was the most thoughtful of men. He
dealt internationally. Companies everywhere. In a multi-
tude of countries. You name it, the country I mean, and
he had a company there. Of course it meant being away
an awful lot of the time."

I can understand why he was away a lot of time,
Strand thought, meanly.

"That's what turned me on to good works," Linda
Roberts said. "Being alone so much of the time. In those
conditions other women take lovers." She laughed again,
breathily, hysterically. "But my husband was not a complaisant man, no, not at all, you couldn't describe him as
being complaisant. Charity fills a great gap in my life, Mr.
Strand, I mean Allen. I mustn't monopolize you anymore.
Nellie Solomon is just dying to talk to you, I can tell, and
I'll just sit here and fall into a stupor."

Mrs. Solomon was seated on his left and he turned
gratefully to her. Once or twice Leslie had looked down
the table during Linda Roberts's monologue and had given
him an ironic, pitying smile.

Mrs. Solomon was eating heartily and silently, her eyes on her plate. Dr. Caldwell, on her left, was talking in a low, confidential tone to Leslie, as Strand had noticed he'd been doing almost all through dinner. Later on Leslie told Strand that Caldwell had moved to the Hamptons to practice because, he said, he could never find a place to park his car when he made calls in the city. He was also deeply interested in music, and she said that he knew a great deal about it and didn't talk nonsense. She said he didn't look like a diplomat to her, but a doctor whose patients were always dying on him.

"Are you here for the summer?" Strand said to Mrs. Solomon, because you had to start somewhere.

"We rent," Mrs. Solomon said. "This is the second summer." She had a soft southern accent. Alabama, Strand thought. "Herb wants to buy a house here."

"It *is* a beautiful part of the world," Strand said.

"If you don't play golf," Mrs. Solomon said.

"What?" Strand asked, puzzled.

"If your name is Solomon," she said, "the club is pretty clubby, if you know what I mean."

"I see," Strand said, embarrassed.

"Oh, it's not too bad," Mrs. Solomon said airily, smiling. She had perfect sharp little white teeth and the smile softened her face. "I haven't noticed any pogroms yet. I guess we'll buy the house. It's only at the club that it makes any difference. Everyplace else you can be a Zulu and you'll still be invited to all the parties. And I guess in fifty years the club'll burn down or everybody will be dead or have a Jewish daughter-in-law." Suddenly, she looked at him strangely. "You're Jewish, aren't you?"

"No." He had been asked that question many times, almost always by Jews. His beak of a nose.

"I'm sorry," Mrs. Solomon said. "Neither am I. Née Ferguson. Nellie Ferguson. I don't know why I thought you were."

"I do."

They grinned at each other.

"I wouldn't have given you my little speech if I thought you were a *goy*. As I said, in fifty years it probably won't

make a smidgen of difference. Fifty years ago, they
wouldn't let the Irish into the club. That's why the rich
Irish set themselves up in Southampton. Fifty years isn't
a long time to wait for a game of golf, is it?" She smiled
again.

Strand decided she was a very pretty woman. If Hazen
had to have a mistress, he would have done a lot better
with Nellie Solomon than with Linda Roberts.

"Actually," Mrs. Solomon said, "I love it here. The
beach is glorious, Russell lets me use his court whenever
I want to—I'm due to play with your daughter tomorrow,
I hear she's somethin'—and it's near enough to New York
so that Herb can dash in when the office calls him. He
loves bein' a Jew. And it helps in the business he's in."

"What business is that?"

"Didn't Russell tell you?"

"No, he merely said there were some nice people coming to dinner."

"He said he especially wanted us to come tonight and
meet you. We broke another date to come."

"I'm glad you did."

"You *are* polite. Russell said as much." She smiled
again. "My Herbert books bands, arranges concerts, rock,
country, jazz, spirituals, schmaltz, you name it, he does
it. You ought to see some of the people who pour through
our house."

"I see," Strand said. He shook his head. Good old
Hazen, something for everyone. He had asked Jimmy to
bring his guitar with a purpose. Perhaps Hazen had
thought that one of the family looked sick, anemic or in
the first stages of some dreadful disease and had invited
Dr. Caldwell to give him a secret diagnosis.

"That's how I met Herbert," Mrs. Solomon said. "I
thought I was a singer."

"How did it turn out?"

She shrugged. "He disabused me. You can't fool ole
Herb when it comes to talent. 'Poor girl,' he said, after
he'd heard me, 'I will have to marry you.'" She chuckled
and looked across at her husband fondly. Then she returned seriously to her food. "I do love to get invited to

Russell's parties here. They're so—so un-East-Hamptonish. He collects oddities—like Herb and me . . ."

"And us," Strand said.

Mrs. Solomon gave him a little childish, conspiratorial smile. "I wasn't goin' to say so."

Strand liked the pretty, frank young woman, with her round, appealing figure, which, if she always ate the way she was eating tonight, would not be so appealing in later years. "He's a most thoughtful host," Strand said, "Russell."

"Marvelous." It came out mahhhvelous. "Have you ever been to his place in New York?"

"No."

"It's just campin' out heah compared to that," Mrs. Solomon said. "It's funny, the feasts he puts out and he hardly takes an insignificant little bite of nourishment himself. . . . Have you noticed that?"

"I have."

"And Herb says that if he had Russell's wine cellar he wouldn't draw a sober breath till the end of his days."

"Everything all right down at your end, Nellie?" Hazen called to Mrs. Solomon.

"Delightful," Mrs. Solomon said. "We were just praisin' you."

"Continue," Hazen said and raised his glass to her, then turned back to talk to Leslie.

"These little green beans are somethin', aren't they?" Mrs. Solomon said, chewing delicately but definitely on a mouthful of food.

"*Flageolets,* that's what they're called," Mrs. Roberts said across Strand. She had not fallen into her promised stupor. "Traditionally," Mrs. Roberts said, "they're always served with gigot in France."

"Thank you, Linda," Mrs. Solomon said. "In Alabama we traditionally serve yams with our gigot." Under the table she pinched Strand's leg, lightly.

Strand tried not to smile too openly.

After dinner, Strand smoked his second cigar. Jimmy, he saw, did not take one when Mr. Ketley passed the box around. They all went out on the terrace to look at the moon over the ocean. Leslie stood next to Strand and he put his arm around her waist. "Having a good time?" he asked.

"Wonderful," she said. "Will you ever be satisfied to eat my cooking again?"

"I'm putting an ad in the *Times* on Monday for a Cordon Bleu cook."

Leslie laughed. "Russell's a fascinating man. He seems to know *everything*. Politics, art, finance, whatever. It makes me feel as though my education has been sadly neglected. And he's *been* everywhere."

"So have we," Strand said. "The Museum of Modern Art, Chinatown, The Bronx . . ."

"Oh, hush, Allen," Leslie said, gently. "I wasn't complaining. But seriously, I *do* think we ought to do some traveling. We could save on other things . . ."

"On what?"

"Oh . . . just other things," Leslie said vaguely. "Russell said I ought to do more with my painting. It's amazing, he's only been in our house twice really and the first time doesn't even count, and he remembers every detail of the two paintings of mine in the living room. He said they were bold and original. Imagine that. My little scratches. I told him I only painted when I was lonesome and he said I ought to arrange to be lonesome more of the time. Do you think he was just being polite and trying to flatter me?"

"No," Strand said. "He doesn't flatter. *I've* always told you I liked your paintings."

"That's different. You're my husband, what could you say, poor man? Do I look all right tonight?" She sounded anxious.

"The lady on my right said you were stunning."

"Stunning how? Stunning stunning or stunning horrendous?"

"Stunning stunning."

"What a nice group of people," Leslie said. "And Jimmy and Caroline are behaving so well."

"Are you surprised?"

Leslie squeezed his arm. "No," she said. "I've had enough of the moon. I'm getting a little cold. Let's go inside."

The others followed them in and Hazen asked Jimmy if he would oblige them with a little music. Jimmy looked doubtfully at his parents. Strand didn't say anything, but Leslie said, firmly, "By all means, Jimmy," and Jimmy went upstairs to get his guitar. Caroline made a little grimace, but Leslie caught it and whispered, "None of that, young lady."

Strand didn't tell Leslie about Herbert Solomon and his position in the music world. It would only make her nervous if she knew that Jimmy was, in a sense, on trial. Jimmy didn't seem nervous at all as he played a few chords to warm up, then started to sing, accompanying himself, in an almost conversational, undramatic voice, songs that Strand had heard on the radio. To Strand's ears, at least, Jimmy sounded no better and no worse than the performers whose records he was told were on all the best seller charts. Solomon seemed to be listening with interest and began suggesting songs for Jimmy to play. Strand noticed that each time Solomon chose a song in a different style from the one before it, so that Jimmy had the chance to show his versatility and range, as well as his knowledge of what songs had been popular in the last five years or so.

"Very nice," Solomon said, when Jimmy finished, on a last, small, diminishing note, and Mrs. Solomon applauded and Mrs. Roberts said, "Bravo! Bravo!" Leslie was smiling, obviously pleased, and even Caroline seemed impressed.

"Thank you very much, Jimmy," Hazen said. "The next time I'll invite a bigger audience."

The party broke up soon after, with Jimmy holding on to his guitar and taking the Caldwell girl off in the station wagon to the bar in Bridgehampton and Caroline going up to bed, after making a date to play some singles early in the morning with the young man who had sat beside her at dinner.

As the Solomons prepared to leave with Dr. Caldwell

and his wife, he said to Strand, "The boy is serious about his music, isn't he?"

"It seems so," Strand said.

Solomon nodded. "Russell has my office phone number. If Jimmy is interested, tell him to call me during the week sometime."

"That's very kind of you," Strand said.

Solomon shrugged. "It may come to nothing. There're thousands of kids who own guitars and have a good ear. Anyway, let him call."

Tactfully, Strand went upstairs with Leslie, leaving Mrs. Roberts, who had said she wanted a nightcap, alone in the living room with Hazen.

"Why did Mr. Solomon say that about telephoning?" Leslie asked when Strand had closed the bedroom door behind them.

"He's in the music business," Strand said, and repeated what Mrs. Solomon had told him about her husband.

"Wasn't it thoughtful of Russell to have him over tonight to hear Jimmy?" Leslie said.

"Very."

"Do you think he and that Mrs. Roberts are . . . ?" She didn't finish the sentence and Strand grinned. "You know what I mean," Leslie said.

"Yes."

"Well?"

"At a guess, I would say not," Strand said. "I don't think she would take the time off from talking to do any mistressing."

Leslie laughed. "You mean she's not to *your* taste."

"No. But I know somebody who is."

"That pretty little Mrs. Solomon. You two seemed to get along awfully well together."

"We did, indeed," Strand said. "But that wasn't whom I meant."

"Faithful, dear man," Leslie said and kissed him. "I'll be in bed in a jiffy."

He was awakened by the sound of moaning. Leslie was asleep in his arms. They had made love slowly and for a long time and the moans brought him up from profound, satisfied depths. It was dark in the room and just before he woke the moans blended in his sleep with the steady rumble of the sea. Gently, he took his arm away from under Leslie's head and got out of bed. The moans were coming from the next room, where Caroline was sleeping. He put on a robe and went into the hallway, where a lamp burned. Barefoot and silent, he went to Caroline's door. The moans were clearer now. The rooms of Hazen and Mrs. Roberts were in the other wing of the house and Strand was thankful that whatever was bothering Caroline would not disturb them. He opened her door. In the light from the hallway he could see she was twisting about convulsively in her bed and moving her arms in front of her face as if to ward off an attacker. Swiftly, he went over to the bed and took her in his arms. "There, there," he whispered. "It's all right. You're all right."

Caroline opened her eyes, her face rigid with fear. "Oh, Daddy," she cried and clung to him.

"You've just been having a bad dream," he said. "I'm here. There's nothing to worry about."

"Oh, Daddy," she wept, "they were going at you, with knives, they were laughing, I couldn't do anything about it, I tried and tried . . ."

"Sssh, sssh."

"I'm so frightened." She held him tight.

"There's nothing to be frightened about. Anybody's likely to have a crazy dream once in a while."

"Don't go away. Please don't go away."

"I won't go away. You just go back to sleep."

"I don't know what I'd have done if you hadn't come in." Suddenly she laughed. "Your beard's scratchy."

"I'm sorry."

"I love it," she said sleepily and in a moment she was asleep again.

He sat holding her in his arms for a long time. When he was sure that she was sleeping peacefully, he put her down gently and covered her and went out of the room, closing the door behind him. He heard steps on the stairs and saw Jimmy coming up, carrying his guitar.

"Hi, Pops," Jimmy said. "What're you doing prowling around at this hour?"

"What time is it?"

"After three," Jimmy said. "It was a big night. Anything wrong?"

"Caroline had a nightmare, that's all."

"My music." Jimmy grinned. "I didn't know it was *that* powerful. Is she okay now?"

"Fine."

"Poor kid," Jimmy said. "Well, good night. Sleep well."

But it was a long time before Strand could fall asleep again. The sound of the ocean seemed ominous now and Leslie's even breathing seemed frail and precarious and heartbreakingly dear to him in the quiet strange room where they had made love but which was no longer secure from invasion.

He woke late and alone in the morning, feeling tired and unrefreshed. When he went downstairs, Mr. Ketley told him everybody had gone to the tennis court. He wasn't hungry, so he just had a cup of coffee. The day was muggy and he decided to take advantage of everybody's absence to take a dip in the ocean and wake himself up.

When he came down in his swimming trunks and robe, the terrace and the beach were still deserted. The sea wasn't too rough, just small waves curling over and breaking about ten yards from shore. Strand dropped his robe and trotted across the fine white sand into the water. He walked out toward where the waves were breaking, the water cold and up to about his waist. He was thoroughly awake now and enjoying himself as he stood, letting the waves wash over him. He swam a little, thinking, I should join the Y and swim at least three times a week, it would do me good.

When his arms began to feel a little tired he put his feet down on the smooth sand and started to walk in. But he found he couldn't move an inch toward the beach. The water was swirling around him and he had difficulty remaining standing. Then, suddenly, his feet were swept out from under him and slowly and inexorably the tide began to take him out. He tried not to panic, but thrashed wildly with his arms to fight the current. He had never felt so tired in his life and he was swallowing water. Shouting would do no good; there was no one to hear. He looked at the big house, so close to him and with no sign of life in it.

Then he saw Conroy come out on the terrace, a newspaper in his hand. Conroy sat down and unfolded his paper, not looking toward the beach.

"Conroy!" Strand managed to call. "Conroy!" He saw Conroy look around him puzzledly, as though he couldn't make out where the call came from. Then he saw Strand, who waved frantically, unable to shout anymore and fighting to keep his head above water.

Conroy turned and waved toward the house, then ran down to the beach, stripping off his sweater as he ran. He was in Bermuda shorts and barefooted. He plunged in and swam toward Strand. As he reached him, he said, "Easy does it, Mr. Strand," in a flat, surprisingly calm voice. "Just turn over on your back and let yourself float. I'll take hold." His lank hair was plastered against his head and his arms were thin and pale.

Strand turned over on his back. The sun glittered in his eyes through a haze of foam. He felt Conroy's hand under his chin, supporting him. Conroy swam with his free arm, slowly, slowly, not toward shore, but trying to keep parallel with the beach. The current pulled them farther out to sea. Strand was gasping, short painful intakes of air and water. The land kept receding, far, far off.

He raised his head and glimpsed someone running toward the water, carrying something. After a moment, he realized it was Linda Roberts and that what she was carrying was a coil of rope. He saw her plunge into the waves, lost sight of her.

Then, suddenly, the current released the two men. Conroy gasped. "Okay," he said, "we're out of it now. Just keep calm." He started to tow Strand slowly toward the beach, panting painfully with each stroke. We're not going to make it, Strand thought, we're both going to go under. He wanted to say something to Conroy but he couldn't talk. Then something hit the water near them with a splash and Conroy reached out. It was a rope that Mrs. Roberts, now up to her waist in the water, had thrown to them. Strand was sure he had been in the water for hours and the beach didn't seem to be getting any closer, but at least it wasn't slipping away anymore.

"We'll make it now," Conroy said, grasping the rope. His arm holding Strand took on a new strength. Slowly, Mrs. Roberts strained on the rope. Foot by foot, inch by inch, they approached where she was standing. When they reached her, she and Conroy dragged Strand through the surf and finally he was lying on the rough sand of the beach, trying to smile up at Mrs. Roberts, whose flimsy dress clung wetly to her bony frame. But his face seemed to have frozen and he couldn't smile.

Conroy dropped down beside him, his eyes closed, his chest heaving.

"You got caught in a sea pussy," Mrs. Roberts said, pushing her wet hair away from her eyes, her voice sounding as if it were over a telephone far away, on a bad connection. "They're freak eddies, one of the main attractions of this coast."

Then he blacked out. When he came to he felt a face above him, lips clamped against his, a warm breath blowing into his mouth. The kiss of life. The phrase wandered foolishly through his mind. Mrs. Roberts stood up. She seemed to be floating above him, somewhere between land and sky, in a red mist.

Now Conroy was floating above him, too, in a red mist of his own. "He's alive," Strand heard Conroy say, still on the bad telephone connection.

The worst pain he had ever felt in his life was tearing at his chest and shoulders and he could not breathe. "Conroy," he said faintly, "it hurts. It hurts here . . ." He managed to touch his chest. "I'm afraid I . . ."

A half hour later he was in the intensive care room of the Southampton Hospital, with Dr. Caldwell leaning over him, saying to someone whom Strand couldn't see, "Heart . . ."

"A man exactly your age," Dr. Prinz had said.

After that he didn't hear or remember anything for a long time.

8

Voices became clearer. She sounds foolish at times, but I assure you she's not foolish. The kiss of life. He recognized faces. Identities merged. He recognized himself. The world moved closer.

It was two weeks before he was out of the hospital. Dr. Caldwell had proved efficient. Dr. Prinz had come down from New York and looked grave. A great heart specialist, called by Hazen, had flown down from the city by helicopter and had been encouraging. The doctors had tested and probed and whispered together in the corridor. Conroy, ashen-faced navigator of the deeps, had been helpful in matters of transportation. Eleanor had canceled her trip to Greece and was staying at Hazen's house with Jimmy. Leslie had started driving back and forth from New York when the worst was over, so that she could continue with her lessons and be with Caroline while she took her final exams.

The pain was gone now, but Strand still felt so weak it took a great effort to lift his arms. Hazen had driven him to the big house on the beach, where he and Mr. Ketley had carried him up to the bedroom.

He had been told by all the doctors that he needed rest, a long rest. He had let himself be handled like an infant, allowing others to make decisions about him. He did not think of the future, but accepted what was told him, what was given him to eat, the medicines they gave him to take, the installation in the big bedroom overlooking the sea on the second floor where he could look at the Renoir drawing. He was wearily grateful to everyone and didn't take the trouble to speak.

He could live to be a hundred, the doctors told him, if he took care of himself. He had always thought that he did take care of himself. Nobody had told him about sea pussies or the malevolent power of the ocean. There was a letter on his bedside table from Judith Quinlan. He hadn't opened it. He wondered if he had yet thanked Conroy or Linda Roberts for saving his life. Time enough when his strength came back. He was not used to illness, but relapsed into it with dreamlike pleasure. His body was for the time being no longer his responsibility.

People talked to him, Leslie, the doctors, Eleanor, Jimmy, Caroline, Hazen, Mr. and Mrs. Ketley. A moment after they had spoken he didn't remember what they had said. He smiled benignly at everyone, believing that his smile was reassuring. He was not interested in reading or what was happening to the country or anybody else's problems, or the weather. It was the most beautiful summer in years, someone said, he couldn't remember who, but the climate in the big, luxurious room was always the same.

The principal of the high school came to visit him and told him not to worry about the department. "I know you're going to be better," the principal said. "Just take your time and when you're ready to come back just give me a call on the telephone. Your place will be open." He was not in the mood for telephones and he did not worry about the department.

There were always flowers in the room during the day but he never knew their names and didn't ask.

A cot had been put in his room for Leslie and he did not question why, after so many years of their sleeping together, she now spent her nights in a different bed.

He slept more than he had ever slept in his life.

One evening, when he began to feel better, he told Leslie that everybody should have at least one heart attack.

She laughed. She was thinner and there were lines in her face that he had never seen before.

Herbert Solomon sent over a cassette machine, with selections from Beethoven, Brahms, César Franck and songs by Joan Baez, Bob Dylan and a man named Cohen. Strand didn't ask for the machine to be turned on.

Linda Roberts sent a big book about the Midi, with handsome photographs. He didn't open the book.

Caroline told him she thought she had done well on her exams. He was involved in other examinations and didn't ask her what tests she had taken. He did ask her, though, about the man from Truscott.

"It seemed to go all right," Caroline said, without enthusiasm. "He timed me twice and said he thought they'd accept me. He said he'd talk to Mr. Hazen." She shrugged. "It's not important."

Her face, too, had grown thinner, he noticed, and she looked as though she cried often. He would have liked to comfort her, but the effort was too great. She said Alexander and Mrs. Curtis sent their best wishes and Mrs. Curtis a box of cookies she had baked herself. He told Caroline to eat the cookies.

Giuseppe Gianelli sent him an enlarged photograph of Eleanor, standing on a dune, in a blowing denim dress, laughing against the sky, with spikes of grass around her bare legs. With it, there was a note that Leslie read to him. "Something beautiful to look at in the dark hours. And a tonic for all hearts." He had signed the note, "Your poor poet contractor friend, Giuseppe."

"He's a fine young man," Leslie said, as she put the photograph on the bureau, where Strand could see it from the bed. "We've had some long talks together. He's crazy about Eleanor."

From time to time, idly, Strand looked at the photograph. He wondered what Giuseppe Gianelli had said to his daughter to make her laugh like that against the open sky.

Sometimes, late at night, he heard Leslie playing on the piano downstairs, softly. He didn't know if she was playing for herself or if there was anybody else listening. He meant to ask, but then when she came up to bed, forgot.

Hazen came into the room from time to time and stared

at him soberly. "I must remember," Strand said to Hazen, "only to visit people who include strong swimmers in the guest list. I must also remember to thank Conroy and Linda. Above and beyond the call of duty, wouldn't you say?"

Hazen didn't answer the question. Instead he said, "I've already thanked them in your behalf. I gave a thousand dollars to Conroy—money means everything to him, he saves like a pack rat—and a little gold bracelet to Linda. A bauble."

"Now," said Strand, uncomfortable with the information, "now I know what my life is worth. A thousand dollars and a bauble."

Hazen looked at him curiously. "Everything has its price," he said curtly. "Which does not necessarily correspond with its value. I would advise you not to be embarrassed by money. Which brings up another question. Are you well enough to talk?"

"Just," said Strand.

"Did you know that after the first ten days the doctors said you were going to pull through and be able to lead a normal, although fairly quiet life?" Hazen said.

"I don't know. But it's good news."

"It certainly is. But it means that you will have to think about the rest of your life. If you take what they say seriously." Hazen sounded almost accusing. "Which would not mean going back to your job in September as though nothing has happened."

Strand suppressed a sigh. He had known that one day, not too far in the future, he would have to face this, but he had used the invalid's prerogative of postponement.

"I don't suppose," Hazen went on, "that a New York City high school disability pension would go very far, especially in these days of inflation."

"Subway fare," Strand said.

"Exactly. I hadn't wanted to talk to you about this so soon, but there are other considerations . . ." He waved vaguely. "I have taken the liberty of talking to the headmaster of a small school in Connecticut about you. Dunberry. It's about two hours from New York, north of New

Haven. My father endowed the school handsomely both during his life and in his will. He had known at college the man who became its headmaster and admired him. The son is the present headmaster and is inclined to think kindly of whatever suggestions I happen to make. It's a small school—just about four hundred boys—and run on old-fashioned lines, which I approve. It might be just the place for your friend Jesus Romero, too. You could keep an eye on him."

"You never forget anything, do you, Russell?" Strand said in honest admiration.

Hazen shrugged the compliment off impatiently. "The classes are small and your work load would be moderate," he said. "About twelve hours a week, at least the first term, the headmaster told me. And a comfortable old apartment comes with the job, which in these days is better than income—considerably better. And when I told the headmaster—Babcock is his name, by the way, an excellent fellow, I'm sure you'll like him—about your wife, he said he has long been wanting to institute a music appreciation course and he was sure she would be most valuable. And the strain of living in a quiet little school town is infinitely less taxing than fighting the battle of New York. Am I tiring you?"

"A little," Strand admitted.

"It's just that there really isn't much time to lose," Hazen said apologetically. "The school session is just two months off and the faculty has to be confirmed. Another thing, Babcock will be visiting friends at Montauk next week and he could drop over and have a talk with you, which would save you a trip to Connecticut."

"It all sounds very promising," Strand said wearily. "Of course, I'd have to discuss it with Leslie first."

"I've already told her about it," Hazen said. "She approves wholeheartedly."

"She hasn't said anything to me about it," Strand said. "Or maybe she did and I don't remember. I don't remember a lot of things these days, you know."

"That'll change," Hazen said confidently. "Anyway, she

wanted me to talk to you about it first. She didn't want to influence you unduly, she said."

Strand nodded. "Ever since I got out of the hospital she's treated me as though I'm made out of old china."

Hazen laughed. "I noticed," he said. "That will change, like everything else, as you grow stronger. Once you're able to get out of bed and can walk around you'll be surprised how different everything will look."

"I don't want any more surprises, thank you," Strand said.

When Hazen left the room he allowed himself the luxury of the sigh that he had suppressed while the man was there. He would have to think about the rest of his life, Hazen had said. Among other things that meant money. Always and persistently—money. He had known that what was happening to him was expensive, but for the first time in more than thirty years he had not asked what anything cost. But soon the bill would be presented and it would have to be paid. He sighed again.

He closed his eyes and dozed. When he awoke he remembered vaguely that Hazen had been in the room and had spoken about a school. But he didn't remember the name of the school or where it was or the name of the man who was coming to interview him or if Hazen had mentioned anything about salary. He lay back and dozed again.

The morning Dr. Caldwell said he could go downstairs he insisted upon dressing, although Leslie tried to convince him it would be easier just to put a robe on over his pajamas. "I will not have Russell Hazen's terrace look like the front porch of an old folks' home," he said. He also shaved himself. It was the first time he had looked at himself in a mirror since the accident, as he described the event to himself. He was pale and very thin and his eyes looked enormous in the gaunt face, like two question marks in dark ink. While he was in bed, Mr. Ketley had shaved him every other day and he had been spared mirrors.

Dressing, he moved slowly and carefully, sensing that

the bones and arteries in the envelope of imperiled flesh
were fragile. But he moved. Leslie clutched his arm as
he went down the staircase, holding on to the banister,
and Mr. Ketley walked backwards before him, as though
afraid that he would suddenly pitch forward and would
need to be caught.

On the terrace in the warm sunlight he lay on the
reclining chair, propped up on cushions, with a blanket
over his knees, grateful for the sunshine and the breeze
off the ocean. Everything looked and felt mint new to
him, the small white clouds in the summer sky, the color
of the sea, the air in his lungs. "You're out of the woods,"
Dr. Caldwell had told him. "If you take care of yourself."
Taking care of himself, Dr. Caldwell had explained, was
not climbing the stairs more than once a day, eating wisely, refraining from alcohol, sex and anxiety, and, most
important of all, not allowing himself to get excited.
Strand had promised to take care of himself. "I will devote
myself to getting a tan," he told Caldwell, "and remaining
unexcited."

Caroline said everybody commented on how brave he
was. He did not ask who everybody was and did not feel
either brave or cowardly.

Lying there, with Leslie sitting beside him, holding
his hand, he suddenly found that he had been interested
only in himself for so many weeks. "Tell me everything," he said to Leslie, "about everybody." It was as
though he had just returned from a long voyage to a place
cut off from all outside communication. The Valley of
the Shadow. Could it be reached by Western Union, satel-
lite, the human voice? "First—you. What are you doing
about your lessons?"

"I'm taking care of them," Leslie said evasively.

"How?"

"I've crammed them into one day a week," she said.
"It's easy in the summer. So many people are out of town."

He nodded. "How's the house?"

"Fine," Leslie said. "Mrs. Curtis dusts three times a
week."

"Caroline?"

Leslie hesitated. "She found out yesterday she's been accepted in Arizona. She won't go, she says, if you say no."

"I won't say no," Strand said.

"She's stopped playing tennis. She gave all her tennis clothes and her racquet to a girl friend."

"Why did she do that?"

"She said she was tired of the game." Leslie's face was grave and she turned away from Strand as she spoke. "What I think is that she's propitiating the gods." Her voice was flat. "Giving up something she loves in exchange for something dearer. . . . Do you want me to go on?"

"No."

They sat in silence for a while, Leslie's hand in his. Each age to its own particular sacrifice, he thought. If he died, would his daughter ask for her pretty white shorts and cotton shirts and racquet back, disillusioned, no gods left? What atavistic piety had led her into this touching and ludicrous teenage denial? "And Jimmy?" he asked. If Jimmy had given up the guitar, how would the gods weigh it against the tennis racquet?

"He's in New York," Leslie said. "He had an appointment to see Herb Solomon. Believe it or not, Jimmy was too shy to call Solomon himself and Russell made the date."

"Maybe we ought to put Russell on a yearly retainer as general manager of the whole family," Strand said. "I wonder how we got along all these years without him."

"I'm glad to see you're getting better," Leslie said. "You're recovering your sense of ingratitude."

"I'm grateful enough," Strand said. He paused. "I suppose. You must thank him in my name for all of us. He cuts me off every time he thinks I'm on the verge of talking about it."

"I know," Leslie said. "He won't let you mention it. I tried once or twice. He was very brusque with me. I don't know whether he was angry or embarrassed."

"Did he tell you he gave Conroy a thousand dollars and Linda Roberts a gold bracelet for pulling me out of the drink?"

"No," Leslie said, "but they did."

"Don't you think it's a curious way of compensating

people who after all risked their lives to save a comparative stranger?"

"A little," Leslie admitted. "It's his way. He's a closed kind of man. He can't *show* emotion, he can only act it. With money, favors . . . symbols."

"Still," Strand said, "it makes me feel peculiar. Like something in an ad from the Lost and Found columns—Misplaced: One middle-aged schoolteacher, somewhere in the Atlantic. Reward offered if returned in passable condition."

"Don't ever let him know that's the way you feel about it. Generosity is his hobby, it helps offset what he feels about his work. We were talking about it the other night and he told me in a lawyer generosity is considered a weakness. It's easy to see he couldn't stand anybody's thinking he was a weak man."

"He told me he'd spoken to you about that school thing," Strand said, pleased that his memory was coming back. "He said you approved."

"More than that. I kissed him for it."

"There's no need to go to extremes," Strand said dryly.

"It's the perfect solution," Leslie said. "For all of us."

"You love living in New York," he said. "How do you think you'll feel stuck in a small, sleepy town surrounded by four hundred or so adolescent boys?"

"I'll survive," Leslie said. "Anyway, it's not important. What's important is keeping you alive and well. And New York is only a couple of hours away. I'll manage."

"Maybe when that man comes to look me over . . ."

"Mr. Babcock."

"Mr. Babcock. Maybe he'll decide I'm not the right man for him."

"Don't worry about that," she said. "I spoke to him on the phone and he's overjoyed at the prospect of having you."

"Overjoyed," Strand said. "There's a word."

He sighed, looked around at the blue water of the pool, the immaculate bathing mats, the white dunes, the shining ocean. "We can't stay here until school opens you know.

It's one thing to come here for a weekend and then for an emergency, but . . ."

"He won't let you mention that, either. I've talked to him about it, at least I've *tried* to talk to him . . ."

"Well?"

"I told him I'd take you back to the city as soon as you could be moved."

"Well?"

"He asked me if I was trying to kill you," Leslie said.

"What a nuisance I've become."

"Hush," Leslie said. "Of course, he was being melodramatic, but there's no doubt it's worlds better for you here. The Ketleys, the sea air. We don't have any air conditioning at home and it's sweltering in town. Russell says keeping you here is the least he could do for a man he nearly let drown practically in front of his eyes."

"He has a curious system of values," Strand said.

"Would that there were more like him," Leslie said. "By the way, I'm almost sure it isn't Linda Roberts."

"Linda Roberts what?"

"The reputed mistress."

"Oh, that." Another world. Other bodies. "Why not?"

"He just takes care of her," Leslie said. "And her money. He's the executor of her husband's will. Her husband left her a fortune, but Russell says that if she'd been abandoned to her own devices she wouldn't have a penny left. She's a soft touch for anyone with a hard luck story. He says she's afflicted by leeches. He's kept her from getting married twice to men who were after her money. He takes care of her because she has a good heart and because her husband was a close friend of Russell's and she's lonely. That's why she talks so incessantly when she gets a chance, he says. More generosity. In his own style. With his time, his affection, everything."

"He is that," Strand said. "But why would that prevent . . . ?"

"I saw him walking along the beach with Nellie Solomon."

"So?"

"There's a certain way a man and a woman can walk together when they think nobody is watching."

"Oh, come now, Leslie."

"He's walked along the beach with me," Leslie said, "and I've seen him walking along the beach with Linda Roberts and with Eleanor. I assure you there's a difference. A great difference."

"You're not gossiping, are you?" Strand asked, although he knew Leslie never gossiped.

"It's just an intuition," Leslie said. "Don't take it for divine revelation."

But he was sure she was right. He felt a twinge of envy for Russell Hazen and was disappointed in Nellie Solomon. The crosscurrents around a dinner table. He remembered Mrs. Solomon's light pinch on his leg when Mrs. Roberts had made the remark about France.

"Good for him," Strand said. He wondered if Herbert Solomon was a complaisant man. He did not look the type. Strand wished everybody well. He remembered Judith Quinlan's unopened letter and knew he, too, was guilty. The sexual revolution, with its lighthearted couplings, was for the young. He was involved in a sterner doctrine. He closed his eyes, feeling the heat of the sun on his lids, and they were quiet for a while.

Another subject. "I'm sorry," he said, "that I spoiled Eleanor's vacation."

"Greece'll still be there next year," Leslie said.

"Did she think I was going to die?" He spoke with his eyes still closed. "Is that why she stayed?"

"I don't know what she thought," Leslie said. "She just wanted to stay. She's back at work now. She didn't take the extra week off. I think we're going to have some important news from her soon."

"Like what?"

"Like her telling us that she's going to get married."

"How do you feel about it?"

"The usual. Sad and glad. They're a beautiful couple."

"Is that enough?"

Leslie sighed. "We won't know for perhaps twenty years."

"We were half a beautiful couple," Strand said.

Leslie laughed. "I called my parents to tell them about you and they sent their best wishes. My father said he thought you didn't look like a healthy man even the first time he clapped eyes on you."

Strand chuckled weakly. "Palm Springs hasn't changed him."

"He said it's a wonder *everybody* in New York doesn't have a heart attack. He says we ought to move to Palm Springs, it does miracles for hearts."

"Tell him I'll move to Palm Springs the day he moves out."

"I see you're getting better," Leslie said lightly.

"Anyway, I wasn't in New York when it happened," Strand said. "I was halfway to Portugal."

They were quiet again for a while, Strand still with his eyes closed. "Did *you* think I was going to die?"

"Never."

"Why not?"

"Because," said Leslie, "I couldn't have borne it."

Herb Solomon came out onto the terrace, where Strand was lying. Strand was alone. Leslie was down the beach somewhere with Linda Roberts. Leslie was painting and Linda, he supposed, was talking. Leslie had had a birthday the week before and Hazen had surprised her with a gift of a portable, collapsible easel and an extravagant set of oil paints and brushes. Caroline was working at a veterinarian's clinic in town, and Jimmy was staying in the city for a few days. Hazen was in New York, too. Solomon still looked like George Washington, even in cotton slacks and a polo shirt. He was carrying a big wooden board with something on it wrapped in tinfoil. "Good morning," he said. "I heard you now welcome visitors."

"The more the merrier," Strand said. "Please sit down."

Solomon put the board on a table. "Nellie baked a loaf of bread for you," he said, unwrapping the tinfoil. The loaf was huge and the crust was brown and it smelled delicious. "It's still warm," Solomon said. "She's a great believer in home-baked bread. Unbleached flour, stone

ground, that sort of thing. She says bread should be baked
with love. She thought it might tempt your appetite."

"It does indeed," Strand said, uncertain of what the
protocol should be about accepting a loaf of bread from
the husband of the woman who was reputed to be the
mistress of one's host. Busy hands, in the kitchen and elsewhere. "Thank your wife for me." He reached over and
broke off an end of the loaf and tasted it. It was as delicious as it looked and smelled. "Ummn," he said. "Don't
you want some?" Bread and salt and complicity. The
bonds of friendship.

"I have to watch my weight," Solomon said, seating
himself. Other things, too, Strand thought, are to be
watched. Solomon looked around him with approval.
"You're a lucky man, Allen," he said.

"You can say that again."

"I don't mean being snatched from the briny. I mean
being in a place like this to get over . . . Well, you know
what I mean."

"I do."

"There's nothing Russell Hazen wouldn't do for a friend,"
Solomon said. "The blood out of his veins. And I know.
He's been my lawyer for fifteen years. In the music business I'm something of a giant—but in *real* business, the
sort Russell's firm handles, I'm a pygmy. But he worries
about me as though I'm A.T. and T. There've been a
couple of times I'd have sunk with all hands on board if
it hadn't been for his advice. He's not a happy man"—
Solomon looked around him cautiously—"I suppose you've
heard some of the stories?"

"Some," Strand said, not in the mood for stories.

"He's not a happy man, but he's something rarer—he's
a good man. Good, but unlucky. Amazing, how often those
things go together. I try to keep a sensible balance." Solomon laughed, a deep, rumbling basso. "Russell's afraid
you're not going to take care of yourself." Suddenly,
Solomon's voice was serious. "He's become very attached
to you. Your whole family. With reason, I would say."

"As you said, he's a lonely man."

Solomon nodded somberly. "One night, when he had a

little too much to drink, he told me he knew the moment he'd made the one great wrong turn of his life—when he said, for the first time, 'Yes, Father.'" Solomon made a small grimace. "Old American families. Fortunately, I came from a new American family. Nellie says she thought you were Jewish." Solomon chuckled. "By now she thinks practically *everybody* is Jewish. Have you been married before?"

"No."

"It shows," Solomon said. "Nellie's my second—and last. I have two awful kids. Not by her," he added hastily. "There's a subject—children. To weep vinegar." His face grew dark as he said it. "Talk to Russell sometime. You ought to write a manual, with *your* litter. 'How to Bring Up Human Beings in the Twentieth Century.' It would outsell the Bible. Hang in there, pal. You have a lot to be thankful for."

"I know," Strand said, although he wasn't sure that the reasons he had to be thankful were those that Solomon was thinking of.

Solomon squinted thoughtfully at him, Washington reviewing his troops. Was it at Valley Forge or Yorktown?

"You don't look so bad, considering," Solomon said. "A little thin, maybe. And you're getting a nice tan."

"The doctors say I can live to be a hundred."

"Who wants to live to be a hundred?" Solomon said. "What a drag."

"Exactly my sentiments." Both men laughed.

"I had an interesting talk with your son," Solomon said. "There's a bright boy. Did he tell you he's starting work for me on Monday?"

"No."

"Oh?" Solomon sounded surprised.

"I think he believes I disapprove of his getting mixed up in the music business," Strand said.

"Do you?"

"I don't want him to be disappointed. And it's so chancy. And I haven't the faintest idea of how good he is."

Solomon nodded soberly. "I explained all that to him. I

listened to him again and had some of my people in to listen, too. I put it on the line for him. It isn't Tin Pan Alley, it's Heartache Alley, I told him. Old Chinese joke. For everyone who makes it there're ten thousand who don't. It's a grim life, waiting around maybe years for your chance, and maybe the worst thing is to get your chance and then flop. I put it to him squarely. I told him he had a nice touch and a passable voice, but there was nothing original in the way he played and sang and that his own songs—the ones he wrote himself—were all derivative. I told him that I didn't think he had that something special, that electricity, that makes a performer popular."

"How did he take that?"

"Like a soldier," Solomon said.

"But you said he was going to work for you . . ."

"In the office," Solomon said. "Not as a performer. Oh, maybe in a couple of years, as he matures, he may find a style. A sound, as he says himself. And then, of course, I might be wrong. I've been wrong before." He smiled sourly, remembering mistakes, opportunities missed. "But as I said, he's got a true ear, and he knows just about everything about the current crop of artists, what they're good at, where they fake, what they've done. He'll be very useful, I think, to weed out the hopeless ones who flood into my office and latch on to just the one or two who might go all the way. It's not creative in the way he wants, but it's creative just the same. You understand what I'm talking about?"

"I believe so. And he said he'd do it?"

"Yes."

"It's very kind of you to give him the chance."

"Not kindness. Business. I feel I can trust his judgment. That doesn't happen to me too often with people."

As Solomon spoke, Strand began to develop a new picture of the man. Not the jovial teller of jokes at dinner parties, with the sound of New York in his voice, not the pleasant neighbor delivering a gift of a loaf of bread, but a shrewd, hard-grained man, honest and implacable in his estimates of possibilities, characters, virtues and faults. "Jimmy will be lucky," Strand said, "to have you as his boss."

"I hope he'll think so. And I hope it'll be true. There're a million traps." Solomon stood up. "I don't want to tire you. I'll be moseying along."

"You're not tiring me at all. The doctor tells me I'm to get up tomorrow and start taking walks. A mile a day."

"The fact is," Solomon said, "I have to drive into town. I have to be in the office by two o'clock. There's a singer who just made a recording for us that she's decided she doesn't like or her fag of a husband tells her she doesn't like and she wants to do the whole thing all over again. There will be tears." He grinned, relishing the scene in his office that afternoon in advance. "There will be ultimatums. I will save some fifty thousand dollars. Nellie's staying down here. She'd love to come over and say hello to you."

"By all means."

"I'll tell her. Keep well, Allen. They didn't fish you out of the waves to have you fade on us." He started to leave.

"Oh," Strand said, "I'm afraid I've never thanked you for the recorder and the cassettes."

Solomon shrugged. "Nothing," he said. "I dispense music the way the men with the baskets on Fifth Avenue dispense pretzels. When you're up and around you must come over and have dinner with Nellie and me. She says she grew fond of you in one evening."

"We shared secrets together," Strand said and waved good-bye as Solomon left.

Strand stared out to sea for a long moment, then absently reached over and broke off another piece of bread.

"I haven't noticed any pogroms yet," Nellie Solomon had said at dinner. Jews, murdered and surviving, invited to everything.

Strand took a bite of the bread, tasting the earthy stone-ground wheat.

Baked with love.

He dozed. Dozing, he thought, as the sound of the surf

ebbed from his consciousness, dozing can become a full-
time career

He was awakened by the sound of voices. Leslie and
Linda Roberts were coming up the steps to the terrace
from the beach. Leslie was carrying the easel and the
canvas she had been working on and Linda Roberts was
carrying the big box with the paints and brushes in it and
Leslie's palette. Both women were barefooted, Linda in a
flouncy pink bathing suit, which revealed that she had a
good figure, long-limbed and narrow-waisted. The bony
shoulders and insignificant breasts were fashionable, the
feminine superstructure in vogue in the magazines in
which tall, starved girls posed in the latest gowns. Once
more Strand had doubts about Hazen and Linda Roberts.
Men went in for that sort of thing these days. Maybe both
of them—Mrs. Solomon and Mrs. Roberts. Perhaps Hazen
wasn't as lonely as Solomon had said. Not by half. He
remembered Linda Roberts through the haze of foam,
staggering as the waves buffeted her, her arm raised, the
loop of rescuing rope ready to be thrown—then, as he
dazedly came to, lying on the wet sand, the feel of her
lips on his, breathing life back into his lungs. Yes, she was
much better than fashionable. People were not to be judged
by their talk at dinner tables. One day he would tell her
all this. But they would have to be alone.

Leslie had on a short cotton skirt and a loose, woven
blouse that left her arms bare. She was getting tan, too,
and it became her.

"How did the morning go?" Leslie asked as she reached
the terrace.

"Fine," Strand said. "How about yours?"

"Happily smudging away," Leslie said, putting the easel
down and leaning the canvas against a chair. Strand saw
that she had just blocked in the outlines of a scene of
dunes, with a gray house in the distance, and put in
splotches of different colors here and there as an indication
of what she was going to fill in later.

"I wouldn't call it smudging," Linda Roberts said. "I

just marvel about how sure she is about what she's doing. Even with me gabbing away in her ear all the morning."

"It isn't gabbing," Leslie said to her husband. "She's been to all those museums in Europe that I've never seen and I'm beginning to get an idea of what I'm missing. Linda, don't be modest, you know a great deal about painting."

"Russell keeps after me," Mrs. Roberts said. "He makes me buy pictures. Some of them very curious, indeed. He's the one who made me buy into the galleries here and in Paris. He says I must become a patron of the arts. Patroness? Nobody knows about words like that anymore. Chairman, Madam Chairman, Chairperson, Chairlady. The world is getting just too complicated. Women in the Naval Academy. You'd be surprised how many letters I get from women's organizations asking me to support abortion and God knows what all. Anyway, it's a wonderful way to spend the morning, watching a pretty woman doing something and *knowing* what she's doing."

"I put on a good act," Leslie said.

"And the piano besides," Mrs. Roberts said. "It makes me feel absolutely *stunted*. Now I must go into the village and have my hair done. The beach and the sun and the sea are marvelous and I'm grateful Russell gives me the freedom of the house, but it's sinful what it does to the hair. Leslie, I hope I didn't disturb you about—well, what we talked about."

"No, not at all," Leslie said shortly.

"Well, see everybody at lunch," Mrs. Roberts said, and went into the house.

"What was that about?" Strand asked. "What did you talk about?"

"Nothing."

"Come on, Leslie," Strand said. He could see that she *was* disturbed.

"Nonsense," Leslie said. "She just chatters. Off the top of her head." She sighed. "It was about Caroline's nose."

"Poor Caroline," Strand said. "I have a lot to answer for. Has Linda been talking to Eleanor?"

"No. She thought it up all by herself."

"Well, what in the world can anybody do about it?"

"She thinks Caroline ought to have an operation. Now.
Before she goes away to college. She'd be absolutely beautiful, Linda says, the boys'd fall over themselves chasing
her . . ."

"What's so good about that?"

Leslie shrugged. "It would change her whole way of
looking at life, according to Linda. She quoted chapter
and verse. Nieces of hers, classmates in school, timid little
creatures now living like duchesses."

"Caroline seems to be doing all right down here, nose
or no nose," Strand said defensively. "There's that boy,
that sophomore from Wesleyan, George Anderson, who
comes and picks her up almost every night."

"I don't like him," Leslie said.

"That's beside the point. It's the first time a boy, any
boy, has shown an interest in her."

"He's a spoiled young man," Leslie said, disregarding
what Strand had said. "A boy that age with a fancy car
like that." The boy drove a Corvette. "And the way he
rushes up the driveway and sweeps to a stop, as though
he's a movie star. I don't like him at all. He's barely civil
to any of us and he snarls at Caroline if she's a minute
late and his lordship has to wait. I tell you, I sit up every
night until she comes home and I never did that with
Eleanor and any of her beaux."

"Eleanor was different. Noses had nothing to do with it."

"Who can tell?"

"Anyway," Strand said, "she comes home early and in
one piece, doesn't she?"

"So far," Leslie said gloomily.

"I'd be grateful to Linda Roberts if she kept her opinions to herself."

"You've got the wrong lady for that," Leslie said, laughing. "Now, let's not talk about it anymore. A man who's
just recovering from a heart attack has more important
things to worry about. Eleanor's coming down for the
weekend and I'll have a chat with her."

"You mean you're actually taking this seriously?" Strand
asked incredulously.

"Half," Leslie said. "Oh, Jimmy called this morning. You were sleeping so I didn't wake you. He's got a job."

"I know," Strand said. "Herb Solomon was here and he told me about it. He brought a loaf of bread his wife baked. We're having it for lunch. Mr. Ketley took it into the kitchen."

"That was nice of the Solomons. What do you think about the job?"

"It won't kill him."

"He's awfully young for that sort of work."

"He'll age quickly in that business," Strand said.

Leslie sighed. "I think I'll go to a fortune teller and find out what's going to happen to us in the next five years. Linda has a gypsy in Greenwich Village she says is absolutely fantastic. Horoscopes. She predicted Mr. Roberts's death."

"That's just the sort of thing we need just now," Strand said ironically. "Tell Linda Roberts to stick to being a patron or patroness or whatever of the arts."

"She means well. She's not as foolish as she seems."

"Not by a long shot," Strand said.

"She's unsure of herself and scared about the rest of her life and she still hasn't gotten over the death of her husband and she's uncomfortable with the image of the rich widow and she hides it all by pretending to be frivolous. She'd rather have people laugh at her than be sorry for her. Everybody to his own disguise."

"What's yours?" Strand asked.

"I pretend to be a big grown-up serious woman," Leslie said, "when I really know that I'm only an eighteen-year-old girl who isn't sure if the boys like me or not." She laughed, stood and leaned over and kissed the top of his head. "The sun isn't doing awful things to *your* hair," she said. "I'm going in and getting ready for lunch."

But when she went into the house, he heard her playing the piano, something sad and complicated that he couldn't recognize.

Once, when he had come into their living room while she was playing Bach he had asked what she thought as she sat at the piano. "I hope," she had said, "I am addressing God."

Now, sitting in the seaside sun, tanned to a simulacrum of health, frail and escaped from the tubes, machines and flickering dials of the hospital, he listened to the shadowed and unfamiliar music of his wife, who had been counseled to consult downtown gypsies who had warned Linda Roberts of her husband's end. The stars in their courses, fate in the whirl of planets, death in the corridors . . .

Christ, he thought, fragile in his comfortable, blanketed chair, what is going to happen to me, what is going to happen to us all?

PART TWO

1

He stood at the window of the Hotel Crillon and looked out at the obelisk, the rearing stone horses set in the noble expanse of the Place de la Concorde. In the milky sunlight with the Seine and the Chamber of Deputies in the distance it was almost empty, because, as Hazen had explained when they arrived, everybody left Paris in August. His being there seemed almost miraculous to Strand. When Hazen had told them that he had pressing business in Europe and that a company for which he worked was lending him their corporate Lear jet to cross the ocean and had proposed that since there was room and he detested traveling alone the Strands and Linda Roberts accompanying him, he had immediately said, "Impossible." He had suggested to Leslie that she make the trip on her own, but Leslie had said she wouldn't go without him. He had tried to plead illness, but he had been walking a mile a day on the beach and the truth was that he was fit as a man his age who had been at death's door only six weeks before had a right to feel and Dr. Caldwell had said the trip would do him good. The munificence of Hazen's offer had embarrassed him but Leslie was so painfully anxious to go that he had felt that it would be cruel to deprive her of the experience. Eleanor, too, had said that it was sinful to reject the gifts that a benevolent fate, in the form of Russell Hazen, was offering him. Women, he had thought, accept favors more naturally than men. He had said yes reluctantly, but now, after a week in Paris, strolling slowly along the streets whose names he had known from his reading since he was a young man and sitting in the sidewalk cafés and making his way slowly through

Figaro and *Le Monde,* pleased that he still half-remembered his college French, he was grateful that Leslie had insisted.

Actually, there had been no urgent reason to keep him in America for the moment. Mr. Babcock had visited him and, as Hazen had promised, had been a likable, diffident, rather dusty small man. The interview had been tactfully brief, and after he had outlined the nature of Strand's duties Strand was relieved to see that after all his years of teaching history there was no need to prepare his courses. Leslie had gone to Dunberry to inspect the house they were to live in and pronounced it livable. They needed a car to get to town but Hazen had volunteered the old station wagon and Mr. Ketley had given her lessons in driving it. She was a nervous driver, but she had passed the test at the first attempt and now had her license.

Although from her gallery and her social life Linda knew, as she said, shoals of French, she had advised them that for their first short visit they'd have a better time just seeing what the French had produced and collected during the centuries rather than grappling with the race itself. Taking her advice as wise counsel, they had kept to themselves and escaped the rigors of not quite bilingual socializing. As Linda said, they had been spared the disappointment of comparing what the French had accomplished with what the French had become.

His own sightseeing was limited, as Dr. Caldwell had warned him not to overdo things. His trying to keep up with Leslie and Linda Roberts in their tireless raids on museums, galleries and churches certainly wouldn't have met with Dr. Caldwell's approval. He had quickly fallen into a happy and comfortable routine, spending most of the days by himself. He slept late, waking in the beautifully appointed large room to breakfast with Leslie. When she went out to meet Linda Roberts he would go back to bed and sleep for an hour or so. Then, shaved and bathed, he would walk idly, looking at the windows on the Rue du Faubourg St.-Honoré or the Rue de la Paix, admiring the lush displays of the shops, but with no itch of acquisition. He would meet with the ladies for lunch at a bistro, listening with amused detachment to their descriptions of the treasures they had viewed that morning, then go back to the hotel for a siesta, unhurried, content to let Paris bustle on without him for a while, before going out again to sit on an open *terrasse* with the newspapers, lulled by the sound of a language he could not quite understand, half-reading, half-watching, with a small smile on his lips, the lively show of pedestrians, approving, without lust, of the pretty, well-turned-out women and girls who passed by, and intrigued by the Japanese tourists who like himself were in Paris for the moment.

Hazen himself appeared only at odd times. He flew to a different city almost every day, Vienna, Madrid, Zurich, Munich, Brussels, trying to disentangle, as he put it, multinational chaos. "You won't miss me," he had said to Strand. "Linda knows Paris better than most Frenchmen and you couldn't have a better guide."

Among the things that Linda Roberts knew about Paris was where to find the best restaurants that were open in August, and for the first time since his twentieth birthday Strand found himself gaining weight and going to bed nightly a little drunk on French wine.

Hazen had invited Caroline to accompany them, but Caroline with an unexpected newfound seriousness had said she couldn't interrupt her track training. When she wasn't at the small animal clinic, she worked out for hours every day with the track coach of the East Hampton high school and had already improved her time in the hundred and was working on the two twenty. "I don't dare go," she had said when she was told she was included in Hazen's invitation. "I have the rest of my life to see Europe, but this is the summer I have to get down to at least ten-five. I couldn't stand the thought of showing up in Arizona and being an absolute flop and knowing everybody was asking, 'What is that fat horse doing in the race?' " Hazen had agreed with her and assured Strand that the Ketleys would take perfect care of her. Mr. Ketley had become interested in her new career and had found a book on diet for athletes from which his wife prepared special meals for her.

So it was a man at peace with himself, soberly tasting foreign joys at age fifty, who stood in the late afternoon sunlight at the window of the large room gazing out at the heart of a country he had loved from afar and never hoped to visit.

Hazen arrived that evening from Madrid in time to take them all to dinner at an elegant small restaurant that offered a Burgundian cuisine and the accompanying wines. He was in a holiday mood and joked with the maître d'hôtel about how the prices of La Tache had gone up since he had been there last. Strand didn't see the wine list but from the figures on the *carte* he could guess that the meal for the four of them would cost well over two hundred dollars. When he had been installed in the grandiose room in the hotel overlooking the Place de la Concorde, he had protested mildly to Hazen about his extravagance. "Nonsense, man," Hazen had said. "A taste of luxury is part of the education of any intelligent human being. It teaches him how unnecessary it is."

Easy enough to say, Strand had thought, for a man who has inherited a house with sixteen bedrooms.

Linda Roberts, who had overheard the exchange, said to him later, "Don't thwart his Santa Claus complex. He gets very cross when he thinks people are trying to keep him from distributing largesse to us peasants."

The "us" was diplomatically inclusive, Strand thought, and was typical of Linda's sweetness of nature. His gratitude toward her grew daily as he saw how she devoted all her time to making Leslie's visit as rewarding as possible and how Leslie's face glowed when they returned from an afternoon at the galleries or a visit to the studio of a young painter who, according to Linda, was sure to make a name for himself in the future. "If a person couldn't paint here," she said, her enthusiasm for the city overcoming her usually well-developed critical sense, "he couldn't paint anywhere."

During the meal of *jambon persillé* and *entrecôte marchand de vin* and a hot pear tart, Linda had said, "I've crossed the ocean forty-five times and this is the best time of all." She raised her glass. "I think we should drink a toast to the group that has made it possible."

So they all drank happily to themselves.

Hazen had drunk copiously and by the time they were at their coffee was expansive and jovial. "I have an idea," he said. "I've got three days before I have to fly to Saudi Arabia and I propose we make the most of it. Leslie, have you ever been to the Loire valley?"

"I've barely been to New Haven," Leslie said, flushed with the wine. She had bought a new dress because Linda had said that a girl couldn't just *pass* through Paris but had to have something to show for it, and it was very becoming, deep plum-colored and close-fitting and cut daringly low in front, displaying her Hampton honey-colored skin and the fetching outline of her bosom. "My slinky outfit," she had described it to Strand as she dressed. "I hope you're not shocked."

"I am ravished," Strand had said loyally, not exaggerating by much.

"Why don't we hire a car tomorrow morning and go take a look at the châteaus and drink some Vouvray?" Hazen said. "And if they're still putting on the *Son et Lumière* shows, good old Allen can brush up on his French history."

"At Chenonceaux," Strand said, showing off a little, "Catherine de Medici used to have her prisoners tortured in the courtyard for the delectation of the ladies and gentlemen who happened to be her guests."

"The bloody French," Hazen said.

"From what I've read," said Strand, "they've stopped the practice. At least as a public amusement."

"Now they do it for profit. To Americans. In business and politics. But give them a century or two," Hazen said, "and they'll probably get around to prisoners again. Anyway, they won't be doing it in the next three days, unless the government happens to change or the Communists take over Orléans. What do you say, can we all be ready by ten o'clock in the morning?"

"Russell," Linda said, "you've been gadding around so much, I think you could stand a day or two of just sitting in one place. Why don't we all fly down to Nice and go to my place in Mougins? I hear the weather is divine just now and the garden is at its best."

Hazen scowled. "Linda," he said, with surprising harshness, "Leslie and Allen haven't flown three thousand miles just to sit in a damned garden. They can sit in my garden all they want when they get back. Anyway, I told the pilots they could have three days off. They need the rest."

"We could always fly down to Nice on Air France," Linda said, "like the rest of the human race. And the Loire valley will be jammed with tourists. We'll be lucky to find hotel rooms."

"Let me worry about that," Hazen said, his voice rising.

"It'd be a shame if Leslie and Allen went back home without seeing my little place in Mougins," Linda persisted. "They must be getting tired of hotels by now. I know I am. There's more to France than hotels."

"It's a shame that they have to go back to America without seeing Verdun and Mont-St.-Michel and the cathedral in Rouen and the Lascaux cave and a million other things," Hazen said loudly. "But they only have two weeks. Christ, you're a stubborn woman, Linda."

"Leslie, Allen." Linda turned toward them. "What do you want to do?"

Leslie glanced quickly at Strand, looking for a signal. Strand would have been happier just to remain in Paris doing exactly what he had done since he had arrived there. But the exasperation in Hazen's voice was not to be ignored. "I'm sure," he said tactfully, "that Leslie would love to see your house, Linda. But I know she'd regret missing the chance to see the châteaus."

Leslie gave him a quick, grateful smile.

"There," Hazen said with satisfaction, "it's settled. And no more insane arguing, Linda. If there's one thing I hate it's arguing when you're on a holiday. I get enough arguments at the office."

"Do you ever lose, Russell?" Linda asked gently.

"No." Hazen laughed, his good spirits restored.

"I'm glad I don't work for you," Linda said.

"So am I." He reached for her hand and kissed it

graciously. "So—ten o'clock tomorrow morning. Country clothes."

"Leslie," Linda said, "you know what we can do when we get rid of this brute—we can let him fly his toy plane back to America and we can stay on and go down to Mougins on our own and fly back home in our own good time."

"That would be wonderful," Leslie said. "But I have to go home and start getting ready to move. We have to be at Dunberry by September tenth. Maybe next year. That would be something to look forward to, wouldn't it, Allen?"

"I'm looking forward to it already," Strand said. If there will be a next year, he thought, as he said it.

He lay in his bed watching Leslie, in her nightgown, brushing her hair in front of the dressing table mirror. "It was a nice evening," he said, "wasn't it?"

"Better than nice," she said. "Like all the evenings. Except for that little clash of wills between Russell and Linda."

He lay in silence for a moment. "Tell me," he said, "was I right in saying that you'd prefer going down to the Loire instead of to Linda's place?"

"You were right in saying it," she said, her arm rising and falling in smooth even strokes, "but it wasn't the truth. I'm gorged for the moment with sightseeing. A few days in a garden in the south would have made a perfect ending to our trip."

"Then why didn't you say so?"

Leslie laughed softly. "Darling," she said, "it's his holiday."

"I guess we really didn't have any choice."

"Not for a minute." She stopped brushing her hair and stared at herself in the mirror. "Do you think I look younger than I did two weeks ago?"

"Years," he said.

"I think so, too." She resumed brushing her hair. "Still," she said, "I would like to look at least once at the Mediterranean."

"Next time we come to Europe," he said, "we pay our own way."

"Next time," she said softly. "Who knows if there'll be a next time?"

He was disturbed by the echo of his own thought. Vaguely, he felt that somehow tonight they both needed comforting and he almost asked her to come into his bed so that he could sleep with his arms around her. But he didn't speak. He didn't know whether he should be proud of his prudence or despise himself for his cowardice. He closed his eyes and went to sleep to the silken sound of his wife brushing her hair in the shadowy room.

There was a surprise for Strand and Leslie and Linda Roberts when they came down from their adjoining rooms to the lobby the next morning at ten o'clock. Hazen was waiting for them with a striking-looking blonde, who was holding a smart black attaché case. She was dressed severely in a simple tweed suit and low-heeled shoes. "This is Madame Harcourt." He said the name in the French manner, leaving off the final *t*. "She's from our office here and she's driving us down. She's going to Saudi Arabia with me and we have some business to work out before we leave. Don't worry, you don't have to talk French to her. Her mother's English." He spoke hurriedly, as though a little embarrassed by Mrs. Harcourt's unannounced appearance.

"Mr. Hazen always says that right off, whenever he introduces me to Americans," the woman said, smiling. The businesslike severity of her face disappeared, and her voice was low, pleasant, easy, and her accent was clipped but not obnoxiously British. "It's as though he doesn't want to be accused, even for an instant, of favoring the French."

"She's a lawyer," Hazen said. "I deal with French lawyers only out of dire necessity. Well, the luggage is in the car. Shall we take off?" He started out of the lobby with Mrs. Harcourt and the others following.

"Quite an improvement on good old Conroy, wouldn't you say?" Strand whispered.

"Cosmetically, anyway," Leslie said.

A big black Cadillac was waiting for them at the door and Mrs. Harcourt got in on the driver's side, with Hazen beside her. "Mrs. Harcourt will drive," Hazen said. "I hate to drive and I'd have to jump out of the car before we reached the Pont St.-Cloud if I let Linda behind the wheel and I know Allen hasn't a license and Leslie's too new at the sport for French roads. You all comfortable back there?" Although he had said country clothes, he was dressed in a dark suit and a white shirt, tight around the collar, and a sober tie, making Strand wonder what Hazen would wear to a funeral. Even with the weight he had put on in Paris, his own collar, Strand felt uncomfortably, left an unfashionable gap at his Adam's apple.

"We're fine," Strand said. "Couldn't be better."

Mrs. Harcourt turned on the ignition and the car started off. She drove deftly and confidently through the light traffic.

It was a beautiful morning, sunny but not too warm, and Strand leaned back contentedly, enjoying looking at the buildings of Paris and then at the green rolling country they were in when they passed through the tunnel under the Seine and sped south.

They stopped in Chartres and went into the cathedral. Strand would have liked years of slow study to absorb it, but Hazen was visibly annoyed at a loud group of German tourists who were being addressed, in their own language, at a decibel count suitable for a political meeting, by their guide.

"Let's get out of here," Hazen growled, after they had been there for only ten minutes. "I'm hungry." He refused to have lunch in Chartres, though. "I recommend the cathedral, but not the food." He said there was a wonderful place just off the highway about a half hour away.

They had a fine lunch out in the open air at a table set in a garden and Hazen was jovial again and ordered two bottles of Montrachet to go with the trout, while making a good-humored point of not allowing Mrs. Harcourt to drink any of it because she was doing the driving and the cargo of the Cadillac was precious. She listened politely but hardly spoke while the others talked. She sat quietly, erectly, almost stiffly, as though the holiday atmosphere did not include her and she remained conscious that she was an employee and her employer was present. She locked the car carefully because she had left the attaché case on the front seat.

But as Strand and Leslie were walking back to the car after the others, Leslie said, "It's a fake."

"What's a fake?" Strand asked, puzzled.

"The junior employee and the big boss act," Leslie said. "For our benefit."

"Oh, Leslie."

"You don't have to be a detective to guess what business they have to work out in the Loire valley before they take off for Saudi Arabia."

"I don't believe you," Strand said, slightly shocked by the hostility he sensed in his wife's voice. "And even if you're right, it's no business of ours."

"I just don't like people to think they can pull the wool over my eyes, that's all," Leslie said, her lips tight. "Madame Harcourt! They're a cool pair, those two."

Strand was glad when they reached the car. It was a conversation he had no wish to continue.

They all had rooms on the same floor in the hotel in Tours and Strand noticed the malicious gleam in Leslie's eyes when she saw that their room and Linda's were at one end of the corridor and Hazen's and that of Mrs. Harcourt, again carrying the attaché case, at the other.

"What do you think she's got in that case she lugs around everywhere?" Leslie asked.

"Industrial secrets," Strand said. "Russell told me he's negotiating for a company that's putting in a bid to construct an atomic plant in Saudi Arabia."

"My guess is that it's a douche bag," Leslie said.

"Good Lord, Leslie!"

Leslie merely giggled as she went through the doorway of their room.

Leslie continued to be reserved and cool toward the woman the next day when they visited Chambord and Chenonceaux, but if either Hazen or Mrs. Harcourt noticed it, they didn't show it. But Leslie made no secret of her delight in the glorious piles of masonry and told Hazen, as they stood in the formal garden looking at the gallery of Chenonceaux built on stone columns over the Cher River, "This moment alone is worth the trip." Then she kissed his cheek.

Hazen smiled happily. "I told you this would beat sitting and sweating in a garden while being eaten up by mosquitoes." He glared at Linda. "Next time I hope you'll go where I tell you to without my having to get out a subpoena for you."

"The mosquitoes only come out after it rains," Linda said with dignity, "and it hasn't rained all summer."

"There it starts again. You know you're lying." Hazen appealed to the others. "Will you listen to that? Only after it rains!"

"Please," Leslie said, "please. Let peace and harmony reign. Stop teasing the poor man, Linda."

"He has such a low boiling point," Linda said, smiling, "sometimes I can't resist, just to see how fast the steam starts to spout."

"Low boiling point! Mrs. Harcourt, you've known me for many years and you've seen me tried in important matters, sorely tried in important matters, sorely tried, by low dealing and gross incompetence, and outright chicanery. Have you ever seen me blow up?" By now Hazen, too, was amused.

"You have always been a model of decorum, Mr. Hazen," Mrs. Harcourt said demurely, "in my presence."

"Now you're doing it, too," Hazen said and then joined in the general laughter.

But back in the room in the hotel, getting ready for dinner, Leslie had forgotten the comradely laughter of the afternoon. "I heard something about that Madame Harcourt this afternoon," she said.

"What?" Strand sighed inwardly. He had grown to like the woman. She seemed modest and intelligent and cheerful and her presence seemed to lighten Hazen's moods and make him a more agreeable companion.

"There is no Monsieur Harcourt," Leslie said. "She's divorced."

"How did you find out?"

"Linda told me. The last time she and Russell were in Paris together the junior attorney was there all the time, too. Divorced."

"Divorce isn't a crime. Most of the people anyone knows are divorced."

"I just thought you'd be interested, that's all. You seem so interested in the lady I thought you might be interested in her marital status, too."

"Oh, come on, now, Leslie," Strand said, annoyed, "I'm just decently polite."

"Everybody is so decently polite." Leslie's voice had a dangerous edge to it. " 'You have always been a model of decorum, Mr. Hazen' "—she mimicked Mrs. Harcourt's English accent—" 'in my presence.' *Mr.* Hazen! Do you think she calls him Mr. Hazen in bed, too?"

"Oh, cut it out, Leslie," Strand said sharply. "You're being absurd."

"Don't you snap at me!" she shouted. Then she bent over in her chair, raised her hands to cover her face and sobbed.

Strand was too astonished to do anything for a moment. Then he went over to Leslie and knelt and put his arms around her. "I'm sorry, darling," he said. "I guess we walked around too much in the sun today and we're both a little tired."

She pushed his arms away from her violently, still sobbing, her mascara running. "Leave me alone. Just leave me alone."

He stood up slowly and went to the door. "I'm going downstairs," he said quietly. "When you come down, look for me in the bar."

He closed the door silently behind him.

When the others found him in the bar, Leslie had not yet appeared. He had spent a half hour alone trying to figure out what was wrong with her and had come to no conclusion. She was an emotional woman but not an irrational one and her outburst was mysterious to him. He had never given her reason for jealousy and the times when he had openly admired a pretty woman she had joked with him mildly about it. Too many new and different experiences, he decided, crowded into too short a period. He told the others that Leslie was tired and lying down for a while and that they should begin dinner without her.

They were only on their first course when Leslie came into the dining room. She had redone her face and was smiling and looked serene. "Forgive me for being late," she said as she took the chair that Hazen was holding for her. "It's been a long day. I'm starving. Everything looks and smells delicious. Thank you, Russell. What are you having, Mrs. Harcourt? That looks especially good."

"Hot local sausage and hot potato salad," Mrs. Harcourt said.

"I heard men do like women with hearty appetites," Leslie said and Strand began to worry about her again. "I'll have the same. I'd be much obliged if you'd order it for me. With my French I never know what I'm getting until I taste it."

The dinner progressed normally with a great deal of talk about wine on the part of Hazen and Linda, who defended the wines of Provence, although Leslie put in a few good words for several bottles of California white wines.

"Tomorrow," Hazen announced as they were served their dessert, "we're through with sightseeing. Mrs. Harcourt has a friend in the neighborhood who has a vineyard and cellars where he bottles Vouvrays, and she tells me they're very good indeed and we're going out to his place in the morning and taste a few of them. Everybody agreed?"

Everybody agreed. Strand decided that tomorrow he was going to call Mrs. Harcourt by her first name, if he ever discovered what it was.

"His name is Larimmendi," Mrs. Harcourt said. "The wine man, I mean. He's a Basque, but he fell in love with

Touraine. I went to law school with him, but he decided to give up the law for the grape. A wise man. I nearly married him after I saw all those beautiful bottles in the cellars. He's a charming man but he drinks so much of his product himself, I doubt that he'd be much use as a husband. . . ."

As she was speaking, Strand saw a tall woman in a gray wool coat that exactly matched the silvery color of her hair enter the dining room and stand at the door looking as though she were searching for someone. Then she started toward their table. As she moved toward Hazen, who was sitting with his back to the room, Strand saw that she was an impressive looking woman, with a bony, fine face and a long sharp nose, like the paintings of eighteenth-century beauties in English portraits. She stopped behind Hazen, stared down at him for a moment and then bent over and kissed the top of his head. "Good evening, dear Russell," she said. Her voice was sharp and the emphasis on the "dear" was ironic.

Hazen pivoted in his chair, looked up. "Good God, Katherine, what are you doing here?" He stood up, hastily, dropping the spoon he was holding onto his plate with a clatter, his napkin falling to the floor.

"I came to see how my husband was faring," she said evenly. "In case you've forgotten, that's you, Russell."

The silence after these words was oppressive around the table. Mrs. Hazen's eyes were blank and the pupils curiously dilated and Strand wondered if the lady was drugged.

"How did you know I'd be here?" Hazen's tone was aggressive.

"Not through any fault of yours, dear. Your communications are few and far between, aren't they? Your office was kind enough to tell me. And of course friends in America are quick to let me know of your activities. Legions of friends." She looked deliberately around the table, fixing each of them for a moment with an appraising glance. "Ah," she said, "I see you have your portable harem with you. And this handsome couple must be the Strands, of whom I've heard so much."

Strand stood up, because he didn't know what else to do. Hazen looked as though he were trying to speak but finding it impossible.

"Good evening, Linda," the woman went on. "I'm glad to see you looking so well. I hope dear Russell is taking good care of you."

"Very good care," Linda said, her hands moving in a flustered little gesture. "As always."

The woman nodded. "As always," she said. She turned toward Mrs. Harcourt. "And you, Madame Harcourt, I see that you're still in the lineup, to use a sporting term that might be considered appropriate for the occasion."

Mrs. Harcourt folded her napkin and stood up with dignity. "If I may be excused, Mr. Hazen," she said, "I'd like to go up to my room."

"Of course, of course." Hazen sounded hoarse, as though suddenly afflicted with a constriction of the throat.

Mrs. Hazen turned and watched Mrs. Harcourt make her way across the room and did not turn back to the table until Mrs. Harcourt had gone through the door. "It's admirable," she said to no one in particular, "how she keeps her looks. I do approve of a woman who doesn't let herself go. Russell, don't you think it's about time to introduce me to your new friends?"

"Mr. and Mrs. Strand," Hazen mumbled.

"I'm delighted finally to meet you," Mrs. Hazen said. "I hope you've recovered from your experience with the Atlantic Ocean, Mr. Strand."

"Yes, thank you," Strand said, because it was plain that Mrs. Hazen expected him to say something and might stand there for minutes in accusing silence if he didn't speak. "Largely because of the efforts of your husband and Mrs. Roberts," he said, trying to make the moment socially bearable. "Along with Mr. Conroy, whom I presume you've met. I owe my life to them."

"Ah, the faithful Conroy. Always available. Although I was not aware that service as a lifeguard was included

among his duites." In her way of speaking she sometimes
fell into the ornate rhetorical rhythm that she must have
picked up from her husband. "Yes," Mrs. Hazen said, "my
husband is well known as a saver of lives. Except for those
of his family. But I hadn't known that Linda had added
that to her list of good works."

"Katherine, you're embarrassing everybody in the place."
Hazen looked wildly around him. There was a quartet of
middle-aged English tourists at the table next to theirs and
they were clearly interested in the conversation. "I'm going
to be in Paris tomorrow afternoon. Why don't we talk
there?"

"I won't be in Paris tomorrow," Mrs. Hazen said calmly. "I'm on my way down to the Basque country by car
for a holiday and I find it more convenient to talk here.
Besides"—she moved around the table to Mrs. Harcourt's
vacant chair—"I believe a glass of wine would do me
good. Is there any left in the bottle, Russell?" She sat
down firmly.

"Leslie, Linda," Strand said, "I think it would be wiser
if we moved on."

Leslie half-stood up to leave, but Mrs. Hazen put her
hand firmly on her arm. "Please stay. I would feel terribly
guilty if I thought I was breaking up Russell's charming
little party. And there are things I have to say to our host
that I think you ought to hear. . . ."

"Please take your hand away," Leslie said. "My husband and I are leaving."

Mrs. Hazen kept her grip on Leslie's arm. "If anybody
leaves I warn you I am going to scream," she said.
"Loudly."

Leslie made a move to pull her arm away and Mrs.
Hazen screamed. It was a wild, shattering, sirenlike wail.
When she stopped, the room was absolutely silent and
the other diners sat immobilized, as though frozen in place
by some new and devastating instantaneous industrial
process. Mrs. Hazen smiled and dropped her arm. "Mr.
Strand, Russell, I suggest you sit down, too. And Russell,
the wine is near you." She picked up a glass from the table
and held it out toward her husband. "If you'd be so kind."

"Sit down, Allen," Hazen said hoarsely. "The woman's crazy." He sat down, too. His hand trembled as he took the wine out of the cooler and poured some into Mrs. Hazen's glass.

She sipped daintily. "One thing I must say for you, Russell, you always knew how to choose wines. I must apologize to you ladies and gentlemen for the extreme measures I have had to take, but lesser measures have failed, like letters that have gone unanswered for three years and countless transatlantic telephone calls, and this may be the only opportunity to make my point, with other people present, as it were, to bear witness and be able to recount the truth later on if necessary. Russell . . ." She paused, like an orator on a platform, and sipped once more at the wine. "Russell, what I have to say to you is that I am giving you a choice. I am prepared for one of two actions. I will sue for a divorce and a large, a very large settlement, a *vast* settlement, or I shall kill myself."

"Katherine," Linda said, "that's maniacal."

"Linda," Mrs. Hazen said, "you always talked too much. I see you haven't conquered the habit." Then she addressed herself to Hazen, who was sitting with his eyes closed and his head bent, an old man dozing in a corner. "Russell," she said, "you know that I can take care of myself perfectly adequately so I'm not speaking out of avarice. Frankly, all I want is to hurt you. For all the years of bullying, of ignoring me, despising me, of making love to me as though it was a particularly onerous penance you had to pay . . ."

"Oh, shit," Russell said without opening his eyes or lifting his head. "Shit, shit, shit."

"In a word, since I have given up hope of anything else, I want revenge," Mrs. Hazen went on in the eerie flat tone with which she had begun her tirade, her manner that of a woman reading a prepared and carefully rehearsed speech, "revenge for breaking up the family, casting my daughters out, destroying all their confidence in themselves so they've become promiscuous, foolish tramps whose only ambition is to put as much distance as possible between themselves and their family. Revenge, finally, for killing my son and then trying to put the blame on me. . . ."

Finally, Hazen lifted his head and glared at her. "You pampered him, you turned him into a fairy, you entertained his fairy friends in our own house, you knew he was shooting heroin and God knows what else and you gave him the money to buy the stuff . . ."

"And you made him feel worthless. You couldn't make him into your own glorious captain of industry pious image," Mrs. Hazen said, the words snapping out of her mouth vindictively now, the sound the breaking of glass, "so you abandoned him and let him feel that nobody cared if he lived or died."

Strand tried to hunch into himself, make himself invisible, make himself not hear or understand. He looked across at Leslie. She was weeping, her face contorted. Twice in one night, tears, he thought mechanically. It was all he was capable of thinking.

Suddenly Mrs. Hazen's voice became businesslike. "So. If you make the divorce difficult, if your generosity does not stretch quite far enough to cover your wife, I'll make sure to have your list of conquests well publicized—all those foolish Mrs. Harcourts, the secretaries, the plump little wives of our friends whom you so kindly helped in business and politics, the fluffy actresses who comforted you and helped you forget the frigid embrace of your wife and whose names would make such interesting reading in the newspaper columns."

"You're a witch," Hazen whispered.

"If I am, you made me one. I don't forgive you for that, either. Once more back to the shopping list," Mrs. Hazen said, almost gaily. "You can keep the house in New York. It's a vault and I always hated it, anyway, from the first day, it was haunted by the saintly ghost of your beloved father. But I get the house in the Hamptons, with everything in it."

"I was brought up in that house," Hazen said.

"I will do my best to forget that fact when I move into it and try to make a life in it once more for my daughters," said Mrs. Hazen. "And I hope it will not be too much trouble for you, Mr. and Mrs. Strand, and your brood, to which my husband seems rather curiously attached, to find ample time to remove yourselves and your belongings before my arrival. I hope your taste of a more gracious style of living has not spoiled you for the modest appointments to which you must now return. I like to choose my own parasites as guests, whose tastes and habits are compatible with mine. I'm not fond of guitar players, lady athletes, young women who live openly with men without the formality of marriage, nor am I fond of amateur painters, piddling schoolteachers dangling their young daughters before a foolish old man or Jews."

"You can stop there," Strand said, thinking, Christ, there must be somebody there who sends in a daily bulletin to this weird lady. "You're an ugly and unpleasant woman and we're leaving. I don't care if you scream loud enough to be heard on Long Island. Come on, Leslie. And Linda, I think you must have heard enough, too."

"I certainly have," Linda said, as she and Leslie stood up.

Leslie had stopped crying as Mrs. Hazen had gone on about the family and Strand could see she was furious. But he wasn't prepared, as she turned around, for her slapping Mrs. Hazen as hard as she could, squarely across the face.

"Leslie!" Strand cried. "That's enough."

Mrs. Hazen sat without moving or even putting her hand up to her face, as though she had expected the blow and welcomed it.

"Russell," said Strand, "if you want my advice I'd suggest that you take up your wife's kind offer to commit suicide."

"You will not be let off, you two," Mrs. Hazen said quietly. "He will destroy you with his goodwill. You will slip once and he will disapprove of you and cast you and your hopes and schemes out without a backward glance. Remember my words, you silly, grasping little people, your holiday will soon be over." She was stretching her glass toward Hazen, saying "I do think I'd like some more wine, dear," as Strand, with the women on either side of him, started out toward the door through the hushed room full of diners.

It was a long, long walk.

2

Leslie walked steadily, almost woodenly, her makeup streaked but her expression cold and artificially serene. Linda stumbled as they started up the stairs toward their rooms and Strand caught her by the arm. She was trembling. All the color had drained from her face, the touches of rouge on her cheeks standing out like small wounds. When they came to their door Strand knew that he couldn't let her go to her room and face the rest of the night alone. "Come in with us for a while," he said gently. "What we all need is a drink."

Linda nodded numbly.

In the room, Strand telephoned down for a bottle of whiskey and some ice. He didn't know about Linda but he and Leslie had never drunk out of despair before. Linda fell limply into a chair, as though her bones had liquefied. Her hands shook on the chair's arms. Leslie went into the bathroom, saying "I'm going to repair the ravages of the soirée."

"That awful woman," Linda said, her voice quivering. "And I've always tried to be her friend. I knew she was having a dreadful time after her son . . ." She dabbed at her eyes with a lace handkerchief. "I made sure to see her every time I came to Paris and had her as my guest at Mougins. Those nasty insinuations!" Now she was indignant. "There was never anything like that between Russell and me. Good God, I'm not like that. Allen, tell me, did you ever think for a moment . . . ?"

"Of course not," Strand said, not quite honestly.

"That poor Mrs. Harcourt," Linda said. "Don't you think we ought to ask her to come in here and . . . ?"

"I don't think she wants to see any of us anymore," Strand said. "Or at least, not tonight."

"You don't believe I ever shared any of Katherine's sentiments about Russell and the friends he invited to the house, do you, Allen?" There was a desperate appeal in her voice. "I couldn't stand it if you thought . . ."

"Linda," Strand said, going over and holding her hands, "listen to me. I think you're one of the most decent women I've ever met in my life."

"Thank you," Linda whispered.

"You mustn't take it so hard. The woman's deranged. No one in his right mind would believe a word she says."

"She never was a good wife," Linda said. "She made his life hell. I don't know how he stood her as long as he did. She was constantly putting him down. She has a tongue like a razor. At a party, when somebody would ask him about a case he was working on—you know, he's in the papers all the time, he's in tremendous demand, some of the biggest people in the country, in business, in the government, come to him for advice—well, when he would explain some legal technicality that somebody had asked him about she would sneer at him openly and say 'Stop boring our guests. They all know you're the greatest fixer in the profession.' Fixer! A man like Russell. Of course, you had to feel sorry for her, losing a son like that and seeing how those daughters turned out, but there are such things as human limits. Once there was a senator at the house for dinner, a most respected man, but he belonged to the wrong party as far as Mrs. Hazen was concerned and she said, 'You're a damned, bleeding-heart fool,' right to his face after he said he'd voted for a bill she didn't approve of. How can you expect a man to live with someone like that? And even so, no matter what she says, she was the one who walked out, not him."

There was a knock on the door and Strand opened it to let the waiter in with the whiskey. He poured stiff drinks into three glasses and handed Linda hers. She drank half of the drink in one convulsive gulp. "I'll tell you something," she said. "I don't blame him for Mrs. Harcourt and whatever others there were. In spite of everything,

Russell was the soul of discretion. Whatever he did, he kept to himself. I was absolutely dumfounded when he appeared with Mrs. Harcourt. He must have been at the end of his patience. Although even in just this short time I've gotten to like her, really like her a lot. She's so pretty and considerate." She finished her drink and held out her glass and Strand refilled it. "Frankly, I was pleased for Russell and I never saw him so gay before."

Strand heard the sound of laughter from the bathroom and turned, puzzled, as Leslie came into the room, giggling, her face rearranged. "What're you laughing at?" he asked, trying not to sound angry. With Linda in the state she was, laughter seemed callous.

"I was thinking about my hitting that woman," Leslie said, still giggling. "It was one of the most satisfactory moments of my life. I broke a fingernail on her, too. I didn't know I was going to hit her. It was automatic. Deliciously automatic. Ah, whiskey. Just the thing to make the evening perfect. I may get drunk tonight to celebrate. I'll depend upon you, Allen, to put me safely to bed. I knew Europe was going to be interesting, but I never thought it would be *that* interesting." She raised her glass. "To my fingernail," she said. "And to amateur painters and piddling schoolteachers and their brood and to the Jews. I'm getting to love parties among the upper classes, I really am, they're so *refined*."

"Are you all right?" Strand asked anxiously.

"Tip-top," Leslie said airily. "Tonight has made my summer."

The telephone rang and Strand picked it up. It was Hazen. "Allen," Hazen said, "I'd like to talk to you if you don't mind. Can you come to my room? Just you, please. Are the women okay?"

"I think so. They're drinking."

"I don't blame them. I'd drink too if I weren't afraid my ulcer would kick up, if it hasn't already."

It was the first time Strand had heard that Hazen had an ulcer. He was gathering a great many new facts this evening. "I'll be right over," he said. "Leave some of the booze in the bottle for me," he said to Leslie and Linda.

"Give my regards to the lovebird," Leslie said. Her tone was not friendly. "We'll be here, waiting for the next bulletin from the front."

He was finding out some new things about his wife, too, Strand thought as he walked down the corridor to Hazen's room. There was a streak of toughness in her that he hadn't suspected was there. It might be useful in facing up to the shocks that life had in store for her, but he wasn't sure that he liked it.

Hazen's door was ajar and Strand knocked and went in. Hazen was sunk deep in a chair, scowling. He still had all his clothes on, jacket and vest rumpled now. He had unbuttoned his collar and pulled it open and loosened his tie as though he had had trouble breathing and he didn't look as he usually did, ready for a board meeting or an address to the jury. He glanced up as Strand came in and ran his hand wearily across his face, the scowl vanishing, replaced by a twitch of embarrassment.

"I want to apologize for this goddamn evening," he said. His voice was still hoarse.

"Forget it. I've been through worse."

"I haven't," Hazen said. "That woman's demented. Will you ever forget that crazy scream?"

"She *was* in good voice."

"She loves to make scenes. With me, especially. It's her favorite form of amusement." Hazen stood up and pulled at his collar, loosening it further. He began to pace. "Mrs. Harcourt's packed and left. God knows where she's going at this time of night. I wouldn't blame you if you'd all done the same thing. Well, there won't be any visiting vineyards tomorrow. It's good of you to keep me company in my dark hour. After all those hideous insults. I don't know what I'd do tonight if I couldn't talk to you. First of all I owe you some explanations."

"You don't owe me anything, Russell."

Hazen shook his head, still pacing. "It's true about Barbara. Maybe I was unwise to bring her along. I noticed Leslie didn't take kindly to her presence."

Barbara, Strand thought, finally I know her name.

"I'm very attached to her. And there *was* some legal

work we had to get out of the way." Hazen sounded defiant. "And we weren't hurting anybody. She's a fine woman and I don't know how I'll ever make up to her for what
happened tonight. She came over to the States last year on
business and she spent a couple of weekends at the beach.
But, Christ, there were at least six other people in the
house all the time. My goddamn nosy neighbors. 'And of
course friends in America are quick to let me know of
your activities.' " He mimicked his wife's voice. " 'Legions
of friends.' And all that stuff about you and your family.
How anybody could make something evil out of my be-
friending people like you and lending a little helping hand
here and there is beyond mortal comprehension. There's
no purity left in the world, Allen, none, and no belief in
goodness. Just malice. Endless malice. The sharks who've
drunk my wine and feasted at my table'd tear a man to
shreds for the pleasure of ten minutes' gossip about something that is no business of theirs at all, something as innocent as a newborn babe's first breath. Christ, maybe it'll
be a good thing if I have to give that damned house to
her. Fuck the legions of friends." He was ranting now
and pacing faster and faster.

"*Are* you going to give her the house?"

"What else can I do? That wasn't an idle threat about
suicide. After you left me alone with her she told me she
was already in touch with some lawyer in New York—I
know the man and wouldn't touch him with a ten-foot
pole—and had written out everything, chapter and malicious verse, and instructed him to make sure it got into
the papers after she'd done herself in. My name'd be
dragged in the mud and so would that of a great many
other people and there'd be some perfectly working marriages on the rocks. I'll have to give in. I'll be honest with
you—I hate the bitch and I'd be glad to see her dead but
I'll feel guilty for the rest of my life if she dies because
of me just for a few lousy dollars and a ramshackle old
house that'll be swept out to sea in a couple of years anyway. I'll give her what she wants even if it leaves me pen-
niless. But it won't. She's been rich all her life but you
ought to see the gleam in her eye when she talks about

money. I'll put a tough young lawyer from my office on her and she'll bargain. When she sees the goodies dangling in front of her, suicide won't seem so attractive to her even if it could ruin me. She'll bargain, all right."

"I wish I could help," Strand said, shaken by Hazen's torment.

"You *are* helping," Hazen said. Suddenly he stopped pacing and in a clumsy gesture put his arm around Strand's shoulders, then quickly pulled away as if embarrassed by this display of affection and went on pacing again, as though the only way he could alleviate the pain that had him in its grip was by movement. "Just by being here and letting me get some of this off my chest, you're helping more than you could possibly know. God, I've been bottled up so long, keeping everything to myself, my wife, my worthless children, everything, I was ready to explode. My portable harem! Linda Roberts, for God's sake! We could be on a desert island for twenty years and we'd never even think of touching each other. The bitch knows it as well as we do but she wants to destroy every human contact I ever had or could have. So—there were others. I confess that to you—there were others. What else did she expect? She stopped sleeping with me years and years ago and even before that, from the day we were married, it was like trying to make love to an icicle. It was different before we were married, when my father and her father—they were partners in the firm—decided it would be nice to keep the money in the family and winked at the fact that their upright son and debutante daughter were fucking practically under their eyes. Jesus, was she different then, you'd think she was the hottest thing between the sheets since Cleopatra. But once the ring was on her finger, when I came near her it was as though I was trying to rape a nun. How we ever managed to beget three children is one of the mysteries of the goddamn age. And that's how they turned out, too, although maybe it wasn't all their fault, with a mother like that, full of venom toward their father and insanely infatuated with her brats. Nothing was too good for them, all three of them were given Ferraris when they were eighteen.

Three Ferraris parked in front of the door! Can you imagine anything like that? None of them ever finished college. They came running to their mother crying that the teachers were unfair to them or they were unhappy with the class of students they had to put up with or they wanted to go to Europe for the winter with their lovers. Lovers in the case of my beloved son were conspicuously of the male sex. And they just laughed at me when I tried to reason with them. And their mother would laugh along with them. And it wasn't just the money. When I looked around at the children of friends of mine who had ten times the money we had and saw that they were ambitious, responsible citizens that any father would be proud of and then compared them to the children who bore my name I wept. And blaming me for the boy's overdose! I had to go to San Francisco for a few days and I thought it would be good for him and asked him to come along, but he said he was busy, he couldn't make it. Busy! Christ, all he did was loll around the apartment all day. He never bothered to get out of his pajamas or even shave. He looked like a hermit in the desert with his beard. It must be hard for you, with your kids, to understand how I felt, but I tell you it was like drinking acid day after day, year after year. And if you think for a minute that she let me alone even after she cleared out of the house and went to Europe you couldn't be more wrong. She bombarded me with letters, full of all kinds of threats and accusations and the worst kind of filth, you couldn't begin to imagine how degraded that lady's mind is, it's a sewer, that's what it is. If the postal authorities ever opened one of those letters she'd've been arrested for sending obscene matter through the mail. In the beginning I answered them, trying to reason with her, but it was hopeless. Would you imagine even in your wildest dream that that flower of New York society, that graduate of a fancy finishing school in Switzerland would write in her own hand to her husband and the father of her children that he was a cocksucking, shit-eating liar who should have his balls cut off and stuffed into his mouth for supper? Finally, I just threw her letters away unopened and left word that I would not answer the phone when she called. Wait till I find out who it was in my office who told her I was in Tours. Whoever it was will be fired so fast it will take his breath away and I'll make sure he'll never get a job in the legal profession again."

Suddenly Hazen stopped pacing and threw himself, sprawling, gasping for breath, red in the face, into the big chair and began to sob.

Strand had backed against the wall to keep out of the way of the bulky man careening like a berserk bull elephant around the pretty room with its old Provençal furniture and flower-patterned wallpaper. Now he stood, transfixed, staring, horrified, pitying, helpless, frightened, anguished, as the huge man delivered, in a mad torrent of words, his guilt, his hatred, his shattered hopes. For the moment Strand could not talk, found it impossible to stretch out a hand in friendship or rescue for the man who, he felt, might never be rescued, might be lapsing once and for all before his eyes into a mania as disastrous as that of the woman who had caused it. I'm paying for the summer, he thought. Why me? Then was ashamed of the thought. "Please," he said. "It's over."

"Nothing is over," Hazen said. He was moaning now, the sound choked, an eerie soprano. "It will never be over. Get out of here. Please. Forgive me and get out of here."

"I'm going," Strand said, relieved that he could leave the room, get away from the sound of Hazen's grief. "You ought to take a sedative or a sleeping pill."

"I don't keep any of that stuff around. The temptation would be too great," Hazen said without looking up, but in a calmer voice.

"I could let you have something. One pill."

"One pill." Hazen laughed harshly. "There's a remedy. Cyanide. Thank you. And go."

"All right." Strand moved toward the door. "If you need me during the night, just call."

Hazen looked up at him, his eyes red, his mouth just barely under control. "Forgive me, my friend," he said. "Don't worry. I'll be okay. I won't call."

Strand went out of the room and walked down the corridor toward his room, feeling weary and drained. The prisoners of Catherine de Medici were not the only ones tortured publicly in the valley of the Loire. Leslie had left the door unlocked and he let himself in. There was only one small lamp on and Leslie was under the covers, sleeping, snoring softly, which she did only when she was ill. He undressed silently, but even in her sleep she felt his presence and opened her eyes. He was just about to climb into his own bed when she stretched out an arm.

"Please," she whispered. "Tonight."

He hesitated, but only for a second. If ever there was a time for the warmth of beloved, familiar body against beloved body, this was the time. He slipped off his pajamas and got in beside her. He lay with his arms around her in the narrow bed. "Don't say anything," she murmured, "not anything." She began to caress him, softly. Then they made love, gently, soundlessly, allowing desire and gratitude, the enormous remembered gift of loving, of releasing sex, obliterate the chaos of the night.

Leslie fell asleep immediately after. He lay awake, unable to sleep, his heart suddenly an independent and unruly part of his body, racing wildly. No, he thought, it can't, it would be too much. By an act of will he tried to control the thunder he felt inside his chest, but the heart went on in its unsteady drumming, guided by ominous signals of its own. Despite all his efforts, his breathing became louder and louder, rasping, and he felt he was choking. Unsteadily, he got out of bed, stumbled in the darkness, trying to get to the bathroom, where his shaving kit was, with the bottle of nitroglycerin pills. He tripped over a chair, fell heavily, with a groan, was unable to lift himself off the floor.

The noise awoke Leslie and a moment later the room was lit as she switched on a lamp. With a cry, she leaped out of bed and rushed over and knelt beside him.

"My medicine . . ." he said, between gasps.

She jumped up, ran into the bathroom. He saw the light go on, heard the rattling of bottles, water running. He pulled himself along the floor, managed to sit up, his back against a chair. Leslie knelt beside him again, held his head as she put a capsule in his mouth and tilted a glass against his lips. He gulped thirstily, felt the capsule wash down his throat.

He tried to smile reassuringly. "I'll be all right," he said. "Don't talk."

Suddenly, the harsh sound of his breathing subsided. The attack, if that was what it had been, was over. "There," he said. He stood up. He swayed a little, but he said, "I'm cold, I've got to get back into bed." He felt foolish, standing there naked.

She helped him over to the bed and he fell into it. "Do you want me to call a doctor?"

"No need. I just want to sleep. Please get in beside me and turn out the light and put your arms around me."

She hesitated for a moment, then put the glass and bottle of pills on the bedside table, switched off the lamp and got into bed with him.

When he awoke in the morning, he felt fine. He put his hand to his chest and was pleased that he could barely make out the orderly small pulse under his ribs.

He was having breakfast with Leslie when the phone rang. She went to pick it up. Standing at the table on which the phone rested, she looked refreshed and young, her hair long, hanging down over the shoulders of her dressing gown in the morning sunlight. Watching her, Strand marveled at the resilience of womankind.

"Of course, Russell," she was saying, "I understand perfectly. Don't worry, we'll be ready in an hour." She put the instrument down and came back to the table and buttered a piece of croissant. "We're going back to Paris this morning," she said. "I imagine the Loire valley has lost some of its charm for our host."

"How did he sound?"

"Normal. How did he sound when you saw him last night?" She looked over the rim of her coffee cup at him.

"You don't want to know," Strand said.

"Bad?"

"As bad as could be. Ugly and sad. If you want the truth, it make me sorry we ever met him."

"That bad?" Leslie said thoughtfully.

"Worse."

"Did he attack you?"

"Not personally. Just the whole world." He stood up from the table. "If we have to be ready in an hour I'd better start getting packed and dressed."

The trip to Pàris was grim. Leslie had turned out not to be as resilient as he had thought. The night had finally taken its toll. After breakfast she had begun coughing and looked feverish, her eyes and nose damp. She complained that she was freezing, although she was bundled up and it was a warm day.

Hazen, impeccably dressed in his business suit and outwardly composed, drove. They had barely passed the outskirts of Tours when Strand found himself regretting Mrs. Harcourt's midnight flight. Hazen drove like a madman, going slowly at times but weaving the car across the road, then putting his foot down violently on the accelerator to pass trucks on blind curves, cursing under his breath at other drivers as if they were mortal enemies. He doesn't need pills to commit suicide, Strand thought, holding Leslie's sweating hand, he's going to do it with the internal combustion engine. And he's going to take us all with him. For the entire trip, as their heads snapped with the sudden and unpredictable accelerations of the machine and their bodies rolled from side to side when Hazen swung around turns, Leslie sat with her foot jammed against the foot rest, her legs rigid. Linda, dressed in a smart suit, next to Hazen on the front seat, slept the whole way, as if knowing she was going to be killed that morning, she had decided to die mercifully unconscious. She had not slept a wink all night, she had told the Strands, and she seemed determined to go to her Maker well rested and looking her best.

Somehow they survived the ride and they drew to an abrupt stop in front of the Crillon with the smell of burning rubber accompanying their arrival and Linda saying, as she opened her eyes, "Oh, we're here. What a nice ride, Russell. I had such a good nap."

"French drivers," Hazen said. "It's a wonder any of them are still alive."

"Russell," Strand said, as they all got out of the car, "that's the last time I'll ever ride with you."

Hazen stared blankly at him. "I don't know what you're talking about."

It was time for lunch, but Hazen said he was sorry, he had to get to his office immediately. He waved to a taxi and jumped into it without saying good-bye. Leslie told Strand that she felt ill and just wanted to lie down for the afternoon. Strand, not willing to face lunch alone with Linda that day, said that he was feeling a bit off-color himself and would have lunch with Leslie up in the room. The morning three days ago when they had set out so gaily from the Place de la Concorde now seemed a foggy memory from a distant age.

When the Strands stopped at the desk to get the key to their room, the concierge gave Strand a cablegram. Feeling that any information it would contain could only be disastrous, Strand hesitated before tearing open the envelope. He was annoyed that his hands trembled as he did so. A death would not surprise him. He read it once. Then again. It was from Eleanor. "MARRIED THIS MORNING STOP HAVE QUIT JOB STOP AM HONEYMOONING WITH GIUSEPPE STOP ECSTATIC STOP SO FAR STOP BLESS US IN FRENCH LOVE MR. AND MRS. GIANELLI"

Mechanically, without emotion, Strand looked at the date on the cable. It had been sent from Las Vegas and had arrived the night before. It must have come in at just the moment that Mrs. Hazen had come into the dining room in Tours. Marriages end, Stop, Marriages begin, Stop.

"What does it say?" Leslie asked, worried.

Strand gave her the cable. The print on the flimsy page was pale and Leslie had to hold it close to her eyes to read it.

"Oh, my," she said in a low voice, sinking into one of the lobby chairs. "Las Vegas. What could they have been thinking of? It doesn't sound like Eleanor at all. It's so *tacky*. And why did they have to run off like that? Do you think that boy has something to hide?"

"I doubt it."

"Why didn't they at least wait until we got home? Good Lord, it's only a few days."

"'Maybe they wanted to do it while we were away," Strand said. "So they wouldn't be under any pressure from us to make a big fuss. Marriage is different from what it was in our day." Leslie's parents had insisted on a church wedding and a wedding luncheon and he still remembered the whole day as an ordeal. For days after his face had seemed stiff from the effort of smiling falsely at a hundred people he hoped never to see again. Still, he was a little disappointed in his daughter and he could see that Leslie was hurt. She had been an open and forthright girl and there was something secretive and mistrustful in what she had done. And he shared Leslie's dismay at the idea of the garish marriage mills of Las Vegas.

"And we don't even know where she is," Leslie said, her eyes, already red from her cold, filling with tears, "so that at least we could call them to congratulate them. And no word about Caroline or Jimmy. It's as though she'd completely forgotten she had any family at all."

"Well, there's nothing we can do about it now," Strand said. "And they'll undoubtedly explain what it was all about when we get home. Let's go upstairs. You look as though you've got something more than a cold. I'll call for a doctor."

"It must have been a premonition," Leslie said, as she stood up and they started toward the elevators. "Every time something upsetting is going to happen I come down with something." Usually, Strand smiled when she talked about her premonitions. He didn't smile today. "We should never have come on this trip," Leslie said. "Things would've been different if we'd been there."

Upstairs, he helped her out of her clothes and into a robe, and shivering now, she got into bed.

Just as the doctor was leaving, after telling them he thought Leslie was suffering from a severe bronchial in-

fection and advising that she stay in bed for a few days
and take the medicine he was going to prescribe, the telephone rang. It was Linda. "Allen," she said, "I'm flying
down to Mougins this afternoon. Do you think Leslie is
well enough for the two of you to come with me? The sun
would do her good."

"I'm sorry," Strand said. "The doctor's ordered her to
stay put."

"Oh, isn't that too bad." But from the tone of her voice,
Strand guessed that she was relieved. He felt that way,
too. It was almost as though what they had been through
had left ugly scars on them that would remind them too
vividly of a scene that all of them were trying to forget.
"I'll stay," Linda said, "if you think it will do any good."
But from the way she spoke he was sure that she wanted
to get away—alone.

"Thanks, Linda. That won't be necessary. Have a nice
peaceful time down south."

"I'll keep in touch," she said. "If you see Russell before he leaves for Saudi Arabia, tell him where I am and
that he's not to worry, I'll be in Paris in plenty of time to
fly back to the States with all of you."

As Strand hung up, he was sorry that the airplane had
ever been invented. As a fitting end to the holiday he
would not be surprised if they wound up in the middle
of the Atlantic.

The medicine the doctor had ordered seemed to be
working and the fits of coughing became fewer and fewer
and after twenty-four hours Leslie's fever had abated and
her temperature had returned to normal. Hazen did not
call to say good-bye. Strand tried to call Jimmy in New
York and Caroline on Long Island, but there was no answer at their apartment even though, with the time difference, he had called Jimmy at seven in the morning,
New York time. Mr. Ketley answered the phone at the
beach house and said that Caroline had been gone all day
and had told him that she was invited out to dinner. If
Mr. Ketley knew about Eleanor's marriage, he said nothing about it.

Strand stayed in the room with Leslie most of the time, content to read quietly and listen to the little portable radio Hazen had bought for them during the stopover at Shannon Airport. The chain that carried *France Musique* played fine music hour after hour—Beethoven and Bach and Schubert, remedies from other centuries, made the days pleasant for both of them. Leslie asked him if he thought they ought to try to get in touch with Mrs. Harcourt, but Strand said it would be wiser to give her time to let the wounds heal and wrote her a short note that he hoped was warm and friendly but feared was stilted. It was not an easy letter to write. Somehow, just from being at the table when the woman was attacked by Mrs. Hazen, he felt guilty. He sent the letter to Hazen's Paris office, although it was possible that Mrs. Harcourt had already left it and would never put foot in it again.

By the third day, Leslie was well enough to go out and they splurged and had lunch at Maxim's, around the corner from the hotel, and after that went into the Jeu de Paume Museum and were cheered by the sunshine of the Impressionists. Leslie said that it would be nice if they could bring the couple a wedding present from France. They looked in some of the shops but everything they saw was wildly expensive and they had to settle on going to Bloomingdale's as soon as they reached New York.

When they got back to the hotel they found a message from Russell Hazen. He had phoned while they were out and wanted them to call him at his office. He had left the number.

Strand called from their room. Hazen sounded brusque and hurried. His business voice, Strand thought. "I got back a little earlier than I expected, Allen," Hazen said. "I'd like to leave for New York no later than noon tomorrow. I'll have to stay late tonight at the office but if you and Leslie and Linda don't mind waiting, I'd like us all to have dinner together at the hotel."

"That's fine with us," Strand said. "But Linda is down in Mougins."

"That flighty woman." Hazen was annoyed. "There's no

keeping her in one place. I'll get her on the phone and tell her to get her ass back up here by noon if she wants a free ride home." Hazen's vocabulary, Strand noticed, had been affected, Strand hoped not permanently, by the flood of profanity, both his own and that of his wife, the night in Tours. "And I'll call Conroy and tell him to tell your kids our estimated time of arrival, so they can be there to greet you."

"That's very kind of you," Strand said. "But tell Conroy not to bother trying to reach Eleanor. She got married a few days ago in Las Vegas and she's on her honeymoon and she didn't give us any address."

"Las Vegas, for Jesus' sake," Hazen said. "Kids will do anything for a kick these days. How do you feel about it?"

"Dazed."

Hazen laughed. "I can understand why. I hope she's happy."

"Ecstatic, she said in her cable. So far."

Hazen laughed again. "Well, anyway, give my felicitations to the mother of the bride. I'll try to get to the hotel about nine tonight. That okay with you?"

"Nine," Strand said.

"How is he?" Leslie asked, when Strand hung up.

"The Master's back," he said. "Taking charge."

When Hazen came into the hotel dining room fifteen minutes late, he looked haggard, with hollows under his eyes. His clothes were badly creased, as if he had flown back from Asia Minor in them and had not had time to change. He hadn't shaved, either, and there was a gray stubble on his cheeks and chin, which gave him an oddly disreputable appearance, as though a family portrait of a distinguished ancestor had been defaced by childish vandals. I wonder, Strand thought as he stood up to greet him, how many years an ordinary man could bear up under a timetable like his. But Hazen smiled warmly, baring his even strong teeth. He shook Strand's hand vigorously and bent over to kiss Leslie's cheek before falling back heavily into a chair facing them. "What I need is a drink."

"Did you get hold of Linda?"

"She'll meet us at the airport tomorrow. She dithered, but she'll be there. A martini, please," he said to the waiter.

"How was Saudi Arabia?" Strand asked.

"A waste of time," Hazen scowled. "They're even worse to do business with than the French. They may have clocks, but they don't seem to be able to tell the time. And there're dozens of relatives of various desert princes you have to go through, handing out money left and right, if you want to get anything settled. I'd've done just as well going down to the south with Linda. And how about you? How're you taking the news about Eleanor?"

"Shakily."

Hazen laughed. "He's a nice young fellow."

"That's what I thought," Leslie said. "Up to Las Vegas."

"It's not how a marriage starts that counts," Hazen said sententiously. "It's how it ends up." He scowled again, as though remembering the end of his own marriage. He sipped gratefully at the martini the waiter had put before him. "I needed that. In Saudi Arabia they put you in jail or scourge you or cut off your hand, whatever little pleasantry occurs to them at the moment, for a single cocktail. Try and do business with people like that. And everybody from the so-called civilized world—Americans, English, French, Japanese—are falling all over themselves to get in on the act. When the thing finally happens there it'll make what happened in Iran look like a church bazaar. Mark my words." He drank again, morosely. "I've already warned my clients to lay off and invest their money in something safe, like a patent for a perpetual motion machine." He laughed at his own conceit. "Enough about my affairs. Have you any idea what the newlyweds plan to do, where they're going to live, etcetera?"

"All we know is that in her cable Eleanor said she'd given up her job."

Hazen nodded soberly. "I thought that might happen when I sent the boy down to Georgia."

"Georgia?" Strand asked. "What has Georgia got to do with it?"

"You knew he kept talking about how he wanted to

quit his father's business and set himself up publishing a small-town newspaper and that his brothers were funding him up to a point to get rid of him."

"I remember something like that," Strand said.

"Well, there's a town called Graham in Georgia, used to be a small place, but two big businesses, one an electronics company, the other a packing plant, have moved there from the north and the town's growing in leaps and bounds and my firm represented the editor and publisher of the little daily newspaper there in a libel suit. I went down and pleaded the case myself because it was a freedom of the press issue and important and we won. I got friendly with the fellow, he was a native Georgian, went to college at Athens and all that, but he was a good tough old bird and I grew to like him. He feels he's getting a little age on him and the daily grind was beginning to get to him and he called me out of the blue and asked me if I knew some smart young ambitious fellow with a little cash, not too much, who could take on the daily responsibility and share in the profits. And it just happened that a couple of days before I'd had drinks with Gianelli and Eleanor and he'd told me again how he'd like to take over a small-town newspaper if he could. Eleanor had said she'd take in washing in New York first, but love conquers all, as the Romans put it, and I guess that's why she's quit her job. My friends in Graham must have been pretty impressed with your new son-in-law."

"Georgia!" Leslie said in the same tone in which she had said "Las Vegas" when she read the cablegram.

"It's a nice neat little town," Hazen said. "You'd like it." Then he smiled. "For a week."

"I doubt that Eleanor will last that long," Leslie said, her face gloomy. "I can't see her in the piny woods of the South after New York."

"We northerners have to get used to the idea that civilization doesn't stop at the town line of Washington, D.C.," Hazen said. "Don't look so glum, Leslie. It isn't the end of the world. If it doesn't work out, they're both young and strong and they'll try something else. At least they won't go through life thinking, We had our chance and we were too cowardly to risk it. Speaking of chances, a month or so ago Mrs. Harcourt was offered a job teaching international law at George Washington University and she has now decided to take it." Hazen spoke matter-of-factly, as if he were passing on a piece of news about a casual acquaintance.

"I'm sure she'll be very popular at all those government parties," Leslie said.

Hazen squinted at her suspiciously, guessing cattiness. Leslie merely smiled sweetly.

The waiter, who had been standing next to the table hoping for a break in the conversation, handed them the menus. Hazen glanced at his, then threw it down and stood up. "Forgive me," he said, "I'm too tired to eat. And if I have a second drink they'll have to carry me out. I'm going up to bed. It's been a long day. I think you'd better be ready by about ten thirty tomorrow morning. There's a weather front moving in, they tell me, and the field may be closed in the afternoon. I'm glad to see you looking so well, Leslie. You were a little peaked the other day. Good night and sleep well." He walked, his shoulders bent and looking old, toward the door.

They ordered dinner and ate it in silence.

They met Linda at the airport. She looked well, with a new tan, but flustered. "I'm just no good at changing schedules," she complained. "I'm sure I packed all the wrong things. It's not like Russell at all. He's usually as dependable as the Swiss railway system." After kissing her briskly in greeting and saying "I'm glad to see you made it," Hazen had gone off to make a last call to his office.

It was a raw day, with a little drizzle of rain and irregular gusts of wind sweeping the field. As they walked across toward the airplane Strand looked doubtfully up at the overcast sky. The weather fit his mood. A front moving in, Hazen had warned them. It would probably be a rough voyage. Sunshine would have been inappropriate for the end of this particular holiday. As they got into the gleaming small plane, Strand was afraid that

Leslie would pick that moment to say that she was having one of her premonitions. But she was chatting cheerfully with Linda and there was no sign that the thousands of miles of wild sky ahead of them held any fears for her at all.

The trip was bumpy, but no more. Leslie and Linda dozed, Strand read and Hazen drank. When they stopped to refuel at Shannon, Hazen didn't offer to buy them any presents, but Leslie bought a pink wool shawl for Caroline, although Strand didn't think Caroline would have much occasion to wear it in the balmy climate of Arizona.

They arrived in New York on time and Hazen got them through customs quickly, the inspector deferentially waving them through without asking any of them to open their bags. Conroy and Jimmy and Caroline were waiting for them. Leslie gasped when she saw Caroline. She had a bandage on her nose and her face was swollen and one eye closed and black and blue.

"My God, Caroline," Leslie said as they embraced, "what happened to you?"

"It's nothing, Mummy," Caroline said. "It looks gruesome, but it's just a few scratches. George was driving me home the other night and some idiot bumped into us from behind when we were stopped at a light and I hit my head on the dashboard."

"I knew we never should have let you out with that boy," Leslie said. "He drives like a fool."

"It wasn't his fault, Mummy," Caroline protested. "We weren't even moving."

"Even so," Leslie said.

"Don't take it so big, Mom," Jimmy said. "What's a little black eye between friends?"

"Don't be so debonair, young man," Leslie said. "She could have been disfigured for life."

"Well, she isn't," Jimmy said. "How was your trip?"

"Marvelous," Strand said hastily, anxious to avoid a family quarrel in front of the others.

"Have you seen a doctor?" Hazen asked Caroline.

"There's no need for a doctor," Caroline said querulously, as though she felt she was being unjustly scolded.

"Conroy," Hazen said, "we won't be going out to the Island. We're going to New York and we're taking this young lady to see a doctor. The man's name is Laird and he's the best one in the business for this type of thing."

"Why don't we just get an ambulance with a siren and life support equipment," Caroline said sardonically, "and get the horribly mangled poor beautiful young victim to a hospital where a team of experts at bone setting and open-heart surgery are waiting to save her life?"

"Don't be smart, Caroline," Leslie said. "Mr. Hazen's right."

"Everybody's making such a fuss," Caroline said, sounding like a little girl. "Over nothing. It happened almost twenty-four hours ago and I'm still alive."

"That's all out of you," Leslie said to her. "Just keep quiet from now on and do what you're told."

Caroline grunted. "I hate doctors," she said. But Leslie took her arm firmly and marched her toward the exit, with Hazen at her other side. Strand walked behind them with Jimmy and Linda. "What do you know about all this?" Strand asked Jimmy.

"Nothing. The first I knew about it was just fifteen minutes ago when I saw her. I came from New York and Conroy drove her in from the Island. Mom's just blowing it up into something enormous. And Hazen's just showing what a big shot he is and running everything, as usual."

"Well," said Linda, "at least she didn't lose any teeth. That's something to be thankful for. She's got such pretty teeth."

"I'll ask Conroy to drop me off at the office," Jimmy said. "I told them I'd only be a couple of hours."

"Don't you think you ought to stay with your sister at a time like this?"

"Oh, Pops," Jimmy said impatiently. "For a little black eye?"

"How're you doing at the office?" Strand said, switching the subject, not wishing to argue with his son. He hadn't won an argument with him since Jimmy was twelve.

"Still feeling my way," Jimmy said. "Ask Solomon. He knows better than I do. Anyway, whatever he thinks, I like the job."

Strand was about to tell him that he didn't like the way he dropped the Mister when he spoke about Solomon and Hazen, but suddenly remembered Eleanor's cable. In the excitement over Caroline's injury, it had completely slipped his mind. "Have you seen Eleanor?" he asked.

"No," Jimmy said. "We talked over the phone last week."

"What did she have to say?"

"Nothing much," Jimmy said carelessly. "The usual. That I sounded as though I wasn't getting enough sleep. Sometimes I think she believes she's my mother, not my sister."

"Did she say anything about getting married?"

"Why would she say anything like that?" Jimmy sounded genuinely surprised.

"Because she got married four days ago. In Las Vegas."

Jimmy stopped walking. "Holy cow! She must have been drunk. Did she say why?"

"That's not the sort of thing people put in cablegrams," Strand said. "The family's had a full week."

"You can say that again." Jimmy shook his head wonderingly. They started walking again toward where Conroy was packing their bags into the car in front of the terminal. "Where're they now? I'd like to call her and tell her her loving brother wishes her many happy returns of the day."

"You can't call her. She didn't tell us where she was."

Jimmy shook his head again. "She's devious, that girl. Devious." He put his hand gently on his father's arm. "I wouldn't worry, Pops. She'll be all right. He's okay, Giuseppe. They must know what they're doing. And you'll have a little tribe of angelic bambinos to dandle on your knee."

"I can't wait," Strand said gloomily as he climbed into the big Mercedes, where the others were already installed.

Caroline had a stubborn, set expression on her face and she looked grotesque with the bandage on her nose and the swollen, discolored eye. He leaned over and kissed her. "My dear little girl," he said softly.

"Oh, leave me alone," Caroline said, shrugging away.

It was not a happy group that drove away in the big car in the direction of the city.

As the car crossed the bridge into Manhattan it occurred to Strand that since the first night Hazen had staggered into the apartment, bloody and stunned, he had had more to do with the medical profession than at any other period of his life.

3

Naturally Strand thought, as he listened to the doctor, who was talking to them in his brisk, best-man-in-the-business manner, naturally it was worse than it looked. It was a period when things were worse than they looked.

"The bone's pretty well smashed and the left septum is blocked," the doctor said to Leslie and Strand in the elegant Park Avenue office into which he had called them after he had looked at the X rays and completed his examination of Caroline, whom he had left with an assistant in another room where the assistant was putting on another bandage and drawing samples of blood. "I'm afraid that it will mean an operation," the doctor said. He didn't look afraid, at all. The English language, Strand thought, with all its polite ambiguities. "We'll have to wait a few days until the swelling goes down. I'll reserve the operating room. That is, if you agree."

"Of course," Leslie said.

Strand nodded.

"She'll only have to stay overnight," the doctor said. "There's really nothing to worry about, Mrs. Strand."

"Mr. Hazen tells me she's in the best possible hands," Leslie said.

"Good old Russell." Dr. Laird smiled at this reported vote of confidence. "In the meanwhile, I advise putting the young lady to bed and keeping her quiet. She's too brave for her own good. Will you stay in New York or do you plan to go out to Russell's place on the Island?"

"We'll be in New York," Leslie said quickly.

"Good. The less she moves around the better." He stood up to show that the interview was over. The best man in the business had no time for idle talk. "I'll call you after I make the arrangements at Lenox Hill Hospital, that's just around the corner from here on 77th Street, and tell you when to bring the young lady in." He accompanied them into the waiting room, where Linda and Hazen were sitting, Linda thumbing nervously through a magazine and Hazen staring, his face set, out the window.

"Russell," the doctor said, "might I have a word with you in my office?"

Hazen got up and followed him out of the room. Linda put down her magazine and looked at Strand inquiringly.

"There're some complications," Strand said. "He's got to operate."

"Oh, dear," Linda said. "The poor girl."

"There's nothing to worry about, the doctor told us," said Leslie. "I'm sure he knows what he's talking about."

"Has he told Caroline?"

"Not yet."

"I hope she won't be too upset."

"When she learns that if she wants to breathe normally from now on she has to have an operation, I'm sure she'll be reasonable," Leslie said calmly.

They were still waiting for Caroline when Hazen came out. There was no indication from his expression of what private communication the doctor had had with him. "Is there anything Dr. Laird told you that he didn't tell us?" Strand asked.

"Nothing important," Hazen said. "He hasn't got time to lie. No—all he said was that in a case like this with young girls, when he has to operate anyway, there's always a chance that at the same time, if the patient wants it, he can easily do a little cosmetic job."

"What does that mean?" Strand asked suspiciously.

"Make the nose more esthetically pleasing to the eye is the expression he used. He does a lot of plastic surgery and from what I hear he has a satisfied clientele."

"Why didn't he tell *us* that?" Strand asked.

"Sometimes, he said, parents are apt to get angry at the suggestion. Their vanity is touched. He'd rather that you get angry at me than at him."

Strand glanced at Leslie. She was looking at Linda. Linda was nodding her head vigorously.

"Of course," Hazen said, "you'd have to see what Caroline wants."

"I know what Caroline wants," Leslie said. "She'd be delighted."

"How do you know that?" Strand asked, taken aback.

"We discussed it, long before we went to France," Leslie said, sounding defiant. "Way back, when Eleanor talked about it."

"Why didn't you say something to me then?" Strand demanded.

"I was waiting for the right moment," Leslie said.

"And you think *this* is the right moment?" Strand tried to keep his voice from rising.

"Providential," Leslie said calmly. "Maybe we ought to give a vote of thanks to that boy George for the way he drives."

"I think it's nonsense." Strand knew he didn't sound convincing.

"Allen," Linda said, "please don't be medieval."

"Well, there's one sure thing," Strand said, although he knew he was beaten. "I'm going to talk to the young lady myself."

"Oh, Allen," Leslie said impatiently, "don't make a drama out of it. They do it a million times a year."

"Not in my family, they don't." He turned toward the door to one of the inner offices as Caroline came out with the assistant who had been taking care of her. She had a new rakish bandage tilted over her nose and bad eye.

"How do you feel, baby?" Strand asked.

"I'm breathing my last," Caroline said.

"Don't be flip. We're taking you home. Come on." Strand held the door open and Caroline, holding her mother's arm, went out with Linda. Hazen held back a little, as though reflecting. "You coming?" Strand asked.

"Yes, yes, of course." Hazen seemed flustered.

"Is there something else the doctor told you?" Strand felt that he was surrounded by conspirators.

"No, nothing," Hazen said. "I'll tell you some other time."

What a day, what a goddamn day, Strand thought as he and Hazen followed the others to the waiting car. Millions of people are starving to death and killing each other all over the world and we're worrying about whether a girl's nose should be a quarter of an inch shorter.

The apartment was a mess in the following days. Leslie had started packing immediately for the move to Dunberry and the place was a confusion of barrels and crates and excelsior to protect the dishes and pictures and there were long discussions between Leslie and Caroline, who refused to go out while she still had bandages all over her face, about what to throw out and what to take along. They had had the apartment for twenty-five years and Strand was aghast at the amount of junk they had piled up. Leslie refused to let him help at all because she didn't want him to overexert himself and he couldn't find anything in the confusion. New York was suffering a heat wave, there was no word from Eleanor, and Jimmy was no help at all, appearing briefly at odd hours, monopolizing the telephone when he was home and often not sleeping there but merely rushing in early in the morning to shave and dress for work. Strand was annoyed at what he privately called the boy's distasteful habits, but, heeding the doctor's advice about not getting excited, said nothing about it. He found himself wandering around the streets of New York, reading the newspapers over too many cups of coffee in cafeterias, feeling lonely and at a loss and useless. He had called Dr. Laird's office to find out what the operation on Caroline's nose would cost. He had not been able to get hold of the doctor himself, but had been told by the doctor's secretary, who sounded as though she had been interrupted in the middle of an operation herself, that the matter had already been taken care of. He had called Hazen's office to protest, but Mr. Hazen, he was told, was out of town and could not be reached.

He saw a great many movies, sitting alone in the cool darkness to escape the heat of the streets, and enjoyed none of them. There was one asset in being in New York in August. It made the prospect of moving away from it pleasurable. If he had been twenty years younger, he told himself, he would have gone to the outskirts of the city and hitched a ride on the first car that picked him up and gone anywhere the road would take him.

One afternoon he found himself on the street where Judith Quinlan lived. He nearly went into the hallway of the building and pushed the button of her apartment. Some of the movies he had seen had been pornographic in the extreme, in the new style, and to add to his general discomfort he was subject these days to wild erotic reveries. With his hand poised above the knob on the outside door he pulled back. He imagined headlines: SCHOOLTEACHER FOUND DEAD IN MISTRESS'S BED. He had not lived the life he had led to come to that end. He let his hand drop and walked into the park and sat on a bench and watched the pigeons, who did not seem to mind the heat.

The day before the operation was scheduled Jimmy moved out of the apartment. He scribbled an address. Care of Langman on East 53rd Street. It was convenient, Jimmy said, near the Solomon office. Jimmy did not say whether it was a Miss Langman or a Mrs. Langman or a Mr. Langman and both Leslie and Strand were too embarrassed to ask. Jimmy said it was about time they got rid of the old apartment. It was like carrying 1890 on your back to live there, he said. Strand remembered all the joys, all the sorrows he had lived through in the capacious rambling rooms—the cries of children, the music of the piano, the quiet afternoons poring over books, the smell of cooking—and had told Jimmy to shut up.

He and Leslie took Caroline to the hospital in a taxi on a rainy afternoon. Caroline was as merry as if she were going to a dance. Strand wondered if he would recognize her when the operation was over. He had not been consulted by the best-man-in-the-business about what kind of nose she would finally come out with. Roman, upturned, scooped, like Garbo's, like Elizabeth Taylor's, like the nose of the Duchess of Alba, Mrs. Harcourt?

What would she be like? Your face molded your character, no matter what anyone said. He loved her as she was and believed she was beautiful and knew she loved him. Had she not given up her passion for tennis as a childish offering on some mystical altar to trade for his life? Would she, in her new incarnation, ever offer anything for him again?

Leslie sat sedately on the other side of their daughter in the sweltering taxi, occasionally patting the girl's hand reassuringly. Had he lived for twenty-five years with a woman who had no imagination at all? He wished Eleanor had been there. She would have said something matter-of-fact and sharp and good for his soul. He regarded her absence as a betrayal. Love fled all other responsibilities. He would have one or two things to say to her when she finally showed up. He cursed the day he had gone into the ocean all by himself. Now, he thought self-pityingly, he was on the sidelines of his own life.

They left Caroline in the hospital bed where she would spend the night before being wheeled into the operating room in the morning. Caroline had not hidden her desire to get him out of the room. "You've put on your long face, Daddy," she had said. "Why don't you and Mummy go out and have a nice dinner and go to a concert? You make me feel guilty standing there looking as though the sirens were blowing and you were leaving me alone in an air raid."

The apartment, with books strewn around on the floors and the carpets rolled up and light spots on the walls where pictures had hung for so many years, did not look like home anymore. His voice and Leslie's as they discussed whether they should have dinner in or go out rang hollowly in the stripped rooms. For once, Strand missed the sound of Jimmy's guitar. It was hard to forgive his son's lighthearted and callous farewell. The young, he thought bitterly, spurned possessions, not understanding how much love can accumulate in a battered piano, a chipped vase, a scarred desk, a lamp which had shed light on a quarter century of books.

The family was finished. Now it would be a telephone

call, a scribbled note, from Georgia, Arizona, from an address on East 53rd Street. Children grew and departed. It was the law of life, or at least of the times, but like everything else in the hurried century, it all flashed past in a dizzyingly accelerated tempo. It had happened so quickly. A matter of weeks. A man had burst in, his head bloodied, one evening and all orbits had been tilted. He knew it was unjust to blame Hazen but found it hard to be fair.

Fretfully, Strand turned on the radio. The evening news was on. The news was bad, a report from chaos. He remembered a line from a Saroyan play—"No foundation. All the way down the line." He turned off the radio and switched on the television set. He heard the sound of canned laughter and switched the machine off before the image came on the wavering screen.

He wandered around the apartment, his own ghost. He would have liked to look at the photograph album in which they kept the family snapshots: he and Leslie on their wedding day, Caroline in a baby carriage, Eleanor in cap and gown, her newly won degree in her hand, Jimmy on a bicycle. But the album had been packed away.

Suddenly, the apartment was intolerable to him. He went into the kitchen, where Leslie was opening cans. "Let's go out for dinner," he said. "I want to see other people tonight."

Leslie looked at him strangely for a moment, then put down the can opener she had in her hand. "Of course," she said softly. "Can you wait till I wash my hair?"

"I'm not hungry," he said. "I can wait." Whenever Leslie was troubled, she washed her hair. Her serenity, he realized, was a mask that she had put on for his sake. But he hated the sound of her hair dryer. It was like the sound of ominous engines he heard in the background of his dreams. "I'll wait for you at O'Connor's." O'Connor's was the bar on the corner of their street. He only went into it two or three times a year, when he had unpleasant news to break at home and wanted to postpone the moment.

Leslie came over to him and kissed his cheek. "Don't be melancholy, please, darling," she said.

But all he said was "I could use a drink. And there's nothing in the house. Jimmy must have had some uproarious parties while we were gone."

"They couldn't have been so uproarious," Leslie said. "We didn't leave more than half a bottle of Scotch when we left for Europe."

"Even so," Strand said, knowing he was being unreasonable. As he left, he heard the water running in the bathroom. When Leslie met him at O'Connor's an hour later he still had most of his first Scotch in his glass as he sat by himself at the deserted bar.

They had dinner in a nearby restaurant they had used to like. There were only two other couples in the restaurant and the owner, who knew them, said, "Next August I am shutting down. August is a plague month in New York."

After the meals they had eaten in France the food seemed tasteless, and Leslie found a long hair in her salad. "This is the last time I'm going to set foot in this restaurant," Leslie said.

Last, Strand thought, is becoming the most common word in our vocabulary.

When they opened the door to the apartment, the telephone was ringing. When the next war starts, Strand thought, as he hurried to pick it up, it will be announced to me by that nerve-rasping clanging. Disaster, courtesy of A.T. and T. But it was Eleanor. "I've been frantic," Eleanor said. "I've been calling all night. Then I called Russell out on the Island thinking you might be there and he told me about Caroline. Where've you been? Is she all right?"

"Fine, fine," Strand said, trying to keep the resentment out of his voice. "Where are *you?*"

"My apartment. I just got in this evening. I want to come over."

"What for?" Strand asked, meanly.

"Don't be angry, please, Daddy. All I've done is get married. Can I come over?"

"I'll ask your mother." He turned to Leslie. "It's Eleanor. Do you want to see her tonight?"

"Of course. Ask her if she's eaten dinner. I can fix her something."

"We'll be waiting for you," Strand said. "But your mother wants to know if you've had your dinner. If you haven't she'll rustle up something for you here."

Eleanor laughed. "Good old Mummy. Feed the beasts first and ask questions later. Tell her not to worry, I've put on three pounds since the wedding day." Strand hung up. "She's eaten," he said to Leslie.

"Promise me you won't yell at her," Leslie said.

"Let her husband yell at her," Strand said. "I don't have the energy." He picked up a magazine and went into the kitchen, which had the last light in the apartment by which you could read, and sat at the table and stared at cartoons that did not seem funny in the harsh glare of the neon fixtures, which Leslie had installed when she found that she needed glasses to sew and read.

"Now," said Leslie, "from the beginning."

They were all sitting in the living room, which was most-ly in shadow since all but one of the room's lamps had already been packed. Eleanor had asked about her sister's morale. "Disturbingly high," Strand had said glumly, but Leslie had been reassuring.

Now Eleanor sat on the edge of a hard chair, looking younger and more beautiful than ever, Strand thought, at ease, unrepentant. "The beginning, of course," Eleanor said, "was last summer, not this one, when I clapped eyes on him in somebody's house in Bridgehampton and decided then and there that there was a man I must have."

Leslie looked uneasily over at Strand. He knew that his face showed what he thought of a daughter of his talking in terms like that, married or not.

"After a week, he asked me to marry him," Eleanor went on, a little note of triumph in her voice. "But he told me that sooner or later he was going to get out of New York and go work as a newspaperman in some little town that might be thousands of miles away from the city and he didn't believe that marriages ever worked if the husband lived in one place and the wife in another and I said, 'No, thank you, friend,' and we just—well—we just went on seeing each other. He introduced me to his family and most of them were as nice as could be, but his mother smoldered when she saw me. She was born in Italy and she's Catholic as they come and she goes to Mass Sundays and holidays and whenever there's an excuse in between and while it was all right for her darling son to spend an occasional sneaky weekend with a Protestant temptress, the idea of marriage would send her on her knees, holding a candle, to the nearest statue of the Virgin. Can you imagine it? In this day and age?"

Yes, Strand thought, I can imagine it. In this day and age oceans of blood have been shed because of a belief in one god or another. And the blood of children as yet unborn will flow for the same reasons. In that respect the devout mother of Giuseppe Gianelli was more up to date than his daughter.

"The old lady would get over it, Giuseppe said," Eleanor went on, "and as long as I didn't have to see her it was okay with me and we went our merry way until"—she stopped and her tone became grave—"until he went down to Georgia and the man said he could come and start in on the paper immediately. He called me from Georgia, I suppose Russell has told you about that part . . ."

"He told us," Strand said.

"He said he was taking the job," Eleanor said, serious now, "and that if I ever wanted to see him again I would have to marry him pronto." She sighed. "It was seven o'clock in the evening when he called me from Georgia. I told him I had to think about it. He gave me until the next morning. I can't pretend that I slept well that night. Mummy," she cried, "I can't live without him. What would you have done if Daddy had given you an ultimatum like that—and you knew he meant it?"

Leslie leaned over and touched Strand's hand. "I'd have done exactly what you did, dear," she said.

"You'd have been a damn fool," Strand said.

"No, I wouldn't," Leslie said softly.

"When I called Giuseppe back in the morning, I told

him yes," Eleanor said, her voice so low that Strand nearly couldn't make out the words.

"But Las Vegas," Strand said angrily. "What was the rush?"

"What would you have preferred?" Eleanor got up and paced around the room. "A big wedding with a priest and the relatives singing 'O Sole Mio' and the Mama looking dark Italian curses at the whole family? Frankly, if you must know, neither Giuseppe nor I wanted to give ourselves time to change our minds. What difference does it make? Anyway, Las Vegas was fast—instantaneous marriages— and it was fun. Giuseppe won twelve hundred dollars at blackjack. It paid for the ring. And the hotel. Please, Mummy, Daddy, don't be angry with me. I'm happy and I mean to remain happy. Would you feel better if I stayed in New York and went from one singles bar to another and got my name on the door as Assistant Vice President to the Assistant Vice President of the Overcharge and Complaint Division of the hundred and twentieth biggest computer company in America?"

"Stop raving," Leslie said crisply. She stood up and put her arms around Eleanor and kissed her on the forehead. "If you're happy, we're happy."

Eleanor looked over her mother's shoulder at Strand. "Does that go for you, too, Daddy?"

"I suppose so," Strand said wearily. "Where's your husband now?"

"In Graham, Georgia," Eleanor said. "The fastest growing, greatest little old town in the Sun Belt of the U.S. of A., Rotary Club meetings every Tuesday."

Strand couldn't tell whether she was laughing or crying. "Isn't he coming up here at all?"

"Only under cover of night. He's a brave man, but not brave enough to face Mama for a year or two. Do I have your blessing?" She broke away from Leslie and stood challengingly in front of him.

"I'm not the Pope. Blessings aren't in my line." Strand stood up and embraced her. "But I'll kiss you."

She hugged him fiercely. "Don't you think you ought to offer a toast to the newlyweds now?"

"There's nothing in the house," Strand said crossly. "Jimmy drank it all."

Eleanor laughed and Leslie said, "Oh, Allen."

"Now," Eleanor said, as she sat down comfortably, "the night's still young. Tell me about your holiday."

"It was glorious," Strand said, "but I'm sure you two ladies have a lot to talk about. I've had a big day and I'm going to bed."

Eleanor and Jimmy and Linda Roberts were already in the waiting room of the hospital early the next morning when Strand and Leslie arrived. Jimmy was wearing blue jeans and a black turtleneck sweater and had some sort of gold ornament hanging on a chain around his neck. His working clothes, Strand thought. But for once, at least, Jimmy looked grave. Caroline had just been wheeled up to the operating room, Eleanor said. She had already been under sedation but had waved sleepily once as she was wheeled past in the hall. Strand tried not to think of what was going on upstairs at the moment. The hospital smell was familiar, comforting, to him. He had been through it and had emerged. He had dreamed a great deal while he had been in the hospital, but had not remembered what the dreams were about, except that they had not been unpleasant. He hoped that in his daughter's dreams she won races, accepted trophies, danced in the arms of handsome young men.

Leslie had brought along some knitting and the sound of the needles clicked in the silence. She was knitting a sweater for him, he knew. The last time he remembered her knitting was when she sat beside him in the intensive care room. She was strictly a hospital knitter, he thought. The sweater, he hoped, would not be ready to wear until he was ninety.

The first time Leslie had gone to the hospital—to have Eleanor—he had started reading a Raymond Chandler mystery. As a rule he never read mystery stories, but it had been lying on a table in the hallway and he had picked it up. Leslie's confinement had been short and he had only managed to read a few pages before the doctor had come in to tell him he was the father of a daughter. Later, he hadn't remembered what was in the pages he had read and then when Leslie had to be rushed to the hospital when Jimmy was being born, he had taken along the same book, out of superstition. He had started the book all over again and again had only gotten through a few pages. He had kept the book in a safe place, to be ready for future births, and had taken it along when Caroline was born. But now, in the confusion of their preparing to move out of the apartment, he didn't know where the book was. He would have to find it before Eleanor had her first baby. Maybe then he would finally find out who had killed whom.

Hazen came in after they had been waiting almost an hour. He was tanned and healthy looking, out of place, Strand thought, in a hospital, although he had a bandage on his right hand. He had jammed it in a car door, he explained. He had also talked to Dr. Laird the day before and Laird had said the operation shouldn't take more than an hour and a half, at most, and that there was nothing to worry about. Caroline would be ready to go home after twenty-four hours.

Leslie was knitting faster and faster and the clicking was getting on Strand's nerves. He got up and went out into the corridor and began walking up and down, trying not to look into the open rooms in which people were lying with plastic bags on stands above their beds and tubes in their arms. The laughter of nurses at the end of the corridor offended him.

Hazen came out of the waiting room and paced silently beside him. Hazen cleared his throat, as though to gain Strand's attention. "Allen," he said, "this is as good a time as any to tell you. I don't want to talk in front of the others. First of all, Caroline wasn't in any automobile accident."

Strand stopped walking and stared at Hazen. "What're you talking about?"

"Remember when Laird asked me to come into his office when he got through examining Caroline?"

"Yes. When he told you he could change the shape of Caroline's nose."

"That wasn't all he said. He didn't just examine Caroline.

He quizzed her about what had happened. He told her it couldn't possibly have happened the way she said it had and that as her doctor he had to know the truth. She told him. The truth was that that boy, George, beat her up."

"What?" Strand's knees suddenly felt watery.

"They were sitting in a car all right," Hazen said soberly, "but not on any road. Near the beach. Alone. He tried to undress her and she fought him and he hit her."

"Oh, Christ."

"Filthy little swine. He'll never try anything like that again," Hazen said grimly. "Yesterday I gave him the thrashing of his life." He raised his bandaged hand. "I dislocated two knuckles. It was well worth it. And I went to his father and told him that if I ever saw his son around the Hamptons again, I'd ruin him. And the miserable old man knows I can do it. What's more, he's paying for the hospital and the operation." Hazen smiled grimly at this triumph of negotiation. Then his face grew serious again. "I've been debating with myself whether to tell you or not and finally I came to the conclusion you ought to know."

"Thank you," Strand said dully. "Of course."

"I don't think you ought to tell anybody else. Especially not Jimmy. Jimmy might think he would have to do something about it and God knows what that might lead to. The matter of young Master George is settled and it's best to leave it as it is. I'm afraid it was my responsibility. I invited the little shit to my house and he met Caroline there and it was up to me to take the necessary steps and they've been taken. I apologize to you and to your whole family."

"There's no need for apologies." Finally, Strand found a chair outside a closed door and sank into it, trembling, feeling waves of helpless fury sweep over him. If the boy had been standing in front of him at that moment he would have flung himself at him and tried to murder him, although he had never fought in his life and he wasn't strong enough yet to harm a kitten. But even knowing this he felt dishonored and ashamed that the punishment that should have rightly been his prerogative had been taken out of his hands.

"Are you all right?" Hazen asked anxiously, bending over him. "You're white as a sheet."

"Don't worry about me," Strand said thickly. "Just leave me alone for a minute, please."

Hazen took a long look at him, then went back into the waiting room. Strand was still sitting there, trying to keep his hands from shaking, when Dr. Laird came striding down the corridor. The doctor stopped when he saw him. "It's all over, Mr. Strand," the doctor said. "It came out perfectly. Your daughter will be down any minute now."

"Thank you," Strand said, without rising from the chair. "The others are in the waiting room. Please tell them."

The doctor patted him once on the shoulder, the gesture above and beyond the call of duty of the best-man-in-the-business, and went into the waiting room.

Strand was still there when they wheeled Caroline past him toward her room. He stood up and looked down at her. What he could see of her face which was half covered with bandages looked peaceful and like that of a sleeping and happy child.

He wept without knowing that he was weeping.

4

He was sitting alone in the light of a student lamp with a green glass shade at the big desk in the parlor of the Malson Residence, the house on the campus of Dunberry School for which the registrar had given him the keys. Jimmy had driven him down from New York in a car that he had borrowed from a friend. Jimmy had not been favorably impressed by the creaky old wooden house which, as far as could be foreseen, would be his parents' home for the remaining years of his father's working life. The housemaster's apartment, separated from the boys' quarters in the rest of the house by a long dark hall, was spacious enough, but the furniture was sparse and nondescript and showed signs of long hard use.

"It sure isn't the lap of luxury, is it, Pops?" Jimmy had said after he had carried Strand's bags in.

"We'll throw out most of the stuff," Strand had said. "Your mother's sending down a lot of our things and when she gets here I'm sure she'll make the place comfortable." Leslie had stayed in town because they couldn't leave Caroline alone while her head was still swathed in bandages. Dr. Laird had guaranteed that Caroline would be presentable and ready to travel in two weeks, when she had to go to Arizona for the beginning of her school term, and Leslie had decided to make the trip with her.

"I wish I could stay and keep you company, Pops," Jimmy said. "I hate the idea of you rattling around in this barn all by yourself for two weeks."

"I won't be alone," Strand said. "The boys are due to check in the day after tomorrow."

"How many kids do you have to be den mother to?"

"Only nine."

"God be with you, Pops."

"If I could handle you," Strand said, "I can handle any nine brats they wish on me. We're lucky. Some of the teachers in the big dorms have as many as sixty."

Jimmy laughed. "If any of them give you trouble, call on me. I'll blackmail Solomon into giving me another day off and I'll come down and beat up on them." He looked at his watch. "Well, I've got to be going. I've promised to get the car back before the office closes." Uncharacteristically, he came over and put his arms around his father and hugged him. "Please be serious. Kids can wear a saint down to the marrow."

"After the New York City school system this should be a parade," Strand said.

"Nothing's a parade these days." Jimmy shook his father's hand, scowled at the peeling wallpaper and went out. A moment later, Strand heard the sound of the car starting up and going off. Then the house was silent, a silence, he thought, that he would have to get used to after the constant hum of New York.

There was to be a tea later in the afternoon for the faculty in the headmaster's house. The registrar had given Strand a map of the campus so that he could find his way about. On his route he passed a practice football field, where the boys who were trying out for the team and so had come earlier than the rest of the student body were running through signals, hitting tackling dummies and throwing passes on the beautifully kept rich green turf. The campus itself with its Georgian dormitories and ivied walls looked more like a country club than a school and Strand smiled wryly to himself as he compared it to the grimy buildings in New York in which he had taught and to the hard-packed, dusty and grassless field of Lewisohn Stadium at City College. The stadium had been razed years ago and Strand, who had no nostalgic affection for the college, had not gone back since he had been graduated and had no notion of what buildings had been erected on the spot where undersized ghetto boys had struggled valiantly and usually to no avail on autumn Saturday afternoons.

City College no longer had a football team. Economy measures. Dunberry, it was plain, did not go in for economy measures.

The tea was being served on the lawn behind the headmaster's house, a sprawling white clapboard building with a pillared entrance. The guests were dressed informally and the whole affair reminded Strand of some of the assemblages Hazen had taken him to that summer in the Hamptons. Babcock's wife, a thick, powerful-looking woman in a flowered print dress and a large, wide-brimmed straw hat, took him around to introduce him and he heard a great many names and saw more than fifty faces he would have to sort out later. A surprising number of the guests were either bachelors or spinsters. Leslie, he knew, would regard that as a mark against the institution. She thought of the unmarried state as unnatural for anyone over twenty-five. He regretted that she wasn't there. She always remembered names and he always forgot them.

The people all seemed pleasant enough, although the marks of failure and resignation were on some of the faces, especially those of the older members of the teaching staff, and he guessed from the stiffness of some of his colleagues that they, too, were there for the first time and that the rate of turnover in the school was probably high. Babcock, the headmaster, invited him to dinner with his wife, but he declined, saying he'd pick up something in town, which was only a half mile from the campus. He thought he saw a look of relief on Babcock's face. The man probably saw enough of his staff throughout the school year and was in no hurry to cope with the problem of a semi-invalid stranger who had been wished on him by a man to whom he owed favors.

The walk into town in the summery dusk, with the first touch of autumn spicing the air, was a pleasant one and the little café in which he ate a simple meal was clean and welcoming. A new life, he thought, as he drank his coffee in the nearly empty restaurant. Aged fifty and I'm starting all over again.

God be with you, Jimmy had said.

He ordered another cup of coffee and thought back on what would probably be his last week in New York for a long time. Hazen had called him from his office and told him that he had Romero in his office and that the boy was looking forward to going to Dunberry.

"I don't think you're going to have any trouble with him. We had a nice talk and he listened carefully as I told him how we expected him to behave once he got to the school. He's in the outer office now. I told him to wait until I finished talking to you. I told him he'd be assigned to your house, so you can keep an eye on him."

"Charming," Strand murmured. He half wished that Romero would change his mind.

"He seems meek as a lamb," Hazen said. "He's obviously highly intelligent and motivated. I think he's going to be a credit to us. Anyway, it's certainly worth taking the chance. I told him I'd stake him to a set of new clothes and he was pleased. He needs every advantage we can give him and he certainly can't appear at the school in the kind of clothes he's wearing today. I've made up a list of the sort of things the other boys'd be wearing. I have an account at Brooks Brothers and I wonder if it would be too much bother for you to meet him tomorrow and outfit him."

"Of course not," Strand said. "Leslie wants me out of the house as much as possible these days."

"Good. Ten o'clock, in front of Brooks Brothers. Okay with you?"

"Fine."

"I'll give him the list. My secretary's typed it up and I'll give it to Romero to show you. Of course, you can use your discretion, too. I've just put down the fundamentals. I think five hundred dollars should take care of everything, don't you?"

"I have no idea."

"If you have to go over that, don't hesitate."

"Just tell him that if he packs in that damn football jersey he wore every day to school, I won't acknowledge that I've ever seen him before in my life."

Hazen laughed. "I'll tell him. Well, when I have the time, I'll come down to the school to see how you're both doing. I'm sure it will be a welcome change for you if not for Romero."

As he hung up Strand was not so sure.

The next morning Romero was waiting for him at the Brooks Brothers entrance, which was a surprise in itself. At school Romero was almost invariably late for classes. To Strand's relief, the boy was reasonably presentable. He had had his hair cut and wasn't wearing the football jersey, but instead a battered jacket that was much too large for him.

"Here's the list, sir," he said as they entered the store. It was the first time, Strand noticed, that the boy had called him sir, and he took it as a good sign. "Mr. Hazen said your word would be law." He didn't sound hostile. Perhaps, Strand thought, Hazen had been right in his estimate of Romero's new attitude.

In the store he had the air of a tense and watchful hunting animal as Strand ordered a large traveling bag and Romero was fitted for pants, jackets, sweaters and shirts, shoes and socks and an overcoat. He made no suggestions and accepted what Strand chose without a word. He had grown a little over the summer, but would never be a tall man. Strand hoped that the other boys in the house would not be football players or wrestlers.

Strand was shocked at what everything cost, but managed to keep the bill just under five hundred dollars. However, he doubted that five hundred dollars or even five thousand dollars worth of Brooks Brothers clothing would ever succeed in making Jesus Romero, with his dark, sardonic face and wild, resentful, wary eyes, look as though he belonged in a sleepy New England school which had prepared boys to go to Harvard and Yale and Williams and Dartmouth for over a hundred years.

While the clerks were making up the bill, Romero said, "I got a favor to ask you, sir. Do you think you could tell them to send everything up to your apartment, so I could pick them up on the day I leave for the school?"

"Why?" Strand asked, puzzled.

"If they're sent to my house either my mother or my

brother'll steal them and sell them." He said this without criticism, as though this was to be expected in all families.

"I suppose that can be arranged," Strand said and wrote out his address and told Romero that he'd make sure his wife would be expecting the delivery.

"Thank you, sir."

When they had finished in the store it was time for lunch. Strand thought it was as good an opportunity as any to see how Romero behaved at the table. Fearing the worst, he took him to a small, dark restaurant which seemed to be patronized by clerks and stenographers from the big office building in the neighborhood. In the dark, Strand thought, only he would be able to see just what Romero's manners were like. But his fears turned out to be groundless. Romero ate like a hungry boy, but he didn't wolf his food or mangle it or use the wrong knives and forks. From what he had said about his mother, Strand doubted that it was because of his mother that he ate decorously. Probably, Strand thought, it was the result of watching hours of television, where actors were always sitting down to meals and pretending that they had eaten at "21" all their lives. Score one for television, he thought.

He had to make most of the conversation. When he asked Romero what he had done during the summer Romero merely shrugged and said, "I hung around."

"Do any reading?"

"Some. Most of it crap."

"What books, exactly?"

"I've forgotten the names," Romero said. Strand was sure he was lying. "The only thing that stuck with me was *The History of the Decline and Fall of the Roman Empire.* By a guy called Gibbon. You ever hear of him?" He was glancing across the table at Strand with an expression that on an ordinary boy his age would have been mischievous.

"Yes, I've heard of him," Strand said, not giving Romero the satisfaction of showing that he was annoyed at the taunt. "What did you like about it?"

"I didn't say I liked it. It just agreed with some of my ideas."

"Like what?"

Romero took a package of cigarettes out of his pocket and what looked like an expensive lighter. He offered Strand a cigarette, but when Strand shook his head, he said, "Oh, I forgot. You don't smoke. My ideas . . . well, that nothing is permanent. Those old Romans, they thought they had the world by the tail, they lorded it over everybody and went around telling people how wonderful they were and thought they were doing the poor dopes in other countries a big favor by making them Roman citizens and thought they were real tough bastards and would last forever. So the real tough bastards, the barbarians, the Goths, they didn't take baths or use vomitoriums and they didn't write poetry and waste their time throwing people to the lions and making big speeches and putting up triumphal arches to themselves and they didn't wear purple togas and they came from the wrong side of the railroad tracks and all they knew how to do was wipe out Romans. They were my kind of cats and I rooted for them all the way. And Mr. Gibbon wasn't just writing history. Two centuries before the shit hit the fan he was really writing about the English Empire, where the sun never set, whether he knew it or not, and the fat-ass bastard Americans and it made me realize that when the time comes I'm going to be one of the Goths. And a lot of people who live in my neighborhood and neighborhoods like mine are going to find out they're tough-bastard Goths too, and do their own wiping out even if some of them like me get up and disguise themselves in purple togas from Brooks Brothers."

It was the longest speech Strand had ever heard him make and he couldn't say he was pleased with it, despite the logic and despite the fact that many older and more erudite men than Jesus Romero had written more or less the same thing about Gibbon, although in somewhat politer terms.

"My advice to you, Romero," he said, "is to keep ideas like that to yourself when you have to write essays in your history classes."

He grinned at Strand malevolently. "Don't worry, Professor, I'll wear my purple toga at all times. I wouldn't like to see you kicked out of your job."

Strand stood up and paid the bill and told him he'd see him at the school and that he knew there was a rule there that the only place boys could smoke was in the basement of the main hall. And they had to be seniors at that.

God be with you, Strand thought.

He went out into the balmy night.

Back in the Malson Residence he saw that the maid, whom he had not yet met, had been in and made the twin beds and drawn the curtains. He would have to make sure that Leslie sent their big double bed down with the rest of the things. Since the terrible night in Tours, they had slept together. He wasn't going to start sleeping alone at his age.

Then he sat down at the desk in the living room under the glow of the student lamp and began writing in the student's copy book that he had brought with him from the city.

I am starting a new life and I intend to keep a diary from now on. Perhaps if I put everything down in writing, or at least bits and pieces that may eventually form a pattern, I will better understand what is happening to me. Everything is changing and I am being overtaken by events. Time is pressing me and I feel my age. If history is a means of understanding the past, a small, everyday record of the present may help make some sense of the future.

It is a season of departures. First Eleanor, happily driving off to her new husband and a new profession, leaving the city in which she was born and reared with a brisk kiss and a wave of the hand. Then saying good-bye to Caroline; no happiness there. She is progressing well, the doctor says. Progressing toward what? Since she still is wearing bandages, there is still no telling what she will look like when they are all finally taken off. She is outwardly composed about the whole thing and I heard her humming cheerfully to herself as she went about packing, getting ready for her trip to Arizona. Leslie is going to accompany her and help settle her in, although Caroline is impatient with the idea.

Although I am not happy about having to go off to Dunberry by myself, I am convinced that Caroline should not make the trip alone and have told her so. Her ostentatious

*humming and her composure seemed false to me from the
beginning. My fears were confirmed in the worst possible
way when I passed her closed door one day when Leslie
was out and heard sobbing from behind it. I opened the
door and saw her crouched on the floor in the corner of
the room beating her head against the wall and weeping. I
bent down to her and held her in my arms and after a while
she calmed down. She wiped her eyes with the back of her
hands and essayed a smile. "It's just only once in a while,
Daddy," she said. "Maybe it's the rain."*

*I am also almost equally worried about Leslie. Although
on the surface she is matter-of-fact and in control of herself, there are little things that have changed in her. She
has always been competent and sure of herself, but in the
last days I spent in New York I caught her in moments
when she was remote, irresolute, floating from room to
room with a few books in her arms or carrying sheets of
music as though she didn't know what to do with them and
putting them down in odd places, then hunting for them
distractedly later on, only to put them down again a few
minutes later in unlikely corners.*

*I haven't spoken to Leslie or Caroline or anyone else
about how Caroline had her nose broken. I imagine Caroline would like to forget about it and about lying to us.
And I dread to think what Leslie would do if she knew the
truth. I am still not so sure about myself, either. If I were
to happen to see the boy who hit her and there were a
murderous weapon handy I'm afraid I might use it.*

Strand's hand trembled and he stopped writing and
stared at the last paragraph. His usual neat handwriting
had suddenly degenerated into an almost unreadable
scrawl. He put the pen down and pushed away from the
desk. Time, he realized, had not immunized him against
the almost intolerable rage that had first swept over him
in the hospital corridor when Hazen had told him about
Caroline's confession to Dr. Laird.

Jimmy would say he was overreacting. Parents are made
to overreact. He stood up and went to the French door
that opened onto the garden. He went out and breathed

deeply, trying to calm himself, taking in great gulps of the fragrant night air. He wished he had had the foresight to buy himself a bottle of whiskey.

He looked up at the sky. The stars in the pure darkness above him were bright. A crescent moon was rising and the old trees at the bottom of the garden, their foliage rustling in the light breeze, cast flickering shadows on the dew-damp lawn. If I can forget the past, he thought, or at least manage it, I can be happy in this gentle place.

The next morning he woke early enough to have breakfast in the dining room at the main hall with the rest of the faculty, but he didn't want to try fitting half a hundred faces to the names he had heard the evening before. He walked into town, enjoying the freshness of the morning and the sight of children playing with dogs on the lawns of the neat houses he passed on the way. He bought a copy of *The New York Times*, but a glance at the headlines made him fold the paper and keep it for later reading. The morning, with its sunshine and nature's profligate promise of hope, was no time for this year's news. The evening, with the melancholy of growing darkness and its hint of mortality and endings, was more suitable for the reports from Washington, Iran, Moscow, Jerusalem, and the southern hemisphere.

When he got back to the Malson Residence, trying to curb his natural fast lope out of deference to Dr. Prinz's advice, he found a huge black man sitting on the front steps. The man—no, he thought, he couldn't be more than eighteen, despite his size—stood up politely. "Mr. Strand?" he asked.

"Yes."

"I'm Alexander Rollins," the boy said. "I'm assigned to this house."

They shook hands and Rollins smiled shyly. "I'm on the football team and I've been sleeping in the Worthington Dormitory with the rest of the team, but I thought, if you didn't mind, I'd move in a day earlier. It gets pretty riotous on moving day, they tell me, with mamas and papas messing around and all." He had a rich, slurry voice and a proper New England enunciation and it occurred to Strand that perhaps he should be encouraged to take up singing seriously. He would tell Leslie about him.

"Of course," Strand said. "You're in room number three on the top floor." The registrar had given him a list of nine boys who would live in the house and had paired them off, two to a room, alphabetically, the ninth boy in a small room to himself. Rollins would be sharing the room with Romero. The registrar hadn't told him Rollins was black, or rather, a deep, glowing brown. "I hope you'll like it here."

"I'm sure I will," Rollins said. "I'm new here, too. I'm on a one-year football scholarship. I played for my high school in Waterbury and I wasn't the smartest kid in my class"—he grinned—"and everybody figured that no matter how many times a season I sacked the quarterback, another year at the books would help if I wanted to get into a place like Yale."

"My daughter is on an athletic scholarship to a little college in Arizona," Strand said, suddenly and for the first time proud of that fact. "She's a runner."

"That's more than can be said for me," Rollins said. "I'm a defensive tackle. Mostly I just try to stand my ground." He laughed. "I'll bet your daughter could beat me down under a punt every time. Girls these days . . ." He shook his head humorously.

"I hope she stands her ground, too," Strand said. "In other ways."

Rollins looked at him very seriously. "I hope so, too," he said. "Well, I won't take up any more of your time, sir. I'll just move in my stuff after the morning practice session."

"I'll leave the door open for you."

"There's no need to worry. Nobody steals anything around here."

"I come from New York," Strand said. "Everybody steals everything there."

"So I've heard." The boy shook his head. "Waterbury is bad enough and it ain't a pimple compared to the size of New York. I hope you're happy here, Mr. Strand. Every-

body says this is a right nice friendly place and I hope it
turns out that way for both of us. If you and your wife
ever need some heavy pushing and hauling, furniture and
stuff like that, please call on me. I may not be smart"—he
grinned again—"but I've got a strong back. Now I have
to get over to the field and run my poor sagging butt off."
He moved off with an athlete's easy walk, his close-
cropped head looking too small on the great trunk of neck
which jutted up out of his sweater.

Strand went into the house, thinking about the two R's
—Rollins and Romero. A black boy and a Puerto Rican.
Would Romero, with his street cynicism, think "Of course,
keep the black brother and the not quite white brother
segregated in their nice genteel way"? Would he accept that
it was just an accident of the alphabet? The registrar had
told him that if any of the boys wanted to change rooms
and nobody objected it could be done. But what if all the
other boys were satisfied with the arrangement as it was
and no changes could be made? He didn't know how many
blacks were included in the student body or how they were
selected. Rollins because he could play football, although
Strand was a little shocked that a school with the reputation of Dunberry would recruit its teams so openly. After
all, Dunberry wasn't Notre Dame or Alabama. And Romero because, by a fluke of random conversation, a powerful man had become interested in him. What of the others?
He would have to ask around discreetly what the school's
policy actually was.

He went into the big common room, where there was a
radio and a television set and some bookcases with volumes
stacked haphazardly on the shelves. He started putting them
in order and realized he was looking for a copy of *The
History of the Decline and Fall of the Roman Empire*. If
he was going to have to argue for a year with Jesus Romero
he would have to start by rereading Gibbon and very carefully, indeed. But the only books he found whose authors
began with G were *Inside Africa*, by John Gunther, and
The Affluent Society, by John Kenneth Galbraith, neither
of which he felt would be of much use to him in a debate
with Romero. He could imagine the hoots of laughter if

by chance the boy, with a mother on welfare, picked up the Galbraith book. He took the book off the shelf and carried it into his apartment and put it on the table in the bedroom. If he had found *The Conquest of Mexico* and *The Conquest of Peru,* although they were two of his favorite volumes of history, he would have hidden them, too, as additional fuel to Romero's smoldering assortment of resentments.

He knew that Caroline had an appointment that morning at eight o'clock with Dr. Laird, before he began his day's operations, and while he didn't expect there would be any important developments to report in her condition, he decided to telephone, admitting to himself that he was doing it more to hear Leslie's voice than for information about his daughter. As he dialed he told himself that he would have to ration his calls. At his salary long distance telephoning was a dangerous luxury.

It was Caroline who answered the phone. "Oh, Daddy," she said, "I'm so glad you called. Dr. Laird has turned out to be Santa Claus. He looked at my nose and took some more X rays and he said in a week I can take off all the bandages and I'll look like a human being again. Mummy says we'll have time to come and visit you for a couple of days before we go west. Isn't that something?"

"Santa Claus is right," Strand said. "The next time you see him tell him it's Christmas for me, too. And when you come wear the ugliest long dress you own. There'll be four hundred boys here from tomorrow on."

Caroline giggled. "Oh, I don't think it's going to be *that* startling. But wouldn't it be nice if it was?"

"No," Strand said. "Now let me talk to your mother."

Leslie's voice, too, was cheerful. "Caroline told you," she said. "Isn't it wonderful? And how are *you* doing?"

"As well as can be expected. The people are nice and while the house is an old barn, a woman's touch will do marvels for the place. And you're the woman whose touch is needed."

"All in due time, dear." But she sounded pleased. "Is there anything special you need that we can bring when we come down?"

"Only our bed."

"Incorrigible." But she sounded even more pleased. "By the way, your young friend, Romero, came by just a few minutes ago for his clothes. He said he thought he'd come down today instead of tomorrow. He seemed very eager. I think you're wrong about that boy. His manners were perfect."

"He's a consummate actor. What did Caroline think of him?"

"She didn't see him. You know how she is these days. When she heard the bell ring she locked herself in her room. He asked if he could get dressed in his new clothes in the bathroom. When he came out he looked quite handsome in his small way. He made a strange request. He said he'd left all his clothes in the bathroom and he asked me to burn them."

"If he was dressed the way he usually is, it's not so strange. Enough about him. How are you?"

"Fine." She hesitated. "I have a confession to make to you. Mrs. Ferris, you remember her, she's the headmistress of Caroline's school, called last week and asked me if I could arrange to come in one day a week and give private lessons to the students. She said I could use the music room. There won't be many. I'd only keep the best of my students."

"Why is that a confession?"

"Because I didn't tell you. You had enough on your mind as it was."

"Do you want to do it?"

Leslie hesitated again. "Yes," she said. "Do you think the people at Dunberry would mind?"

"I'm sure it could be fitted into your schedule. I'll ask today."

"Don't do it if it's any trouble, dear."

"It's no trouble at all."

"It would mean I'd have to stay over in New York someplace for the night."

"I guess I can survive one night."

"Are you taking things easy?"

"I'm not doing anything. I drank tea with the faculty

d the boys don't arrive till tomor-
found a big hulk of a football play-
to move the piano around for us. I
to love the place," he said with all the
id muster.

we will." Leslie didn't sound absolutely con-
It's beautiful in New York today. Indian sum-
She didn't say why she thought it was necessary to
port on the city's weather.

"Have you heard from Jimmy or Eleanor?"

"Out of sight, out of mind. But I'll try to get Jimmy to
come down to the school with us. This call must be costing
a fortune. We'll save all the news for when we see each
other. Good-bye, dear."

"Good-bye, my love," he whispered. One night a week,
he remembered, as he hung up.

There was a knock on the door and he called, "Come in."

A plump woman dressed in baggy black slacks and a
sweater stretched tight over an enormous, pillowy bosom
entered. She was carrying a large shopping bag and had a
rosy complexion and dyed blond hair. "Good morning,
Mr. Strand," she said. "I'm Mrs. Schiller. I'm your housekeeper here. I hope you found everything in order."

"Fine, fine." Strand shook her hand. It was soft, but
strong. "You only have to make up one of the beds. My
wife won't be coming along for some days. And two of
the boys will be arriving today. Their names are Rollins
and Romero and they're assigned to room three."

"The boys take care of their own rooms," Mrs. Schiller
said. Her voice was gruff, as though she smoked too many
cigarettes. "I occasionally straighten up the common room
for them when the disorder reaches a certain point. And
once in a while I take a peek upstairs to see if any of the
walls have been torn down." She smiled. She had a warm,
motherly smile. "I passed through the dining room this
morning and noticed you weren't there for breakfast. My
husband works in the kitchen, he's a baker, and I help out
until the full staff is on duty. Would you like me to buy
some things to put in the refrigerator? Snacks, fruit, things
like that? Until your wife arrives?"

"That would be very kind of you."

"If you'd like to make up a list . . ."

"Anything you think I should have will do perf
Strand said. He didn't mention the fact that he would
a bottle of whiskey in the house. He would do the shopp.
for that himself. He didn't know how discreet the woma
was, and he didn't want to take the chance that she woulu
spread the word that the new history teacher was a solitary
drinker.

"Is there anything special you want to tell me?" she
asked.

"Nothing. Oh—one thing. Please don't touch anything
on the desk, no matter how jumbled it looks."

She smiled again. "In a school, where everybody lives
on paper, you learn that lesson right away," she said. "I've
seen some desks that mice could have lived on among the
books and papers and magazines for years without being
discovered. If there's anything you and your wife disapprove of, please let me know right off. The couple who
were here until the summer were too shy to tell me the
way they liked things and I was constantly catching the
lady rearranging furniture and moving plants from one
place to another and looking guilty when she saw me in
the room. I want you and the missus to enjoy living here."

"Thank you very much, Mrs. Schiller. I fully expect to."

"One last thing, Mr. Strand," she said, as she opened the
bag she was carrying and took out an apron, which she tied
around her ample waist, "if ever you want anything special
in the way of baked goods—canapés for a party or a birthday cake—just let me know. My husband likes to do little
odd jobs for the faculty and the boys. It breaks the routine,
he says."

"I'll remember that. I have three children—they're grown
and they won't be living with us but we may be lucky and
have them for visits from time to time and they're all
fiends for chocolate cake." He found that it gave him pleasure to talk to this nice and helpful woman about his
children. "Do you have any children?"

"God has not seen fit to bless us," Mrs. Schiller said solemnly. "But with four hundred boys storming around the

place, it almost makes up for it. Oh, I nearly forgot—be careful about the pilot light on the stove. It's ancient and it has a habit of going out and the gas collects."

"I promise to watch the pilot light like a hawk."

"The house nearly blew up last February. The couple was as nice as could be, but they were a little vague, if you know what I mean."

"I do, indeed. I might be a little vague myself, but my wife is a demon of responsibility."

"Just tell me when you expect her to arrive and I'll cut some flowers and put them around to welcome her. It's a wonder what a few flowers can do for this old house. And I'll have some wood brought in for a fire. Some of the boys make a little extra money clearing branches and cutting down dead trees and sawing them up for firewood. The nights get nippy around here and a fire's a comfort. Well, I won't disturb you anymore. I'm sure you've got a lot of work to do preparing for the invasion. And if you don't mind my saying so, I think you ought to take a little time off and take some walks. It would help your complexion." She sounded more like a nurse who had been in the family for years than a cleaning woman he had just met a few minutes ago. As she went out of the room, Strand felt he had something on the plus side to report in his next conversation with Leslie.

He looked in the mirror over the fireplace. The tan of the summer had vanished from his face and he decided he did look a little greenish. He went out. He would heed Mrs. Schiller's admonition and take a long walk to town, improving his complexion and finding a shop where he could buy a bottle of whiskey.

Romero arrived in the dark, after dinner, which Strand had eaten in town, still postponing the moment when he would have to make small talk over food with the men and women of the faculty. If Leslie had been there he knew that she would have been calling at least half a dozen of them by their first names and would have made estimates of their various characters that later would turn out to be mysteriously accurate. He did not have that quick talent and depended upon time and slowly growing familiarity to develop his judgment of people. It saved him, he told Leslie, from unpleasant surprises.

He was standing at the entrance of the Malson Residence, looking up at the stars, a little reluctant to go into the empty house, when he saw a small figure, carrying a bag much too large for him, toiling across the campus from the direction of the main building. Under the light of the lamps along the asphalt paths he saw that Romero was wearing some of the clothes from Brooks Brothers, slacks and a tweed jacket and a collar and tie.

"Good evening, Romero," he said as the boy came up to him. "I'd just about given up hope of seeing you here today. What happened? You get lost?"

"I never get lost," Romero said, letting the heavy bag down on the lawn and rubbing his shoulder. "Nobody has to send out search parties for me. I met a girl on the train, she was on her way to New London for a job as a waitress and we got into a conversation and she seemed okay, she used to be a stripper, she told me, and we decided to stop off and have an afternoon in New Haven. I never had anything to do with a striptease artist before and I thought this might be the last chance in a long while and I bought her lunch and we saw the sights of New Haven and then I put her on the train again and I grabbed the bus and here I am, ready for further education." He looked around him with distaste. "This place sure is dead. What do they do—shoot everybody who's out on the street after dark?"

"Wait until tomorrow," Strand said. "You'll need a traffic cop to get across to the dining room. Have you eaten? There are some things in the refrigerator."

"I'm not hungry. But I sure could use a drink. Got any beer in the joint?"

"I'm afraid not," Strand said coldly. He didn't mention that in one of the kitchen cupboards there was a bottle of whiskey still in the plain brown paper bag in which he had carried it back from town. "I believe that there's a rule here that the students are not permitted to drink."

"Beer is *drink*?" Romero said incredulously. "What is this, a convent?"

"This is a boys' school," Strand said. "Notice I said *boys*. Here, let me help you with that bag. It looks awfully heavy. I'll show you to your room." He bent to pick up the bag and had trouble lifting it from the ground. "What have you got in here—bricks?"

Romero grinned. "Gibbon's *Decline and Fall of the Roman Empire*. In seven volumes."

As they climbed the stairs to the top floor, with both of them taking turns carrying the bag, Strand said, "Your roommate's already here. He's the only one besides you until tomorrow. He's on the football team."

"I would have brought my football jersey that you liked so much, Professor," Romero said, "but they're retiring my number and putting it in a glass case in the high school gymnasium."

"You'll find, Romero," Strand said, "that your sense of humor will not be admired as much here as it was in New York."

As they neared the top floor they heard rock music, being played very loudly.

"What've they got up there—a disco?" Romero said. "By the way, what's the policy on girls, Professor?"

"I don't believe your striptease artist will be welcomed here," Strand said. "Dunberry is connected to a sister school. But it's five miles from here."

"Love will find a way," Romero said airily.

The door to the room was open and the light from it poured into the corridor. Rollins was lying on his bed with his shoes off and was reading a book. A cassette machine was blaring on a table just a few inches from his ear. But he stood up quickly when he saw Strand and Romero and turned off the machine.

"This is your roommate, Rollins—Jesus Romero."

"My name is pronounced, Haysooss," Romero said.

"Sorry," Strand said. He never had had the occasion to use the Christian names of his students at the high school and he was afraid that his mispronunciation of Romero's name was a bad start for his relations with the boy at Dunberry. "I'll remember from now on."

Rollins put out his hand and after a suspicious glance

Romero shook it. "Welcome, Haysooss," Rollins said. "I hope you like music."

"Some music," Romero said.

Rollins laughed, a deep, rumbling, good-natured sound. "At least you won't take up much space, brother," he said. "That's right considerate of Mr. Strand, considering my size and the size of the room."

"I had nothing to do with it," Strand said quickly. "It's all done alphabetically. Well, I'll leave you two to get acquainted. Lights're supposed to be out by ten thirty."

"I haven't gone to bed by ten thirty since I was two," Romero said.

"I didn't say you had to sleep. Just that the lights have to be out." Strand knew he sounded testy and regretted it. "Good night."

He went out of the room, but stopped a few feet from the door to listen. What he heard came as no surprise to him. "Well, black brother," Romero was saying, in an exaggerated Southern accent, "I see they've got slave quarters and everything on this good ole plantation."

As quietly as possible Strand went down the stairs to his apartment. He looked at the bottle of whiskey in its brown paper bag on the cupboard shelf, but didn't open it. He had the feeling he would need it more on other nights.

5

It would be self-delusion on my part to pretend that what I am doing is actually keeping a diary. The school term is now one week old and I am too tired at the end of each day to do more than glance over notes for the next day's classes or nod over a newspaper or magazine. The first day, when the boys arrived, was pure bedlam—greeting parents who either had special praise or special requests for their offspring or who took me aside to confide that a son had to be watched to make sure he took a certain medicine for anemia every night, or that another had a masturbation problem, or still another daydreamed in class and needed constant vigilance in respect to his studies to help keep up with his grades.

The boys, when I finally managed to sort one out from the other, seemed like an average group of well brought up young people, polite with their elders, if somewhat condescending, and boisterous with each other. I see no particular difficulties in the future with them. Romero and Rollins seem to be getting along splendidly and in fact Rollins has persuaded Romero to go out for the football team, although Romero cannot weigh more than a hundred and forty pounds and Rollins must weigh at least two hundred and ten. But in an impromptu game of touch football the first day on the campus grounds, Romero, who had been standing to one side watching, had been impressed to fill a side which had lost one of the players because of a slightly sprained ankle and ran for a touchdown the first time he got his hands on the ball. I watched him with amazement, since I had never heard him express interest in any sport, as he sprinted and wheeled and cut

*back and squirmed away from the arms of boys twice his
size. He seemed as unpredictable as a wood dove in flight
and his sudden twisting runs left his pursuers panting
helplessly behind him. Perhaps, I thought, half-joking to
myself, it was just this gift that had kept him from being
caught and arrested by the New York City police.*

*That night Rollins talked to him seriously and took him
down to see the football coach and somehow the next
afternoon they had found a uniform small enough for
him and he was on the football squad. Although I feared
what the result would be when he was hit in a real scrim-
mage by a mass of brutes who all towered over him, it
boded well for his acceptance by the other students.*

A few days after the beginning of the term a message
was left for Strand that the headmaster would like to see
him at his convenience. When he went to Babcock's office
he was greeted warmly but nervously. "We have a little
problem," Babcock said. "It's about Jesus Romero."

"Ah," Strand said.

"Exactly," Babcock said. "Ah. It seems that Romero
has been skipping chapel. As you may know, we have to
abide by certain terms which we accepted when we were
bequeathed the endowment fund which kept this school
going when it looked as though it was going to founder
in the 1960s. It was a most generous gift—most generous.
The new field house is a result of it; our library, which is
one of the finest in any school in the East; many other
amenities. . . . The old lady who left us the money in her
will happened to be an extremely religious woman with a
strong mind of her own and one condition laid down in
her will was that every student attend chapel every school
day. She also added the condition that all boys wear
jackets and ties in the dining room. Other schools have
moved away from these customs. We can't. I wonder if
you can reason with Romero before I have to take official
action against him."

"I'll try," Strand said.

"You've seen for yourself, the services are practically
nondenominational. Almost anodyne. There are quite a

few Catholic and Jewish boys enrolled and they seem to
have no difficulties in bending to the rules of the school.
You might mention this to Romero."

"I will," Strand said. "I'm sorry he's causing you all
this trouble."

"There are bound to be worse ones before the term is
up. And not only with Romero," Babcock said.

Strand called Romero in to see him after classes and
told him what the headmaster had said, using all the
headmaster's arguments. Romero listened in silence, then
shook his head. "I don't care about the Jews and the other
Catholics," he said. "I'm my own kind of Catholic."

"When was the last time you went to Mass?" Strand
asked.

Romero grinned. "When I was baptized. I don't believe
in God. If I have to choose between chapel and leaving
school I'll go pack my bag."

"Are you sure you want me to tell Mr. Babcock that?"

"Yes."

"You're dismissed," Strand said.

When Strand reported his conversation with Romero
the next day to Babcock, the headmaster sighed. A good
part of his conversation, Strand realized, was punctuated
by sighs. "Well," he said, "if nobody makes a noise about
it I guess we can live with it."

"There's another thing," Strand said. "It's about my
wife. She has no classes on Wednesday and none until ten
in the morning on Thursdays. Would you think it an imposition if she went into New York each Wednesday? She
has several pupils she doesn't want to give up."

"I quite understand," Babcock said. "Of course."

Strand went out of his office, thinking what a decent
and intelligent and flexible man. Already so early in the
term, Strand had felt how easily and calmly the school was
run, how discipline was kept with very little constraint.
There was an easygoing friendliness between the boys and
the faculty that provided an invigorating climate for the
process of teaching and learning and Strand was rediscov-
ering some of the sense of hope that he had in his early
years as a teacher.

"You're lucky Mr. Babcock is such a lenient man," Strand said to Romero the next day. He had let the boy sweat for a night before telling him of Babcock's decision. "He's going to keep you on. Just don't tell everybody about it. And you might write him a note of thanks."

"Did you ask him if *he* believed in God?"

"Don't press your luck, young man," Strand said shortly.

Romero took a piece of paper out of his pocket and unfolded it. "There's something here you have to sign, Mr. Strand," he said. "It's the permission from my mother for me to play on the football team. I just got it this afternoon."

Strand looked at the paper. It was a form printed by the athletic department, with a space for a parent's signature and one for the signature of the housemaster attesting to the genuineness of the parent's signature. In this case it was merely a scrawled X in pencil. As Strand looked at it Romero looked at him with the challenging direct dark stare that Strand still found uncomfortable. But even then, this evidence of the transition in one generation from an illiterate mother to an adolescent who could argue heatedly about the works of Edward Gibbon made Strand think more kindly than usual of the working of the American public school system.

When he gave the form, as required, to Mr. Johnson, the football coach, a serious and devout young man who conducted prayers before each game in the locker room in which he asked God not for victory but for the safety of the players on both teams, he raised his eyebrows at the X. "I suppose this is legal," he said.

"I would think so," Strand told him.

"Anyway," he said, "the *kid* can read signals." Then, with a smile, "Even though he rarely follows them. He drives the other boys crazy. They never know what he's going to do. If he's called to go around end and things don't look too good for him there, he just turns around and goes through center or even around the other end. He does everything wrong and I bawl him out for it, but it doesn't help much. And it's hard to be too tough on him. At his size it takes guts to even be out there, and then, most of the time he gets away with it. Somehow, he's out in the open and making big hunks of yardage. He's like an eel—nobody can really get hold of him. It's almost as though he's escaping from a lynching party. I don't think he cares whether we win or lose a game, he just wants to show everybody that he's uncatchable. I tell you something, Mr. Strand, in all the time I've played football and coached it, I never set eyes on a kid like this before. He's not like an athlete—he's like some kind of wild animal. It's like having a crazy panther on the squad."

"Is he going to make the team?" Strand asked.

The coach shrugged. "I don't intend to use him much. He's too small to stay in there regularly. Somebody would finally eat him up alive. It's not like the old days. The boys today are monsters, even at our level, and the big ones run just as fast as the small ones. Anyway, the kid can't block or catch passes. If I can teach him how to hold on to punts maybe I'll put him in to run back kicks. Otherwise I'll just use him on special plays when we're praying for a long breakaway run. When I told him I was going to keep him on the squad, I said, almost as a joke, he was going to have a lot of time sitting on the bench, I was only going to put him in when we were desperate. He just smiled up at me—small as he is he's got a smile that would scare a sergeant in the marines—and he said, 'Coach, that's the job for me, I've been desperate all my life.'"

"Is he popular with the other boys?" Strand didn't think it was the time to tell that serious young religious man that he had a Goth in his backfield.

The coach looked at Strand speculatively as though debating with himself whether to tell the truth or give him half an answer. "You have a special interest in the boy, I understand," he said. "He's here more or less because of you, isn't he?"

"More or less. He was in my class in high school and was an extraordinary student."

"Well, if his roommate Rollins wasn't so protective of him, I think somebody would have taken a swing at him by now. He doesn't bother to keep his opinions to himself, does he?"

Strand couldn't help smiling. "Not so you could notice it," he said.

"When he fakes a man out on a run or somebody in front of him misses a block, he—well, he sneers at them. And he has a favorite phrase that's getting on the boys' nerves—'I thought you gentlemen were here to play football.' He divides himself and Rollins from the rest of the team with something he must have picked up in reading English literature. You know how the English newspapers used to report the lineups of cricket games—'Gentlemen versus Players.' The other boys aren't quite sure what it means, but they know it's not complimentary to them."

"Are there any other black boys besides Rollins on the squad?"

"Not this year," the coach said. "The school does everything it can to get blacks to enroll, but not with much success. I'm afraid the school has had a reputation as a WASP stronghold for so many years that it's going to take time to change its image. I think there're only four other blacks in the school and none of them plays football. Last year we had a black instructor who taught history of art and he was well liked, but he never felt at home. Also, he was too high-powered for a prep school. He's teaching up at Boston U now. Good intentions aren't always enough, are they?" He sounded wistful, this big healthy young man whose aims in life Strand would have thought, because of his profession, to ten yards at a time.

The football coach was not the only member of the faculty to be puzzled by Romero. Another young teacher, a quiet woman in the English department by the name of Collins, who had Romero in a course in English and American Literature, fell into step beside Strand as he was leaving the main hall after lunch one day and asked him if she could talk to him for a few minutes about the boy. She, too, knew that he had come to Dunberry because of Strand. He hadn't bothered to correct this notion by telling anybody of Hazen's influence in the affair. If Hazen wanted to take the credit or the blame for Romero's presence on the campus he was perfectly capable of doing so.

"You taught him in New York, didn't you?" she said as she walked by his side.

"If anybody can be said to have taught him anything," he said.

She smiled. "I'm beginning to see what you mean. Did he give you any trouble in class?"

"Let me say," he said, trying to sound as judicious as possible, "that the views he expressed were not always in accordance with those of the accepted authorities."

"The change of schools," Miss Collins said, "hasn't changed his habits. He's got the whole class embroiled in an argument already."

"Oh dear," Strand said. "What about?"

"The first book we discussed was Stephen Crane's *The Red Badge of Courage*," Miss Collins said. "It's a book boys can relate to and the style is admirably plain and prepares the way for a whole genre of American writing. When I asked for comments, Romero kept silent while two or three of the boys explained why they liked the book, then raised his hand and stood up and said, very politely, 'Begging your pardon, ma'am, it's all brainwashing.' Then he made quite a speech. He said that no matter what the writer might or might not have intended, the result was that it showed that you never became a man if you ran away, you only proved yourself if you stood up and fought no matter how sure you were you'd get your head blown off, and as long as people admired books like that young men would go maching off to war singing and cheering and get themselves killed. He said he didn't know about the other boys in the class but if he hadn't kept running away all his life he sure as hell wouldn't be there in that classroom that morning. Running away, he said, was the natural thing to do when you were scared and stuff like *The Red Badge of Courage* was just a lie that old men cooked up to get young men to go out and get themselves killed off. He said he had an uncle who was decorated in Vietnam for sticking to his machine gun in an ambush to let the other men in his platoon get away and now his uncle is in a wheelchair for life and he's thrown his medal into the garbage can." Miss Collins, who had a shy, apologetic manner and a pale troubled face, shook her head as she remembered the incident in her classroom. "I just couldn't cope with that boy," she said despondently. "He made us all feel like uneducated fools. Do you think he really has an uncle who got wounded in Vietnam?"

"This is the first I've heard of an uncle," he said. "He's not above inventing things." If he had been disposed to argue with Romero, an unprofitable exercise at best, he might have reminded him that the author he esteemed so highly, Mr. Gibbon, used the words "military valor," with approval, on almost every page. Consistency, Strand had learned, was not the boy's strong point.

"Do you think that you could tell him that if he has opinions to express that might disturb the other boys he might first come to me privately after class and talk them over with me?" Miss Collins asked timidly.

"I could try," he said. "I don't guarantee anything. Privacy isn't exactly his thing, as the boys say." Suddenly he had a new insight into Romero's character. He was always in search of an audience, even of one, and preferably unsympathetic to him. He seemed to find his emotional outlet in hostility and with it a sense of power over people older and in a worldly sense much more powerful than he. If Strand could foresee a career for him it was as an orator, having to be protected by the police, whipping crowds into frenzies of dissension and belligerence. It was not a comforting vision.

"One of the difficulties in handling him," Miss Collins was going on in her frail, apologetic voice, "is that he always speaks with the utmost politeness, full of *ma'am*'s and *if I may ask a question*'s. And he's the best prepared boy in the class. He's got a photographic memory and he can quote verbatim whole paragraphs from books he's read to support his arguments. When I gave the class a list of suggested books to read for the semester, he tossed it aside contemptuously and said he'd already read most of the titles and the books he hadn't read he wouldn't waste his time opening. And he objected because James Joyce's *Ulysses* and *Lady Chatterley's Lover* weren't on the list. Imagine that, from a boy of seventeen."

"As the saying goes," he said, "he's wise beyond his years. Or vicious beyond his years."

"He said that those two books were among the foundations of modern literature and ignoring them was an insult to the class's intelligence and a denial of the sexuality of the modern man. Where do you suppose he picks up ideas like that?" she asked plaintively.

"From the public libraries."

"I wish there were a more advanced course," Miss Collins said. "I'd put him right into it. I'm afraid he's some sort of genius. I never had one before and I never want to have one again."

"Take heart," he said. "With his temperament he's likely to get into some kind of scrape and be expelled."

"It can't be too soon for me," Miss Collins said, her voice for once decisive. As she walked sadly off to her next hour, Strand was selfishly relieved that for this semester at least Romero was in none of his classes.

Among Strand's duties as housemaster was a biweekly inspection of the boys' quarters, which he made when the boys were out to class. There was the expected range in orderliness—from spinsterly neatness to a kind of infantile playpen sloppiness. The room on the top floor occupied by Romero and Rollins was clean enough, but the division between the halves of the room was so clear that it was almost as though an invisible wall ran between Rollins's side and that of Romero. On Rollins's bed there was a brightly figured Navaho blanket and against the headboard a maroon pillow with a big felt W in yellow sewed on its cover, the major letter he had won playing for his high school team. On his desk, in a heavy silver frame, there was a colored photograph of a grave-looking middle-aged black couple, posed in front of a white front porch, inscribed "From Mom and Dad, with love." Next to it was a photograph of a pretty, smiling black girl in a bathing suit, with the chaste inscription in fine, ladylike handwriting, "In fond remembrance, Clara." On the wall was a large photograph of four huge young men with wide grins on their faces, the smallest of them Rollins himself, all of them wearing varsity sweaters with different letters on them, all of them clearly brothers. Rollins was holding a football, the brother next to him a baseball bat and the two others basketballs, to show that their athletic honors had not been won in only one sport. They were a formidable if friendly group and one doubted that any neighbor would recklessly engage any of them in a dispute.

On the wall above his bed was a large lithograph advertising a concert of Ella Fitzgerald's and on the bedside table was his cassette machine and a row of cassettes, which Strand knew from experience he played at top volume. On the little shelf under his desk was a pile of *Playboy* magazines. Strand had found girlie magazines in other rooms also, but hidden on the floor under the beds. Rollins plainly didn't believe he had anything to hide.

On the shelf of his closet, which had been carelessly left open and in which his clothes were rather haphazardly arranged, there were a half-dozen cartons of chocolate marshmallow cookies, which made Strand smile as he thought of the moments during the night when the pangs of hunger awakened that huge body and his groping through the dark to the cache of childish sweets which would keep him going until breakfast.

By contrast, Romero's side of the room was bare and Spartan. The blankets were the olive drab wool ones issued to every boy and the bed was made with military crispness. There were no photographs and no magazines in evidence and the desk was bare except for a note pad and a neat row of sharply pointed pencils. It was as though Romero had resolved that nothing that he left behind him would reveal any fact to anyone who might be in a position to judge him. His clothes were arranged perfectly in his closet and on the shelf there was the famous 1909 edition, edited by J. B. Bury, in seven volumes, of *The History of the Decline and Fall of the Roman Empire,* which Strand knew to be of considerable value as a collectors' item and which had added so much weight to Romero's bag on the day of his arrival.

With the difference in tastes of the two young men, one had to wonder how it came about that they could live so harmoniously in one small room and seek out each other's company with such pleasure, as they did at all times.

Curious about how exactly Romero had come into possession of the set of Gibbon and if he knew how valuable the books were, Strand left a note asking him to visit him after football practice that afternoon. By school rules, Strand had to grade the condition of each room in the house and post the grades on the house bulletin board. The numbers ran from one to ten and he marked down ten for Rollins's and Romero's room, although there was something vaguely disturbing about that invisible wall between the two beds.

Romero came into the living room of Strand's apartment fresh from a shower and, as usual, neatly dressed and controlled in his movements. Strand made him sit down and before broaching the matter of the books he asked him a few questions about his classes and about the football team, which was to play its first game that Saturday. He said he liked the classes and thought he was doing well enough in them. He said he doubted that he would get to play in the game, but that he liked the coach, although he thought he lacked imagination. Very frankly, he told Strand that he had told the coach that if he didn't get to play at least for a few minutes by the second week of the season, he was going to drop off the squad and concentrate on his studies.

Strand asked him, routinely, if he had any complaints and he said none. He said that Mr. Hazen had written him that he had deposited a certain sum to his account at the school bank and that he was allotted ten dollars a week of it for spending money, as were all the other boys in his form. He said he had written a note to Mr. Hazen thanking him for his generosity. Strand told him that he could thank Mr. Hazen in person, as he was driving down with his wife and daughter to visit the school on Saturday morning. "I guess I'm in for another speech," he said, smiling, but without malice.

Then Strand brought up the matter of the books. "You know," he said, "they're quite valuable."

"Are they?" he said ingenuously. "That's good news."

"How did you happen to come by them?" Strand asked.

He looked at Strand, as though weighing his answer. "I stole them," he said matter-of-factly. "It took me nine trips down to the secondhand bookstores on Fourth Avenue to pick them up one by one." He stared coolly at Strand, as though waiting for comment. Strand kept quiet and he said, "Those clerks in those stores wouldn't last ten minutes on the street. They'd be robbed naked and they wouldn't know it until they caught pneumonia."

"Do you want to tell me at just which stores you picked them up, as you put it?" Strand asked.

"I don't remember their names," Romero said and stood up. "Is there anything else, sir?"

"Not right now," Strand said.

He went out. Strand sat at his desk, staring at the dusk growing deeper outside the window, faced with a moral problem that he did not want to try to solve. I must not get obsessed with that boy, he thought. I have other things to worry about.

The big Mercedes, with Conroy at the wheel, drove up to the entrance of the Malson Residence just before lunchtime on Saturday morning. Strand was on the steps of the house to greet Leslie and Caroline and Hazen as they got out of the car. Caroline was holding a small, wriggling black Labrador puppy. Strand was shaken by emotion at seeing his wife and daughter again but did not wish to make a scene of husbandly and parental affection in front of the two boys from the house who were watching from the steps.

For the moment, he avoided looking at Caroline. "Where's Jimmy?" he asked. "I thought he was coming with you."

"At the last minute Mr. Solomon sent him out to Chicago to take in some group that's performing out there,"

Leslie said. "It means he's rising in the firmament, he tells me. He'll try to call you when he gets back. He sends his regards."

"Good of him," Strand said dryly. Then, still without having taken a good look at Caroline, he asked almost gruffly, as he patted the dog, "Where did you pick *that* up?"

"Mr. Hazen gave him to me. Two days ago. When Dr. Laird took the bandages off." She put the dog down. Smiling, but a little nervously, she touched her nose with the tip of her finger. "How do you like the job?"

"Fine," he said. He thought she looked beautiful, but then he had always thought she was beautiful. "It actually looks real."

Caroline laughed. "Oh, Daddy," she said, "can't you curb your enthusiasm?"

"The important thing is," Strand said, "what do *you* think?"

"I think the ugly duckling has turned into a swan," Caroline said gaily, as they went into the house. "I dread to think of what I'm going to do to the fellers from now on."

"There's no need to exaggerate," Leslie said, looking sternly at the two boys who were examining Caroline with evident interest. "The operation was a success, but you're not a movie star yet. And you'll have to get over the habit of staring at yourself in the mirror a hundred times a day." But she spoke affectionately and Strand could see that she was almost as pleased with Caroline's new appearance as the girl herself.

She was not as pleased with the appearance of the apartment, although Mrs. Schiller had put flowers in vases at strategic places in the living room. "I hadn't realized this place was quite so desolate," she said, "although it'll look better when we move our stuff in. But it certainly can stand at least a coat of paint."

"I'll talk to Babcock about it," Hazen said. "I'm sure the school won't go bankrupt if you have the painters in here for a couple of days."

"I wouldn't like to seem picky," Leslie said. "Right from the beginning."

"I'll tell Babcock it's my own idea," Hazen said. "You'll get your paint."

"It's time for lunch," Strand said. "We'd better go over to the dining room. I told them you were coming and they've set up a visitors' table with some other parents. We have the first game of the football season today and quite a few people have come down for it. By the way, Russell, our protégé Romero is on the squad."

"What does he play—water boy?" Hazen laughed.

"No, seriously," Strand said, as they started out of the house and walked along the path to the Main Hall. "He may not get in today but the coach told me he expects to use him in spot situations."

"How is he doing generally?"

"I believe he's keeping up with his classes," Strand said cautiously. "I try not to look as though I'm meddling, but he seems conscientious enough and he doesn't horse around in the study hours here like some of the other boys."

"You'll have to give me a list of his teachers. While I'm here I should have a word with them about him. I'm sure they're not used to boys like that and I wouldn't want them to be hard on him out of a lack of understanding of his background."

Remembering Miss Collins, Strand thought it might be more rewarding if Hazen had a word with Romero and appealed to him not to be too hard on his teachers. He didn't think it was wise to tell Hazen that, nor to mention anything about the set of Gibbon in Romero's room. Hazen might fly into a rage and have the boy thrown out immediately and the experiment, which Strand now felt he had a stake in, would be over before it had a chance to begin.

He dropped behind the others to take Leslie's arm and walk beside her. She smiled at him gratefully. "I missed you so much," she whispered.

"I, of course, have been having the time of my young life here alone," Strand said. "You have no idea what the orgies are like at teatime in the faculty common room."

Leslie squeezed his arm. "You do look well," she said. "It seems as though this place is going to agree with you."

"It does. I hope it's going to agree with you."

"If you're happy here," she said, "I'm going to be happy here." But there was a note in her voice, the slightest of inflections, that indicated doubt, reluctance, a shadow of fear.

When they entered the dining room, which was already filled with boys, Strand could tell by the way the boys stared at Caroline, with the puppy wobbling on a leash beside her, that the operation had indeed been a success. He noticed that Caroline even walked differently now. If he had to put a word to it, he decided, it would be haughtily.

After lunch, at which Hazen was pleased to find himself seated next to a man he knew from Washington who had something to do with the oil lobby and with whom he conversed animatedly, Strand walked Leslie back to the house, because she wanted to take a nap, while Hazen and Caroline and Conroy went over to the football field. "Are you sure you don't want me to stay with you?" Strand asked as he watched Leslie take her shoes off and lie down on one of the beds.

"There's plenty of time later," Leslie said. "I'm sure they'd be offended if you didn't watch their game. And I've met enough people for one day."

He bent down and kissed her forehead, then set out for the field. There were perhaps a thousand spectators in the open wooden stands but Hazen had kept a place for him next to Caroline. Hazen and Conroy sat on her other side. The game had already begun, but Hazen said nothing much had happened yet. "Which one is Romero?" he asked.

Strand scanned the bench. On one end, alone, with quite a space between him and the nearest player, Romero sat, bent over, staring at his hands hanging loosely between his knees and never looking at the field, as though he had no connection with what was happening there. "Number 45," Strand said.

"God, he's *tiny*," Hazen said. "Next to those other kids

he looks as though he should be in nursery school. Are you sure somebody's not playing some sort of practical joke on him?"

"The coach takes him quite seriously."

"The coach must be a sadist," Hazen said glumly. "I think we ought to take an insurance policy out on him, full coverage, hospital, doctors and funeral expenses."

"That might be the only way you'd ever get any return on your investment in him," Strand said, thinking of the five hundred dollar bill at Brooks Brothers and the ten dollar a week allowance.

Hazen grinned across Caroline as Strand said this, taking it as a joke. Strand himself was not sure, after he had said it, that he really meant it as a joke.

The game was raggedly played, with many fumbles, missed plays, dropped passes and blocked kicks. A man behind them, whose son played tight end and dropped two passes in a row, kept saying "What do you expect, it's the first game of the season."

Whatever the quality of the play, it was pleasant sitting out there in the warm early autumn sunshine, watching swift young men racing across the fragrant green turf. There was none of the savage passion of professional football or of the games between the big-name universities and the only penalties were for offsides and too much time in the huddle and when one boy on the Dunberry team had the breath knocked out of him momentarily, the boy who had hit him knelt anxiously beside the injured boy until he sat up. Caroline, the puppy squirming in her lap, cheered loyally for Dunberry and smiled provocatively at some boys from the other school who turned around and booed her good-naturedly. "Just leave your name and telephone number," one of the boys said, "and we'll get even with you."

"You can get it from my father." Caroline pointed her thumb at Strand. "He teaches here."

The boy laughed. "Sorry, sir," he said. "But I'll have a pencil and paper with me later on in the field house."

Tea was to be served after the game in the field house for the students of both schools and their parents. Strand didn't doubt that the boy would show up with his pencil and paper, but Caroline would be in Arizona in three days, Strand would be happy to tell him.

There was a lot of scoring and toward the end of the last quarter the other school was leading 26 to 20. The boys on both benches were standing now, cheering on their teammates, but Romero still kept to himself, seated, studying his hands. When the whistle had blown, indicating only two more minutes to play, the coach strode down toward Romero and spoke to him. Romero stood up slowly, almost leisurely, put on his helmet and trotted out onto the field. The other team had the ball on its own forty yard line and it was fourth down and eight yards to go and a punt was the obvious play.

Romero took up his position at safety, on his own twenty yard line, his hands negligently on his hips. When the kick came and the ends came rushing down on him, he juggled the ball, then dropped it. There was a groan from the stands as it bounced erratically toward the sidelines, Romero chasing it, the opposing team's red jerseys in hot pursuit. He grabbed the ball on a dead run, then suddenly stopped. Two of his opponents flew past him helplessly. Fleeing, he ran back almost to his own goal line, then veered just as it seemed he was about to be tackled and ran, twisting, toward the opposite sideline. He evaded another tackler, Rollins threw an opportune block, and suddenly he was in the clear, running close to the sideline with no one near him and the red jerseys helplessly outdistanced. He crossed the goal line, even slowing down contemptuously for the last ten yards, stopped and carelessly tossed the ball to the ground.

"Well, I'll be damned," Hazen said, speaking loudly to be heard over the cheers of the crowd. "I thought I was sending a student to Dunberry and it turns out I sent a rabbit."

Romero's teammates crowded around him, clapping him on the back and shaking his hand, but he submitted to the gestures of approval rather than acknowledging them. It was only when he started trotting back toward the bench

and Rollins grabbed him and lifted him as though he were
a child that he permitted himself a smile.

As he went off the field he waved once, casually, without glancing toward the stands, where everyone was standing and applauding.

He trotted slowly toward the bench, his face calm, and
went to the place at the end where he had been sitting for
almost the entire game. He took off his helmet and once
more sat staring at his hands hanging loosely between his
knees. As the teams lined up for the point after touchdown the coach came over and patted him on the shoulder, but he didn't look up even then.

The place kick was wide and there was just time for a
final kickoff when the time ran out with the final score
twenty-six to twenty-six. Romero hurried to the field house
to shower and dress before he could be reached by the
crowd of fellow students who rushed after him.

Tables and chairs had been set out in the field house,
and there was a long buffet with small sandwiches and
cakes behind which faculty wives stood to pour tea.
Strand and Hazen sat at a table while Caroline and Conroy went to get the tea. Strand smiled as he saw the boy
who had asked for Caroline's address at the game quickly
intercept her and walk with her to the buffet.

There was a quiet murmur among the groups of parents
and students and a general sharing of pleasure in the way
the afternoon had turned out.

As he watched the polite movement of the hearty, con-
vivial middle-aged men and their handsomely turned out
wives, Strand suddenly had the feeling that by some un-
acknowledged bond they were all related to Russell Hazen.
They were the bankers, the lords of trade and commerce,
the chairmen of the boards, the quiet movers and shakers,
the judges and interpreters of the laws, the managers of
great fortunes and institutions, the architects of political
victories, the men who had the ear of senators and law-
makers, their children the princelings of a class which in
America would not admit it was a class but, as Romero

would recognize, comprised what the old Romans honored as the equestrian order.

As for the teachers, both men and women—the men deferential or at least reticent in manner, struggling against humility, the women willingly being of service—they were like the learned slaves imported to the capital to instruct the privileged young in virtue, valor and the arts of government.

As the students and guests of the school passed the table, Strand heard Romero's name mentioned several times with approval. Strand was not sure if it was the praise bestowed on a gladiator who had shone that afternoon in the arena or a token that the equestrian order was open from time to time to barbarians of merit.

He shook his head impatiently, displeased with the way his thoughts had run, and stood up to greet Johnson, the football coach, who was approaching the table, a smile on his face. Strand introduced the coach to Hazen, who also stood. "Too bad you fellows couldn't make that extra point," Hazen said.

The coach shrugged. "I tell you, sir, I was happy to settle for a tie today. That boy is something, isn't he? I was ready to kick him off the squad right then and there when he started running back toward our own goal." He laughed. "But nothing succeeds like success, does it? Two or three more runs like that and we'll have to change the name of your house from the Malson Residence to Romero Gardens."

"Frankly, Mr. Johnson," Hazen said, "Mr. Strand and I are more interested in the boy's attitude toward his studies than his exploits on the football field. What do you hear about him from his teachers?"

"Well," Johnson said, "the coaching staff keeps a pretty close watch on how our boys are doing in their studies. We aren't one of those schools that look the other way when an athlete falls behind in class. So far, I'm happy to say, the word on Romero is most satisfactory. He's highly intelligent, they say, and is always thoroughly prepared in class. He's somewhat argumentative, as you probably know"—Johnson smiled—"but always polite and clever

in the way he states his positions. Of course his . . . uh
. . . background is considerably different from the usual
run of Dunberry students, so his teachers realize that there
must be a certain give and take in the way he has to be
handled, but I'd say that if he continues as he's begun
there's nothing to worry about. Except that he doesn't
seem to be interested in being liked by his fellow students
or the boys on the squad and except for his relationship
with Rollins he doesn't seem to want any friends."

"I'll have a little talk with him," Hazen said. "Allen,
let's take him to dinner with us tonight. The restaurant at
the inn where I'm staying in town is quite good and maybe in a different atmosphere he'll unbend a bit. And I'd
like to get Caroline's opinion about him. I haven't the
faintest notion of how he reacts to girls who have been
—ah—more gently reared than the girls he's been used
to."

Strand wondered what Hazen would say if he told him
about the striptease artist on the train and the afternoon
in New Haven. "Well," he said, "I haven't seen him with
any girls, either here or back in the city, but Mrs. Schiller,
our housekeeper, says he's her favorite. He treats her like
a lady, she says, which is more than she can say about
most of the other boys. And he's the neatest boy she's
ever had anything to do with in all her years at the
school."

"I'd say that's a good sign," Hazen said. "Wouldn't
you?"

"Yes, I would," Strand said. "A very good sign."

By this time the members of the two squads had come
into the field house, fresh and rosy from their showers
and swarming hungrily around the buffet table. "Do you
see him?" Hazen asked. "If he's here, I'll invite him
myself."

"I don't think he's here," Johnson said. "He was the
first one out of the locker room and I heard him say to
Rollins that he'd meet him later back at the house. Tea
parties obviously are not his favorite form of entertainment."

Strand saw Rollins carrying a plate piled with sandwiches away from the buffet table and waved to him to come over. As Rollins approached, he looked a little embarrassed to be caught with the evidence of gluttony on his plate, but grinned and covered the sandwiches with his hand jokingly. "Caught red-handed, sir, I'm afraid. All that open air sure gives a man an appetite."

"Rollins," Strand said, "this is Mr. Hazen. He was instrumental in getting your friend Romero to come to Dunberry."

"Glad to meet you, sir." He put his plate down on the table and shook Hazen's hand. "This afternoon, at least, you're the most popular visitor on the campus."

"Congratulations on your game," Hazen said.

"Thank you, sir. We didn't win, but we didn't lose either. We'll do better later."

"That was a nice block you threw on Romero's run," Johnson said. "He'd have been nailed if you hadn't made it."

"Well, coach," Rollins said, grinning again, "us players have to show the gentlemen we know how to help each other."

"Rollins," Johnson said sharply, "I think you and Romero could drop that private joke of yours from now on. We've all had enough of it."

"Sorry, coach," Rollins said quietly. "I'll pass the word along." Carrying the plate piled with sandwiches, he walked off toward a group of his teammates. Rollins, Strand thought, deadly blocker, nighttime devourer of chocolate cookies, another candidate for the equestrian order.

PART THREE

1

For the first time since Leslie got back from Arizona, she is not here with me in the evening. She is in New York, where she goes every Wednesday to teach her pupils in Caroline's old school. Until now she has driven back after her lessons, getting in as late as eleven o'clock, after the long trip from the city. This time she has arranged to sleep over in the apartment of the dean of the school and get up early enough tomorrow to be here for her scheduled ten o'clock class. The railroad connections are inadequate and she has to drive the old station wagon Hazen has loaned us to and from the city. She is still a nervous driver and the two trips crowded into one day have turned out to be too much for her and she invariably has arrived back here with nerves frayed by the glaring lights of the nighttime traffic and suffering from a violent headache. The traveling isn't the only thing that disturbs her. The clatter of the boys around us, the wild bursts of adolescent laughter, the shouts in front of the television set in the common room, the thuds of playful scuffling, the wailing of canned music, are painfully reflected in the tautness around her eyes and the lines at the corners of her mouth and she is resorting to aspirin frequently and taking daily doses of the Librium the school doctor has prescribed for her.

I am of two minds whether her keeping up with her pupils in the city is good or bad for her. I know she is stimulated by them and she says that one of her girls, aged twelve, gives promise of developing into a concert pianist. When she speaks of this girl a tone of elation, rare these days, comes into her voice. She is pessimistic about the

*value of her classes in Dunberry. There isn't a boy, she
says, who's interested in anything musical beyond rock or
disco.*

Even at moments like this one, when the late evening
quiet has fallen on the house, she moves restlessly around,
moving bits of furniture, clipping dead flowers out of the
vases, thumbing through books and magazines and throwing them down impatiently. She plays the piano only during school hours when the boys are out of the house and
she has no classes. When she has any time free she goes
out to paint, but returns home with canvases smeared
savagely in disgust with what she has done.

Our apartment still looks bare and temporary. Leslie
has not as yet put up any of her paintings. She says she is
shy about having any of the boys or faculty think that she
considers herself an artist, although I don't believe that is
the reason. To me she seems poised for flight, although
I'm sure she does not think so, and her paintings on the
walls would be symbols of unwanted permanence.

On one of her visits to New York she had lunch with
Linda Roberts, who told Leslie she might be going to
France for a week or ten days and invited Leslie to accompany her. I told Leslie I was sure the school would
allow her the leave and that the trip would do her good,
but she said it was out of the question. When I tried to
persuade her, she became impatient and asked me if I was
trying to get rid of her. I denied this as nonsense, but, and
I hate to admit it, her brief absence now is soothing. It
presents an opportunity, which I am taking, to reflect at
leisure for once, to sit at my desk here in the room and
reflect upon the small events of the autumn.

The evening after the game in which Romero made his
first appearance on the field for Dunberry we all went to
dinner at the inn at which Hazen and Conroy were staying.
Romero, neatly dressed and wearing a tie, sat next to
Caroline at the table. They seemed interested in each other
and Hazen, while regarding them intently at certain moments, left them to their own conversation. The next
morning, before he left for New York with Leslie and
Caroline, he told me he was favorably impressed with

Romero's manners and asked me to sound out Caroline about what she thought of the boy. I had no chance to talk to her before they left, but told Leslie to speak to Caroline and find out what she could.

We had our furniture from New York by that time, and so Leslie and I could sleep in the same bed, but after what had happened in Tours we slept stiffly as far away from each other as possible. We said nothing about it, although we both knew we would have to come to some final decision on the subject of our sexual appetites and the impossibility of pretending that abstinence had not changed the character of our marriage. With all that, we woke in the morning lying in each other's arms.

He put down his pen. He had been writing for more than an hour at the old desk in the light of the student lamp. Weary, but knowing he would not be able to sleep, he sat, slumped in his chair, staring out the window.

The first snow of the season was beginning to drift down in the November darkness. The lights were out in the rest of the house and the noise of the radios and cassettes and the thunder of the boys' feet above the Strands' quarters finally was stilled. When Leslie was home she could not wait for the blessed moment when riot turned into silence. Usually during those hours Strand merely sat in a big easy chair reading or staring into the fire that took the bite off the autumn nights, as the house cooled down with the fire in the furnace banked for the hours of sleep.

He heard what he thought was the sound of a car arriving outside the house. It sounded like the engine of the old Volkswagen Leslie drove. He jumped up and went to the window and looked out, thinking that perhaps Leslie had changed her mind about staying overnight in New York. But there was no car, just the snow and the dark windswept campus. With a sigh, he went back to his desk.

He had heard that sound the evening that Leslie had returned from Arizona and had almost run to the door to greet her. They had thrown themselves into each other's arms, he remembered, not caring if there were boys watching them or not. She was glowing with pleasure at seeing

him again and he could tell by her expression that all had
gone well on her trip.

They had sat on the couch, his arm around her, until
well past midnight as she told him what it had been like
in Arizona.

"Caroline is sure she'll love it there. She likes the college—it's very pretty and certainly not anything like City
College—and the other girls on her dormitory floor were
nice and friendly. We talked and talked—endlessly. Just
being alone together for a few days, with no one else in
the family to get my attention, seemed to have opened
some sort of dam. Maybe we should have done more of
that, both of us, with all three of the children."

"What did she have to say?"

"Well, for one thing, she was very impressed with your
Mr. Romero."

"Russell will be pleased to hear that." Strand was not
so sure that he was equally pleased. "What impressed her?
That crazy run he made in the football game?"

"She didn't even mention that. She said he seemed
gentler and shyer than most boys."

"That will come as news to Romero," Strand said dryly.

"She said that she sensed that he had no desire to be
like the other boys in his classes."

"There's hardly any danger of that."

"It was impossible for him, anyway, he told her. He
was going to amount to *something*, he said. He didn't
know just what it was going to be, but it was going to be
something. Just about every other boy in the school was
on rails, he told her . . . Caroline said his tone was scornful . . . they had everything all mapped out—go to Harvard or Yale, then to business school and into their daddy's
firm, be a lawyer, be a bank president, get into the big
bucks and retire at the age of fifty-five and play golf.
They're all in for big surprises, though, he said. He had
one big advantage over all of them—*nothing* was going
to surprise him. They were going to teach him all the
tricks . . ."

"Who're *they*?" Strand asked.

"He didn't tell Caroline that. He just said that he was

going to beat them at their own game and *his* own game and any game that was going. Caroline said he was very intense about it all, as though he'd been thinking about it for a long time and she guessed it was the first time he'd had a chance to talk to anyone about it."

"She guessed wrong," Strand said. "I got a little dose of it, too. Not exactly the same, but close enough." He remembered the conversation about the Goths.

"And he thanked them for it, he said. They were educating him. Just like the fellahin in Algeria who got educated at the Sorbonne and then kicked the French out of the country and the smart Arab kids who got educated at Harvard and Oxford and turned around and made the British and Americans bleed for oil like stuck pigs when they took off their business suits and put on their desert robes."

"And what did Caroline think about that pleasant piece of information?"

"She told him she thought he was just trying to put on a show for her benefit—that he'd read it all someplace and he was just sounding off to be a big shot."

"That must have flattered him," Strand said.

"Caroline said he glowered at her and she thought he was just going to get up and leave. But he didn't. He said, sure he read it someplace, he'd written it himself after he'd been at the school for a week and asked himself what the hell he was doing there. He sure wasn't there to run back kicks."

"He probably wasn't lying," Strand said. "About writing it himself. It sounds like him."

"Then he asked her where she was going to school and when she told him about her athletic scholarship, he laughed. Two accidental jocks, is what he said. He knew what he was running away from. What was *she* running from? Then he said, even after the touchdown that afternoon, he would have quit the team, but was only staying on for his friend Rollins's sake. Games were for kids, he said."

"Johnson will not weep into his beer if he quits," Strand said.

"Who's Johnson?"

"The football coach. Romero kept telling people he didn't have any imagination and the word got back to him."

"I know you think he's a difficult young man," Leslie said, "but I never heard Caroline go on like that about anybody. She said it was the most fascinating evening she'd ever had in her life and when she got back home here after dinner she sat down and wrote out everything she remembered about it."

Another keeper of journals in the family, Strand thought. Perhaps it was a hereditary disease. "She seems to have remembered every word," he said.

"There's more to come," Leslie said. "When Caroline told him she wanted to be a veterinarian, he said that she was trying to save the wrong species. He knew where she should practice when she got her degree—in his old neighborhood in Manhattan. It was teeming with animals, he said, herds of them, on two legs, all of them sick. He said she'd be a lot more useful there than giving pills to deworm Pekingeses. Caroline thought that he was making fun of her, but then he asked her, very seriously, if it would be all right if he wrote her. Caroline asked what he would want to write her about, and he said politics, murders, graft, poverty, the color of peoples' skin, the lies of history, napalm and the hydrogen bomb, running back punts. . . . When you were his age, did you ever hear talk like that from anybody that young?"

"No," Strand said. "Times were different then."

"He said that he'd also practice writing a love letter or two."

"The bastard," Strand said.

"Oh, Allen, it's just a boy trying to show an attractive girl that he's more sophisticated than he is. And by the time they ever see each other again they won't even remember each other's names."

"What did Caroline say—about the love letters, I mean?"

"She told me she said she didn't think it would do any harm." Leslie smiled as she said this, as though reassured

that her shy daughter had finally caught on to the rules of
the female game. "The boy wasn't kidding," Leslie said.
"When we got to the college there was a letter from him,
waiting for Caroline. She read it and gave it to me. It
didn't have a date or start with Dear Caroline or Dear
Anything. It was just word for word the speech he'd made
to her about the Algerians during dinner. It wasn't even
signed. Caroline said it was the first love letter she'd ever
received. Of course she laughed at it, but she said she was
going to keep it and show it to the other boys to improve
the level of their conversation if they ever said any of the
usual stupid thing to her." Leslie scowled a little then. "I
do hope she isn't turning into a coquette. Just about every
male on the campus stared at her every place we went."

"You were the one who said she should have the nose
job," Strand said.

"Those are the risks you run," Leslie said, but not
lightly. She shook her head, as though to get rid of fears
about her daughter. "She'll probably change ten times before we see her again. With or without us."

"You haven't said a word about how Eleanor is doing,"
Strand said. Leslie had flown to Georgia for a few days
after Arizona to visit the young married couple. "Is she
happy?"

"Very," Leslie said, "as far as I could tell. Although the
town is stultifying."

"Leslie, darling," Strand said, smiling, "that's what you
say about just about anyplace that isn't New York."

"I don't say it about Boston or San Francisco or even
Atlanta," Leslie defended herself.

"Anyplace under a population of a million. I didn't ask
about the town. I asked about Eleanor and Giuseppe."

"Well, they seem to be delighted with their work,"
Leslie said grudgingly. "They feel they've improved the
paper a hundred percent and they seem to devote sixteen
hours a day to it. They have a big old house which looks
as though it's falling down. It's like a cross between Tobacco Road, cleaned up for the movies, and an antebellum
plantation. Eleanor says it's perfect for newlyweds. When
they have an argument they can sleep in bedrooms so far

apart they have to communicate with each other by short-wave. I only got to talk to them in fits and starts. Whenever we sat down to a meal, the telephone rang and one or the other of them would have to charge out and do something. It would drive me crazy, but they both seem to be thriving on it. When I tried to find out if they were making or losing money they immediately changed the subject. They seemed to be crazy about each other and I suppose that's the main thing." She wriggled out of his encircling arm and said, "Goodness, it must be past midnight. Is there any hot water? I must take a bath, I've been traveling all day."

"There's hot water. At least I think so. Don't you want a drink first, to celebrate being home?"

"Maybe after the bath. I'll signal when ready." She bent over and kissed him. "Did you miss me?"

"What do you think?"

She laughed and went in and in a moment he heard the water running.

When he went in a few minutes later, she was already in bed, her hair brushed and shining. He undressed and got into the bed and snuggled up to her. He began to caress her, but she pulled away gently. "I'm afraid, darling," she said. He didn't have to ask what she was afraid of. Dr. Prinz had warned him. Even obeying Dr. Prinz's orders, pampering and denying himself at the same time, he was still subject to sudden fits of fatigue when he could hardly make himself walk across the campus or face a class.

"Of course," he said, and moved to the other side of the bed. This is impossible, he thought. Tomorrow night I'll sleep in the other room.

From then on, without discussion, Jimmy's narrow old bed in the other bedroom was made up for him each night.

Well, he thought, as he sat at his desk, remembering in front of the fire, that was a good night in our marriage, considering everything.

He sighed, stood up, stretched, put a log on the dwindling fire because he was not yet ready for sleep and went into the kitchen and poured himself a drink of whiskey and water.

He went back into the living room, carrying his drink. Above him he heard the sound of footsteps. The old wooden house creaked and groaned and all movements were betrayed through its beams. He was sure that there was a certain amount of prohibited visiting after hours among the boys. He did not wish to learn what the nocturnal traffic meant. An illegal cigarette perhaps, the passing of a marijuana joint from one hand to another, homosexual experiments, the sharing of smuggled liquor, a more or less innocent rap session. A dedicated and conscientious teacher, he thought, would steal upstairs as quietly as possible and catch the culprits at their teenage crimes and bring down upon their heads appropriate punishment. What appropriate punishment was for any crime in this day and age would be difficult to figure out. At least in the public school system he hadn't had to worry about what his students did once they left his classes. As always, you had to live in consideration of a balance between profits and losses. As long as his charges didn't burn the house down, a benevolent blind eye was a useful piece of equipment. He hadn't asked the other teachers what their systems for maintaining order were and nobody had volunteered any advice to him. He wondered what a teacher from Eton or Harrow, schools where caning, as far as he knew, was still practiced, would think of his conduct. Would such a pedagogue march boldly up the stairs, uphold the law, grimly mete out so many strokes of the cane for smoking, so many for drinking, so many for talking after hours? How many for buggery? None, from what he had read. Go, and do thou likewise. Strand grinned at the thought. His own son was no older than some of the boys in the house and Strand had never punished him except by a sharp word, rarely spoken. If Jimmy had gone to Dunberry or Eton or Harrow instead of to a public high school, would he now be immersed in the world of bearded guitarists and orgiastic millionaire rock stars doomed to die before the age of thirty from overdoses of heroin or uppers and downers?

He put his drink down on the desk, seated himself, hesitated, then picked up his pen and began to write.

I have been musing upon the differences between the old-time system of education in the English language and the permissive order we have now in which students are awarded degrees for some of the most inconsequential dabbling the tutorial mind can imagine. When one thinks of the poets, philosophers, statesmen, and soldiers turned out by the old British system and by the church-oriented colleges of the United States that have endured since colonial times, it is difficult to believe that we are doing as well for our children as our ancestors did for theirs. We live in the most curious of times, where at the same moment liberalism has gone amok in our educational systems while discipline and repression have gone amok in most of the world's political systems. The two things must be somehow linked, although it is too late in the night for me to find those links. The English schools found place for eccentrics: do we find place for scholars? Gentlemen? Poets? It is a nice subject to bring up with Romero. Or should I merely go to the headmaster and tell him that the boy is dangerous and a threat to us all and have him dropped from the school immediately? But I know I won't do it. I am affected as we all are here, as Russell Hazen is, too, by the liberal superstition which, with all that has happened, still impels us decently or guiltily to spend our treasure and our goodwill in educating and even arming our own Arabs, our own fellahin, our invited Iranians. I will not discuss this in the faculty common room over tea. I am the odd man out among them, as it is, and when they ask me about my career in the public schools they sound as though they were asking questions of a man who has spent the best years of his life in a combat zone.

On the whole, though, they are good people, lacking in that quality, ambition, which so often makes people repugnant.

The word ambition itself leads to endless speculation. Just last week Hazen telephoned me, ostensibly to apologize for not being able to come and visit us and to find out how I was doing. I told him, not completely candidly, that everything was going along splendidly. Then he said he had a little problem to talk to me about. It was not about his divorce problems or the pretty lady lawyer from Paris, as I half-guessed it would be, but about Eleanor and Gianelli. I told him that when Leslie had visited them she thought they were doing very well. Hazen was of a different opinion. He had talked with his friend the publisher, who had warned him that the two young people were too ambitious by far, changing routines that had made the paper prosper for almost a half century, firing old hands, bringing in know-it-all kids from eastern schools of journalism, antagonizing the townspeople by their high-handedness. Eleanor, it seems, was being blamed even more than her husband. "They say she's leading her husband around with a ring in his nose," Hazen said the publisher told him. "And he complains that they treat him as though he's a fragile relic from another century. He may be exaggerating," Hazen said, "but it wouldn't be amiss if you could advise them to show a little patience."

I promised to do what I could. I didn't tell him that I didn't have much hope of influencing Eleanor and felt that I would have to get Gianelli off to one side in a private conversation if I wanted to try to do anything with him. Besides, they have no plans that I know of to visit here and a trip to Georgia would only be a useless expense.

When I put the phone down, I sighed involuntarily. When one is poor in one's youth, even if later on one is quite comfortably fixed, thinking about money is an activity which can send one into a state that borders on anything from a slight uneasiness to terror.

I had never had any illusions about being rich and I hadn't longed for the toys and choices of wealth. I was never a gambler and knew that the windfalls of luck would never be mine. I had chosen a profession for love of teaching, for the opportunities of scholarly leisure, for the assurance it had seemed then to offer of a decent if modest *style of living. As I rose in the school system my salary increased proportionately and met all our reasonable needs, with the prospect that when I was forced to retire the blows of old age would be softened by an adequate pension. Like most Americans I was not prepared for the spiraling realities of inflation. The disasters it had caused for the middle classes of the countries of Europe could not descend, we thought, upon America. As a historian I knew we were not immune to change, but I shared the common belief that if America was no longer a fortress in military terms, our monetary system, at least, would resist invasion in our lifetimes. On a more personal level I had never imagined that at the age of fifty a nearly mortal illness would make me alter my entire mode of life and force me to earn my bread in a different place and under radically different rules.*

If I had continued working until retirement age in the public school system, my pension would have been fair enough. Under ordinary circumstances, although we would have had to move to a smaller apartment, I could suppose that we could survive comfortably, even a little better than comfortably, with enough left over to be able to visit a child who lived a thousand miles away from us, when the necessity arose. My salary here is much less than I was earning in the city and even though we get the house rent-free, if I had to buy a new suit or Leslie needed a new coat, it would mean some close and anxious planning on our part. Leslie of course doesn't complain, but I would be fooling myself if I thought that some of the tension reflected in her face is not . . .

The phone rang. He stared at the instrument stupidly. Calls that late at night were frightening, especially since Leslie was not in the house with him. He let the phone ring two more times before he picked it up, trying to control the shaking in his hands.

But it was only Russell Hazen. His voice was reassuringly normal. "I hope I'm not waking you, Allen," he said.

"Actually," Strand said, "I was sitting at my desk catching up on my work."

"Don't overdo it," Hazen said. "One heart attack is enough."

"I agree with you there," Strand said, relieved that there were no accidents to report, no crises to be attended to.

"It's just that I've been so busy," Hazen said. "I've just gotten in from a conference. And I wanted to catch you as soon as I could."

"What is it, Russell?" Strand asked. "Have you been talking to your friend in Georgia again?"

"No. I haven't heard from him, so I guess things have been going better down there. Actually . . ." He hesitated for a moment. "Actually, it's about me. It's nothing very important, but it just possibly might involve you, too." He laughed a little oddly. He sounded embarrassed, Strand thought. "You remember that oil man—at least that lobbyist I met at lunch when I was up at the school . . . ?"

"Yes," Strand said.

"Something a little unpleasant has come up. He's been called before a Senate committee down in Washington that's investigating the use of improper influence on legislators . . ."

"I haven't read anything about it in the papers."

"It hasn't reached the papers yet. But a friend who's in a position to know has given me some private information."

Strand couldn't help thinking that once more, as always, Russell had a friend who was in a position to know or do something useful for him.

"The man's in hot water," Hazen went on, "and he's trying to shift blame. They haven't anything definite to load on him, but some drunk at one of those goddamn Washington parties was overheard babbling that he'd heard the oil man boasting that he'd persuaded a certain senator to switch his vote on a big offshore exploratory drilling proposal and that a company my firm happens to represent had promised to put up an important sum of money to make sure the senator saw the light. And he mentioned my name. According to my information he told the committee that we had met by design at the school—his kid is in one of your classes, I think—Hitz is his name . . ."

"C scholar, verging on D. Actually, he's in my house.

Not likable. A big fat oaf of a boy, given to bullying the younger ones."

"Anyway, aside from saying—or at least he was reported as saying—that we had planned the meeting at Dunberry, Hitz said I had taken him aside and discussed the deal with him, the lying sonofabitch."

"I'm sorry to hear this," Strand said, "but why're you telling it to me?"

"Because, Allen," Hazen said, "if anybody comes around to ask you questions or if you have to testify, I'd like you to swear under oath, if necessary, that I was with you or someone in your family at all times when I was at the school and nobody ever heard anything at all about votes or deals or law firms . . ."

"Russell," Strand said, as quietly as he could manage, "I wasn't with you every minute and neither was Leslie or Caroline."

"You don't think I'd be capable of anything like that, do you?" Hazen's voice on the telephone was getting loud, with a hint of anger in it.

"No, I don't," Strand said honestly.

"It's a vendetta," Hazen said. "Against me. You don't know what the infighting is like in Washington. In my work, there's no avoiding rubbing some people—powerful people—the wrong way and if they see even the smallest, most ridiculous chance of getting me discredited, they'll jump at it."

"What can they possibly do to you? There's no proof of any kind, is there?"

"Of course not." There was no questioning the sincerity in his reply. "But you have no idea of how it can look in the newspapers and how delighted some of my colleagues in the Bar Association would be to have my scalp. Probably nothing will come of it, Allen, but if you do by some chance come up for questioning I'd be most grateful. Well, I've said enough. You do what you think fit."

"Russell . . ." Strand began.

"I'd rather we didn't talk about it any longer." His tone was decisive. There was a short silence which Strand was not tempted to break. When Hazen spoke again the usual friendliness was in his voice. "Oh, by the way, I saw Leslie last week. I called the school in New York and invited her out to lunch. There's a young boy, the son of a friend of mine, who shows some talent and I wanted to talk to her about the chances of her taking him on. She looked splendid. Has she said anything to you about the boy?"

"No," Strand said. The truth was that she hadn't told him about seeing Hazen at all.

"Ask her about him. The father is waiting for an answer. Well, it's been great talking to you. And please don't worry about me. Probably the whole thing will dry up and blow away in the next week or so. Take care of yourself, friend. And I promise, I'll come out and pay you a visit, probably on Thanksgiving, if not before. I miss you, old friend, I miss you a lot."

When Strand hung up, he sat staring at the telephone. Slowly, he finished his drink and turned off the lamp and went to the back of the apartment, where the bedrooms were. He looked into Leslie's room, where the wide old-fashioned bed he had shared with Leslie since the early days of their marriage looked comfortable and comforting. Jimmy's bed was narrow and his sleep there was haunted by dreams in which he felt tied down, imprisoned. He nearly decided to sleep in the big bed this one night, then thought better of it and went into his own room and slowly undressed and got in between the cold, shroudlike sheets.

He was awakened by a sound in the next room. He rubbed at his eyes blearily, automatically looking at the fluorescent dial of the clock on the bedside table. It was after four. The sound in the next room was steady and for a moment he just lay there, puzzled, wondering what it was. Then he realized it was a woman sobbing. He threw back the blankets and jumped out of bed and ran into Leslie's room. She was sitting in the dark, bent over on the big bed.

"Leslie," he said, "Leslie, for the love of God . . ." He switched on a lamp. He couldn't see her face.

"No lights," she cried, "please, no lights." Suddenly she seemed small to him, shrunken. He turned off the lamp and kneeled in front of her and put his arms around her waist. "Leslie," he said, "what is it?" Then, worriedly, "What are you doing here? I thought you were staying overnight in New York. What happened? Did you just get in? It's past four o'clock . . ."

"Don't scold me," she said. "I can't stand being scolded tonight. I'm home. Isn't that enough?"

"Darling," he said soothingly, "I'm not scolding. I'm worried. I want to help . . ."

"Hold on to me. Just like that. And don't say anything for a while." She laughed hysterically. "Can't a lady cry once in a while without calling out the police? Forgive me." She stroked his hair. Her hand was trembling. "I'm calming down. Believe me, it's nothing. Nerves. Idiocy. Now, you do something for me. Leave me alone for a minute or two. Go into the kitchen and make us a nice drink. Then I'll put on the light and fix my face and comb my hair and I'll come into the kitchen and we'll have a sneaky nightcap and a cozy little fireside chat and you'll see that there's nothing to get upset about. I'm a little foolish, but you've known that all along and there's no drastic change. Really. And put on a robe and slippers. You're shivering. Go ahead. *Please* go ahead."

Slowly, reluctantly, he stood up and went into his room. He put on a robe and slippers and walked down the dark hall toward the kitchen, switching on lights as he went. He poured two whiskeys, put a lot of water in his and a few drops in Leslie's and sat at the table and waited, looking out the window, seeing his reflection blurred against the dark glass and the snow drifting slowly down, white deliberate dust threatening winter in the beam of light from the old-fashioned kerosene lamp, now wired for electricity, that hung over the kitchen table.

I'm not going to be good for much in the morning, he thought, and then was ashamed of his selfishness. His first class was in American history and he tried to remember what he had intended to say about the Federalist papers because he didn't want to think about what Leslie's appearance, hysterical and at that hour of the night, might mean.

When Leslie came into the kitchen she was in a night-gown with a robe over it and her hair was in order and her face almost composed.

"Here," he said. "Here's your drink."

"Thank you," she said in a low voice. She tried to smile at him. It was like a flickering signal seen from thousands of yards away.

"Darling," he said, "what is it? Did you have an accident?"

"No," she said. "Only about a dozen near-misses. It's the first time I've driven in snow. The car takes on a life of its own."

"Did anything happen back in New York?"

"Nothing special." She sat down suddenly and took her glass in both hands, like an infant, and brought it up to her mouth and sipped at it thirstily. For a moment, in a flicker of memory, like a superimposed picture, he saw Judith Quinlan, in the steamy coffee shop, holding her cup to her lips with the same gesture. "By the time I'm eighty," Leslie said, "I suppose I'll develop a taste for Scotch. Still, from what I've read, they give it to the survivors of ship-wrecks, so it must have a life-supporting value. No, nothing special happened. I had a nice dinner with the dean and we played some Chopin duets and she told me about what a wonderful man her husband had been and how she has missed him since he died and what a credit to the school Caroline was and apologized for the fact that the school had no regular athletic program, because if it had, Caroline might have had chances for scholarships at colleges all over the country and how she looked forward to other evenings like this when I would stay over because it was so dreary sitting alone reading and sleeping alone in an empty apartment. No, nothing special—except that I had a vision. The vision was of my being like her, sitting alone reading at night and hating to go to bed alone . . ."

"Your husband isn't dead, darling," Strand said gently. "Although I must say he tried." The wry little joke did not make her smile.

"No, you're not dead," Leslie said. Her voice was flat, exhausted, without timbre. "And I don't think you're going to die. What I'm afraid of is that we're floating apart. We're like two people in the water, in different currents, slowly being pulled away from each other. Finally, you're gone and there I am like the dean, waiting for one of Jimmy's duty telephone calls or Eleanor's telegram on my birthday or a clipping from an Arizona newspaper saying that Caroline has tied the school record for the hundred yard dash. Suddenly, I couldn't bear lying there alone in the middle of the night in a strange bed with you more than a hundred miles away. I had to make sure I could find you, touch you . . ."

"Darling," Strand said, "I'm here. I'll always be here."

"I know it's irrational," she went on in the same dead tone, "but we're both so distracted these days, I have the feeling we're leading somebody else's lives. We don't sleep together, we don't even eat our meals together, we're drowning in a sea of boys, I have the most awful sexual dreams, other men, leering boys . . . And then on the road home a drunken man passed me, he was angry because I hadn't pulled to the side quickly enough for him, and he shouted insults at me, then dropped behind me and kept right after me, with his high lights on and blowing his horn and I went off the highway at the first exit because I was frightened of him and I got lost and I wandered around all over Connecticut on dark little winding roads and there wasn't a light showing in any of the houses I passed and the car skidded on the snow and I just missed hitting a tree . . . I had the crazy feeling that the car was trying to kill me, that it was my enemy and I was going to stop it and get out and sit by the side of the road and freeze to death, but then I saw a sign and I was just off the highway and here I am. For the rest of the night, at least, I feel safe again." She smiled wanly at him and sipped her drink. "Don't look so troubled, dear. I'm sure I'll come back to my senses in the morning. Go to bed now. You have to get up in a couple of hours." She leaned over and kissed him. "Go. Please. You look exhausted. I'm home and I'm safe and things will look different in the light of day."

He was too tired to argue with her and he put down his glass, which he had hardly touched, and dragged himself into his room and, shivering again, got under the covers without taking off his robe.

Later, he heard, or thought he heard, the sound of a piano being played softly, far away.

2

Classes were cancelled for the Wednesday afternoon before Thanksgiving and Leslie and Allen were packed and ready at noon when Conroy drove up in the Mercedes. They had been invited to spend the weekend in Hazen's house on the beach and while Strand would have preferred merely lazying around the quiet campus, with all the boys away for the holiday, a conversation he had had with Babcock, the headmaster, about Leslie the week before had made the invitation come at a fortunate moment.

Babcock had asked Strand to drop into his office and had fussed uneasily at his desk, lighting and relighting his pipe, pushing his glasses up and down from his forehead and rearranging papers while talking, with many false starts and embarrassed clearings of the throat, about the system of grading Strand was considering for his students and about the kind of schedule he preferred for the next term, which was still two months off. Finally, he had gotten around to the reason for his asking to see Strand. Apologetically, he said, "Allen, I don't want to worry you unnecessarily—and I don't want to seem to be prying into something that's no business of mine—but Leslie . . ." He sighed. "You know we all admire her immensely and we were delighted when she offered to take the class in music appreciation and I don't know where we could hope to find anyone as well qualified as she is to take her place. . . ."

"Please," Strand said, "just what are you trying to tell me?"

Babcock sighed again. The work of the term had made his face even wearier and grayer than it had been and Strand couldn't help but be sorry for the man as he nervously fussed with his pipe and avoided looking directly across the desk. "It seems that her behavior in recent weeks . . . well, there's nothing *extreme* about it, I hasten to say . . . but, I mean, she . . . she doesn't seem to be quite herself, if you understand what I mean. . . . Something . . . I couldn't say what it is and maybe you could help . . . Her behavior is a little . . . bizarre is much too strong a word, of course, but it comes to mind. . . . She has stopped abruptly in the middle of a sentence in the classroom. . . . Of course it's the boys who report this and one must take their gossip with a grain of salt . . . and just walked out of the room, without saying when or if she expected to return. And she has been seen by members of the faculty walking across the campus crying. It might be that she's overworked, although her schedule is minimal, as it were. . . . I just wondered if I might suggest a little holiday for her . . . a few weeks off. . . . Miss Collins, who is something of a musician herself, has offered to fill in temporarily. . . . Naturally, it is the policy of the school to continue salaries during—ah—sick leave. Oh, dear, I find it so difficult to strike the right tone . . ."

Strand felt sorry for the gentle, overburdened, slight man, and at the same time helpless about Leslie. Around the house, since the night she had arrived and awakened him she had merely been subdued, a quiet, receding presence moving listlessly, without complaint, from one room to another.

"It's not overwork," Strand said. "It's a combination of things, I would say. . . . I don't think you should blame the school in any way."

"Thank you, Allen. I wasn't sure how much you've noticed. Sometimes, those who are closest . . ." Babcock left the sentence unfinished. "The atmosphere of a school, when the term has been going on so long, when the season wanes, as it were . . . November can be trying to the strongest souls—the sense of confinement for a sensitive woman . . ."

"We've been invited to Russell Hazen's house in the Hamptons for the Thanksgiving weekend," Strand said. "Our son may join us, there will be people there who

interest her. . . . Perhaps that will be all she needs."
Strand was anxious to get away from the sight of the
weary, anxious face behind the desk. "It may help. If it
doesn't—we'll see. Actually, a good friend of hers has
asked her to go to Europe with her. So far, she's refused
—but if I let her know that you suggested a little vacation
might do her good—I'll be as tactful as possible. . . . You
don't mind if I wait until the weekend is over before I talk
to her about it, do you?" As he said it, he knew he was
postponing. Out of cowardice? Fear of bruising Leslie even
more?

"Anything that you feel is the wise course to pursue.
You're in the best position to judge," Babcock said. There
was relief in his voice that the matter, at least for a few
days, would be out of his hands. "And you know, I'm
sure," he added delicately, "that if between you and your
wife you feel that some psychiatric help would be useful,
there's a very good man who comes up from New Haven
when we need him, who might . . . You'd be surprised how
many times we have felt it necessary to talk to him. For
teachers and students alike. Sometimes I think that we are
all too close, we sit in each other's laps, so to speak, day
in and day out, egos are rubbed raw, tempers flare, melancholy sets in, the approach of winter . . . so many things
to consider, so many stresses . . ." One last sigh and he
turned back to shuffling papers on his desk.

When Strand left the office, he walked slowly across
the campus. As he passed students, other teachers, who
said hello to him, he weighed their greetings, wondering
who had spoken to Babcock about Leslie, what they felt
about her, who snickered secretly at her behavior, who
pitied her, who said poor woman, the husband's fault . . .

Perhaps a psychiatrist, Babcock had said, out of the
goodness of his heart and the modern totemic belief that
words could cure ills that words had not caused and were
beyond the reach of the remedies of language. What could
Leslie tell the man from New Haven? I have been uprooted,
my dear man, suddenly and without warning, from the city
in which I was born and in which I have lived all my life;
overnight my children, to whom I have devoted the great-

est part of my emotion, have gone their own way; I am
deafened by the clamor of that constantly renewed tribe
of barbarians—boys in their teens—whose values are as
strange to me, and as hostile, as that of the savages of the
forest of the Amazon. And, since you are paid to hear
the darkest truths of the troubled soul, I shall not hide
from you that now, I, as a woman in her forties, at a time
when, I am assured by the authorities of your profession,
I am at the height of my sexual desires and capacity for
satisfaction, am forced to sleep alone. I shall not bore you
with my dreams. I am sure you can easily guess their
nature.

As he crossed the campus, Strand shook his head, tortured. What was the approved procedure for a psychiatrist
at this juncture? What was he likely to suggest? Divorce?
Violent exercise? Drugs? Other men? Masturbation?

He decided that if he finally had to cope openly with
Leslie's problem—and, he realized, his own—whatever
else he might say, he would not bring up the subject of
psychiatry.

In the days before Thanksgiving he said nothing to
Leslie about what Babcock had told him, acted as normally
as he could, as though he sensed nothing was wrong, the
outburst in the kitchen had never occurred.

Now, in the cold November noon, as he and Leslie
greeted Conroy, in the holiday atmosphere of boys racing
off jubilantly to four days of freedom, he felt reassured.
Leslie looked lovely, he thought, smart and young in her
heavy beige wool coat with the collar turned up around her
face, alive and eager and flushed with color from the wind.

He held her hand in the back seat as Conroy started
the car and they wound around the campus to the stone
gates which marked the limits of the school grounds and
out onto the open road. As they left the school behind
them he felt as though a great weight had been lifted from
his shoulders.

The weekend, they all agreed, was a great success. The
Solomons, whose beach house was closed for the winter,

were there and Linda Roberts, all of them pleased at seeing each other again and feeling lucky that the sun was shining and the weather warm enough to have cocktails on the terrace with the salt autumnal wind off the calm sea. Jimmy had brought along his guitar and entertained them, especially Herbert Solomon, with imitations of some of the more obstreperous performers among Solomon's clients. Hazen had been a relaxed host and if he was worried about his wife or the investigation in Washington he hadn't shown it. Leslie had brought along her painting kit and portable easel and with Linda accompanying her had gone down the dunes and started a landscape that Linda assured her would wind up hanging on the walls of a museum. Linda was more exuberant than usual. The gallery in Paris with which her New York gallery was associated had asked her to bring over a representative show of twentieth-century American paintings for an exhibition and Linda had gotten the last two of fifty canvases for which she had been negotiating for three months and would be leaving for France within a week. She repeated her invitation to Leslie. "They're paying the way for me and an assistant. You'd make a marvelous assistant. When it comes to hanging the show, I'll need an American to back me up against all those impossible Frenchmen. And we'll take along your dune painting and in the program notes we'll write that you're our new, marvelous one hundred percent American discovery. All the other paintings are signed by people whose names end in *ski*."

Leslie had laughed and said, "Pipe dreams, Linda. I've had my Paris trip this year."

"Allen"—Linda had appealed to Strand—"make her say yes, she'll go."

"If she won't," Strand said, "*I'll* go."

"You don't look like an assistant *anything*," Linda said. "It'd be such fun, Leslie."

But Leslie shook her head, still smiling. "I'm a working woman. There are four hundred boys in Connecticut waiting for me to explain to them on Monday what A flat minor means."

But Strand could see that Leslie was tempted. Before the

weekend is up, he decided, he would tell her about Babcock's suggestion.

Hazen, who had been down on the beach with Mr. Ketley inspecting the damage a storm had done to a jetty the week before, came up to the terrace where they were standing, wrapped in sweaters and coats, watching the sunset. Hazen was dressed in heavy corduroys and a ski cap and mackinaw, his face whipped to a high color by the wind. He looked as though he had never been in an office in his life. He smiled benignly at his guests. "It'd be perfect," he said, "if your kids were here, too, Leslie. The *other* kids, Jimmy. No offense meant by calling the brood kids. You know what would be nice—telephoning them and saying 'Happy Holiday.'"

"There's no need going to all that expense," Strand said. "They're okay."

"Nonsense," Hazen said. "I insist."

So they trooped into the house and telephoned Caroline in Arizona and Eleanor and Giuseppe in Georgia and there was a general hubbub as they took turns at the two linked phones in the downstairs living room and the small library.

Leslie had sounded lighthearted as first Caroline and then Eleanor gossiped with her over the phone. Taking turns, they all said hello. The only wrong note came when Leslie and Strand were talking to Caroline and Leslie said how much they missed her and Caroline said, "East Hampton isn't for me. I don't like the boys there."

"Now, what in the world does that mean?" Leslie said testily. Strand knew what it meant. Caroline had not forgotten the night in the parked car when George had torn at her clothes and broken her nose. Would never forget.

"It doesn't mean anything," Caroline said. "I'm happy as a lark out here. Arizona is divine."

After that they all went upstairs to get ready for dinner. Solomon and Strand were the first ones down and while Strand stood in front of the driftwood fire, blazing high and spitting blue and green sparks, Solomon fixed himself a drink. With a sigh of satisfaction, Solomon sank into an easy chair and spoke about Jimmy. He told Strand that Jimmy was a great favorite around the office and with a wry smile intimated that Jimmy was having an affair with one of his stars, a woman by the name of Joan Dyer, who until Jimmy came into the business had been the most difficult of all his singers. "She's been a different woman since she clapped eyes on the boy," Solomon said. "I'm doubling his salary for devotion to the cause of Solomon and Company above and beyond the call of duty. She's been a man-eater with everybody else in the office, including me. A tigress. Her tantrums are a legend in the business. I'd been seriously thinking of letting her go even though she sells more records than anybody else I've got."

"How old is she?" Strand asked.

"Thirty-five, thirty-six."

"Isn't he a little young for her?" Strand was not pleased with the news, although if he had been asked why, he couldn't have explained his reasons.

"Apparently not," Solomon said. "Don't worry about Jimmy, though. He's amazingly level-headed for a boy his age. Hasn't he said anything to you about her?"

Strand shook his head. "Jimmy doesn't boast about his conquests. If he has any. For all I know he's still a virgin."

Solomon grinned. "Don't bet on it."

Strand didn't smile. "I was still a virgin at his age," he said.

"Different professions," Solomon said, "different moralities." He shrugged.

"Thirty-five," Strand said. "Is she married?"

"There's a husband around somewhere, the second or third, I think. Don't look so shocked, Allen. Show business . . ."

"Do me a favor," Strand said. "Don't say anything about this to Leslie. I'm afraid it might disturb her. She still thinks of him as her little innocent child."

"She's in great form these days, Leslie," Solomon said, "isn't she?"

"Great." Solomon might be an astute judge of talent but as a barometer of the ups and downs of female weather he was hardly reliable. Strand remembered Leslie's guess that Hazen and Nellie Solomon were lovers and he wondered if Solomon was any better at measuring his wife's emotional level than he was of Leslie's.

Although Leslie was putting up a brave front Strand had the uneasy feeling that her show of good spirits was the result of politeness rather than an indication of any real change in her mood. He was not the only one to sense this. Jimmy, who had driven Nellie Solomon into the village to do some shopping at the drugstore, had gotten Strand aside when he returned to quiz him about Leslie. "Is Mom okay?" he asked. He looked worried.

"Of course," Strand said, sharply. "Why do you ask?"

"Something Mrs. Solomon said in the car. She said when Mom didn't realize anybody was watching her, she looked—melancholy was the word she used. And when she talked to people she seemed distant, as though she was behind some kind of curtain, Nellie said."

"Have *you* noticed anything?"

"I'm a dope," Jimmy said. "Mom always seems the same to me, except when she's bawling me out about something. And she hasn't bawled me out even once this weekend." He grinned. "Maybe that's a bad sign."

"If you have any more private conversations with the lady," Strand said, angered at the accuracy of Nellie Solomon's observation, "tell her your mother couldn't be better."

Jimmy looked at him curiously and Strand knew that he had been too vehement in his reassurance. "Will do," Jimmy said and dropped the subject. Another curtain in the family, Strand thought. Between my son and myself.

Somehow, throughout the rest of the weekend, there had never seemed to be a proper moment for telling Leslie about the conversation with Babcock. And so far Leslie had not volunteered any comments about her lunch in New York with Hazen. The curtain Mrs. Solomon had spoken about had dropped long before Thanksgiving.

They reached Dunberry late. There had been heavy traffic, people going home from the holiday to be ready for work on Monday morning. They had dropped Linda off at her apartment near Hazen's house on the East Side,

because she was late for a supper she had promised to go
to. Jimmy had said good night and had gone off on a date.
The Solomons had driven to the city in their own car.
Hazen had insisted that Leslie and Strand come up to his
apartment for a bite to eat. He had called from the beach
and had the butler leave some food on the sideboard in
the dining room. It had been a pleasant and easy meal,
cold chicken and salad and a bottle of white wine. Hazen
had sent Conroy home but had ordered a limousine to
take the Strands to Dunberry. Strand had protested at the
extravagance, and as usual Hazen had waved away his
protests.

"It was a wonderful holiday, Russell," Leslie said as she
kissed Hazen good-bye at the door. "I feel like a new
woman."

"We must do it again," Hazen said. "Maybe a whole
week or ten days, even, at Christmas, if I can make the
time. Try to get the kids down there, too. They make that
wreck of a house feel young again."

In the back seat of the limousine, Leslie put her head on
Strand's shoulder and dropped off to sleep. If he had been
going anyplace but back to Dunberry he would have felt
completely at peace. With Leslie's soft breathing so close
to him and the uneventful but happy four days behind them
he felt that he could honestly go to Babcock and tell him
that he thought that Leslie's crisis, whatever its causes,
had passed, that she could be depended upon to perform
her duties at the school in a normal fashion and that it
wouldn't be necessary for her to apply for sick leave. He
told himself that while Mrs. Solomon had made a shrewd
guess about Leslie, she had exaggerated her estimate of
Leslie's vagueness and occasional small fugues out of all
proportion. But he knew that his thinking in part was in-
fluenced by selfishness. The thought of being without her
for weeks or even months was dismaying.

He felt Leslie stir at his side and lift her hand from his
shoulder. "Are we there yet?" She sounded like a sleepy
child.

"Nearly."

"What a nice vacation. Never-never land, Long Island,

Zip Code 119 something." She laughed softly. "I could spend the rest of my life there. Just painting and looking at the ocean and not thinking about anything, surrounded by those nice, rich, generous people." She laughed again. "Would you be bored?"

"I doubt it," he said. "I might take up golf. Or basket weaving."

"It was good of Russell to start making plans already about our coming out for Christmas. With the whole family." She sat up suddenly. "Why do you think Caroline said on the phone that she'd never come to the Hamptons again?"

"She said something about boys . . ." Strand purposely made it sound vague. He hoped that Leslie would never find out exactly what that meant. Better to let her wonder than have her know about Caroline's struggle in the car and the near rape and the brutal fist. "Maybe she's found some young man in Arizona and her interests lie in another direction now." His words sounded to him as though he was speaking through cotton wool.

"I'm going to write her a good strong letter," Leslie said. "She knows we wouldn't go without her on her vacation and it's selfish of her to ruin it for all of us for some foolish little whim."

"I'm sure she'll see the light and come around," Strand lied.

When the car drew up in front of the Malson house Strand saw that there was a light at the window of one of the bedrooms on the second floor. It was past ten thirty and all lights were supposed to be out but it was likely that some of the boys had gathered to swap stories about the weekend. He got out of the car and started toward the house, the chauffeur following with their bags. Just as he reached the door it swung open violently and a boy, barefooted and in pajamas, ran out, nearly knocking him over. Before he could move, another boy burst out of the door in pursuit. This one Strand could recognize. It was Romero, dressed in jeans and a sweater. Neither of the boys made a sound. By the light of the front door lamp, Strand saw that Romero had a knife in his hand.

"Stop!" he shouted. "Stop right where you are."

"Oh, my God," Leslie cried.

Neither of the boys stopped. The first boy, much larger than Romero, dodged behind a tree, cut off to the right. Romero, running swiftly, soundlessly, caught up to him and jumped on his back and they both twisted and fell to the ground. Now Romero was on top, sitting on the boy's chest. Strand ran over to them, shouting, and managed to grab Romero's wrist, which Romero was holding at shoulder height, his hand grasping the small knife.

"Are you crazy?" Strand said, pulling at the wrist, struggling, feeling how thin and at the same time how powerful, like a cable alive with electricity, the arm was. "Romero. Drop that knife."

As though hearing his name had brought him to his senses, Romero let the knife fall, turned and looked up at Strand. "All right," he said. His voice sounded strange and calm. "It's over." He stood up.

Then Strand saw that the boy on the ground, who was sobbing in big convulsive gasps, was Teddy Hitz. There was blood all over Hitz's face and more blood was pumping from a slash on his cheek.

"Leslie," he said, as calmly as he could, "will you go in and phone the doctor and then Mr. Babcock and tell them to get over here as quickly as they can. Hitz is hurt."

"Not enough," Romero said.

"You shut up," Strand said, as Leslie ran into the house. "Driver," he called to the chauffeur, who was standing frozen near the door, still holding the bags, "will you come help me here?" He kneeled next to Hitz, whose sobs were subsiding. "Okay, Hitz," he said, "he's dropped the knife." He took out his handkerchief and put it against the cut on Hitz's cheek. "Can you hold on to it yourself?"

Hitz nodded, blubbering, and put his hand up to the handkerchief.

"Holy Jesus Christ!" The chauffeur had come over to them and was staring down at the bleeding boy. "What goes on here?"

"I taught the sonofabitch a lesson," Romero said. Now

Strand could see that his face, too, was bloody, and he spoke thickly, as though his lips were swollen.

"That's enough of that, Romero," Strand said. Then to Hitz, "Do you think you can walk?"

Hitz nodded and sat up. Thank God, Strand thought. Hitz weighed over two hundred pounds and the driver was a small old man and Strand doubted that between them they could have managed to have carried Hitz even as far as the door.

"*Madre!*" Romero said disgustedly, "a little scratch like that and he makes a fucking massacre out of it."

"You keep quiet," Strand said, standing up and taking Hitz's hand to help pull him to his feet. "And I advise you to start thinking hard. There are a lot of questions you're going to have to answer."

"I want a lawyer," Romero said. "I have a right to a lawyer."

Even as he got Hitz to put his arm around his shoulders, saying "Just lean on me and walk slowly," Strand nearly laughed. A lawyer. In Romero's neighborhood, he realized, ten-year-old children knew all about lawyers.

Romero wheeled around and walked quickly into the house. He had the lights of the common room on and was sitting on a table, swinging his legs, when Strand and the driver got Hitz, staggering dramatically, into the room. "You'd better lie down," Strand said to Hitz, "and keep your head up." The handkerchief was now drenched in blood.

He helped Hitz stretch out on the battered couch of the common room and prop his head against the arm. "Mrs. Strand is calling the doctor," Strand said to him. "I'm sure you'll be all right." Then he said to the driver, who was standing in the middle of the room, shaking his head, muttering, over and over, "Goddamn kids, goddamn kids." "You can go now, driver. Everything's under control. You've got a long way back to town." He wanted to get rid of the man. The fewer people involved in this little mess the better. He was glad that Hazen hadn't made Conroy drive them out. He could imagine the story Conroy would have to tell his employer if he had been there.

"Okay, I'm leaving," the driver said. "I ain't got any special desire to be here all night when the police come."

Police. Strand hadn't thought of that.

"You might want to hold on to this." The driver held out the knife. It was a Swiss army knife and the blade had blood on it. "I picked it up outside. If you can, keep my name out of it. I don't want to get mixed up in no court case if I can help it . . . having to drive out to Connecticut on my own time every time a lawyer makes an objection. It's enough trouble driving in New York as it is."

"Thanks," Strand said and took the knife. The blade was only about three inches long. It didn't look like much of a weapon, but Hitz's blood was still coming through the handkerchief he was holding to his cheek.

"This yours?" he asked Romero as the driver went out.

"Who knows?" Romero said. He grinned malevolently.

Strand looked at him closely for the first time in the neon glare of the common room. Romero's lips *were* bruised and swollen. The flesh around his right eye was puffing up and already beginning to discolor and he had to squint to see out of it. "Anybody can buy a knife like that in any hardware store," Romero said. "They sell them by the million. I've had one since I was nine. Never leave home without it, like they say on the television."

"Listen, Romero," Strand said quietly, "you're in trouble and I want to help you. You've got to believe that, because I'm afraid you're going to need all the help you can get. Now tell me what happened. Before the doctor gets here and Mr. Babcock and the police."

Romero took a deep breath, stopped swinging his legs. "He beat up on me. I went down to his room on a personal matter and he beat the shit out of me. He weighs sixty pounds more than me, so I thought we ought to meet on more equal terms." He grinned again, his swollen and battered face grotesquely twisted.

"What was the personal matter?"

"Personal," Romero said.

"He accused me of stealing his money," Hitz said. His garishly striped pajamas were streaked with blood. "I'm not going to let a little sneaky spik make accusations like that and get away with it."

"What money?" Strand asked, looking from one boy to the other.

"*My* money," Romero said. "And some letters. He broke open my tin box and he took my money and the letters."

Leslie hurried into the room. "Allen," she said, "the doctor and Mr. Babcock are coming right over." She stared at the bloodied boy on the couch, Romero's disfigured face, the knife still open in Strand's hand. "Oh, it's too much," she said softly. She turned and rushed out of the room, down the hall to their apartment.

"What letters?" Strand demanded again.

"Private letters," Romero said. "From a girl friend. I don't like to have my private letters read by anybody. Especially shits like him."

"I never saw any of your letters," Hitz said.

"You fucking liar," Romero said and Strand moved to get between the table on which he was sitting and the couch. But Romero didn't get off the table. "You made fun of them when I came to your room. You read them, all right. Romeo Romero you called me, you fat shit."

"Shut up," said Strand.

"I never saw any letters," Hitz whined. "I don't know what he's talking about."

"All right," Strand said, "let's forget about the letters for the time being. How much money do you say it was, Romero?"

"Three hundred and seventy-five dollars."

"What?" Strand said, surprised. "How much?"

"Three seventy-five."

"Where did you get that much money?"

"I want a lawyer," Romero said.

"I'll tell you where, Mr. Strand," Hitz said. "He runs a crap game two or three nights a week in his and Rollins's room. And a lot of the fellers think he uses loaded dice. Him and Rollins both. A spik and a nigger. That's the kind of school you're running and don't think I'm not going to let everybody know about it. My father's a big wheel in

Washington and he knows every newspaperman down there and plenty in New York . . ."

"You'd better keep quiet, Hitz," Strand said, despising the fat, blubbering boy. "Concentrate on keeping your mouth shut and stopping the bleeding." He sighed as he thought of what the night's disaster would look like in the newspapers and what it would sound like at the next meeting of the Dunberry Board of Trustees. "*Do* you and Rollins run a crap game in your room at night?" he asked Romero.

"Leave Rollins out of it," Romero said. "He's got nothing to do with it. He just happens to be my roommate."

"Where is Rollins?"

"Asleep. He doesn't know anything about what's happened. He came home tired and went to sleep."

"You didn't tell him anything about what happened?"

"If I told him he'd've gone down and killed Hitz with his bare hands. And he'd be out on his ass in the morning. And there'd be no college for him, no pro ball. He's got enough trouble being black. I don't want to see him wiped out just because he's my friend."

"Let me ask you a question, Jesus," Strand said. "Why do you think Hitz here took your money?"

"If there ever *was* any money," Hitz said. "This little greaseball's been trying to get me since the beginning of the term. I don't like some of the types they're letting into this school nowadays and I don't hide it. This is a free country and I can say what I want . . ."

"I think you'll be better off holding your peace, Hitz," Strand said, trying to sound impartial and patient and knowing he was not succeeding. "Now, Romero, what made you think that it was Hitz who took your money and nobody else?"

"I got private information."

"What sort of information?"

"Confidential."

"Who told you?"

"I said confidential," Romero repeated.

"Did you find the money in Hitz's room? Or the letters you spoke of?"

"No," Romero said.

"Sure he didn't," Hitz said. "Because I didn't take any-thing. If *anybody* took anything. That man's crazy, Mr. Strand, he's got a hate on against the whole world, especial-ly if they're white. If the teachers here had the guts of a rabbit, even, they'd all say, every one of them, including you, that they wished that this little bastard had never *heard* of Dunberry."

"You be careful of your language, fat boy," Romero said, "or I'll carve your other cheek and cut your ass for dessert."

The threat reminded Strand that he was still holding the open bloodstained knife. He closed it and dropped it into the pocket of his overcoat. "Romero," he said, "you're not doing yourself any good by talking like . . ."

The door opened and Dr. Philips and Mr. Babcock came in. Babcock stopped dead as his eyes took in the scene. "Oh, dear," he said.

The doctor nodded to Strand, looked curiously at Ro-mero, then bent over Hitz and said, "Let's see what we have here." He took the soaked handkerchief from Hitz's face and dropped it on the floor, squinted through his glasses, bending down over Hitz's head and touching the wounded cheek lightly. "I'd better get him to the infirmary," he said. "It's going to take some cleaning and sewing. Quite a bit of sewing."

"It hurts," Hitz said, his lower lip quivering.

"Of course it hurts," the doctor said. "It's supposed to hurt." He was a brusque man, competent and quick and not known to coddle adolescents. He opened his bag and took out a big bandage pad and taped it over the wound. It turned red immediately. The doctor took off his coat. "Put this on and get up and I'll walk you to my car."

"I don't know if I can walk. . . . I lost a lot of . . ."

"Nonsense," the doctor said. "Get up on your feet. It's just superficial. Your beauty won't be marred."

Hitz made a show of dizziness as he pushed himself off the couch. The doctor helped him on with the overcoat and buttoned it up. Romero, his head bent, watched through lowered eyelids, his eyes dark and scornful. "Maybe he needs morphine," he said. "So he can bear the awful pain."

"That's enough out of you, young man," Babcock said. It was the first time Strand had heard a note of severity in the headmaster's voice.

"Babcock," the doctor said, stopping at the door, his hand lightly on Hitz's arm, "I suggest you call the police."

"The police," Babcock said distractedly. "Oh, dear. Do you really think it's necessary?"

"If I want to keep my license to practice," the doctor said, "and if you want to keep your school, it's necessary."

"Of course," Babcock said. "It's just that . . . Nothing like this has ever come up before. Of course. I'll call."

"Tell them to meet us all at the infirmary. There'll certainly have to be an inquiry. In the meantime, young man—" He stopped and stared at Romero. "I know you, don't I? From the football team?"

"Yes," Romero said. "You told me I was crazy to play."

"What's your name . . . ?"

"Romero," the boy said.

"Consider yourself under a citizen's arrest. And I'm the citizen. I'll see you all at the infirmary."

There was silence for a moment as the doctor and Hitz went out. Strand was glad that he no longer had to look at Hitz's bloody face. Babcock sighed and stared down at the couch and raised his glasses to his forehead then pulled them down again. Strand noticed that Babcock wasn't wearing a tie. It was the first time he had seen him tieless. He probably had been in bed with his stout wife when Leslie's call came and had dressed hurriedly.

"The couch will have to be cleaned," Babcock said. "It's all bloody. What should I say to the police?" He sounded helpless. "I have no idea of what happened. Is there a phone here?"

"There's a pay phone in the basement," Romero said.

"Thank you," Babcock said. He started toward the staircase leading to the basement level, then stopped. "Oh, dear," he said, patting his pockets, "I left all my money on the dresser. I was in bed and . . . Allen, do you . . . ?"

Strand dug into his pocket. There were only bills. "I'm sorry," he said.

"You can call the police emergency number," Romero said. Strand had the feeling that Romero was enjoying himself. "They'll come in three minutes, sirens and lights, the whole business."

"They'll wake everybody up," Babcock said. "I don't think we need . . ."

"I'll go into the apartment and make the call from there," Strand said.

"I wish I knew what this is all about," Babcock said plaintively.

"I'll fill you in later." Strand went down the hall and into his own living room. Leslie was sitting at the piano bench, but not playing. She turned when she heard Strand come into the room. "Well?" she said.

"It's a mess. I haven't time to tell you now. Nothing really serious." As he said it he wished he could believe it. "I have to call the police." He looked up the number in the directory on the table next to the phone and dialed. The man on duty said his name was Leary, Sergeant Leary. "Sergeant," Strand said, "could you send somebody over to the Dunberry infirmary as soon as possible?"

"What is the nature of the incident?" Sergeant Leary asked.

"There's been a . . . a dispute . . . a scuffle, between two of the boys. One of them has been hurt . . ."

"Does it require an ambulance?"

"Oh, I don't think so. The doctor's examined him. A superficial wound. A cut." He cleared his throat. "One of the boys had a knife."

"At *Dunberry*?" Leary sounded shocked. The crime rate in the village and its environs was not rich in midnight stabbings.

"It was the end of the holiday." For the honor of the school, Strand thought that he had to make some sort of apology. "None of the staff was on duty. Can you send someone?"

"There'll be a man down there—the infirmary, you said?"

"Yes."

"What side of the campus is that on? East? West?"

Strand felt confused. He closed his eyes and tried to remember on which side of the campus the sun rose. He said, "East," to Sergeant Leary and the sergeant said, "Okay. Is the perpetrator in custody?"

For a moment, Strand didn't associate the word with the events of the evening. Then he remembered Romero. "Yes," he said, "we are holding the perpetrator."

As he hung up, Leslie laughed. The laugh had a little crack in it. "You sound like a detective in a movie," she said.

"Darling," Strand said, "I think you'd better not wait up. I have to go to the infirmary with Romero and Babcock, and the police'll be there and God knows how long it's going to take. I'll tell you all about it when I get back."

"Perpetrator," Leslie said. "I wonder how many perpetrators we have on the campus. I wish I could see the alumni bulletin of the year 2000 and see how many graduates of Dunberry are behind bars at that time."

"I'm sorry, dear, that you . . ."

"It's not your fault," she said. "Try not to stay up too late. You have to get up early in the morning."

He kissed her and went back into the common room. Behind him he heard Leslie locking the door.

3

When they got to the infirmary, with Romero walking between the two men, the doctor had just finished cleaning out the wound along Hitz's cheek and was injecting a local anesthetic, preparatory to taking stitches. Hitz was moaning and shedding tears. Romero looked at him scornfully, but said nothing. He sat down on a stool and took out a package of cigarettes and lit one and began blowing smoke rings. The doctor was too busy with Hitz to notice it at first, but when he did, he glared at Romero and said, "No smoking allowed in here, young man."

"Sorry," Romero said as he stubbed out his cigarette. "And thanks. You've probably just saved me from cancer, Doc."

"Save your jokes for the police," the doctor said and started threading a needle. Hitz watched him fearfully. "You allergic to penicillin?" the doctor asked him.

"I don't know."

"Well, we'll take the chance." The doctor dusted the wound with the powder. "Your cheek numb yet?" He pushed his forefinger in its rubber glove hard against the cheek, above the wound. "You feel that?"

"I guess not."

Strand had to turn away as the doctor stitched at the long gash with swift little jabs of the needle and deftly tied the first knots. He was ashamed of himself for being squeamish, especially since Babcock and Romero followed the operation with interest.

As Dr. Philips was finishing up and taping a bandage on Hitz's cheek, the door opened and a policeman came in. He looked as though he had just gotten reluctantly out of bed. "The sergeant says there's been an offense committed," he said. "What is the nature of the offense?"

"I'm the nature of the offense," Romero said. "I cut him."

"You're under arrest. It is my duty," the policeman said formally, "to tell you that anything you say may be used against you and that you have the right to call a lawyer."

"That's what I want, a lawyer," Romero said. "Do you know a good one? The nearest one I know is on 137th Street in New York."

The policeman ignored him. "Has the weapon been recovered?"

Strand took the knife out of his pocket and handed it to the policeman.

"Thank you," the policeman said. "It'll be needed for evidence. You finished, Doc?"

"Yes," the doctor said, stripping off his rubber gloves.

"We'd better be getting down to the station," the policeman said. "Put out your hands, kid."

Romero smiled and put out his hands. "Afraid I'll jump you in the squad car, officer?"

"Felonious assault with a deadly weapon," the policeman said. "You better start taking it serious."

"Junior size, please," Romero said as the policeman brought out a pair of handcuffs.

"Do you think it's absolutely necessary, officer?" Babcock said. "I'm sure he'll behave . . ."

"S.O.P., sir," the policeman said. "Standard operating procedure. It's in the manual."

"Oh," Babcock said. "In the manual." He sighed.

"March, kid." The policeman jerked at the handcuffs and Romero got off the stool.

"You don't need me, do you?" Dr. Philips asked.

"Did you witness the offense?"

The doctor shook his head.

"Okay. Later on, you may have to describe the wound. But we won't be needing you anymore tonight."

Babcock, Strand and Hitz, the tears still streaming down his face, followed the policeman, who kept his hand on Romero's elbow as they went toward the door.

"Romero," the doctor said, "from now on I advise you to stick to football for your exercise."

"I'll get my car, officer," Babcock said, "and we'll meet you at the station."

They watched as the policeman pushed Romero into the back of the squad car and locked the door. There was a metal mesh between the front and rear seats, and Romero looked like a small caged animal blinking at the light over his head. The policeman got behind the wheel and drove off. Babcock sighed. "I'll go get my car," he said. "I'll just be a minute. I don't think Hitz ought to do much walking in his condition." He started off across the campus.

Strand was left alone with Hitz. "Stop sniffling," Strand said, annoyed at the boy.

"He'd've killed me. I'd've been dead now if you hadn't happened to come along."

"If he was trying to kill you," Strand said, "I think he could have picked up something a little more dangerous than a pocketknife with a two and a half inch blade."

"You wouldn't think that little knife was so undangerous if he'd come at you with it—or at your wife. Or that stuck-up daughter of yours who was at the football game," Hitz said, wiping his streaming nose with the back of his hand. "You'd be screaming bloody murder about protecting society from the spiks and niggers."

"I'm afraid your vocabulary and mine don't contain the same words." Strand wished that he could get Hitz into a dark corner and slap the teary face.

"I'll tell you one thing," Hitz said, "they better put him away for a good long time or they'll hear from my father . . ."

"I don't think the judge will be worried about your father. Tell me, Hitz," Strand said, "*did* you take the money and the letters?"

"I never touched them. I don't know anything about them. You don't have to believe me. Go search my room and see if I'm telling the truth. He just came into the room and started yelling. I didn't even know what he was yelling about. I know he's your pet, you think he's so damn smart, the ghetto genius. Everybody knows about him. You want to hear what the other fellows call him? 'Jojo, the Jungle Boy. The Great Experiment!' Trying to turn a baby gorilla into a human being. Now you see how your experiment turned out, Mr. Strand?" Hitz's voice went shrill, in a hurried crescendo. "And who's paying for it? Me! You got any more noble experiments you want to play around with, I advise you to do them someplace else. And stick to test tubes."

"I don't need any advice from you, Hitz," Strand said. "I'm sorry it happened and very sorry you were hurt. But I'm not sorry enough to stand here and listen to any more lectures about society from you. Just keep quiet now and get ready to tell the police just how it happened, without any philosophical observations."

"He could've killed me," Hitz muttered, getting in the last word.

The lights of Babcock's car swept over them as the car pulled up. Hitz got into the back and Strand into the front beside Babcock.

When they got to the police station, Romero was standing in front of the sergeant's desk, the handcuffs off, the young policeman next to him. "I'm not saying anything until I get a lawyer," Romero repeated over and over again. "I don't even have to tell you my name."

"We know your name," the sergeant said patiently.

"There's the criminal." Romero pointed at Hitz. "He's a thief. I want him charged. Grand larceny."

"We'll come to that in due time," the sergeant said calmly. "You have the right to make one telephone call. To your lawyer if you want."

"I can't afford a lawyer. That sonofabitch stole all my money. I got six dollars on me. You know where I can find myself a lawyer in the middle of the night for six bucks?"

The sergeant played with the pocketknife which was on the desk before him, opening it and snapping it shut. "We'll get you a public defender tomorrow. Meanwhile, Jack," he said to the policeman, "put him in a cell. I'll get the story from these three gentlemen here and we'll book the kid in the morning."

"All right, friend." The policeman gripped Romero's

arm and escorted him toward the back, where Strand could
see two cells, both empty.

"Now, young man," the sergeant said to Hitz, "you
begin . . ."

It was nearly three in the morning before the sergeant
had finished quizzing them, making them retell their stories
over and over again as he noted down their answers on a
form he had taken from a file against the wall behind him.
"All right, gentlemen, thank you and good night," he said
finally. "You can go now. There's a session at the courthouse tomorrow and the boy can go before the judge and
he'll appoint a lawyer for his defense."

"I'll get the school lawyer for him," Babcock said. "But
now can't we take him back to the school with us? If you
release him in my custody? I'll stand responsible for getting him here in the morning."

"I'm afraid not, sir," the sergeant said. "It'll be up to
the judge to set bail. And Jack," he said to the policeman,
"will you escort Hitz back to the school and search his
room? I'd appreciate it if you two gentlemen went along
and witnessed the search. Sorry, Hitz—we have to see if
there's any evidence to back up Romero's charge against
you. Of course, if you refuse to let the officer in your
room, you're within your rights. We'll have to get a search
warrant. But we can't get that till morning and we'd have to
keep you here overnight."

Strand thought he detected a gleam of malicious pleasure
in Sergeant's Leary's eyes as he said this. The sergeant had
not been amused by Hitz's whining version of the events
of the night and had stared thoughtfully at the boy when
Hitz referred to his father's influence in Washington.

"Anybody who wants can search my room," Hitz said
loudly. "And me. Anytime they want. I got nothing to
hide." He began turning out his pockets, strewing loose
change and dollar bills on the desk and banging down his
wallet with a flourish.

"That's fine," the sergeant said when Hitz had finished.
"You can pick up your money. I'll type all this up and
you can all sign your names to it in the morning."

Hitz got into the car with the policeman, and Strand

and Babcock followed in Babcock's car. "What a dreadful night," Babcock said wearily, at the wheel. "Nothing like this has ever happened at Dunberry before. We've had some petty pilfering, of course, but violence like this . . ." He shuddered. "It's a mercy you and your wife came along when you did. Otherwise, the good Lord alone knows what might have happened. I hope Leslie wasn't too upset, although I must say she seemed admirably calm when she called me on the phone."

"She rises to the occasion," Strand said.

"What do you really think are the rights and wrongs of all this?" Babcock said. "I don't mean the knife part. With all the charity in the world I can't forgive a boy using a weapon against a classmate. But what do you think—was it a hideous misunderstanding or what? Did Romero tell you why he thought that it was Hitz who stole the money? Did you ask him?"

"I asked him," Strand said.

"What did he say?"

"He said it was confidential. Whatever that may mean."

"You must be terribly disappointed," Babcock said. "Romero was coming along so well."

"I don't feel disappointed," Strand said flatly. "I feel guilty. Guilty as hell. It was a case of faith overcoming judgment, I'm afraid. He belongs on the streets, not at a school like this. I confused raw intelligence with civilized behavior."

"You mustn't take it on yourself. Or Mr. Hazen, either." Babcock took a hand off the wheel to touch Strand gently on the arm. "It was just an unfortunate combination of circumstances. Nobody could have foreseen it. Frankly, when the term began I didn't think the boy would last out the year. But not for anything like this. I thought he might be bored, maybe insubordinate, unable to respond to discipline . . . Never anything like this. Do you think they'll put him in jail?"

"I hope so," Strand said bitterly. "I would, if I were the judge."

"There, there, Allen," Babcock said softly. "Why don't

we suspend judgment until we know all the facts in the case?"

"I stopped suspending judgment when I saw Romero running after Hitz with a knife in his hand."

They drove in silence for a few moments and then Strand said, "The trustees are bound to give you a rough time. If they demand a sacrificial offering, you can put the blame on me and you'll have my resignation the same day."

"I doubt that it will go that far," Babcock said, but he didn't sound convincing as he said it.

The policeman was waiting in his car with Hitz in front of the Malson house as they drove up. They all went through the empty common room and up the stairs to the first floor together. Strand was surprised that none of the other boys were up. The struggle in Hitz's room and his flight downstairs and out onto the campus must have been silent, deadly silent. Hitz had the room to himself. Whether it was due to his father's influence or to the fact that none of the boys would share quarters with him, Strand didn't know.

The room was small and, aside from the blood on the rug and the unmade bed, eerily neat. Strand and Babcock stood at the door because there wasn't enough space in the room for them all as the policeman methodically opened drawers, looked under the bed, threw back the blanket, turned over the rug, went through the pockets of Hitz's clothes hanging in the closet.

"Nothing," he said, after ten minutes.

"I told you," Hitz said. He had been ashen in the infirmary and at the police station, except for the streaks of blood on his cheek and along his neck, but now the color had returned to his face. "You could've saved yourself the trip. I told you I didn't take his money."

"I think you better get into bed and get some rest, sonny," the policeman said. "I'll be going now."

They left Hitz in his room, calm now and triumphant, and descended the stairs together. Strand said good night to the policeman and Babcock in the common room. Alone, he let himself drop into a chair for a few minutes.

He felt too exhausted to face Leslie without some interval of quiet.

He closed his eyes and tried to recall the exact movements of the policeman as he searched Hitz's room, going over the possibilities that the man might have overlooked just the one place that the money could be hidden. If he had found it, it would not have proven that Romero was innocent of a crime, but it would have been a mitigating circumstance, would have made Romero's attack on Hitz less senseless, less savage and inexcusable. But as he ticked off from memory the places the policeman had looked, Strand could think of no corner that had been missed. He sighed, opened his eyes, stood up, looked for a long time at the bloodstain on the common room couch where Hitz had lain with Strand's handkerchief pressed against his cheek. The handkerchief was still on the floor where the doctor had dropped it to look at the wound. The blood was dry now, a dark rust color, the cloth stiff. Strand bent and picked it up.

He turned off the light and went down the dark hall toward the door to the apartment. He remembered that Leslie had locked the door and fumbled in his pocket for the key. But when he put it in the door he found that the lock was open. He pushed open the door and went into the living room. All the lights were on.

"Leslie," he called. "Leslie!" He went into her bedroom. The lights were on there, too. The door to her closet was wide open. He saw that most of her clothes were missing. Then he saw the note on her dressing table.

He picked it up, his hand trembling, stared at it. The handwriting was hasty, not like Leslie's usual fine script at all.

Dearest,

Forgive me. I just couldn't stand staying here another night. I've called Linda and asked her if she really meant that she would take me along with her to Paris. She said she did and I told her I'd drive into New York right away and be ready to leave with her tomorrow. Please don't worry about me, my darling. And please, please take care of yourself. And above all, don't blame yourself for anything. I love you with all my heart,

Leslie

He put the note down carefully, smoothed it out with his hand. Then he closed the closet door, put out the lights, and went into his room, undressed and got into bed. He did not set the alarm. Babcock would understand that he could not face a class that day.

"Of course, the whole school is talking about it," Babcock was saying. It was eleven o'clock in the morning and they were driving in Babcock's car toward the courthouse. Strand had awakened early, but had stayed in the apartment, disregarding the bell for breakfast and the ringing for the change of classes. He had tried to call Linda's apartment, but the line had been busy each time he had dialed and he had finally given up. Leslie had not called him and he had sent a telegram to Linda asking her to phone him. He knew it was foolish to worry that Leslie might have had an accident on the way into the city. If anything had happened, somebody would have gotten in touch with him. But he could not get over the vision of Leslie, agitated and distraught, wandering off the road and crashing into a tree and lying bleeding in a ditch. He had also called Hazen's office but had been told by a secretary that Mr. Hazen had left early that morning for Washington. Conroy had driven him to the airport, the secretary had said, and she did not know where Mr. Hazen could be reached or when he would be back. "Naturally," Babcock said, driving slowly and carefully, "the Hitz boy spread the news as soon as he woke up this morning. With some lurid exaggerations, I would imagine, from what has come back to me. And he telephoned his father and his father got me on the phone and was most—ah—emphatic with me. What he actually said was that if I tried to whitewash the scandal—that's the word he used, scandal—he'd have my job. He also threatened to sue the school for criminal negligence for ignoring a known danger—that's Romero, of course—and to close us down. And to make sure that I knew that he was not—ah—absolutely happy, he said that if his son was forced to answer to a charge of theft he would name us as codefendants in a criminal libel suit. It's not the most obliging of families." Babcock smiled wanly. His face was gray and strained, his eyes red-rimmed and watery. His hands clenched the wheel so tightly that his knuckles showed white.

"You've had a busy morning," Strand said.

"I've had worse," Babcock said. "There was the morning eighty boys woke up vomiting and with extreme cases of diarrhea. We thought it was typhoid. It turned out to be the pastry we had for dessert the night before. The theory is that schoolmasters live to a ripe old age." He laughed softly. "Outdated wisdom."

"What do you expect you'll have to do?" Strand asked.

"I'm afraid the first thing we'll have to do is expel the boy. Romero. If we don't we'll probably lose half the enrollment of the school."

Strand nodded. "He brought it on himself."

"It's a tragedy just the same," Babcock said. "The next thing I hope to do is keep him out of jail some way. Try for a probationary period, at least. I've called the school lawyer and he's already seen Romero and is meeting us at the courthouse. I had hoped to avoid it. That's why I tried to get in touch with Mr. Hazen to see if he knew somebody else around here. If the parents—especially the ones like Mr. Hitz—get wind of the fact that we're paying the school's money for Romero's defense . . ." He shrugged and left the sentence unfinished. "How is Leslie taking it all?"

Strand had been waiting for the question, although he had hoped it wouldn't be asked. "Rather hard, I'm afraid. She's taken advantage of your kind offer of a sick leave and will be gone for a couple of weeks."

"She's left already?" Babcock's eyebrows went up in surprise.

"Yes."

"I don't blame her. If I could, I'd leave too." Babcock smiled wearily. He maneuvered the car into a parking place in front of the pillared, white clapboard courthouse. "A handsome building," he said. "Built in 1820. What woe has paraded through its corridors."

The lawyer for the school was named Hollingsbee. He was waiting for them at the door to the courtroom. He was fat and florid, in a beautiful dark suit. His voice matched his appearance, round and actorish. "They'll be bringing the boy in shortly," he said after acknowledging Babcock's introduction to Strand with a courtly nod. "I've spoken to him and I fear we have a difficult case on our hands. Romero won't cooperate at all. He's not going to testify. He told me he won't open his mouth. In court he says he won't even say why he did what he did, even though he told the police Hitz stole his money. Let 'em do their worst, he told me, what good would it do to talk? He says I'm the talker in the operation, I can say whatever I want. He seems to know more than is good for him about the law. He says he can't be forced to incriminate himself and he's not going to do it. He's sorry he talked as much as he did to the police. His attitude is sullen— perhaps understandably so—but it won't win sympathy in court. A little sign of contrition would be useful." The lawyer shrugged. "But that doesn't seem to be within his range. He says Mr. Strand here saw him running after Hitz with a knife and that he admitted both to Mr. Strand and the police that he used the knife on Hitz. He says everybody in the courtroom would laugh at him if he pretended he didn't cut Hitz. In fact, if you want to know what I think, he's proud of it and wants everybody to know he did it. He refuses to tell me why he suspects Hitz of being the thief. He says he's always known he'd wind up in jail one day and he has lots of friends who've been there and he's not afraid of it. His attitude, I have to tell you, will not sit kindly with the judge. Or with the jury, if it comes to that. He's over eighteen and he'll be tried as an adult. And we're pleading in a small town in Connecticut, not New York or Chicago, where knifings of this kind, obviously not with the intent to kill, are considered an almost normal part of everyday life. I'll do my best, of course . . ." The lawyer's voice sank to a melancholy register. "But I'm not optimistic."

"What are you able to do?" Babcock asked.

"Play on the boy's background. Brought up in a slum, with a broken and poverty-stricken family, etcetera, etcetera. The usual. Destruction of a promising career in a moment of emotional imbalance, that sort of thing. Not much."

"What can we do to help?" Babcock asked.

The lawyer made a small, helpless gesture with his hands. "Act as character witnesses for the accused. Bring up whatever you think might be useful. Remember you will be under oath."

Whatever he said about Romero's character, Strand knew, would never be the truth. Would he mention the stolen volumes of *The History of the Decline and Fall of the Roman Empire?* Not if he wanted to keep the boy out of jail.

As they were standing there, Hitz came down the hall. The big bandage on his cheek made a dramatic pattern on one side of his face. He bulged out of his clothes. Strand saw that his fly was open. Hitz looked at the three men resentfully, but stopped and said, "Good morning, Mr. Babcock." He ostentatiously ignored Strand. "My father said he was going to get in touch with you, sir. Did he reach you?"

"He reached me," Babcock said.

"He was very upset when I told him what happened," Hitz said.

"So it seemed," Babcock said. "Well, shall we go in?"

"Don't think I'm going to make things easy for Romero," Hitz said. "Or you, Mr. Strand."

"Thank you for the warning," Strand said. "And zip up your fly. You don't want to be held in contempt of court, do you?"

Hitz's face went red and he was struggling with the zipper as Strand led the way into the courtroom, where Sergeant Leary was waiting to testify. Among the few spectators Strand noticed a young woman whom he recognized as a reporter for the town newspaper seated in the first row, a writing pad on her lap and a pencil in her hand. Babcock saw her, too, and whispered, "The news has spread fast, I'm afraid. She's not here to watch the judge handle parking tickets."

Romero came in with the policeman who had arrested him. At least, Strand thought, he's not in handcuffs. He looked small and frail in the dark sweater Strand had bought him at Brooks Brothers. He smiled as he passed Hitz and said good morning to the headmaster and Strand. The lawyer accompanied him to a table set in front of the judge's bench.

The judge entered from his chambers and they all stood up. The bailiff declared the court open and they all sat down, except for the lawyer and Romero and the two policemen, who stood in front of the bench.

The district attorney read the charge in a monotonous drone. Romero looked around the courtroom curiously, as though he was not interested in what the man was saying but was intrigued by the architecture of the old hall.

The district attorney finished and the judge asked, "How does the defendant plead?"

"Not guilty, Your Honor," the lawyer said quickly.

Romero looked at the judge sardonically. The judge peered down at him over the steel rims of his reading glasses.

"I don't recognize the jurisdiction of this court," Romero said.

Strand groaned. TV, he thought, a thousand hours of TV lawyers.

The judge sighed. "We will not go into that at the present time, Mr. Romero. I remand you for trial in custody of the court. I set bail at ten thousand dollars."

Strand heard Babcock gasp. He only half listened as the lawyer argued for a reduction in bail and the acting district attorney emphasized the gravity of the case and the danger to the plaintiff if the defendant, who had admitted his act of violence and showed no remorse for it, was allowed to roam free.

"The bail stands at ten thousand dollars," the judge said. "Next case, please."

The reporter was scribbling busily as Romero, between the policeman and the lawyer, walked down the aisle toward the door. As the trio passed Hitz, Hitz raised his middle finger in a derisive, obscene gesture. Romero stopped walking and for a moment Strand was afraid he was going to leap at Hitz. But Romero merely said, loudly enough for the whole court to hear, "Your time will come, fat boy." Then he allowed the policeman to lead him out of the room.

"Oh, my God," Babcock said. He shook his head sadly. "I dread to think of what that young lady is going to write for tomorrow morning's paper." He took off his glasses and wiped them with his handkerchief, as though he was trying to erase what the glasses had witnessed in the courtroom. "Well," he said, "we'd better be getting back to the school."

On the way back in the car he said, "Allen, do you think Mr. Hazen would be willing to put up the bail money?"

"Ten thousand dollars?" Strand said. "I wouldn't like to hazard a guess."

When he got back to the campus it was the lunch hour and Strand was grateful that he wouldn't have to face any of the students or faculty as Babcock dropped him off in front of the Malson house. Getting out of the car, he felt as though his legs were giving way under him and he was afraid he would not be able to make it to the door. "If you don't mind," he said to the headmaster, "I would like to skip meals and classes for a day or two."

"I understand," Babcock said. "If I could, I'd skip meals and classes for a year."

"I'll try to get in touch with Mr. Hazen. If I do, I'll let you know what he says."

Babcock nodded and drove off. Strand went into the house. Mrs. Schiller was down on her knees, with a brush and a bucket of soapy water, scrubbing at the couch. She stood up when Strand came in. "What a business," she said. Her plump, maternal face, which always seemed to be flushed from standing in front of some invisible oven, was pained. "In twenty years here, there's never been anything like this." She looked around, as though she was afraid of being overheard. "I have to tell you something, Mr. Strand. But you have to promise that it won't go any further."

"Is it about what happened last night?"

"About last night. Yes."

"I promise."

"Can we go into the apartment?" She spoke in whispers. "I haven't been upstairs and one of the boys might've decided not to go to lunch and I wouldn't want anybody to hear."

"Of course," Strand said and led her down the hallway and unlocked the door and opened it. She followed him into the living room.

"Mr. Strand," she said, "I don't know how to say this, but I'm afraid it was my fault." She was near tears.

"What was your fault?"

"Romero stabbing the Hitz boy."

"How could that be?" Strand asked sharply.

"When I came in last night to turn down your beds, it was during the supper hour and the boys were all out of the house, I thought. I heard a radiator knocking and I went upstairs to turn it off. It was in the hall, right at the head of the stairs. The valve was stuck and I was working at it when I saw a boy coming out of Romero's room. It was young Mr. Hitz. I asked him why he wasn't at supper. He said he wasn't hungry, he'd had some hot dogs on the road on the way back to school. And he went downstairs to his room. I thought nothing of it. The older boys are allowed to miss supper at the end of holiday nights. I went home, we have a little house just off campus, and Mr. Schiller and I were watching television and we were just about to go to bed when there was a knock on the door. Jesus Romero was there. It must have been after eleven o'clock. He seemed calm enough. He's a cool boy at all times, mature for his age, if you know what I mean. At

least I used to think so . . . until all this happened . . ."
Her lips and double chins quivered.

"What did he want?"

"He said he'd just come in. He'd been on a trip, he said,
for the weekend, and he'd missed connections getting back
to Dunberry. He said something was missing from his
room, a book he needed for his first class in the morning.
He didn't seem overly concerned, except I should have
guessed it was something important, his coming to my
house so late at night. Only what with the holiday and the
television and all, I just wasn't thinking." She shook her
head sadly. "He wanted to know if I knew anything about
the book. Well, Mr. Strand . . . If I'd dreamed what was
in his mind I'd have kept my peace till doomsday. But the
boys have a habit of going into each other's rooms and
borrowing things—books, ties, a sweater . . . So I said I'd
seen Mr. Hitz coming out of his room at supper time. Now
I could cut my tongue out for being so foolish." She was
weeping now.

"Don't blame yourself, Mrs. Schiller," Strand said.

"I've been partial to Jesus since the beginning, Mr.
Strand. He's such a gentleman with me and he's so neat
and the other boys—at least most of them—treat him like
a stray dog and I thought I was being helpful. He asked
me if Mr. Hitz was carrying anything and I tried to remember, but I couldn't and I told him."

"How did he react to that?"

"Very calm, Mr. Strand. Not a hint of anything really
wrong. He just said thank you and that he hoped he hadn't
disturbed me and Mr. Schiller and went away and I thought
nothing of it until this morning when I heard . . ." The
tears were pouring now down her full cheeks.

Strand put his arms around her broad shoulders. He
could feel her trembling. "There, there," he said helplessly.
"It's not your fault."

"I don't know if Jesus has told anybody that I was the
one who told him that Mr. Hitz was . . ." She couldn't
go on.

"He hasn't told anyone. Not me or Mr. Babcock or the

police or his lawyer or anyone else. In fact, he made a point with me about its being confidential."

"If young Mr. Hitz hears that I was the one who set Jesus on him and he tells his father . . . Mr. Schiller and myself love it here and my husband would be a lost man if the father used his influence . . . he's a powerful man, Mr. Strand, and he's on the Board of Trustees . . ."

"I'm sure Mr. Babcock would never let it get that far," Strand said. "I don't think you have to worry about it. I won't say anything and young Romero seems determined to keep your name out of it and even if he reported what you said you saw, it wouldn't be any kind of evidence in court . . ."

"It's not the evidence I'm afraid of." She wiped at her eyes with both hands. "It's Mr. Hitz and the Board of Trustees. Oh, well—" She tried to smile. "Crying won't take back the words I said, will it?" She picked up her apron and scrubbed at her damp face with its hem. "I should be ashamed of myself. Making such a fuss, when you and Mrs. Strand've gone through so much, it's a blessing *you* didn't get stabbed coming between them the way you did. I guess I made a mistake about the Romero boy. You can't get the leopard to change his spots, can you?"

"He's not a leopard, Mrs. Schiller," Strand said.

"A figure of speech, sir," she said hastily. She looked at him warily. "There's another thing."

"What's that?"

"I was cleaning out the trash bin for papers in the basement this morning," she said, "and I found some letters. In a girl's handwriting. I'd heard already that Hitz said Romero accused him of stealing some letters and I took a look at them. They were addressed to Jesus. They were love letters, very frank, very explicit, very physical, if I may take the liberty to say so, Mr. Strand—girls these days use language that we never even knew existed when we were young. There's something you ought to know—" She hesitated, as though making a decision, looked uneasily at Strand. "They were signed Caroline. Of course there are many Carolines these days, it's a very popular name, but I know your daughter is named Caroline."

"What did you do with them? The letters?"

"I put them in the incinerator, Mr. Strand," Mrs. Schiller said. "I didn't think you or Mrs. Strand would want to read them."

"Thank you," Strand said. "It was thoughtful of you. Is there anything else you want to tell me?"

Mrs. Schiller shook her head. "Just to tell Jesus that I appreciate his keeping my name out of it all."

"I'll tell him."

"I understand Mrs. Strand has gone," Mrs. Schiller said. "Her bags aren't in the apartment. If I could fix you a bite to eat . . ."

"That's kind of you. It isn't necessary, though. I can take care of myself."

"If you change your mind, just call me," Mrs. Schiller said. "Now I better be getting back to work and see if I can't scrub the blood off the couch."

She made a fat little bow, adjusted her apron and went out of the apartment.

For the first time since he had read the note on the dressing table in the bedroom, Strand was glad that Leslie wasn't there.

4

He was awakened by the ringing of the telephone. He had lain down to nap with his clothes on just after his talk with Mrs. Schiller. As he got off the bed and stiffly started in toward the living room, he saw that it was already dark. He had slept away the afternoon, his dreams confused and menacing. He fumbled in the darkness for the telephone. It was Leslie. "How are you, darling?" she said. "How is everything?" She sounded calm, normal.

"As good as can be expected," he said. "How are *you?* I tried to call this morning."

"We had some last-minute shopping to do for the trip. We were out all day. We're leaving from Kennedy tomorrow." She paused. He heard her take a deep breath. "That is, unless you need me back at the school."

"No, darling," he said. "You come back when everything has blown over here."

"Is it bad?"

"It's . . . well . . . complicated."

"Is Romero there? In the house, I mean."

"He's in jail."

"That's good. At least for the time being. I don't want to sound vindictive, but I wouldn't like him to be roaming around the house in his state."

"The judge set bail at ten thousand dollars."

"Is that a lot?"

"It is if you don't have it. I'll write you all about it. Where will you be staying in Paris?"

"At the Plaza Athenée. The gallery made the reservations. Linda's decided we're going to travel in style." She laughed a little nervously. Then she became serious again. "Have you spoken to Russell?"

"I couldn't reach him."

"Do you think he'll put up the money?"

"I imagine so. He's bound to feel responsible."

"I hope *you're* not feeling responsible."

"I'm feeling numb," he said. "By the way, what time is it? I fell asleep right after noon. Last night was exhausting. I probably would have slept through until morning if you hadn't called."

"It's after six. I'm sorry I woke you up. Darling, are you sure you don't want me to get in the car and drive back?"

"I'm sure," he said. "I doubt that I'll be such good company for the next few weeks. You stay as long as you like."

"I wish I could do something to help."

"Knowing that you're out of this business and having a good time will help me more than anything else."

"If you talk like that, I'm afraid I'll break down and cry," Leslie said. "You're the kindest man in the world, Allen, and everybody takes advantage of it. Including me. Most of all, me."

"Nonsense," Strand said brusquely. "How's Linda?"

"Twittering. You know how she is about France. Maybe she has a lover hidden away on a side street."

"Give her my regards. And have a great time. The two of you."

"What do you want me to bring you back from Paris?"

"You."

Leslie laughed, a low, warm sound a hundred miles away. "I knew you'd say that. That's why I asked. *Je t'embrasse*. I'm working on my French."

"I love you. Just don't forget that in any language."

"I won't," Leslie whispered. "Good night."

"Good night, my dearest." Strand put down the phone, reassured that all was well, at least with Leslie. He put on the lights, then went back to the telephone and considered it. Should he call Hazen now? He leaned over to pick up the instrument, then let his hand drop. He felt too tired to answer the questions he knew Hazen would put to him. He knew he should go into the common room and see what the boys were up to and answer their questions, too, but decided to let it wait until the morning. If he had to face Hitz again that day, he had the feeling that he would finally hit him.

He heard the peals of the chapel bell for dinner and suddenly realized he had eaten nothing all day.

He went into the kitchen and looked into the refrigerator. There was nothing much in there, just some eggs and bacon and a half container of milk. But it would have to do. Dinner at a table full of boys in the crowded dining hall was an ordeal to be avoided, even if it meant going to bed hungry. And he was not up to the long walk into town, where he might be recognized by someone who had been in the courtroom that morning. He was frying the bacon when the telephone rang again. He took the pan off the fire and trudged back into the living room and picked up the phone.

"Allen?" It was Hazen.

"Yes, Russell. How are you?"

"I just got in from Washington and I was told you called this morning."

"Are you standing, Russell?"

"Yes, I happen to be standing. Why do you ask?"

"Because it's a long, complicated story and you'd better be comfortable when you hear it."

"What's wrong?" Now he sounded alarmed. "Is Leslie all right?"

"She's fine. She's at Linda's. She decided she wanted to go to Paris after all," Strand said. "It's Romero. Have you sat down yet?"

"I'm down."

"We had just gotten back from New York—were just in front of the house—when two boys came running out the door," Strand said. "One was chasing the other. The one who was doing the chasing was Romero and he had a knife in his hand . . ."

"Goddamn fool," Hazen said. "They'll kick him out of school for that."

"And the boy who was being chased was young Hitz . . ."

"Christ," Hazen said, "I hope I never hear that name again for the rest of my life . . ."

"You will, Russell, you will . . ."

"The old man has given some added lurid details to the Justice Department and that's why I had to go down to Washington. But tell me the whole story. Don't leave out any of the details."

When Strand told him that three hundred and seventy-five dollars had been stolen from the box in Romero's room, Hazen exploded. "Three hundred and seventy-five dollars! Where in hell did he get three hundred and seventy-five dollars?"

"Hitz says he ran a crap game in his room several nights a week after lights-out."

"And you knew nothing about it?" Hazen said incredulously.

"Not a thing."

"What in blazes goes on in that school?"

"I imagine the usual."

"Go on," Hazen said icily. He broke in again as Strand was telling him that Romero said that he had reason to believe that it was Hitz who took the money. "What reason?" Hazen asked.

"He wouldn't say. He said it was confidential."

"Confidential," Hazen snorted. "If I'd been there, it wouldn't have been all that confidential, I assure you! Not for five minutes. Do you have any clues?"

Strand thought of Mrs. Schiller's pleading, tear-choked voice. "None," he said. He didn't mention her story about finding the letters. If Hazen wanted to come down to the school and try to break Mrs. Schiller or Romero down, he would get no help from him. "You want me to go on with the rest of the story?"

"I'm sorry," Hazen said. "I'll try not to interrupt again."

It took fifteen more minutes before Strand came to the last scene in the courtroom and he was telling Hazen about Romero's refusing to testify in his own defense.

"The school lawyer, a Mr. Hollingsbee, pleaded with

him," Strand went on. "But he just stood there and refused to change his mind. He told the judge he didn't recognize the jurisdiction of the court."

"Mr. Hollingsbee must be one hot lawyer," Hazen said ironically, "if he can't even argue an eighteen-year-old kid out of making a horse's ass of himself like that. No wonder he can't get out of that little hick town. Where's Romero now?"

"In jail," Strand said. "The bail is ten thousand dollars." He heard the sharp intake of breath at the other end of the line.

"That's damn steep," Hazen said. "But in the judge's place I'd have made it twenty. That kid deserves to have the book thrown at him, if only for ingratitude. I hate to say this, Allen, but I'm afraid you've been a little remiss in disciplining that boy and at least making sure he couldn't get his hands on any weapons."

"I'm sure you're right," Strand said, not showing that he was offended by the rebuke and the tone in which it was uttered. "I've been remiss about many things and undoubtedly will be remiss about many more. But it's stretching the point a bit to call a pocketknife a weapon. But that's past history. Right now, a boy whom we plucked out of his own environment and put here . . ."

"With the best of intentions," Hazen said loudly.

"With the best of intentions," Strand agreed. "But he's behind bars now, with no family to look to for help, and unless someone with a charitable turn of mind"—he knew Hazen wouldn't like this, but continued—"and the ability to raise ten thousand dollars comes up with the money, he'll stay there till the trial, which may be months from now, and . . ."

"Are you suggesting, Allen, that *I* put up the money?" Now Hazen was frankly angry.

"I'm in no position to suggest anything."

"That's wise," Hazen said. "Because you'd be suggesting that I act like a damned idiot. If you had the money would *you* do it?"

"Yes." He was surprised that he had said it. The sleep had erased his anger and all he remembered was Romero, small and defenseless, being led down the courthouse aisle by the policeman.

"Then it's a good thing you're poor, because you'd be plucked naked in less time than it would take the ink to dry on your I.O.U. I've been in the business world since I was twenty-three and one thing I've found out is that anyone who throws good money after bad is a fool."

"Russell," Strand said, "I don't like to do this, but I'm asking you to lend me the money. I understand why you feel it's not up to you. If it hadn't been for me, you'd never have known Romero was alive. If the burden is on anybody, it's on me. I'm just as mad as you are, but I still feel responsible. I'll repay the money one way or another. We can save more than we've been doing and Leslie's parents would probably be good for some part of it and Jimmy's got a good job . . ."

"As a friend, Allen," Hazen said, "I'm going to refuse. You know what that miserable little gutter rat would do if he was turned loose—he'd vanish. You'd never see him or your money again. Nor would the police. He'd disappear into the ghetto like a ghost, with a million of his countrymen ready to swear that they never even *knew* him."

"I'd take that chance," Strand said quietly.

"Not on my money. And I hope not on yours. I think this conversation has gone on long enough."

"So do I, Russell. Good night."

It sounded as though Hazen had smashed down the telephone on the other end of the line.

One thing is certain, Strand thought as he went into the kitchen, there'll be no Hamptons this Christmas. He put the bacon back on the fire and broke two eggs into another pan. Tomorrow he would ask Mrs. Schiller to do some shopping for him. He didn't know when Babcock would insist that he go back to his regular duties, which included dining in the hall with the boys assigned to his table, but he knew he was in no hurry to take up the routine again and he knew he would not volunteer. And no matter what else might happen, he had to eat.

After he had finished his meal he was still hungry and

for a moment he thought of going up to Rollins's and Romero's room and raiding Rollins's cache of cookies, but, he thought, grimly, there had been enough crime recently to last the school through the year.

He was reading in the living room when there was a tentative knock at the door. He opened it and saw Rollins standing there, bullnecked and wearing the tie and jacket that was compulsory apparel for the evening meal at the school, a condition of which Strand, who had been annoyed for years with his son's haphazard style of dress, approved. Rollins's brown, dark, fine-down athlete's face, which always seemed too small for the massive shoulders and the thick neck, was grave. "I don't like to disturb you, Mr. Strand," he said, his voice low, "but if I could talk to you for a moment . . ."

"Come in, come in," Strand said.

In the living room Rollins folded his long thick legs under him as he sat in a chair facing Strand. "It's about Romero." It seemed to pain the huge boy to get the words out. "He acted foolish and if he'd have woke me up I'd have taken care of it and there wouldn't've been any cutting. I know Hitz and a little threat from me would have settled matters satisfactorily to all concerned without any knives. There might have been a slap or two, but folks don't go to jail for fighting or get expelled or anything like that. But I know Romero and he's a good man, Mr. Strand, whatever he's done he don't deserve jail. I went down there to see him but the man said only family. Well, I'm the only real family that boy has, according to some of the stories he's told me about his mother and father and sisters and brother, they ain't even worth a telephone call and they'd gladly leave him to rot until he's old and gray. You're a smart man, Mr. Strand, you know what jail'll do to a boy like Romero. When he came out he'd be on the streets for the rest of his life and he won't be satisfied with any knife, either, not where he'd been hanging out, he'd have a gun in his belt and God knows what sort of dust in his pocket and he'd be better known to the cops than their own mothers. . . . You know as well as I do, jails don't turn out citizens, they manufacture outlaws. There's too much to that boy to make him into an outlaw, Mr. Strand . . ." He was pleading earnestly, speaking slowly and solemnly, an underlying tone of desperation in his voice.

"I agree with you, Rollins," Strand said. "When it first happened I was angry with him, very angry . . ."

"He knows how much you've done for him, Mr. Strand," Rollins said. "He's told me time and time again, even though I know he hasn't told you. He's not a thank-you kind of boy. It goes against his character. I imagine you guessed that."

"I guessed it," Strand said dryly.

"But he was grateful just the same. Deeply grateful."

"He has a queer way of showing it."

"Hitz beat up on him. Over two hundred pounds. I'm not saying I go along with knives, but Romero—well—the way he was brought up, the places he was brought up, the things he had to do keeping from being thrown off a roof or being found dead in the river, he was—well—he has a different code from the gentlemen here. I'm sure you could find it in your heart to forgive him."

"It's not up to me to forgive him, Rollins," Strand said gently. "It's the headmaster and the faculty and Mr. Hitz's father and Hitz himself and finally the Board of Trustees."

"Man," Rollins said, "they sure bring in the heavy guns when somebody like him gets into trouble, don't they?"

"I'm afraid we have to expect that," Strand said. "There's nothing much I can do."

"I hear they put the bail at ten thousand dollars."

Strand nodded.

"They sure laid it on him, didn't they?" Rollins shook his head.

"The judge was an old man." Strand didn't know why he said that.

"One thing he should have learned—stay out of the white man's court." For the first time, Rollins let his bitterness show.

"I don't think it would make any difference in this case."

"That's what you think." There was a derisive twist on Rollins's lips. "Him and me, we don't read the same books as you folks." Strand noticed that he had become increasingly ungrammatical, as though the stress of the moment had erased his education and uncovered a more primitive level of speech.

"As I said, I would like to help, but . . ." Strand shrugged.

"I understand," Rollins said quickly. "There's no way *you'd* have ten thousand dollars laying around loose."

Strand refrained from smiling at Rollins's assumption that all school teachers were impoverished.

"No, it happens that I don't."

"What I was thinking . . . Mr. Hazen . . ." Rollins said, glancing sideways at Strand as he brought out the name, testing. "He's a nice man from what I've seen of him and what Romero has told me. And with that big Mercedes and the chauffeurs and all . . ."

"Rollins," Strand said, thinking that at the moment, no matter how else he would describe Russell Hazen, he would hardly use the word "nice," "if Romero tells you of any hopes he has in that direction, tell him to forget them."

Rollins frowned, the lines creasing in his forehead. "You mean you talked to Mr. Hazen and he turned you down."

"You could say that."

"Well, then—" Rollins stood up. "No use talking here. We got to look somewhere else." He paced up and down, the old boards creaking under his weight. "Would it be okay if I took the day off tomorrow? My schedule's light on Tuesday and I'm up in all my courses. It'd be different if the football season was still on. The coach wouldn't let you off of practice if you had raging pneumonia and a temperature of a hundred and five. Classes're different." He grinned and looked five years younger than when he had come into the room. "I'm not what you might call an absolute necessity in the classroom."

"May I ask what you expect to accomplish in one day?"

Rollins's expression changed. His face closed down. "I thought I'd take a little trip to my hometown, Waterbury, and look around a little. There's folks I know have some experience in this kind of thing."

"I don't want you to get into any more trouble," Strand said. "You're in plenty of trouble as it is—after all it's known the crap games took place in your room, too."

"Mr. Strand, that ain't even a pimple on my nose," Rollins said. "There been crap games in this here school since the day it opened. Maybe they'll put me in the kitchen doing the dishes for a week, maybe they won't do nuthin'. Is it okay for the day?"

"I'll tell the headmaster I gave you permission."

Rollins put out his hand, and Strand shook it. "Mr. Strand, this place needs more people like you, that's for sure. I never told this to any teacher before, but I enjoy your classes and I'd be lying if I said I wasn't learning something I think is important for me in them. A lot more important than blocking and tackling and you can tell the coach I said so."

"I'll tell that to the Board of Trustees the next time I come up for a promotion."

"You tell them that," Rollins said. "You tell them Rollins said so. And if you see Romero, you tell him he's got friends. Now I better leave you alone. I took up enough of your time as it is. And don't worry, there won't be any more crap games in this house while you're here."

Strand walked him to the door, wished he could say something more to the boy, something to encourage him, a word to let him know that he admired his forthrightness and loyalty, but he felt it would embarrass Rollins, so he kept silent and closed the door behind him.

After a late breakfast the next morning, prepared for him by Mrs. Schiller, who was looking even more mournful than she had the day before, Strand heard the telephone ring.

It was Babcock. "Have you read the newspaper yet?"

"No."

"Good. Don't."

"That bad?"

"The news story was bad enough. The editorial was worse. The editor of the paper has always been on our back." Babcock's voice took on a nasal, back-country ring. "The idle scions of the rich in an anachronistic enclave of valuable town land, pampered by a low tax rate, encouraging the vices of a selected group of spoiled children, scouting the law, hostile to the tax-paying, hard-working citizens who make up the population of our town, a dangerous example to our high school students, etcetera, etcetera, etcetera." He returned to his own soft diction. "He has Romero's picture on the front page, accompanied by his lawyer, on the school's payroll, as the caption helpfully points out, being taken into a squad car by a policeman after the arraignment. The picture makes him look like a hit man for the Mafia, or at least the way they look in the movies. And next to it there's one of us coming out of the courtroom. Somehow it seems as though we are smiling. Do you remember smiling?"

"No."

"Did you see any cameramen outside the courthouse?"

"No."

"They must have used a telephoto lens. The wonders of modern photography." Babcock laughed shortly. "I called the paper and told the editor Romero had already been expelled from the school, but it was just throwing a bone to the lions. The article promises that they will follow the case closely. Every boy at breakfast and every teacher had a copy of the paper. They had all the facts on Romero. The reporter interviewed Hitz. At length, obviously. That Romero was here on a scholarship. Free ride for criminals, they call it. The misguided sentimentality of New York bleeding hearts, exporting their problems to the innocent, old-fashioned countryside. They didn't mention Hazen, but they spelled your name correctly. As a final blow to your reputation, they mentioned that you spent your summers in East Hampton, a haunt of wealth and dissipation. The editor must have gotten his degree in journalism from a correspondence school in Hollywood. It was on the Hartford morning TV news, too. A somewhat more sympathetic treatment, but still nothing to make parents rush to enroll their boys at Dunberry. Sometimes, I must admit, I regret the advances in our communications systems."

Strand could imagine him sitting at his desk, struggling with his pipe and forgetting to keep it lit and pushing his glasses up and down distractedly.

"By the way," Babcock said, "did you speak to Hazen?"

"Last night."

"What did he say?"

"Romero is on his own."

"No bail?"

"Not a penny."

Babcock sighed. "That poor deluded boy. Another thing. The FBI in New Haven called my office. They want to interview you, they say. It can't be about Romero. Whatever he did, it wasn't a federal offense. Have you any idea why they want to talk to you?"

"Not until I hear what they have to say."

There was a peculiar silence at the other end of the phone. Then Babcock said, "Well, we have to live through it. If you can stand it, Allen, I think you had better go back to your classes and make an appearance at meals. If you remain incommunicado it makes it seem as though you have something to hide."

"I see what you mean."

"If I may make a suggestion, try to avoid answering too many questions. The line that might be wise to take is that you consider it lucky that you arrived when you did, that it kept things from becoming more than a minor incident. The less you say about guilt and innocence, if I may presume to coach you, the better it will be for all concerned. In your place I would refrain from speculating about whether Hitz took the money or not."

"Of course. I have no way of knowing, anyway. I'll be at lunch today and will take my classes this afternoon."

"That's very good of you," Babcock said, relieved. "I knew I could depend upon you. And if any newspaper people call you, I'd appreciate it if you just told them, No comment."

"I hadn't intended to make any speeches."

"Forgive me for seeming anxious," Babcock said. "My

head is in such a muddle. You'll be happy to know that Hitz won't be at lunch or in any of the classes. His father called last night and said he wanted his son on the first plane to Washington. To see a *real* doctor, is the way he put it. We shipped him out before breakfast."

"Thank God for small mercies," Strand said.

"So I'll see you at lunch?"

"At lunch," Strand said. He hung up the phone.

The note was delivered in the middle of his last class by Babcock's secretary. There were two gentlemen waiting in the headmaster's office to see Mr. Strand. Would he please come to the office as soon as the class was over? Strand pocketed the note and went on lecturing about the expansionist policies of President Theodore Roosevelt.

Neither the lunch nor the afternoon classes had been as bad as he had feared. The boys had looked at him curiously and the teachers he had happened to meet murmured that they were sorry about what had happened. They had been warned, Strand was sure, not to discuss the case and not to bother Mr. Strand. If anything, Strand felt an undercurrent of sympathy. Although Romero undoubtedly had been the object of scorn by a certain clique in the school, Hitz he knew was universally disliked. The football coach, Johnson, even whispered as he passed Strand on the campus, "I wish Romero had gone just a little bit deeper."

When the class was over, at four o'clock, Strand walked slowly over the bare, yellowed campus, the last dead leaves blowing in the cold November wind. Two gentlemen, he thought. The FBI must be wealthy in manpower if they sent two armed representatives of the bureau to question a fifty-year-old teacher of history who had never ever been issued a parking ticket in his life.

"They're in with Mr. Babcock," the secretary said when he entered the office. "You're to go right in, Mr. Strand."

All three men rose to greet him as he came through the door. The FBI men were youngish, one blond, one dark, neatly barbered and dressed in dark suits, unexceptional looking. He guessed they were young lawyers who had despaired of succeeding in private practice and who also liked to carry guns. Babcock mumbled their names, which Strand didn't catch, and the two men shook hands gravely with him.

"These gentlemen," Babcock said as they sat down, the two men facing Strand, "have been discussing the rise of juvenile delinquency with me." He talked nervously. "It seems that in recent years the FBI has found that increasingly juveniles, or at least young men under eighteen, have been involved in crimes of great magnitude and violence that cross many state boundaries and therefore come under their jurisdiction."

"We've read the papers this morning," the blond young man said, with a smile that Strand took as meant to be reassuring, "and we know about the Romero case. Of course"—again the frosty tolerant smile—"that hardly rates as a crime of great magnitude or national concern. We were just answering some of the headmaster's questions, waiting for you to be free. We're here on a different matter." Both men looked at Babcock, as though they were identical puppets on identical strings.

Babcock rose from his desk. "If you gentlemen will excuse me," he said, looking at his watch, "I have a conference in the science department and I'm late already. I'll tell my secretary you're not to be disturbed."

"Thank you, sir," the blond man said.

Babcock went out and the dark agent produced a package of cigarettes and offered them to Strand. Strand said, "No, thank you, I don't smoke."

"Do you mind if I smoke?"

"Not at all."

The dark man lit up.

"Please put your mind at rest from the beginning," the blond agent said. "We're just looking for a little information that you may or may not be able to provide. We understand you know Mr. Russell Hazen."

"He's a friend of mine."

"You occasionally spend time at his house in East Hampton and you occasionally see each other in New York?"

"That is correct."

"He came to visit you on the third Saturday in September with your wife and your daughter and one of his secretaries?"

"He came to see a football game."

"You had lunch with him in the school dining hall?"

"I sat at the table with my boys. He was at the visitors' table."

"With Mrs. Strand and your daughter?"

"Yes."

"Were they sitting on either side of him?"

"I don't remember."

"You then sat next to him at the football game and were accompanied at the game by your daughter?"

"Yes." The FBI must teach their agents the art of asking useless questions, Strand thought. He hid his irritation with the two men.

Now it was the dark man who took up the line of questions. If Strand had closed his eyes he couldn't have distinguished one voice from the other.

"You saw him in conversation with a Mr. Hitz, from Washington?"

"Yes."

"Where?"

"At the visitors' table."

"Did you recognize Mr. Hitz?"

"Only later. His son, as you know, is in my house, and the father came over to me briefly after the game and introduced himself and asked me how his boy was doing."

"Did you overhear any of the conversation between Mr. Hazen and Mr. Hitz at lunch?"

"They were twenty yards away and there was a great deal of noise in the hall." Now he showed that he was annoyed. "What could I have heard?"

"But Mrs. Strand conceivably could have heard what the conversation was about?"

"Conceivably."

"Is Mrs. Strand with you?" The blond man took the relief.

"She's in Europe."

"May we ask what she's doing in Europe?"

"Smuggling dope." Strand was sorry he had made the joke as soon as he saw the expression on the faces of the two men. "I'm sorry. I was being frivolous. I'm not used to police interrogations. She's on a holiday."

"When will she be back?" The blond man's tone did not change.

"Two weeks, three weeks. I'm not sure."

"Is she in the habit of taking two or three weeks vacation in the middle of the school term, leaving her classes?"

"This is the first time." Strand resolved to hold his temper.

"Isn't it expensive—holidays like that?"

"Terribly."

"Have you any outside income?"

"A small pension from the New York City school system. Do I have to answer questions like that?"

"Not today," the blond man said. "Perhaps later. Under oath. Does your wife have any other income aside from what she earns here at Dunberry?"

"She teaches piano one day a week in the city. And occasionally her parents send small gifts of money."

"Small? How small?"

"Small." Suddenly he decided to be stubborn. "Very small."

"Would you venture a figure?"

"No."

"Does she also receive gifts from Mr. Hazen?"

"He loaned her a car. A 1972 Volkswagen station wagon to go in and out of the city and do her shopping in town."

"Nothing else?"

"Nothing."

"Mr. Hazen is not financing this particular holiday in Europe?"

"No."

"Are *you* paying for it?" The other man jumped in as though he had discovered a sudden light in the darkness.

"No."

"Who is?"

"When she gets back you can ask her yourself."

"Would you be kind enough to let us know where she's staying in Europe? We have agents there who would save her the trouble of hurrying home to talk to us."

"I'm not going to spoil her holiday over something that has nothing to do with her. I told you she was in Europe. I'll say no more."

The two men looked at each other as though they had scored a point and were congratulating themselves. "Let us go back a little, Mr. Strand," the blond man said calmly. "Mrs. Strand was at the table at lunch, presumably next to Mr. Hazen. You all ate dinner together in the Red Top Inn. Am I correct?"

"Yes."

"Was Mr. Hitz present?"

"No."

"Could you say with certainty that you did not overhear Mr. Hazen and Mr. Hitz discussing a business deal while you were with him that day?"

"Yes."

"Would you hazard a guess about whether Mrs. Strand or your daughter overheard anything of that nature or heard from Mr. Hazen directly about such a conversation?"

"There again, you will have to ask Mrs. Strand. And my daughter. Now, if you'll tell me what this is all about, perhaps I can be more useful to you."

"If you buy *The New York Times* tomorrow morning"—the blond man smiled in advance of what he was about to say—"I presume it reaches this outlying center of culture—"

"We get three copies every day in the library."

"Read it and it will enlighten you somewhat." He started to get up and then sat down again. "One more question. In your opinion, is there any possibility that the Hitz boy's stabbing by a protégé of Mr. Hazen's might have had anything to do with presumed conversations of a criminal nature between Mr. Hazen and Mr. Hitz senior?"

"That's the most asinine thing I've heard in years," Strand said angrily.

"We are instructed to ask asinine questions, Mr. Strand,"

the blond man said smoothly. "That's what we're paid for."
He and then the dark man stood up. "Thank you for your
time. And read the *Times* tomorrow morning," he said
as they went out.

Although it wasn't warm in the headmaster's office,
Strand was drenched with sweat.

The door opened and Babcock came in. He looked like
an aged worried monkey. Academics, Strand thought
irrelevantly, were not by and large a handsome race.

"What was that all about?" Babcock asked.

"I'll tell you just about as much as they said," Strand
said, for Hazen's sake not quite telling the truth. "They
said to read *The New York Times* tomorrow and you'll
know."

"The FBI was up here once before," Babcock said
worriedly. "Way back, during the Vietnam War. They
were checking to see if a young instructor we had on the
staff who'd signed some sort of petition was a Communist. They were very unpleasant."

"These gentlemen were most pleasant," Strand said. "The
next time they come they may not be. Thanks for the use
of the office."

As he hurried across the campus he pulled up the collar
of his coat against the cold. A harsh wind was sweeping
in from the northeast, with flakes of snow mixed with
sleet, and the bare limbs of the campus trees were shivering in the polar blasts. The six o'clock bells pealed from
the chapel tower. At that moment Leslie was in the car
approaching the airport to board the plane for France. He
stopped and whispered a small prayer for the safety of all
planes aloft that night in the winter storm.

Then he walked quickly toward the Malson house to
shower away the dust of the school day and dress and get
ready for dinner.

5

Rollins usually ate at Strand's table, but this evening he did not appear for dinner. Even though he had the day off, the school rule was that the boy had to be back by seven o'clock. But Strand wasn't going to put him on report as he was supposed to do. Rollins had enough on his mind without being called into the headmaster's office to explain his absence.

Strand didn't like to speculate on what Rollins might be doing in Waterbury in his attempt to get Romero out of jail. The manner in which he had spoken of the people he might see who knew how to handle matters like that had made it plain that Rollins was not intending to apply for a loan at a bank or sell stock to make up the amount of the bail. Strand had a confused notion that Rollins was speaking of people who were not quite within the law or were frankly outside it, people who in return for a favor given to Rollins would certainly demand a greater favor in return. Scenarios of bribery, numbers running, arson, all the categories of ghetto crime with which readers of newspapers and watchers of television had become sadly familiar, ran through Strand's mind as he sat decorously at the dinner table with the scrubbed and politely dressed boys who, at least at table, remembered the manners their nurses and mothers had drummed into them. The black boys who had been in his classes in high school had not been conducive to making him believe in the absolute probity of what the newspapers called ethnic teenagers, when they didn't call them hoodlums. Rollins was, he knew, absolutely honest ordinarily, but in a situation like this, with his friend abandoned as he was now by the authorities, with his fate, as Rollins believed, in his, Rollins's, own hands, Strand had the uneasy feeling that he had made a mistake in allowing Rollins to leave the campus. The boy's absence fed his fears and after dinner he nearly went over to speak to Babcock and tell him that he thought that it might be a good idea to telephone Rollins's parents and warn them to keep a watchful eye on their son.

But the thought that Rollins, who trusted him, would lump him in with all the other adults in the Establishment who were leagued against people like Romero and himself made Strand hesitate and then decide against saying anything. He had been touched by what Rollins had said to him and valued Rollins's opinion of him and he told himself, One more night won't kill anybody.

He stayed up late, trying to read, and made two trips to the top of the house to look into Rollins's room to see if perhaps he had come back without checking in. But both beds were empty. He kept looking at his watch. With the time difference between New York and Paris, it would be six in the morning Paris time, midnight Eastern Standard Time, before Leslie's plane landed. He knew he wouldn't be able to sleep until he could call Air France at Kennedy and find out that the plane had arrived safely.

He had another call to make before the night was over, but kept postponing it. To Russell Hazen. Hazen had been abrasive in their last conversation and Strand found it hard to forgive the accusations shouted at him over the phone, but the man after all was his friend and the debt he owed him, Strand admitted to himself, far outweighed the small and really justifiable outburst of bad temper. He knew Hazen would not welcome what he had to tell him about the interview with the FBI agents. But Hazen deserved to be warned and sooner or later the call would have to be made. I'll wait till he gets in from dinner, Strand thought, easing his conscience, it'll be time enough. As long as I tell him before he reads the paper in the morning.

He waited until ten thirty, then dialed Hazen's home number. There was no answer. He let the phone ring ten times, then hung up.

He was relieved for the moment but still jittery. He picked up his book and read the same paragraph over and over again without making any sense of the words on the page. He closed the book and went into the kitchen and got out the bottle of Scotch that had been standing in the cupboard since he had bought it at the beginning of the term. He poured a generous slug into a glass, added ice and water, and was sitting in front of the fire in the living room, with the glass in his hand, listening to the wind snapping at the windows, when he heard a knock on the apartment door. He hurried over to the door and opened it. Rollins was standing there swathed in a football hood, his face rimed with frost, looking as though he had suddenly grown old and was sprouting a white beard. He was blowing on his hands, but smiling.

"Come in, come in," Strand said.

"Thank you, sir," Rollins said.

Strand closed the door behind him. Rollins went and stood in front of the fire, warming his hands. "I had to walk from the bus station," he said, "and I nearly froze my bones. This fire sure is a cheerful sight." He looked sidelong at the glass still in Strand's hand. "There just wouldn't happen to be any more of that stuff from where it came from, would there?"

"Well," Strand said, "it's a cold night . . ."

"You ain't exaggerating, Mr. Strand. Any college wants me to play ball for them better be below the Mason-Dixon Line. Or in Hawaii."

"It's against the rules, of course. If anybody finds out . . ."

"I will go to my grave first," Rollins said, with suitable solemnity.

"You stay there and warm up," Strand said and went into the kitchen. He poured a generous dose of whiskey and added only a little water to the glass and brought it back to Rollins. Rollins held it, the glass looking tiny in his huge hand, and rolled the liquid around, gently admiring it. He lifted his glass. "To the gentleman who invented it." He drank a great gulp, sighed contentedly. "That takes the nip out of winter, doesn't it?" Then he became serious. "Any developments since last night, Mr. Strand?"

"No. Except that Hitz went to Washington to see a doctor."

"Eighteen years too late," Rollins said grimly. Then his face brightened. "I got some developments, though. Hot developments."

The phrase was worrisome. "Just how hot?" Strand asked.

"I didn't hold up no bank, if that's what you're afraid of. Legitimate. Strictly legitimate." Rollins took out his wallet. It was bulging. "Here it is," he said. "Ten thousand dollars. In legal tender. Tomorrow morning I'm going to go down to the jail and get Romero out of there quick as a greased pig and there's enough left over so I'll be able to give him the best damn lunch that poor skinny sonofabitch ever sat down in front of."

From the slurred way Rollins was speaking, Strand guessed the whiskey in his hand was not the first drink of the boy's evening. "Going to the jail won't do much good," Strand said. "I'm sure there are all sorts of legal formalities. His lawyer has to be warned to expect you. With the money. If, as you say, it's not hot."

"On the head of my mother."

"He'll do it the way it has to be done," Strand said, pretending to a knowledge of the law that he didn't have, but guessing that if a black boy in a football hood showed up with ten thousand dollars, the process would be slow, to say the least. "I'll have Mr. Babcock call him. I don't know where his office is. In fact," he said, "I don't even know where Romero is at the moment. They've probably moved him somewhere. To a proper prison."

"There ain't no proper prisons, Mr. Strand," Rollins said.

"Will you answer a question?"

"Yes." Rollins sounded reluctant.

"Where did you get the money?"

"Do you really have to know?"

"I don't. But the authorities might be curious."

Rollins took another big gulp of his whiskey.

"I raised it," he said. "From friends."

"What friends?"

"Don't you trust me?" Rollins said plaintively.

"I trust you. But there are other people involved."

"Well, I laid out the case—" Rollins hesitated. "To my family, if you want to know. My mother, my father, my brothers. We ain't on the edge of poverty, exactly, Mr. Strand, we're not starving, even though I look scrawny . . ." He grinned. "My father's chief engineer at the waterworks. One of my brothers owns a garage. My mother is chief nurse at the Intensive Care Unit in the hospital. Another of my brothers is in real estate. And my oldest brother is an assistant vice president in a bank in New York and plays the market like a xylophone. The family ain't exactly sharecroppers, Mr. Strand."

"You amaze me, Rollins," Strand said. "You never told me a word of all this—or anybody else in the school."

"I didn't want it to be held against me," Rollins said, laughing. "I didn't want people to be expecting me to be smarter than I am and holding my record in school up against my family's. It's tough enough when we all get together for dinner and they begin to get on my back for being a shiftless, no-good black jock. My biggest brother, he was offered a tryout with the New York Knicks, that's a basketball team, and he turned it down, he said he didn't want to earn his living running and sweating in public like a slave of the pharaohs and having his knees operated on every summer. If my family thought I was aiming at trying to play pro football, they'd kick me out like a leper. They're bookish, Mr. Strand, fanatical bookish, and they're so set on improving themselves—and me—it near drives me crazy." He finished his drink. "You got any more in that bottle in the kitchen by any chance, Mr. Strand?"

"Do you mean to say that your *family* gave you the money?"

"Loaned, Mr. Strand," Rollins said earnestly. "Loaned is the word."

"And if, after you get Romero out of jail, he runs off?"

"They'd stuff me and hang me up as a trophy on the

wall for ten years," Rollins said. "But he's not going to run away."

"How can you be so sure?"

"He's my friend." It was said with the utmost quiet simplicity. "Anyway, I can't see Romero being allowed to hang around *here* when he gets out on bail."

"No," Strand admitted. "He's already been expelled."

"They don't waste no time on little things like being innocent until proven guilty around here, do they?"

"Do you blame them?"

"Sure I blame them," Rollins said soberly. "I blame everybody. But he won't run away. Not if he knows it's my money. Besides, where's he going to run to? His family? He doesn't even know where they are. His brother wrote he was splitting, going out west, and they didn't know where the sisters've gone to and his mother had to move, but he didn't say where. Makes no difference—he doesn't want to go near any of them. Anyway, I'm telling him he's coming to live in my family's house until the trial and nobody, not even Romero, could get away from my brothers if they had a mind to keep him in place. Now, can I have that drink?"

"I'll get it for you." As he took Rollins's glass and went back to the kitchen, Strand was surprised to feel the tears in his eyes. He made Rollins's drink stronger this time. His own glass was still half full. Before tonight, the last time he had had the bottle in his hand was the night Leslie had been lost on the road back from New York and had been near hysteria when she stumbled into the house to awaken him. "A certain medicinal value," he remembered she had said. One could say that tonight, too, medicine had its uses.

If he had been asked why he had tears in his eyes, he would have been hard put to find an answer. Rollins's unwavering adherence to the bonds of friendship? His family's blind generosity of spirit? Their silent defiance of the capricious indifference of the white man's world? Their quick acceptance of the needs of their youngest member, hardly more than a boy, and his estimate of what it was right and just to do? Strand remembered the phrase Rollins had quoted his brother using—"running and sweating for the pharaohs." Strand didn't know how often the Rollins family went to church, but their act was a Christian rebuke to the men and women sleeping in the pretty, ivied houses that night, people who went to chapel each evening to celebrate charity and the brotherhood of man. And a rebuke, too, to the vengeful, powerful man in the great duplex apartment on Fifth Avenue, surrounded by his glorious paintings.

As he went back into the living room carrying Rollins's refilled glass, he made a decision. "Rollins," he said, handing the boy the whiskey, "I don't like the idea of nobody else chipping in to help. Maybe, if we had the time, we might collect a few dollars on the campus, although I doubt it. But we don't have the time. In the morning, you come down to the bank with me and I'll give you two thousand dollars of my own toward the ten. It's only a token, but sometimes tokens are necessary." He knew he had three thousand dollars in his account. His total wealth. It would have to do him for more than a month. There would be no Christmas presents this year. No matter.

Rollins looked studiously at his glass. "Amen," he said, surprisingly. "What time you figure to be free in the morning to go to the bank?"

"After breakfast."

"What about your classes?"

"Force majeure," Strand said. "I'll explain to the head-master."

"Force—what's that?"

"An act of God," Strand said. "Freely translated."

"I wouldn't want Romero to stay in that jail one minute longer than he has to."

"He won't. One condition, though. Nobody's to know about my contribution. Especially not Romero."

Rollins looked quizzically at Strand. "I understand your reasons," he said.

Strand doubted that he did. He himself was not sure of his reasons. "On second thought," he said, "I think it'd be better if we didn't bring Mr. Babcock in on this for the time being. He might think it's unwise, or he might insist on talking to your parents—"

"You mean you think he wouldn't believe me," Rollins said.

"The possibility exists. And he may be under pressure to leave Romero where he is. I think you'd better do this on your own. The lawyer's name is Hollingsbee. He's in the Hartford book. I'll call him first thing in the morning to be ready for you. If you have any trouble, call me."

"I don't expect any trouble." Rollins finished his drink quickly. "I'd better be getting to bed." He started to leave.

"One more thing, please," Strand said. His throat felt constricted and he coughed. "About those letters that Romero said were stolen. Do you know anything about them?"

"He didn't read them to me, Mr. Strand," Rollins said, "and I didn't ask. He kept them locked up. Every once in a while he would take them out and read them to himself with a sort of sappy expression on his face. Then he'd put them away and lock them up again."

"You don't know whom they were from?"

"From the way he looked I would guess they were from a girl." Rollins laughed. "It's a cinch they weren't from bill collectors. Anyway, I could tell he prized them. Do you want me to ask him who they were from?"

"No. It's of no importance. Well, good luck. And thank your family for me."

"That might help. They ain't all that crazy about my getting them to fork over all that dough. And my mother and father were against my coming here on football scholarship in the first place. But they're on Romero's side, and that's the main thing." He patted the bulge in his hip pocket. "Got to make sure it's still there," he said, a little embarrassedly. "I'm sorry I made such a dent in your booze. See you in the morning, sir."

He was weaving a little as he went out of the apartment.

It had been a long day. He had started out tired. He had dozed a little during the night, but had awakened at six to call Air France. Air France had told him that Paris was fogged in and no planes were landing there as yet and that the New York flight had had to put down in Geneva and was waiting there for conditions to improve. He had called after that at twenty-minute intervals, but the message was always the same. Then, just before breakfast they had told him that Leslie's plane had been diverted to Nice. Her trip was not beginning on a fortunate note.

At breakfast, he had told Babcock that he would have to skip his first classes. He didn't give any reason and Babcock had looked at him oddly and had been markedly cool when he said "I do hope that we can settle back into a sensible routine soon again," and had turned away abruptly.

The long walk into town with Rollins to the bank in a biting wind had left him gasping and twice he had had to ask Rollins to stop while he regained his breath. Rollins had watched him anxiously, as though he was afraid that he would drop where he stood. "My father has heart trouble, too," Rollins said. "My mother's after him all the time to slow down."

"How do you know I have heart trouble?" Strand asked.

"Romero told me. He said they were afraid you were going to die." Rollins looked at him with childlike curiosity. "If you don't mind my asking, what was it like—I mean, when you felt yourself . . ." He stopped, embarrassed. "I've been knocked out a few times myself and the funny thing was it didn't hurt while it was happening—I just felt as though somehow I was floating through the air, altogether peaceful. I just wondered if maybe it's like that. I'd feel better about my father if it was like that for him . . ."

"I hadn't thought about it," Strand said, trying to remember what he had felt as he collapsed on the beach. "Now that I look back on it, that *is* how I felt. It's a comforting thought. To tell you the truth I didn't want to come back."

"Well," Rollins said emphatically. "I'm real glad you did."

Strand smiled at him. "So am I."

At the bank, he had cashed the check and given the two thousand dollars in new hundred dollar notes to Rollins. Rollins didn't put them in his wallet immediately, but stood there, looking uncertainly down at them in his hand. "You sure you want to do this, Mr. Strand?"

"I'm sure. Put them away."

Rollins folded the notes carefully into his wallet. "I better be getting along," he said. "The bus for Hartford leaves in ten minutes. Maybe you better take a taxi back to the school."

Strand had taken a taxi from the town to the school once. It had cost five dollars. "I'll walk. The exercise will wake me up. Good luck with Mr. Hollingsbee. I called him and he's expecting you."

"Be careful, please, Mr. Strand," Rollins said. He strode quickly down the windy street as Strand pushed his wool muffler higher around his neck. At the corner Rollins stopped, turned and looked back. He waved once, then turned the corner and disappeared.

Shivering and with his ungloved hands feeling like two lumps of ice in his overcoat pockets, Strand walked in the opposite direction along the main street going out of town. There was a drugstore on the corner that sold newspapers. He went in and bought the *Times*. The story was on page three and was short. "Justice Department Investigates Charges of Influence Peddling in Washington" was the one-column headline. The story itself was tentative. It had been revealed to the *Times* through reliable sources, it ran, that a prominent New York lawyer, Russell Hazen, had had conversations with a registered lobbyist for the oil industry about the possibility of rewarding an unnamed congressman for a favorable vote in committee on an off-shore drilling bill. The conversation had been taped off a tapped telephone wire in Mr. Hitz's office. The tap had been legally obtained on a warrant from a federal judge. The Justice Department declined to say if an indictment would be sought. The investigation would continue.

Poor Russell, Strand thought. He felt guilty at having given up after one call trying to reach Hazen to warn him of the FBI's visit. It was not the kind of story a man would want to come on unsuspectingly as he opened the paper at the breakfast table.

Strand closed the paper and dropped it back on the pile. He had paid for it, but he didn't want to read about the murders, the executions, the invasions, the bankruptcies that seemed to make up most of each morning's news these days.

He went out of the store into the cold, gray street, where other pedestrians were hurrying, bent over, against the wind. He had foolishly not worn a hat. He pulled the muffler away from his neck and, using it as a shawl, wound it around his head and tied it in a knot under his chin. As he started off again, his eyes tearing from the cold, he thought of all the photographs he had seen in newspapers of refugee women, their heads wrapped in shawls, shuffling along on dusty roads.

By the time he got back to the school, dragging himself along, cursing the wind, he was sure he wouldn't be able to last through his classes till five o'clock. Somehow, though, he managed it, sitting at his desk while he lectured, instead of striding up and down as he usually did, and speaking slowly and laboriously. Then, during his last class, the headmaster's secretary came into the room and told him that he should come over to the office as soon as possible. He cut the class short and went down to the headmaster's office. Romero was there and Rollins and Mr. Hollingsbee.

Romero's mouth was still split and swollen and a bruise on his forehead was lumpy and discolored. But he stood erect and defiant as he glanced once at Strand, then lowered his eyes and stared at the floor.

"Allen," Babcock said, "we've all been trying to persuade Romero to cooperate with Mr. Hollingsbee. Without success. I've told Romero that under the circumstances I have no choice but to expel him from the school as of today. If he is willing to cooperate, I might be able to suspend him provisionally to await the outcome of the trial. Mr. Hollingsbee thinks that with luck he might have Romero put on probation. In that case, I believe I might be able to allow him to come back to the school on probation here, too, to finish his year. Perhaps you can do something with him."

"Romero," Strand said, "you're playing with the rest of your life. Give yourself a chance, at least. I don't like reminding you of what you owe to Mr. Hazen and myself, but I have to do it. Between us we have a large investment in you. And I'm not talking about money. A moral investment. It's callous of you not to feel that you should try to protect it."

"I'm sorry, Mr. Strand," Romero said, still staring at the floor. "Everyone knows what I did and why. I'll take the consequences. I'm not going to weasel out. Everyone's wasting their time arguing with me."

Strand shrugged. "I'm afraid that's it," he said to Babcock.

Babcock sighed. "All right, Romero," he said. "Pack your things and get out. Right now. You can't stay here even one more night."

"I'll drive the boys back to Waterbury," Mr. Hollingsbee said. "Rollins, maybe your parents will be able to do something with him."

"They sure will try," Rollins said. He took Romero's elbow. "Come on, hero."

Mr. Hollingsbee and Strand followed the boys out of the room and out onto the campus. They made a little cortege as they walked across to the Malson Residence. "Before you came," Hollingsbee said to Strand, "Babcock read the riot act to Rollins, too. About not reporting the crap games in the room. He put Rollins on probation for the rest of the year. That means he can't play on any of the teams. The track coach isn't going to be happy when he hears about it. Rollins is the number one shot-putter of the school. It won't help him any getting a scholarship for college, either."

"Do you have any children?" Strand asked.

"One daughter. Thank God she's married." Hollingsbee laughed.

Strand couldn't help wondering if the man had ever read any of his daughter's letters to her husband or to any other man she knew.

"How about you?" Hollingsbee asked. "How many children do you have?"

"Three. So far they've managed to stay out of jail."

"You're ahead of the game." The lawyer shook his head. "Kids these days."

When they got to the house Strand was relieved to see that the common room was empty. Romero started for the stairs, but Strand stopped him. "Jesus," he said, "one last time . . ."

Romero shook his head.

"All right, then," Strand said. "Good-bye. And good luck." He put out his hand. Romero shook it. "Don't take it too hard," he said. "Just one more stick on the fire." He started toward the door, then stopped and turned. "Can I say something, Mr. Strand?"

"If you think there's anything more to say."

"There is. I'm leaving here, but I don't think you'll be here much longer, either." He was speaking earnestly, his voice low and clear. "This place is staffed by time-servers, Mr. Strand. And I don't think you're a time-server."

"Thank you," Strand said ironically.

"The other teachers are grazing animals, Mr. Strand. They graze in peace on grass . . ."

Strand wondered where in his reading Romero had picked up that phrase. Unwillingly, now that he had heard it, he recognized the justice.

"You hunt on cement, Mr. Strand," Romero went on. "That's why you understood me. Or at least half-understood me. Everybody else here looks at me as though I belong in a zoo."

"That's not fair," Strand said. "At least about the others."

"I'm just telling you my opinion." Romero shrugged.

"Are you finished?"

"I'm finished."

"Go get your things," Strand said. He was disturbed and did not want to hear any more. At least not today.

"Come on, Baby," Romero said harshly to Rollins, "let's clear out the ole plantation. Massa's selling us South."

Strand watched Hollingsbee and the two boys go up the

stairs, then went down the hall to his apartment. The phone was ringing in the living room. He had almost decided not to answer it but then, thinking that it might be Leslie calling from France to reassure him that she was all right, he picked it up.

It was Hazen. "Did you read that goddamn story in the *Times* this morning?" He sounded drunk.

"I did."

"Reliable sources." Hazen's voice was thick. "Any two bit shyster lawyer in the Justice Department leaking to a crappy newspaperman and suddenly it's a reliable source. My God, if you tapped a conversation between Jesus Christ and John the Baptist they could make it sound like a federal offense."

"I tried to call you last night and warn you about the *Times*. There was no answer."

"I was at the fucking opera. And when I'm not home my goddamn valet is too lazy to move away from the bar where he's drinking my liquor to pick up the phone. I'm going to fire the sonofabitch tonight. How did you know about the *Times*?"

"There were two FBI men here yesterday, questioning me about you. They told me to look at the *Times* this morning."

"What did they want to know?"

"If I'd heard you talking to Hitz about a deal."

"What did you tell them?"

"What could I tell them? I said I didn't hear anything."

"You could have sworn, for Christ's sake, that you were with me every minute and you knew damn well I didn't say a word about any kind of business with Hitz."

"We went through this before, Russell," Strand said wearily. "I told them what I knew. No more and no less."

"Go to the head of the honor roll, Sir Galahad," Hazen said. "When are you going to come down out of the clouds and hang your halo on the door and learn to play with the big boys on the street?"

"You're drunk, Russell. When you're sober, I'll talk to you." Strand quietly put down the receiver. He was shivering. The cold of the day seemed to be embedded in his bones. He went into the bathroom and turned on the hot water in the tub. He inhaled the steam gratefully as he started to undress. There was a ring on the doorbell. He turned the water off, put on a bathrobe and went barefooted to the door. Dr. Philips was standing there, with his little black bag in his hand.

"Do you mind if I come in, Mr. Strand?"

Strand had the impression that the doctor was on the verge of putting his foot in the door for fear that it would be slammed in his face.

"Please."

Philips came in. "I hope I'm not disturbing you," he said. "But Mr. Babcock called me a few minutes ago and said he thought I ought to take a look at you."

"Why?"

"May I take off my coat?"

"Of course. Did Babcock explain . . . ?"

"He said he was worried about you, he thought you didn't look too well," Philips said, as Strand helped him off with his coat. "He told me about your history with a heart problem and if it's all right with you I'd like to do a little checking." He glanced obliquely at Strand. "The truth is your color isn't all it might be today. I know you've been under stress and . . ."

"I've lost a little sleep the last few nights," Strand said curtly. "That's all." He was certain that no matter what happened he didn't want to be put back in a hospital again.

Dr. Philips was taking a stethoscope out of his bag and the apparatus that Strand had become all too familiar with, to take his blood pressure. "If we can just sit over here at the desk," Philips said, sounding, Strand thought, like a dentist assuring a patient that probing for a root canal nerve wouldn't hurt, "and if you'll take off your robe . . ."

Strand threw the robe over a chair. He still had his pants on so he didn't feel as foolish as he would have sitting naked in his own living room. "You certainly aren't obese," Philips said dryly as he put the cold stethoscope to Strand's chest. The instructions were familiar, too. Cough. Hold your breath. Breathe deeply, exhale slowly. Aside from

the brief commands, Philips said nothing. After the chest
he put the stethoscope to Strand's back. Then he wrapped
the rubber sleeve of the blood pressure machine around
Strand's arm and pumped it up, let the air out, watching
the gauge intently, then repeating the process. Your life
on a bubble of air, Strand thought, as he watched the
doctor's impassive face. Or on a slender column of mer-
cury, that unstable element.

When Philips was through he still remained silent while
he put the gadgets away in his bag. Shivering, Strand put
on his bathrobe again. "Mr. Strand," Philips said, "I'm
afraid Mr. Babcock is a keen diagnostician. Your breathing
is very shallow and there's a worrisome sound to your
lungs. Your heartbeat is irregular, although not too bad.
Your blood pressure is very high. Do you remember what
it was when they released you from the hospital?"

"I don't know the numbers, but my doctor said it was
high normal."

"It is no longer within the normal range, I'm afraid.
Are you taking anything to keep it down?"

"No."

Philips nodded. "If you'll come by the infirmary tomorrow morning I'll give you some pills that should work.
Just one a day should do the trick." He dug into his bag
and came out with a small bottle. "Here's something to help
you sleep. Don't worry—it's not addictive."

"I'm really not afraid of becoming a drug addict at my
age," Strand said.

"Addiction is not only a teenage disease, Mr. Strand,"
Philips said coldly. "There's some liquid in your lungs,
too . . ."

"It's a wonder I'm still walking around, isn't it?" Strand
said, trying to sound amused at the minor misfunctions of
his refractory body.

"A little walking is fine. It's even prescribed. Although
I'd stay indoors until it gets a little warmer. I'll give you
a diuretic, too. I don't want to alarm you. You've recovered remarkably from what Mr. Babcock has told me
was a massive attack. But emotion—stress, as I mentioned

before—plays a great part in conditions like this. If possible, I'd like to see you take things more calmly."

"What should I have done when I saw one of the boys in my house chasing another with a knife—sat down and played the flute?"

"I know, I know," Philips said, reacting to the ring of anger in Strand's voice by talking more slowly and calmly than ever. "There are situations when what a doctor advises sounds foolish. I'm not an extravagantly healthy man myself, but there is advice I give myself that I can't hope to follow. Still, if possible, try to put your problems into some larger perspective."

"How do you make out when you put your problems into some larger perspective?"

Philips smiled sadly. "Badly."

Strand knew from what Babcock had told him that Philips was a widower. His wife had been killed in an automobile accident five years before. He had had a prestigious practice in New York City and had been a professor at Cornell Medical Center. When his wife had died he had given it all up, practice, hospital, office, apartment, friends, and the rest of his family, and had gone off for a year to live alone in a cabin in the Maine woods. He had come to Dunberry, where he had frankly told Babcock that he wanted to have a practice that made minimum demands on him and where his responsibility was limited and where none of the friends and associates he had known when his wife was alive would crop up to remind him of his happier days. As he had just confessed, when he had put his problems into a larger perspective he had fared badly.

"Sprained ankles and adolescent acne," he had told Babcock. "That's about as deep into medicine as I want to go for the rest of my life."

Remembering this dissipated Strand's irritation with the man for coming over unasked to examine him and highhandedly prescribing for him, meddling, as Strand had felt when he saw the doctor at his door, with matters that were not really any concern of his. After all, Strand was not a child and he had his own doctors to whom he could appeal if he felt it necessary. He tried to imagine what Hazen's reaction would have been on the phone if the doctor had answered it and counseled him to put Washington and the FBI into a larger perspective.

"I understand from Mr. Babcock," the doctor was saying, "that you're the most conscientious teacher in the school. That has to mean overwork and overworry. If I may make a suggestion, be less conscientious. Try to let things slide here and there. And don't run after boys with knives if you can help it." He smiled as he said it. "Rest as much as you can. Mentally even more than physically. One more question. Do you drink much?"

"Hardly at all."

"Take a whiskey now and then. It can put things into a rosier light, aside from opening up the capillaries." Philips struggled into his coat. Just at the door, he turned. "What do you think will happen to the Romero boy?"

Strand thought for a moment. "Rollins says that if he goes to jail he'll wind up on the street and he won't be carrying a knife, there'll be a gun in his belt and dust in his pocket. I guess what he means by dust is heroin or cocaine. My feeling is that it's either that or he'll lead a revolution somewhere."

Philips nodded soberly. "Mercy is the scarcest virtue on the market," he said. "We're all such bunglers, aren't we? Well, sir, good night. And sleep well."

Sprained ankles and adolescent acne, Strand thought, as the door closed behind the doctor. Romero hardly fitted into those categories.

Strand went into the bathroom and put the small bottle of pills Philips had given him on the shelf. Nepenthe by the nightly dose, he thought. Retreat to forgetfulness. Civilization's answer to religion and ambition.

He turned the hot water on again, once more grateful for the swirling steam, taking deep breaths. Then the phone rang again. Annoyed, he turned the tap off and went back into the living room. "Hello," he said brusquely.

"You don't have to snap my head off." It was Leslie, her voice amused though far away. "I know you don't like to talk on the phone but you might as well tear it out of the wall if you answer it like that. Nobody will ever dare call you twice."

"Hello, dearest," he said. "God, it's good to hear your voice. Where are you? The last I heard from Air France, you were wandering all over European air space."

"We finally landed at Nice," Leslie said, "and now we're in Linda's place in Mougins. She said as long as we were so close it would be a shame if I didn't see it. It's heavenly. I wish you were here with us."

"So do I."

"How are things on the battlefield?"

"Picking up," he said ambiguously.

"What does that mean?"

"Romero's out on bail and he's staying with Rollins's family in Waterbury."

"Who put up the bail?"

He hesitated. "Friends," he said.

"Was it Russell?"

"He's not Romero's friend." Strand did not add that at the moment Romero didn't think Strand was his friend, either.

"I guess it's better all around that way, don't you?"

"Much better."

"Are you taking care of yourself? Are you lonely?"

"I hardly notice that you're not here," he said, laughing, or at least making an effort to laugh. "Mrs. Schiller is pampering me outrageously."

"I worried about you all over the Atlantic."

"You should have worried about the pilot. You're lucky they didn't put you down in Warsaw. I'm fine."

"Really?"

"Really."

"You sound tired."

"It's the connection. I intend to take up skiing tomorrow. The paper promises snow." It took an effort to be flip, but he made it. If Leslie had been there, he would have told her all, or almost all, of what he had been through that day. But worries, he knew, were multiplied by the square root of distance and Leslie was three thousand miles away.

"What are you doing now?" Leslie was saying. "I mean at this particular minute?"

"I'm about to step into a hot bath."

"And I'm going to jump into Linda's pool tomorrow. Imagine being able to swim in November. When we retire I think we ought to live in Mougins."

"If you find a nice little place for around a million dollars while you're down there, put a deposit on it."

Leslie sighed. "It would be nice to be rich for once, wouldn't it?"

"Thoreau never saw the Mediterranean," Strand said, "and he was happy on a pond."

"He wasn't married."

"So I've heard."

"If I let myself go," Leslie said, "I think I would turn into a frivolous, luxury-loving woman. Would you be able to bear me?"

"No."

She laughed again. "I do like a man who knows his own mind. I've talked long enough. This call is costing Linda a fortune. Are you happy?"

"Never happier," he said.

"I know you're lying and I love you for it." There was a sound of a kiss over the scratchy wire and Leslie hung up.

Strand put down the phone and went into the bathroom and finally sank into the warm water of the bath. My private small sea, he thought as he dozed in the steam. Like Thoreau, he would be content with a pond.

6

He was surprised when he opened the door of his apartment after the last class of the day and saw Hazen standing in the living room picking a magazine off a bookcase shelf. Strand had not heard from him since the drunken conversation on the phone more than a week ago.

"Hello, Allen," Hazen said. "I hope you don't mind. Mrs. Schiller let me in." He put out his hand and Strand shook it. "I brought you a little gift." He gestured toward the table behind the sofa, where two quart bottles of Johnnie Walker, Hazen's favorite Scotch, were standing.

"Thank you," Strand said. "They're bound to come in handy."

"I came to apologize for my bad temper over the phone." Hazen peered at him warily, as though unsure about how Strand would react.

"Forget it, Russell," Strand said. "I've already done so."

"I'm glad to hear it." Hazen's manner became hearty. "Misunderstandings are bound to crop up from time to time—even between the best of friends. And I was a little nervy about the piece in the *Times*."

"How is it going? I haven't seen anything more in the papers."

"There hasn't been anything more," Hazen said. "I guess they decided the fishing expedition was a flop. Justice has probably decided to drop the whole thing."

"I'm glad to hear it. Can I fix you a drink? I'm afraid I'll have to give it to you out of your own bottle. I finished ours a week ago."

Hazen looked at his watch. "Well, I guess it's just about drink time. If you'll join me . . ."

"I could use one, too," Strand said. "This is drinking weather. I nearly froze walking across the campus." He went into the kitchen to get ice and glasses and a pitcher of water. Although Dr. Philips had prescribed a drink now and then, when Rollins had finished off the last bottle, Strand had not bothered to go into town to get another one. He tried to stay indoors as much as possible during the cold spell, but he could have asked Mrs. Schiller to buy a bottle of whiskey when she went into town to shop. It wouldn't be Johnnie Walker. There was a limit to the amount of pampering he could fit into his budget.

Hazen had opened one of the bottles when Strand got back to the living room and Strand poured them each a generous drink. They touched glasses and drank. The immediate warmth in his gullet made Strand resolve that from then on he would have a drink each day before dinner.

Mrs. Schiller had laid a fire on the grate and Strand touched a match to the crumpled newspaper under the grate and watched as the flames began to lick up toward the kindling. He warmed his hands for a few moments before he went over to the table in front of the window where Hazen had installed himself. It was snowing lightly outside in the dusk, making a winter pattern on the half-frosted panes. Hazen's profile was reflected off the glass and the two images of the man himself and his reflection gave a curious double impression of him. The real face was relaxed, friendly; the reflection was etched on metal, cold and austere, like the head of an emperor on a coin, a wielder of power to whom applications for mercy were useless.

As Strand sat down opposite him at the table, Hazen peered at him thoughtfully. "Allen," he said softly, "I have come to ask forgiveness. Not only for what I said on the telephone to you. For my treatment of Romero. I've had plenty of time to think it over and realize what my responsibilities are. I was up in Hartford today and I spoke to the judge and found out that it was the Rollins boy who went bail for him. How he got the money is a mystery to me, but no matter. The judge said he got it in one day. I tell you, I felt ashamed in front of that hard old man. I told him I was going to take a personal interest in the case and would come to the court to take the case myself and explained the circumstances of how I met Romero through you and what we both thought of his capabilities and his extraordinary background. No matter what he looks like, the judge is not a monster, and he remembers my father from the time he, himself, was just a young lawyer breaking in. What he agreed to do was lift the bail and free the boy on my recognizance." Hazen smiled bleakly. "I guess he didn't happen to read *The New York Times* that day. He made conditions, of course. Romero has to report weekly to the hospital for psychiatric tests and treatment. I've already told this to Hollingsbee and Hollingsbee will get Rollins's money back for him tomorrow."

Two thousand dollars back in the bank, Strand thought. There *would* be presents for Christmas. "Russell," he said, "I can't tell you how good I feel about this. Not only for you. For you, of course. And for me, too."

Hazen looked a little embarrassed. He took a gulp of his drink. "It isn't all pure saintliness of character, Allen," he said. "Hitz and Company will pass a few unhappy days. That will not exactly displease me. Tell me, now that the kid looks as though he may get a break, what did he say to you that you said was confidential, about why he thought it was Hitz who took his money and letters?"

"It wasn't he who told me."

The lawyer's inquisitory tone came back into Hazen's voice. "Who told you?"

"I promised I'd keep it to myself."

"Promises." Hazen wrinkled his nose in disgust. "They're the bane of a lawyer's existence. Did anybody find the letters?"

"No," Strand lied.

"What could there be in a kid's letters that could be so damned important?"

"Think back to when you were eighteen, Russell."

"My father read every letter I received until I went to college."

"Romero doesn't even know if his father is alive or dead."

"The judge had better wake up on the right side of the bed the morning of the trial," Hazen said, "or the psychiatrist better find out Romero is the most disturbed kid in Connecticut and at the same time as harmless as a pussycat if he's not ready to do time. The judge was agreeable today but if the prosecutor lays it on, there's no telling . . . Professional courtesy is one thing. The law's another. Ah, well . . ." He sighed. "I've done my best. At least I can go to bed tonight with a clear conscience. It hasn't been an easy time for me."

"Not for anybody," Strand reminded him.

Hazen laughed. "Egotism is not the least of my faults."

"No, it's not."

The smile on Hazen's face became a little strained. He looked thoughtfully across the table at Strand again. "What do you really think of me, Allen?"

"A lot of things. Naturally. You've been insanely generous and helpful to us all. I imagine that you wouldn't be surprised that I have interlocking feelings—gratitude and" —he hesitated—"resentment."

"Nonsense," Hazen said. "You're not like that."

"Everybody's like that," Strand said quietly.

"Christ, for the most part, it was only money. I don't give a shit for money."

"You can say that. I can't."

"Let's forget about the gratitude and resentment and all the hogwash. What else do you think about me?"

"That you're an unhappy man."

Hazen nodded gloomily. "That's no lie. Who isn't these days? Aren't you?" His tone was challenging.

"On and off." Strand realized that Hazen was serious and felt that he should be serious in return. "But on balance, I feel that the happy days in my life have outweighed the unhappy ones. I don't have that feeling about you."

"And you're right. By God, are you right!" Hazen finished his drink, as though to wash out of his mouth the words he had just spoken. "This is just the sort of talk for a cold winter's evening, isn't it? Would you mind if I made myself another drink?"

"Help yourself."

Strand watched the big man as he rose from his chair and crossed to where the bottles and pitcher of water and the ice were standing. The old hockey player was still there, broad, virile, vaguely menacing, willing to take blows and return them. He made his drink, then wheeled at the table. "How about you? This minute? Are you happy now?"

"It's not the sort of question I usually ask myself."

"Ask. For old times' sake." Hazen sounded mocking.

"Well, for one thing, I'm glad you came. I felt our friendship was being undermined and I didn't like that," Strand said, speaking deliberately. "I feel it's repaired now and I feel better about that. About other things . . ." He shrugged. "When Leslie's not around, I miss her. I haven't yet gotten over not having the children present and I miss them, too. What's happened at the school is unpleasant and I still don't think I exactly fit in here yet, but I prefer to hope that given time that will improve. The work is easy and for the most part rewarding. The people are . . . well . . . polite and helpful. For the future, yes, I expect to be happy, reasonably happy."

"The future." Hazen made a derisive, blowing noise. "The future is going to be goddamn awful. The way things are going in the world."

"I wasn't thinking about the world. I can be pessimistic about the world and selfishly optimistic about myself. I've found that when a man steps back from very nearly dying and resumes what can be called a normal life, optimism is almost an automatic response."

Hazen came back with his glass and sat down at the table again. He looked out the window. "Miserable night," he said. "No wonder the whole country's moving south. Sometimes I think every city in the Northeast, Boston, New York, Philadelphia, will be a ghost town in fifty years. Maybe it wouldn't be such a bad idea. Okay, Pollyanna—" For a breath he sounded as he had when he shouted at Strand over the telephone. "Everything is coming up roses, Mr. Strand says. The news of the century. So nothing else is bothering you?"

"Of course there is." Strand thought of Leslie's flight in the middle of the night from Dunberry, of the letters signed Caroline, burned in the basement incinerator, of Eleanor, leading her husband around by the nose in Georgia and arousing the antagonism of the townspeople, of Jimmy, aged nineteen, involved with a pop singer almost twice his age, who had already gone through two or three husbands, of his own forced celibacy. "Of course there is," he repeated. "Family things. Routine." He knew the word was false. "But I'd rather not discuss what they are or even dwell on them. My dreams remind me of them and that suffices."

Hazen nodded, his head like a heavy, off-balance pendulum. "Tell me," he said suddenly, "have you ever thought of suicide?"

"Like everybody else."

"Like everybody else." Again the heavy, swinging nod. "Hell, this is a sorry conversation. The drink. It's unusual for me. Usually drink makes me feel good."

Strand remembered the grotesque scene the first night at the Hamptons when Hazen had arrived drunk late at night and snarled and bellowed and railed against his profession, his family, the world. He wondered how a man ordinarily so intelligent could have such a misconception about himself.

"Anyway," Hazen said, with a plain effort at geniality, "the ladies aren't here to watch us making self-pitying idiots of ourselves. I talked to Linda in Paris and she says they are having a marvelous time. They're delighted that the Christmas holiday in the Hamptons is definite."

"Is it?" Strand asked, surprised.

"I guess I forgot to tell you. Can you get your kids?"

"I haven't asked them yet." He didn't tell Hazen that after their argument he had resolved not to go. "Are you sure Leslie hasn't got other plans?"

"Linda asked her—she was in the room when I called—anl I could hear her say it was a great idea."

"I'll get in touch with the rest of the family." The pros-

pect of ten days away from the school, away from the
weight of the presence of four hundred boys, alone when
he wanted to be with Leslie on the quiet beach along the
shores of the Atlantic, lifted his spirits. "I'm sure we'll
have a wonderful time." He smiled. "See what I mean by
being able to be pessimistic about the future of the world
and still be optimistic about your own? At least for ten
days. Just keep us from watching the television news programs and reading the *Times* and it will be Eden."

The bell of the apartment rang and Hazen looked at his
watch. "That must be Conroy. I sent him to the main hall
to keep warm while I talked to you. It's going to be a long
drive back to the city in this weather. Thanks for the
drinks." When they shook hands, he held Strand's for an
extra moment. "I'm glad I came. I'm too old to turn
friends into enemies."

"I wasn't your enemy, Russell."

"Well, you damn well should have been." Hazen laughed
and went out.

Strand sat down at the table, feeling the glass of whiskey
sweating in his hand, and looked out through the patterns
of frost on the windowpanes at the thickening snow. He
thought of the great cities of the North Hazen had spoken
of, half in jest, the winds looting the glass and concrete
avenues, the population fleeing. He, too, in the first winter
of his imminent and sea-wracked old age, longed for the
South.

There were three letters waiting for him the next day
when he got back from his last class. Mrs. Schiller had put
his mail in a neat little pile on the table behind the sofa in
the living room. It had stormed all day. On the walk across
the campus snow had gotten into his shoes and down the
collar of his overcoat, so before he opened the letters he
took off his coat and shoes and socks, dried his feet, put
on slippers and changed his shirt. He had been soaked once
before that day, after lunch, and his throat felt dry and
raspy and there was a peculiar hot throb in his chest. Perhaps he would take Dr. Philips's advice and go into New
York on Saturday and have Dr. Prinz take a look at him.

Then, remembering the inner warmth of the Scotch the evening before with Hazen, he made himself a whiskey and water without ice and took the first sip before he went back into the living room and picked up the letters. One, he saw from the envelope, was from Caroline, another from Leslie, and a third had no name or return address. He usually read Caroline's letters with a small, indulgent smile on his face. They were short and bubbly and obviously hastily written and were merely signals that she was alive and enjoying herself and loved her parents. But he had had no word from her since the day he had heard from Mrs. Schiller about the letters in the basement trash basket.

He opened her letter first. There was no mention of Romero. Caroline reported that she was having a great time, that she had been chosen as the queen for the Homecoming Game of the new basketball season, that she had made two intellectual friends, a girl who was majoring in philosophy and another who was certain to be the editor of the college literary magazine in her junior year, that the coach of the track team thought that if she applied herself she could beat out the girl who always came in first in the two twenty and that she had been invited to spend the Christmas holidays with a family in Beverly Hills but had declined because she couldn't wait to see her Mummy and Daddy. She had also received a postcard of the Eiffel Tower in a letter from Mummy and thought it was most self-sacrificing of Daddy to spend all that time in dreary Dunberry alone while Mummy gallivanted in Paris. There were five crosses at the end of the letter, above her signature.

There was a postscript, "Mummy wrote that we're all invited to Mr. Hazen's house in the Hamptons for Christmas and I decided that it was childish of me to tell you that I would never go there again. The past is the past and I'm none the worse for having been hit in the head by a dashboard there. In fact I'm much the better for it. Nobody would have dreamed of electing me Homecoming Queen if my nose hadn't been busted."

Well, Strand thought, at least she knows how to stick

to a story. It was too late now—if it hadn't always been too late—to let her know that he knew it wasn't a dashboard that had hit her.

As he put the letter down, Strand remembered Mrs. Schiller saying that Caroline was a very popular name these days.

He opened Leslie's letter, saw it was a long one.

Dearest,

    I have the most enormous news. You are now married to a wealthy woman. Comparatively speaking, of course. What's happened is that I've sold the dune painting I started over Thanksgiving in the Hamptons. Linda was as good as her word and hung it in the show. It was the first one sold. It might have something to do with the fact that it was priced at only two thousand dollars ($2,000!!! It sounds like a lot more in francs) and all the rest started at five and went sky-high after that. I've also sold a water color that I did in a few hours in Mougins. Linda says she didn't believe anyone could do something new with the Riviera as subject and somehow I managed it. Even more dazzling—the man who bought it is a painter himself, a well-known painter in France, and he's invited me to his studio and told me that if I want to paint from live models there I could do so at the same time he's working. Incredible, isn't it? I feel like somebody's maiden aunt who does embroidery in her spare time and is suddenly told she's producing works of art. Linda says that if I go on in what she calls "my new style" (ha-ha) and work hard she'll definitely give me a show in New York next year. I've been working on a big canvas of a courtyard I wandered into, only it doesn't look like a courtyard on the canvas, it looks like a medieval dungeon. "Lit by an unearthly light, like Balthus, only American," is the way Linda describes it, but you know how she exaggerates. I've never felt like this before. The brush seems to move by itself. It's the most peculiar and wonderful feeling. Maybe it's something in the air. Now I think I know why painters had to come to Paris sometime in their careers, the earlier the better. If I'd have come when I was eighteen, I don't think I'd ever have touched the piano again.

I'm on such a high, dear man, as though I'm soaring, that I hate to leave before I have to. Linda's suggested that we stay on here longer than we planned and arrange to meet you at Kennedy the day you're due at Russell's. You have to pass the airport anyway on the way out and to tell you the truth, a little extra time away from Dunberry will fortify me for what I have to face when I get back.

I know it sounds selfish, but it's only a few days, and it's not like Gauguin leaving his family to paint in the South Seas, is it? Of course, if you want me to come back sooner, just send me a cable.

In the meantime, if you can do the family chores and get in touch with the kids and tell them where we can all assemble for the holidays, it will ease my mind.

I hope you're taking care of yourself and that you miss me as much as I miss you. Please let me know as soon as possible what you decide.

Please don't think that because I have the crazy idea that I have a chance to be a good painter I will turn into a bad wife. If I had to make the choice you know what it would be. I am no Gauguin.

Give my blessing to the kids when you speak to them.

> Linda sends her love and I send
> you everything I have. Until the
> blessed holiday,
>
> Leslie

Strand put the letter down slowly, trying to sort out his emotions. He recognized pride, jealousy, an obscure sense of loss among them. If she were willing to give up the music to which she had devoted her life what would be the next thing she would forgo? He would send her a cable of congratulations later, when he had time to compose a fittingly joyous message.

He looked around him. The room suddenly seemed bleak, a seedy bachelor's quarters. He certainly was not soaring.

Absently, he tore open the third letter.

Dear Mr. Strand,

I am not going to tell you my name. I am the wife of an instructor in the biology department in the college which your daughter, Caroline, attends. I am the mother of two small children.

He stopped reading for a moment. The handwriting was narrow and neat. Much could undoubtedly be discovered about the character of the woman who wrote it by an expert in graphology. He felt a little dizzy, sat down, still holding the letter. The handwriting was very small and he had been straining to read it. He fished for his glasses and put them on. The handwriting now loomed large. Ominously large.

My husband has become infatuated with her. She is the flirt of the campus and the boys crowd around her like hungry animals. My husband has told me that if she'll have him, he'll leave me. They had arranged to go to California together over the Thanksgiving holiday, but at the last moment she went off with a boy on the football team. She flits from affair to affair, I am told, although the only one I can be sure of, because I have been told so by my husband, is the one with him. In other days she would have been thrown out of school after the first month. Times being what they are and educators having given up all pretense at discipline or the practice of decency, she is coddled and cossetted and most recently has been elected the queen of the basketball Homecoming Game. Up to now, she has promised my husband that she will finally make the trip with him to California during the Christmas season. I am reduced to the pitiful state of praying that once more she will jilt him. He is neglecting his work and ignoring me, except when we argue, and paying no attention to our children. He is on a small salary, since he is only an instructor, but I know he lavishes expensive gifts on her.

I know that you, yourself, are a teacher and understand how easily a man's career can be destroyed by professional neglect added to an open indiscretion. I understand, also, how when a girl lives away from home for the first time, the attentions of the male sex, especially when the girl is as young and pretty as your daughter, can turn her head, to her everlasting regret later on.

I have no idea of what you know about your daughter's behavior or how much you care about her future, but for her sake and mine and that of my family, I beg you to do whatever you can to make her realize how cruel and irresponsible she is being and restore my husband to the bosom of his family.

The letter was unsigned.

The bosom of his family. Strand read the line, with its biblical echo, over again. He thought of prairie churches, Sunday evening prayer meetings. He knew one thing the biology teacher didn't know—he would be jilted for Christmas as he had been jilted for Thanksgiving. Compliments of the seasons.

He opened his hand and the letter fluttered to the floor. Through sleet and snow and gloom of night, the daily bread of affliction is delivered to our door six times a week by the ever faithful United States Postal Service. Thank God for Sunday.

A biology teacher, he thought. He, himself, had been a teacher of history and Leslie had been in his class, at Caroline's age, demure and beautiful in the first row, and he had lusted after her. Was he to feel guilty? At least he had waited a decent year after she had been graduated and had called at her family's apartment with the intention of marriage. But the biology teacher, too, no doubt intended marriage.

What could be said to his daughter? And who could say it? Not her father, he thought, never her father. Leslie? He guessed what Leslie would say—"She's a big girl. Let her work out her own problems. We'll only make it worse. I'm not going to sacrifice my relations with my daughter for the sake of a randy old fool of a hick biology teacher." If he showed Leslie the letter, she probably would say anybody with a handwriting like that was bound to lose her husband.

Eleanor? Eleanor would tell her, "Do what you want to do." Eleanor had always done exactly that.

Jimmy? Possibly. He was the closest in age to Caroline, moved in the currents of the same generation, was protective of his sister. But with his thrice-married thirty-five-year-old singer, Caroline would probably laugh at him if he brought up the subject of morality. Still, Jimmy was worth a try.

Strand finished his drink. It did not help the dry rasping of his throat or the hot thrust of pain in his lungs. He stood up and went over to the phone and dialed Dr. Prinz's number in New York. Dr. Prinz said it was about time he called. He would see him at eleven Saturday morning. He would have to get the early train.

Then he called Jimmy's number in New York. For once, Jimmy was in.

"Jimmy," Strand said, "I have to be in New York Saturday morning. Can we have lunch? I have some things to talk to you about."

"Oh, Dad," Jimmy said, "I'm sorry. I have to leave for Los Angeles Saturday morning. Business. I'd love to see you. Can you come down for dinner Friday night?"

Sons by appointment only, Strand thought. "I'm through with my last class at three o'clock on Friday," he said. "I can get into New York by six o'clock. Fine. I'll have to stay over, though. I have a checkup with the doctor on Saturday morning."

"Anything wrong?" Jimmy immediately sounded anxious.

"No. It's routine." Strand felt a cough collecting in his throat and controlled it. "Can you get me into a hotel?"

"The Westbury is near me. It's on Madison Avenue, around 70th Street. I'll book you in there."

"It sounds expensive." He had once had drinks in the bar of the hotel with Leslie on an afternoon when they had been at the Whitney Museum nearby. It had been too luxurious for him. The other people at the bar were the same sort as the guests at the parties Hazen had taken them to in the Hamptons.

"No matter," Jimmy said airily. "My treat."

"I can stay at some cheaper place."

"Forget it, Pops. I'm in the chips."

Nineteen years old, Strand thought, and in the chips. When he was nineteen he had stayed at the YMCA. "Well," he said, "if it won't break you."

"I'll reserve the bridal suite."

"The bride's in Paris," Strand said. "Save your money."

Jimmy laughed. "I know she's in Paris. She sent me a postcard. The Mona Lisa, at the Louvre. I guess she wanted to remind me that she's my mother. And that not all art was produced by electric guitars. I'll pick you up at the hotel."

He sounds at least thirty years old, Strand thought as he hung up. He went into the kitchen and fixed himself another drink. If one drink was good for him, perhaps two would be twice as good.

The French restaurant Jimmy took him to was quietly elegant, gleaming with snowy tablecloths and large arrangements of cut flowers. The headwaiter fawned over Jimmy and bowed politely when Jimmy introduced Strand as his father, although Strand thought he detected a momentary flicker of disapproval in the man's eyes. Beside Jimmy, lean and immaculate in a dark suit, narrow at the waist, which looked as though it had been made in Italy, Strand was conscious of his unpressed old tweed jacket, the loose fit of his collar, his baggy flannels, as the headwaiter led them to a table. When he looked at the prices on the menu he was aghast. He had been aghast, too, when he asked the room clerk at the Westbury the price of the room that had been reserved for him.

"Your son's taking care of it," the clerk had said.

"I know," Strand had said testily. The trip down to the city had been uncomfortable. The train was crowded and overheated and the only seat he could find was in the smoking car and the man next to him smoked cigarette after cigarette and only looked at Strand curiously when Strand had a coughing fit. "I know my son's taking care of it," Strand said to the clerk. "I just would like to know what it costs."

The clerk told him and Strand groaned inwardly, thinking, My son will also be the youngest bankrupt in the United States in one year.

When Jimmy appeared a half hour later, Strand hadn't chided him about his extravagance. In fact, he hadn't had the time to talk to him about anything. "We're late," Jimmy had said, after saying "Pops, you look great. Joan's expecting us for a drink. It's just around the corner. She wants to meet you."

"What for?" Strand asked sourly, annoyed at Jimmy's tardiness. He took it for granted that Joan was the name of Jimmy's thirty-five-year-old mistress or whatever she was.

"Maybe she wants to see the oak from which the acorn was dropped."

"Is the lady having dinner with us?" With her at the table he could hardly bring up the subject of Caroline and her biology teacher.

"No," Jimmy said, hurrying him out of the hotel. "Just a drink. She has to pack for the trip tomorrow."

"Trip? Where is she going?" Strand asked, although he knew.

"California," Jimmy said nonchalantly. "With me. She hates to travel alone. She can't cope."

When he was introduced to Joan Dyer in her gaudy, all-white apartment twenty-two stories high, with a view of the East River, Strand thought she looked like a lady who could cope with anything, including fire, flood, famine and finance. She was a tall, skinny woman with no breasts and enormous wild dark eyes, heavily accented with purple eye shadow. She was barefooted, with yellowish, splayed toes, and was wearing gauzy black pajamas through which Strand could see the pinkish glow of bikini underpants. She didn't shake the hand that he extended to her but said, in a deep, powerful, almost masculine voice, "Do you mind if I kiss the father?" and embraced him and kissed his cheek. He was enveloped in a wave of heavy perfume. Whatever he ate for dinner would have to be highly seasoned to compete with the fumes that clung to his clothes. He knew, too, that he would have to wipe off the purplish lipstick before he went anywhere else. This was all at the door, which Joan Dyer opened herself. When she led them into the enormous living room, Strand saw that Solomon was standing there, next to the chair from which he had risen to greet them. "Hello, Allen," Solomon said. "Jimmy." There was a cold edge to his voice when he said "Jimmy." It did not escape Strand. "Well," Solomon said, "I've had my say, Joan. You'll both regret what you're doing."

The woman waved a languid, disdainful hand at him. Her nails, long and predatory, were painted purple, too. "Herbie," she said, "you're beginning to bore me."

Solomon shrugged. His face was deeply tanned and his hair looked almost white over the deep color of his forehead. Strand would have liked to ask him where he found sun in New York in December, but the expression on his face was not conducive to idle conversation. And Jimmy's face, too, had a stubborn look to it that Strand had become accustomed to by the time Jimmy was eight.

"Allen," Solomon said, his voice gentle and friendly now, "if you're staying in town can we have lunch tomorrow?"

"I'd like that very much," Strand said.

"Sardi's," Solomon said. "One o'clock. It's right near my office. West 44th Street."

"I know where it is."

"I'll reserve a table." Solomon left without looking at Joan Dyer or Jimmy and without saying good-bye.

"Ships that pass in the night," Joan Dyer said as they

heard the distant closing of the front door. She smiled a purple smile at Strand. "And now, can I give you a drink? I must warn you, though—it's carrot and celery cocktail juice. I refuse to poison my guests with alcohol and cigarettes."

"Thank you, I'm not thirsty," Strand said, somehow reassured about his son's companion, who, because of her profession, he had automatically supposed was addicted to marijuana, at the very least. A woman addicted to carrot juice could hardly be considered a danger to a young man like Jimmy.

"Do sit down," Joan Dyer said. "I want to take a good look at you. Jimmy's spoken so much about you. You've raised a marvelous son," she said as Strand sat down, sinking almost to the floor on the soft low white couch and wondering if he was going to need help to get up off it. "In our profession the young men are usually runaway children, immature, resentful of their parents, misunderstood talents. It's a breath of fresh air to see you two together. I mean it, Mr. Strand."

"Joan," Jimmy said, with authority, "why don't you cut the bullshit?"

The woman gave Jimmy a baleful stare, then smiled her dark smile at Strand and went on as though Jimmy had not interrupted. "From the look of you, Mr. Strand, Jimmy must have gotten his intelligence, his sense of personality, from you. From the moment I saw him I had a feeling of serene trust, a feeling that finally I had found the man—a child in years, perhaps, but a man, nonetheless, whom I could depend upon, whose judgment in both personal and professional matters was intuitively right. What I've just said will explain the unfortunate little scene you've just witnessed between Herbie and us. I'm sure Jimmy will fill you in on the details. And, now, if you'll forgive me, I must finish my packing. It's the crack of dawn tomorrow and to the airport, so please don't keep my dear Jimmy up too late tonight, Mr. Strand. And I do hope that you will come out and visit us in California soon with your beautiful wife, whose photograph Jimmy has shown me. What a lucky family. I was a waif, tossed around from relative to careless relative, so I can appreciate a family . . ."

"Damn it, Joan," Jimmy said, "your father still owns half of Kansas and your mother has a racing stable."

"I am a waif in spirit," the woman said with dignity. "It is why the audiences respond with such emotion when I sing. I sing to the loneliness of the American soul." She came over to Strand and gracefully swooped over him and kissed his forehead. "Good night, dear father," she said and flowed out of the room.

Strand struggled to get up from the couch and Jimmy came over and gave him his hand and pulled him up.

"What was all *that* about?" Strand asked.

"It was one of her nights," Jimmy said. "You never know which one you're going to get. The waif, the grande dame, the anarchist, the little girl with a bow around her waist and a lisp, the femme fatale, Mother Earth . . . You name it," he said, grinning, "and it's in her repertoire. And don't take the carrot juice too seriously. She asked me if you drank and I said no, so she became a health nut for an evening. The next time you see her she's as likely to be roaring drunk as not. If that's what it takes to make her sing like an angel, which she does, the only thing is to sit back and enjoy the act. Come on, Pops, let's go to dinner. I'm starving."

The restaurant was nearby and they walked to it. As they walked, Strand asked Jimmy what was wrong with Solomon, but Jimmy had shrugged and said it was a long story, he'd tell him over dinner.

Seated at the table to which the headwaiter had led them, Jimmy ordered a martini. In some places, Strand knew, Jimmy would have had to produce his I.D. card to get a drink. Not here. Strand shook his head when Jimmy asked him if he wanted a drink. The second whiskey he had had the night of the three letters had left him with a headache and he hadn't had a drink since.

"Now," he said, after they had ordered and Jimmy was sipping at his martini, "what was all that about with Mr. Solomon?"

Jimmy drummed his fingers impatiently on the tablecloth. "It's nothing," he said. "His nose is out of joint because we're leaving him. He'll get over it."

"Who's we?"

"Joan and me. Her contract's run out and she's had a better offer. On the Coast. Her second husband has a music company out there and they're friends again. It means a lot of bread. For both of us. Twice what old man Solomon was paying me and a piece of the action and that can mean millions with a dame like Joanie girl. And she won't make a move without me. She was ready to leave Herbie anyway before I came . . ."

"He told me he was about to fire her. Until you came along."

"Did he?" Jimmy said carelessly. "Somehow, she fixed on me. We have the same vibes. She won't even sing *do re me* unless I approve. The good old second husband is young and he knows what the kids're doing and that's ninety-nine percent of the business these days. Not like old Herbie. The tide has passed old Herbie by. He's washed up on the beach, only he hates to admit it."

"He was very good to you."

"It was money in the bank for him. I don't owe him anything. Gratitude in the trade is like putting a knife in a guy's hand and giving him lessons in how to slit your throat. I like the old fart, but business is business." Jimmy ordered a second martini. "Joan and I are going to have our own imprint. So we get the credit and the name without putting up any of the dough. And I'm my own boss. No running around like a messenger boy if old Herbie decides he wants a report on a new country singer down in Nashville or out in Peoria. You and Mom can come out to Beverly Hills and swim in my pool."

Strand looked soberly at his son. "Jimmy," he said, "I find all this thoroughly distasteful. I never thought I'd say these words, but I'm ashamed of you."

"Pops," Jimmy said, without anger, "not everybody can be a Knight of the Round Table like you. Camelot is kaput, even if the news hasn't reached Dunberry yet. Now, on the phone you said you had something you wanted to talk to me about. What is it?"

"Nothing," Strand said shortly. "I've changed my mind. I wanted you to do something for me. For the family. Now I believe I made the wrong choice." He stood up.

"Where're you going?"

"I'm leaving."

"Your dinner's going to be here in a minute. Sit down."

"I'm not hungry."

"Don't you even want my address in California?" There was a wailing tone in Jimmy's voice that reminded Strand of when Jimmy was small and had fallen and skinned his knees and come running home to be comforted.

"No, Jimmy, I don't want your address. Good night." Strand walked across the restaurant toward the checkroom. He got his coat and while he was putting it on, he looked back and saw that Jimmy was ordering a third martini. He went out and walked a few blocks along the cold streets to the Westbury and took the elevator to his room and lay down in the darkness. The telephone rang twice before he fell asleep, but he didn't answer it. Among the things he regretted about the evening was that he would have to allow Jimmy to pay for the room because he didn't have enough cash with him to pay for it himself.

7

Dr. Prinz didn't look any graver than usual as he sat behind the desk after the cardiogram, the blood pressure examination, the stress test, the X rays. Strand took that as a good sign. "Well, Doc?" he said.

"Everything is pretty good," Prinz said, "as far as we can tell. The blood pressure's still a little high, but not scary. But . . ." He stopped.

"But what?"

"I don't like the way you *look*. Your complexion, something about your eyes. If I hadn't seen you, if I was one of those great specialists who never see a patient and just have X rays and the results of the tests to go by, I'd say that for a man your age who has had a bad heart attack, you're in surprisingly good shape. But I'm not a great specialist. I'm a poor old G.P. and you're my friend and I've seen you in better days."

Strand laughed. "I've seen you in better days, too," he said.

"You bet you have. But I'm not your job and you're mine. It doesn't show in the tests, but I'd guess you've been sleeping poorly . . ."

"It's a good guess," Strand said.

"And that you're under some sort of nervous strain . . ." Dr. Prinz looked at him sharply, as though to surprise him into a confession.

"A bit," Strand admitted.

"I don't like to sound like one of those quacks who prescribe sedatives every time a society lady goes into a tizzy because she's not been invited to a party," Prinz said, "but I think a mild dose of Librium two or three times a day

might do you good. A year off on a beach would do you
more good, but I don't suppose you're likely to have one."

"Not likely," Strand said dryly.

Prinz scribbled on a prescription pad and pushed the
scrap of paper over the desk. "Have it filled and see if it
helps. I have the impression of fatigue. It may be mental,
it may be something else. Maybe the next time you come
in we'll make some thyroid tests. Between the thyroid
gland and the cerebellum there's sometimes a curious conspiracy. Well . . ." he sighed. "No miracles this Saturday."

"One more thing," Strand said, feeling embarrassed.
"Sex . . . ?"

Prinz looked at him sidelong, the first real glint of sympathy, mixed perhaps with amusement, behind his glasses.
"No prescriptions," he said. "It might kill you and it might
make you feel like a twenty-year-old fullback. Tell Leslie
I miss the string trios."

"Thanks for everything." Strand stood up and Prinz
stood, too, and walked with him to the door of the office.
"By the way," he said, "how is your friend Hazen?"

"Friendly." Dr. Prinz must have had too busy a month
to read *The New York Times*. "Running the country as
usual."

Prinz nodded. "I'd hate to have him as a regular patient.
He's one of those fellers, if I told him he had a disease, by
the next time I saw him he'd have read all the literature
on the subject and would lecture me on why he had it or
didn't have it and why my treatment was fifty years behind the times. And he'd have me call in twelve specialists
from Johns Hopkins and California and Texas for consul-
tations. Still"—he laughed—"the rich *do* live longer than
we do. Take care of yourself, Allen." He opened the office door for Strand. "And moderation in all things. The
Prinz recipe for a long and moderately happy life."

He walked downtown along Central Park West carrying
his small overnight bag, because he had checked out of
the hotel. It was a mild day, the pale sunlight making the
naked trees in the park trace patterns of lacy shadows on
the brown grass. He felt an unaccustomed lift of freedom.
He had no duties to concern him except that of living until

his first class on Monday and he was strolling through his native and beloved city in tolerant weather, amidst children liberated from schoolrooms, aging bicyclists in bright clothes heading for the park, comfortable couples with placid weekend faces advancing unhurriedly toward lunch. He had been presented with a clean bill of health, or at least a conditional one. It might be called a draw between him and death. There would be a rematch later on, but noonday New York beside the great park in the sunlight was too pleasant a time and place to think of that now. A troop of children, very serious on horseback, for whom he had to halt to allow them to cross the avenue to the bridle paths beyond, added to his pleasure.

He passed the street where Judith Quinlan lived and wondered if she were in her studio at that moment and speculated on what she might be doing. Washing her hair, listening to music, preparing to go to a matinee? He had finally read the letter she had sent him when he had come out of the hospital. "Please get well," she had written. "And if there's anything you need, if there're books you want or gossip of the school or a friend to read to you, please let me know."

He had not answered the letter and now he felt a twinge of guilt. For a moment he almost stopped, to turn down her street and ring her bell. But if he was going to walk all the way to Sardi's and get there by one o'clock to meet Solomon, there would be no time for Judith Quinlan. Thinking of her, he realized that he missed her trotting to keep up with him after school and the cups of coffee they had shared in the shops along their route home and he came as near as he ever could to blushing when he remembered the one time he had gone up to her apartment and she had served him a drink and opened his shirt and put her hand on his chest. The tingling sensation made him smile and a young woman walking in the opposite direction smiled sweetly in return. Gallantly, he tipped his hat. Her smile broadened at the gesture and he continued walking with a fresh lilt to his steps, although as he approached the restaurant where he would meet Solomon he was sorry he had made the date. He did not feel like discussing his son that day.

During lunch, Solomon did not mention Jimmy. He asked about Leslie and Caroline and Eleanor and her husband and inquired solicitously about Strand's health and told him about a friend of his, aged sixty, who had had an even worse attack than Strand and now played three sets of tennis daily. In answer to Strand's question about his tan, he said that he'd just come back from California, where he'd spent a week lying in the sun by the pool at the Beverly Hills Hotel, waiting for a rock singer to make up his mind on a deal. The deal had finally fallen through, but the tan had made the trip worthwhile. When he talked seriously, it was about Hazen. Solomon no doubt was as busy as Dr. Prinz, but he found time to read the papers. He had called Hazen to find out if there was anything he could do—he, too, knew many people in Washington— but Hazen had assured him that it was all blowing over and there was nothing to worry about. "I'm not so sure," Solomon said to Strand. "A friend of mine works for the UPI Washington bureau and he tells me that *something* is cooking, but he doesn't know just what as yet. I'm concerned about Russell. They're hitting him in his most vulnerable spot and the one thing that he's proudest of— his reputation. With all that he's seen and done he's never had to fight for it in his whole life and he may blunder into a trap. I tried to suggest that he go to a lawyer who's helped me and some of my friends out of shadowy cases —cases like his—plagiarism suits, doubtful breach of contract, slander and libel, payroll padding, unrealistic income tax returns, imaginative bookkeeping, blackmail, bribing union officials—the necessary underside of the law, as it were, that keeps the wheels of business turning. But when I mentioned the man's name, he just snorted and said he wouldn't soil his hands with a shyster like that." Solomon shook his head sadly. "He may wake up one morning and find that he's a broken man, if not in court, then on the front page of the *New York Post*, even if he's done nothing that's really against the law."

"Do you think he *has* done something against the law?" Strand asked.

Solomon smiled at him as he would at a credulous child. "Allen," he said, "you're a student of history. In all our history—in all the world's history—has there ever been a powerful, ambitious man who has not—well—stretched the law here and there, out of pride, righteousness, religion, impatience with a bureaucracy, the desire to be acclaimed, what have you? As a joke, my wife calls my business King Solomon's mines. Do you think I got where I am by dotting every *i* and crossing every *t*?"

"What you're telling me is that you think Hazen has put himself into a position where the Justice Department is right to go after him, is that it?"

"I'm suggesting that it is possible," Solomon said gravely. "If you could get Russell to listen to my advice about the lawyer I told him about, you would be doing him a great service."

"He thinks I'm an absentminded professor with a mind like a spinster librarian's. Do you think he'd listen to me?"

Solomon laughed. "No."

They were at their coffee now and Strand could see that Solomon's mood had suddenly changed and that he was looking at him speculatively, as though he was making a decision about him. "Frankly, Allen," Solomon said, "I didn't ask you to come to lunch to talk about Russell Hazen. Have you spoken to Jimmy?"

Here it comes, Strand thought, bracing himself. "Yes," he said. "Last night."

"Did he tell you he's leaving me?"

"Yes."

"Did he tell you why?"

"He did." He tried to sound neutral. "The gist of it seems to be that he wants to improve his position." Despite himself, he knew that he was trying to defend his son.

"Improve his position," Solomon said thoughtfully. "I guess you could describe it that way. Temporarily."

"A quite peculiar woman, to say the least," Strand said. "I think she's got him hypnotized."

"I'm afraid it's the other way around, Allen. She's the

one who's hypnotized. Of course, sex has a lot to do with
it. She's been dropped by every man who's ever come near
her and Jimmy makes a great show of being in love with
her."

"Show?"

"Allen," Solomon said patiently, "you've seen the lady.
Would you ever fall in love with her?"

"I'm not nineteen years old," Strand said, knowing it
was the weakest of arguments.

"The whole idea is Jimmy's," Solomon said. "He told
me as much. He came to me a month ago and made the
proposal to me: their own imprint, a share of the profits,
no interference from me in selection of material, playing
dates, accompanying bands, the whole shebang. Pretty
good for a nineteen-year-old boy whom I took in as an
apprentice just a few months ago to please a friend. He
said he'd give me a month, up to the date her contract
ran out, to consider his proposition. If I said no, he'd
take her away from me. She's the biggest money earner
we've got, but I said no. I may blackmail a little myself
from time to time"—Solomon smiled wanly—"but I do
not submit to blackmail. I told him he was fired, but Dyer
put up such a hysterical performance—she was in the
middle of a recording session that would take at least three
more weeks even under normal conditions—that I had to
keep Jimmy on for another month. But he's out now. I
just wanted to make sure you knew why."

"Thank you," Strand said sadly.

"I hope it won't affect whatever friendship you feel for
me."

"It won't," Strand said, although he knew better.

"The music business is a rough trade," Solomon said.
"Cutthroat at times. But people, especially young people,
think they can go all out, run roughshod over everybody,
ignore all codes. They're mistaken. I'm afraid your Jimmy
isn't strong enough, and never will be, to accumulate
enemies so early on. He'll have his little moment of glory,
Allen, but the slide will commence and there'll be no
stopping it. I'm not happy about it. In fact it saddens me

that I know my prediction will come true. The lady's a
menace, a bomb waiting to explode. Her voice is going and
she knows it. She needs to be protected and Jimmy couldn't
protect his own mother from getting wet in a drizzle. She's
desperate and manic-depressive and some new young
genius will come along on a night when they're booing her
off the stage or when the telephone stops ringing and she's
ready for one of her suicide attempts. If you can persuade
Jimmy to come to his senses I'll take him back. In time I
can turn him from a novice into a professional. And it's
not for my sake, it's for his. You believe that, don't you,
Allen?" Solomon stared hard across the table. "Don't you?"

"I believe it," Strand said. "Last night I told him what
he's done was distasteful—I'm not in the habit of using
strong language, as you know, and that was pretty strong
for me. I told him I was ashamed of him and I got up
from the table and left him there. But I know there's nothing I can do with him. Either the last few months have
changed him or he was always like this but I didn't recognize it. Whatever it is, he's going to go his own way." He
remembered what Jimmy had said about gratitude. Like
putting a knife in a guy's hand, he had said, and giving
him lessons in how to slit your throat. "My son has moved
out of my life," he said gently to the tanned, reasonable,
forgiving man across the table from him. "All I can do is
wave good-bye. I'm sorry."

Solomon reached over and touched his hand. "You know
what we need?" he said. "A brandy. The best brandy in
the house."

They had the brandy and then Solomon said he had an
appointment with a composer in his office. "He's a little
crazy," Solomon said. "He will only come to the office on
Saturday afternoons. It's his lucky day, he says. I've missed
two trips to Palm Springs and a skiing weekend because
of the sonofabitch. Want to go into the music business,
Allen?" He smiled.

"No, thank you," Strand said, and watched the man
make his way through the restaurant to the door, the perfect image of success and hearty well-being, waving genial-

ly, with a papal gesture of benediction, to friends at the
tables he passed.

He was at Grand Central Station, waiting for the three
twenty-one train to Connecticut. A young couple—a tall
boy and a pretty, much smaller girl—were kissing good-
bye, as though whichever one of them was traveling was
going to be gone for a long time. Strand stared at them,
amused but a little embarrassed at the public sexuality of
the embrace. On the walk across town from the restaurant
he had been thinking about Jimmy, embarked on God
knew what kind of adventure, on a wave of sex, of Caroline, that improbable home-breaker, tormenting all the
men around her, if the anonymous wife of the biology
teacher was to be believed, of Eleanor, stuck away in a
small town in Georgia because, as she had said, she could
not live without the one man she had chosen and who had
chosen her. The prospect of spending the rest of the weekend alone on the deserted wintry campus seemed bleaker
than ever. The city had revived old juices in him. For the
first time he resented Leslie's absence. Soaring, he remembered from her letter. He, too, could soar if he were in
Paris. He turned away from the couple, still locked together, and went to the side of the station where there was
a bank of telephones. He looked up the number in the
Manhattan directory, hesitated, then put a dime into the
slot and dialed. He waited for ten rings. There was no
answer. Judith Quinlan was not home. He hung up the
phone, fished out his dime, hurried back to the platform
gate, which was now open. He got into the last car just
before the train glided out of the station. As he looked
for an empty seat he saw the small girl who had been
kissing the boy at the gate. She was crying, dabbing at her
eyes with a handkerchief.

Women are lucky, he thought as he sat down in front
of her. They can cry.

For a moment he considered getting up and sitting in
the seat next to the girl to console her, perhaps console
himself. But he had never picked up a girl in his life and
he doubted that he could start now.

Forlorn and unhappily virtuous, a sinner in intention and already suffering from a sinner's remorse, without having tasted any of sin's pleasure, cursing himself for not having had the sense to call when he awoke that morning to announce to Judith Quinlan that he was in New York, he stared morosely out the window as the train rose from the tunnel under Park Avenue and rumbled on the overhead tracks in the failing winter sunlight.

When the train came to New Haven, where he had to change for the line going north, he saw that the girl had long ago stopped crying, had done her face carefully with fresh powder and rouge and was talking animatedly with a young man in a long fur coat who had boarded the train at Stamford.

It made him remember Romero and his striptease artist. In essential matters, like speaking to strange young women on trains, Strand thought, Romero was infinitely more learned than his history teacher.

The weather mocked him. It was a sunny, brisk Sunday morning and the few boys who had stayed on the campus for the weekend were playing touch football, their cries reaching him through the open window, merry and young. He had never had the talent or time to play games when he was their age and the young voices outside his window in the autumnal sunlight made him think sorrowfully of the lost, beautiful days of his youth, days that had passed unappreciated when he was their age.

He was restless and lonely. During the term he had had tea in the Red Top Inn on fine afternoons when he and Miss Collins had walked into town together. He had enjoyed the quiet melody of her voice, her abstention from school gossip, and her modest explanations of what she was doing in the book she was writing on American novelists of the 1930s. Twice she had brought along papers that Romero had done for her class that she thought were particularly fine and had blushed when Strand had complimented her on getting the best out of the boy. He decided to ask her to lunch, but when he called her number, her old mother, who lived with her, told him that she

had gone into New York for the day. I'm having no luck
with English teachers this weekend, he thought ironically
as he hung up.

He wanted desperately to talk to Leslie. But it would
only spoil her holiday if he told her about Caroline's letters and Jimmy's move to California and his reasons for
going there. If he called her, he knew she would ask him
for news about the children and he would have to lie and
she would detect the tone of falsehood in his voice and
the conversation would undoubtedly end badly. Besides,
transatlantic calls were forbiddingly expensive and he knew
he would regret his impulse, even if the conversation with
Leslie went smoothly, when the bill came in at the end of
the month. The ads of the telephone company in magazines always showed happy parents calling happy children
far away, but they did not include a warning that it was a
dangerous habit that schoolteachers on small salaries were
not encouraged to indulge.

He did not envy Hazen his house on the beach, his
marvelous paintings, his freedom to travel and dine in great
restaurants, but he did envy him the unthinking way he
could pick up a telephone and have long conversations
with people in California, England, France, whomever
and wherever. With a touch of malice, brought on by his
self-pitying mood, he thought that with all his command
of the long distance wires, Hazen hadn't succeeded all
that well in communicating with his own wife and children.

He remembered that it had been Eleanor who had told
him of Hazen's son's death from drugs. He hadn't heard
from her for more than a month and decided it was about
time he spoke to her to find out if she could make it to
the Hamptons for at least part of the Christmas holiday.
She was not loquacious on the phone and the call to
Georgia might be thought of as a necessary modest expense. He looked in his address book for her number. He
had it twice—once under Strand and the other under
Gianelli.

He dialed the number. It was answered on the first ring,
as though whoever was there had been impatiently await-

ing a call. It was Giuseppe's voice at the other end of the line. He sounded brusque as he said hello.

"Giuseppe," Strand said, "this is Allen. How are you?"

"Oh . . . Allen." Now Giuseppe sounded disappointed. "I'm okay. I guess."

"Is Eleanor there?"

There was silence at the other end and Strand wondered if the line had been cut. "Giuseppe," he said, "are you still there?"

"I'm here," Giuseppe said, "but Eleanor's not." He laughed strangely. It occurred to Strand that perhaps his son-in-law was drunk. It didn't seem likely, though, at eleven o'clock on a Sunday morning.

"When do you expect her back? I'd like her to call me."

"I don't expect her back."

"What?" Strand said loudly. "What are you talking about?"

"That I don't expect her back, that's all." His tone was hostile now.

"What's going on down there?"

"Nothing. I'm sitting in my goddamned house and it's raining in Georgia and I don't expect my wife back."

"What's happened, Giuseppe?" Strand tried to make his voice soothing.

"She's gone."

"Where to?"

"Don't know. Into the blue. Just gone. Her last words were, by a great coincidence, 'Don't expect me back.'"

"Did you have a fight?"

"Not really. More like a slight difference of opinion."

"What's the story, Giuseppe?"

"I'll let her tell you," Giuseppe said, his voice flat and listless. "I've been sitting here for five days and nights since she went, going over the whole thing in my head again and again and I'm tired of it. She's bound to get in touch with you eventually."

"Is she all right?"

"When she left she was sound in mind and body, if that's what you're worried about."

"You must have some idea . . ." Strand stopped. There

had been a click at the end of the line and then dead wire. Giuseppe had hung up. Strand stared dazedly at the telephone in his hand.

Through the window he heard a boy's voice calling excitedly, "Cut! *Cut!*" and then a sardonic cheer which meant that the boy who had run out for the pass had dropped it.

Eleanor had been home for dinner the night that Caroline had brought Hazen, dazed and bloody, back from the park. She had gone off in the taxi with Hazen at the end of the evening, the evening when Hazen had said in parting from Strand, "I must tell you something that perhaps I shouldn't say—I envy you your family, sir. Beyond all measure."

Strand doubted that Hazen would say as much to him on this bright Sunday morning when, if he were asked where his children might be found, he could give the address of only one out of three. And if he, himself, wanted to visit his youngest daughter, he would first make sure that she was in her own room and alone when he arrived.

There was a battered station wagon with Georgia plates parked in front of the Malson Residence when he came back after the last class the next day. He blinked at it as though it was an apparition, then made himself walk slowly, with dignity, into the house.

Eleanor was sitting in the common room talking to Rollins. She still had her coat on and there was a large suitcase on the floor beside her chair. She didn't see him because she was half-turned away from the door. Strand hesitated a moment, feeling a wave of relief surge over him as he saw her looking relaxed and normal, as though it was the most routine thing in the world to come up unannounced, from Georgia, to drop in for a visit with her father.

"Eleanor," he said quietly.

She swung around and jumped up and they met in the middle of the room. The embrace was brief and she kissed him lightly on the cheek. "Dad," she said, "I'm so glad to see you."

"Have you been here long?"

"Only about fifteen minutes. And Mr. Rollins was kind enough to keep me company."

Strand nodded. He found it difficult not to put his arms around his daughter and hold her tight in love and relief. But two boys came clattering down the stairs and then stood there staring curiously at them. "Let's go into our place," Strand said. "Is that your bag?"

"Yes. I hope you won't mind having me around for a few days." She smiled. Her smile, which was frank and generous, had always affected him deeply, especially as she grew older and had taken to practicing looking stern and businesslike. "I've heard from Mother and know she's not getting back till Christmas and I thought you might like company."

"I certainly do."

Rollins picked up Eleanor's bag and with the three boys at the bottom of the stairs watching them, they went down the hall to the apartment. Rollins put the bag down in the living room and Eleanor said, "Thank you."

"Mr. Strand," Rollins said, "I have a letter for you. From Jesus. I went home for the weekend and he asked me to give it to you."

"How's he doing?" Strand asked as he put the letter down on the table. "Is he behaving himself?"

"In my family there ain't no choice. He's doing fine," Rollins said. "He's the new household pet. He's working in my brother's garage pumping gas. He got word last week that the trial is set for January seventh, but it doesn't seem to worry him much. Miss, Mrs. Gianelli, I mean, if there's anything I can do for you around the school, remember, I'm right here."

"I'll remember." Eleanor had taken off her coat and was looking around the room critically. "It's not very grand, is it?" she said when Rollins had left.

"It looks better when your mother is here."

Eleanor laughed and came over and hugged him, this time a real embrace. "You don't change, do you, Dad? Now," she said, "what I'd like is a nice, strong cup of tea. Show me where things are in the kitchen and sit down and take it easy. You know"—her tone became serious—"you don't look as well as you might. You're not overdoing things, are you?"

"I'm fine," Strand said curtly. He led her into the kitchen and sat down while she set about making tea. "Now," he said, "I think you ought to tell me about yourself. I talked to Giuseppe yesterday."

She sighed and turned around from the stove. "What did he tell you?"

"Just that you had left and he didn't know where you were and you told him not to expect you back."

"That's all he told you?"

"He hung up on me."

"Well," Eleanor said, "at least he's breathing."

"What does that mean?"

"It means that they've been threatening his life. Our lives."

"Good God. Are you serious?"

"*They're* serious. A week ago they planted a bomb on our porch and blew out all the front windows and the door. We were out at the time. Next time, they've told us, we'll be in when they visit."

"Who're *they*?"

Eleanor shrugged. "Pillars of the church. The mayor, the police chief, the mayor's brother-in-law, who runs a construction company that does work for the town, a couple of lawyers who run the judges . . . You name them, they're *they*. Giuseppe came in there and in a couple of months he dug up enough on the whole crowd of them to put them in jail for a century. He got Watergate fever. He sounded as though his so-called investigative reporting was saving the whole nation from an invading army. It was all the usual small-town stuff and it *had* been going on since the Civil War and people lived with it all right and they just got annoyed with us northerners, and Italian northerners to boot, coming in and starting a fuss. But then he got onto some federal cases and the threatening telephone calls in the middle of the night started to come in. I tried to get him to see that pinning a fine on a man who's being paid twice over for laying a sewer line wasn't worth getting killed for, but he's stone-headed stubborn and now after the bombing he's out for revenge, too. He's bought a shotgun and he sits in the living room in the dark with it across his lap. And the sad part of it is that he's not a particularly good newspaperman and the paper probably could be put out better by a parcel of high school kids. As for me, things I had to do for the paper were demeaning, they were so trivial. We made a mistake, I told him, and I didn't believe in being party to a double suicide because of it. I gave him one day to think it over after we got the last telephone call. I told him I was going whether he was coming with me or not." She had been speaking flatly, without emotion, but now her face worked and her voice choked a little. "He said he didn't need the one day. So I left."

"What a rotten story," Strand said. He stood up and went over to the stove, where Eleanor was pouring water from the kettle into the teapot, and put his arm around her. "I'm so sorry."

"Marriages break up every day," she said. "For worse reasons. Where's the sugar?"

He took down the sugar and they sat at the kitchen table with their cups in front of them. "Why didn't you let me know before? Where've you been all this time?" he asked.

"I wanted to make sure I wasn't going back to him before telling everybody the happy news," Eleanor said. "That took some time. Then I wanted to find a place to live and get a job, so nobody would have to worry about my being a burden on the community up in the frozen North."

"Have you found a place to live and a job?"

She nodded. "My old firm. I start on January second. And they've raised my salary. And my name's on the door. Maiden name. Eleanor Strand, Assistant Vice President." She grinned boyishly. "In my case absence made the corporate heart grow fonder."

They drank their tea in silence.

"Do you think if I called him and spoke to him it would help?"

"You can call him," Eleanor said, "but it won't do any good. He won't come back up here with his tail between

his legs and have to confess to his brothers that he's a
failure, that he's lost their money, and have to beg to be
taken back in the family business by them. He'd rather
come back in a casket."

"What are you going to do about him?"

She looked steadily at him. "I'm going to try to forget
him. If I can't, I'll go back and get blown up with him."
She stood up. "Now," she said, "I'd like to freshen up a
bit. Which is my room?"

"Here, I'll show you." They went through the living
room and Strand picked up the bag and led her toward
the bedrooms. On the way along the hall, they passed the
small cubbyhole which was Strand's bedroom.

"Why can't I sleep here?" Eleanor said.

"That's my room." He opened the door to the master
bedroom. "And this is your mother's. Yours while you're
here."

Eleanor looked at him. He hoped that the look he saw
in her eyes was not pity. "Oh, Dad," she said, throwing
her arms around him and weeping on his shoulder, "isn't
everything *awful?*"

The little spell of tears was quickly over and she said,
"Forgive me," and he left her unpacking her bag. He went
into the living room and saw Romero's letter lying on the
table and picked it up. He gazed at it for a moment, sure
that whatever was in it would not add joy to his day. He
slit the envelope and took out the two pages. It was written
on paper that had Rollins Garage, Repairs and Body Work
at the top. The handwriting was small and round and neat
and easy to read.

Dear Mr. Strand,

This is just to thank you for everything that you
and Mr. Hazen tried to do for me. I see now that you
were wrong to help me and I was wrong to let you do
it. Whatever side you and Mr. Hazen and Mr. Babcock and all the others are on, I'm not on it and never
could be. I'd come out a fake gentleman and all my
people would see the fake and they wouldn't come

near me for the rest of my life. That isn't what I want, Mr. Strand. Going to prison, if that's what I have to do, will fit me better to understand my own people and do something with them and for them than ten years of fancy schools and snooty universities could do. I have to educate myself, my own way. I'll read the books I want and draw my own conclusions and they won't be the conclusions I'd come away with from Yale or Harvard or anyplace like that. The libraries are open and if I can't find the book I want in them I can always steal it. When I remember the look on your face when I told you how I got the set of Gibbon I burst out laughing even now.

I know you think I'm sick or something harping on Puerto Rican, Puerto Rican. But you wouldn't have done what you did for me for any white boy in your class, no matter how smart he was. What you did for me you did because whatever I was, I wasn't white. At least by your standards. I'm no good at taking handouts and I'm glad I figured out that was what I was doing. Finito.

I know what you'll say—that Rollins doesn't mind taking handouts and that he'll turn out to be a successful citizen, a credit to Dunberry, to his family, his race, and the fourteenth amendment of the Constitution of the United States of America. Just because we both have dark skins doesn't mean we're the same. His family made the big jump upward long ago and all he has to do is climb higher. I'm in the mud at the bottom of the pit and there isn't a ladder around anywhere in sight.

One thing you deserve to know. The letters Hitz stole were from Caroline. They were love letters. It started as a joke, but then it stopped being a joke. At least for me. I thought she meant what she was saying. It turns out she didn't. I went out to her college the day after Thanksgiving because she said she'd like to see me and I told her I was coming. She wasn't there. I was left standing with my suitcase in my hand like an idiot. When you see her tell her she better not play jokes on any other fellows.

For the first time in the letter, which was more clearly written than anything written for his classes all term, Strand saw the hurt, scorned adolescent in the last paragraph. There were only two more lines.

If you're a friend of Fatso Hitz, you tell him that if I go to prison he better hide when I get out.

Yours sincerely,
Jesus Romero

Another battle lost, Strand thought. To be expected. Young as he was, Romero had recognized his predestined role in life—the Goth outside the gates, too proud to conspire from within. History, after all, was on his side. Strand sighed, rubbed his eyes wearily. Then folded the letter neatly, put it back into the envelope and tucked it in his jacket pocket. One day he would show it to Caroline.

8

Christmas was on a Monday and the holiday began at noon on Friday. Strand and Eleanor could drive down from the school and still be in time to meet Leslie's TWA plane at Kennedy. Hazen had called during the week and Strand had told him that it wasn't necessary to send the car to Dunberry. Caroline was flying into Kennedy around one o'clock on TWA and would wait in the terminal and the whole family would drive out to East Hampton together. Hazen had spoken to Romero and said the idiotic kid still insisted on not cooperating when he went into court on January seventh. He had also told Hazen he was satisfied with Mr. Hollingsbee and didn't want Hazen to waste his time coming out for the trial.

"The kid's hopeless," Hazen had said wearily, "and nothing any one of us can do is going to help him. Oh, well —see you on Friday afternoon."

It had been pleasant having Eleanor around the house although Strand could see that it was only with considerable effort that she maintained an appearance of calm cheerfulness. He knew it was for his sake and was grateful for it. He tried not to notice the way she jumped up and ran to the phone when it rang and the tension in her voice as she said hello. But it was never Giuseppe on the line and she never called Georgia. Late at night, when she thought he was asleep, he could hear her prowling around the house.

Twice when she was out of the house, he had tried calling Giuseppe but Giuseppe had hung up on him each time. Strand didn't tell Eleanor about his attempts.

She had asked for all the news of Caroline and Jimmy. Leslie had written her a letter, which she had received just before she left Georgia, and she knew of Leslie's triumph with her two paintings and of her extending her stay in Paris. She said Leslie had sounded like an excited young girl in her letter and that it had been amusing and had touched her. She said she always knew her mother had a real talent and was happy it had finally been recognized, even if it was only for two paintings so far. "You watch," she told Strand, "she's going to work like a demon now, you'll be lucky if she takes enough time off to make you a cup of coffee in the morning."

Strand had carefully edited the news about Caroline and Jimmy. The burden of waiting and dreading to hear from Giuseppe, or, even worse, from someone else on the paper, was enough for her to bear, Strand thought, without her having to worry about her sister and brother. So he showed her Caroline's letter in which she wrote about being voted the Homecoming Queen. She laughed as she gave the letter back to Strand. "She's come out of the cocoon with a bang, my little sister, hasn't she?"

"You might say that," Strand said. If he had shown her the letter from the biology teacher's wife and the letter from Romero, and she discovered just how great the bang was, he doubted that her reaction would have been quite so pleased.

As for Jimmy, Strand merely said that he'd gone to Hollywood on a new job and was making a lot more money than he had been getting on the old one. He also told her that Jimmy had become a fancy dresser and was becoming accustomed to three-martini lunches.

Eleanor made a wry face when she heard this. "Onward and upward, I guess. Winning all hearts and minds on the way. At least he isn't turning into a complete bum, as he gave every sign of doing when I was in New York. Does he send you any money?"

"We don't need it," Strand said shortly.

Eleanor looked at him gravely. "You could stand a

couple of good suits, too, you know." But she left it at that.

The drive into Kennedy from the school in the old station wagon was an agreeable one. The weather was fine, there was very little traffic, Eleanor was a good, careful driver, and they had time enough so that they could stop off and have a leisurely lunch outside Greenwich at a very nice inn whose advertisements Eleanor had seen in *The New Yorker*. Both she and Strand were amused by the glances they drew from the other diners as they came in—admiring for her and either envious or disapproving for him.

She squeezed his hand and whispered, "They think you're an irresistible old man sneaking off for a dirty weekend with your secretary."

"Maybe I'll try that one day," Strand said, laughing. "Being irresistible. Only I'll have to hire a secretary first." But when she went into the ladies' room to comb her hair he thought of Judith Quinlan and the girl on the train with the young man in the fur coat and wondered just what a dirty weekend was like and if ever in his life he would have one.

When they went down to the exit from Customs to wait for Leslie and Linda to come out, they saw that Caroline was already there. Caroline squealed as she ran toward them and hugged first her father, then her sister. "Daddy," she said reproachfully, "you never told me. I thought she was still languishing in Georgia. What a great surprise! Where's your beautiful husband, Eleanor?"

"Languishing," Eleanor said. She took a step back. "Let me take a look at you."

Caroline struck an exaggerated model's pose, legs apart, one hand on her hip, the other in a dancer's gesture over her head. "How do you like the new me?"

"Pretty classy," Eleanor said. "Now I'm glad my husband's in Georgia." As she said it, she glanced warningly at Strand and he knew that she wasn't going to tell Caroline why Giuseppe was in Georgia and what she feared would happen to him there. "You've lost some weight, haven't you?"

"They run me to death every day," Caroline said.

"It becomes you."

Actually, Strand thought Eleanor's "classy" was a sisterly understatement. He was sure it wasn't merely fatherly indulgence that made him think that Caroline, her face fined down, her eyes bright with health and happiness, her skin a clear, athletic glow, her long legs shapely and firm, was one of the prettiest girls he had ever seen in his life. With her new nose and her recently acquired assurance, she no longer bore any resemblance to him, but now looked breathtakingly like Leslie when Leslie was her age. He couldn't think of a more flattering comparison. Remembering the letters that he would eventually have to talk to her about, he searched for signs of depravity. He found none. She looked untouched, youthfully innocent.

As the travelers came trickling out of Customs, Hazen hurried up. "Hi, everybody," he said, shaking Strand's hand and hesitating a second as Caroline came up to him and hugged him and waited to be kissed. Then he kissed her cheek. He hesitated more than a second when Eleanor greeted him, but then kissed her, too. "I was afraid I was late. The traffic out of the city is fierce. Friday night before the big holiday. It's a good thing Linda's always the last one off any plane. Between forgetting things and having to go back to look for them and getting her face prepared, the plane's just about ready to take off again by the time she gets out."

When Leslie and Linda came out and Leslie saw Eleanor with the others, tears sprang to her eyes and she stopped walking for a moment. Strand was surprised. Leslie usually kept a tight control on her emotions and it wasn't like her to cry on happy occasions. Then she rushed toward them and kissed them all. Linda kissed everybody, too, amid smiles and laughter and chatter about baggage and who was going to ride in which car and congratulations all around on how well everybody looked.

Once out of the terminal building they decided that

Caroline would drive with Linda and Hazen while Strand and Leslie would go with Eleanor in her Volkswagen. The driver, a strongly built youngish man in a chauffeur's uniform, helped load all the baggage into the back of the Mercedes and on the roof rack.

"Where's Conroy?" Strand asked.

"I'll tell you later." Hazen made a face as though he had tasted something sour and got into the car. Leslie and Strand were left alone on the curb as the Mercedes drove off and Eleanor went to the parking lot to get her car. Strand stared approvingly at his wife. She seemed to have shed ten years and he thought she could easily pass as Eleanor's prettier older sister. And not much older. Impulsively, he kissed her.

She smiled up at him, still in his arms. "I didn't know you've gone public."

"I couldn't resist. Paris has put a new bloom on you."

"It certainly hasn't done any harm." Then her face became grave. "Allen," she said, "I shouldn't spring this on you so suddenly, but I'm so full of it I can't really think of anything else. I was going to write you about it, but I thought I had to see the expression on your face when I told you about it—"

"What are you going to tell me, that you took a lover in Paris?" He hoped he had managed to keep his tone light enough.

"Allen," she said reproachfully, "you know me better than that."

"It's been a long time. A lady might be excused." But he sighed with relief.

"Not this lady. No, it's more serious than a lover. What I want to ask is this—do you think there's any chance that you could get a job in Paris, at least for a year? There's an American school there and I'm sure Russell knows somebody on the board."

"There's the small question of money," Strand said. "Airplane fares, a place to live. Little things like that."

"We could swing it," Leslie said. "I'd be chipping in. The gallery owner promised to finance me, on a very small scale, of course, for a year if I come back and work with the artist who bought my paintings. Working beside him and listening to him has given me a whole new vision of what art can be. I have the feeling that at last I'm finally on the verge of being somebody."

"You always were somebody, Leslie." Now he felt bruised and shaken.

"You know what I mean. Do you want us to spend the rest of our lives in a backwater like Dunberry?" She spoke softly, without emphasis, but he could sense the desperation behind the question.

"I haven't thought much about the rest of our lives. Up to now, I've been content to live from week to week."

"Oh, dear," Leslie said, "I've bothered you. Forget what I said. I won't say anything more about it. Tell me about Eleanor." She spoke briskly, as though the idea of Paris was a frivolous one and easily forgotten. "Where's Giuseppe?"

"I'll let her tell you about it."

"There's trouble." It was not a question.

He nodded.

"Bad?"

"It might be very bad. I don't know yet. Get her off to one side. She doesn't want Caroline or Russell to hear about it. Here she is," he said, as the Volkswagen drew up to the curb.

He sat in the back to give Eleanor a chance to talk to her mother. Eleanor spoke softly and he couldn't hear what she was saying over the noise of the old car. From time to time, though, he heard Giuseppe's name. Although Leslie was not presenting him with an ultimatum as Eleanor had done with Giuseppe, Strand felt that like Giuseppe he was facing a similar choice—go with his wife or stay behind—alone. He had not interfered with his children's choice of careers and he could hardly be less generous with his wife. He was not facing a bomb as Giuseppe was, but looking at things through Leslie's eyes he could understand that Dunberry was not much more attractive to her than the Georgia town from which Eleanor had fled was to their daughter. He would see what could be done about Paris.

Once he had reached this decision, the idea of exchanging Dunberry for Paris, if it were possible, began to intrigue him. He closed his eyes, lulled by the motion of the car, and imagined himself sitting at a café table on an open terrace reading a French newspaper in the sunshine and smiled. After all, fifty was not *that* old. Generals who led armies at that age were considered young men. It would be a challenge, he knew, but there hadn't been enough real challenges in the last few years, if you could forget the heart attack. And he had emerged from that with a deep feeling of triumph. He knew that both Eleanor and Caroline would approve if they made the move, if only because it would give them an excuse to visit France.

Eleanor's low murmur stopped. Then he heard Leslie say, loudly, "You did exactly the right thing. It's monstrous. And if I see him I'm going to tell him so. If he's foolish and stubborn enough to want to risk his life, that's his business. Asking you to risk yours is ghoulish." She turned in the front seat and said, "Allen, I hope you've told Eleanor the same thing."

"In the strongest possible terms," Strand said.

"Have you tried talking to Giuseppe?"

"I telephoned twice. He hung up as soon as he recognized my voice."

"Have you told Russell about it?"

"I think this had better just stay in the family."

"I guess you're right," Leslie said, but she sounded dubious.

He wondered if in the low conversation in the front seat Eleanor had told her mother what she had told him—that she was going to try to forget her husband and if she couldn't she was going back to him. He hoped Eleanor had not gone that far. If she had, Leslie's anxiety about Eleanor's possible return to Georgia would destroy all the pleasure she was getting out of her newborn success in France and her plans for the future, pleasure that would be multiplied many times over when he had the chance to tell her that he would see about getting a place on the faculty of the American School in Paris.

It was dark when they reached the house on the beach. The sea could be heard in a low steady rumble and the stars were sparkling in the frozen black crystal of the sky. Strand took a deep breath of the cold salt air and felt his throat and lungs tingle as he inhaled.

Hazen was sitting in one of the twin high-backed leather wing chairs that flanked the fireplace. A driftwood fire sent out sparks of electric blue and green. In a corner was a Christmas tree, its branches adorned with tinsel and colored glass globes that reflected the changing light from the fire. The tree filled the room with a piny forest aroma. Hazen had a drink in his hand and poured a whiskey and soda for Strand while the women went upstairs to unpack.

"I forget how wonderful this place is," Strand said. "Then, when I come back, it hits me with a rush." He sat in the chair opposite Hazen, feeling the welcome warmth of the fire on his legs. "I'm going to thank you now—for the whole family—for this holiday and then shut up about it once and for all."

"Thanks," Hazen said. "Especially for shutting up about it. It's too bad Jimmy couldn't come along."

"He's in California."

"I know," Hazen said. "Solomon told me."

"Did he tell you anything else?"

Hazen nodded. "Solomon's making too much of it. An ambitious young man grabs his chance when he sees it. I'm sure Solomon did worse things when he was Jimmy's age. And so did I. Don't be moral about it, Allen."

"Camelot's kaput, Jimmy said, when I voiced some objections."

Hazen laughed. "That's one way of putting it. It's been kaput for a long time."

"How're things with you?"

"The usual little annoyances." Hazen shrugged. "I fired Conroy."

"I wondered why he wasn't at the airport."

"I found out my miserable wife was paying him to keep

tabs on me. That's how she knew so much about you and your family in Tours that night. Talk about morality . . ."

Poor gray-faced, all-purpose Conroy, Strand thought, remembering the embrace of the thin arm in the pounding surf, the embarrassment between them when Strand had tried to thank him for saving his life, the disdainful check for a thousand dollars for services rendered from Hazen, Hazen's words. "Money means everything to him. He saves like a pack rat." There had been no thought of reward when the man had plunged into the waves as Strand was being swept out to sea. Morality on varying levels. He knew there would be no use in asking Hazen to change his mind and give Conroy another chance. Betrayal outweighed past gallantry.

"If I may ask," Strand said, "how are the divorce proceedings going?"

"Badly. She calls my lawyer twice a day from France. She's driving a hard bargain. And she keeps threatening that if I don't give in very soon, she's going to blow the whole thing open in the papers." He looked bleakly at Strand and seemed as if he was about to say more, then rattled the ice in his glass and said, "Conroy's told her I've made out a new will. Like an idiot I had him witness it. Of course he doesn't know what's in it—it's in the private safe in my partner's office and my partner's the only one besides me who's read it. I typed it myself. But she knows it's a new one and she says she won't sign anything unless I show it to her." He smiled bleakly. "Merry Christmas, one and all." He took a big swallow of his drink. "You'd think a man my age wouldn't be surprised anymore by one more piece of evidence of the world's evil. But Conroy, after all these years . . ." Hazen shook his head. "When I fired him he said he was glad he was going, he'd hated me from the first day he saw me, only he didn't have the guts to quit. You have no idea of the amount of venom stored up in that quiet little drab man. He told me he'd had a homosexual affair with my son and my son told him that eventually he was going to commit suicide if I lived long enough because that was the only way he could be free of me. I picked Conroy up and threw him bodily out of the office. If I could have opened the window, I'd have thrown him out of it. From now on I'll hire a chauffeur for business and drive myself when I have private matters to look after. I've hired a pretty twenty-two-year-old girl to be my confidential secretary. At least, being a woman, if she hates me it will show early and I'll be able to get rid of her. Ah, enough of my troubles. We're here to relax and enjoy the holiday. I need another drink. How about you?"

"I'm fine, thanks." Strand watched, with pity in his heart, as the robust, unbowed man went over to the bar and poured himself another whiskey with a steady hand. As Hazen filled his glass he said, "Caroline has turned into a real beauty, hasn't she?"

"I can only give you a father's opinion. Yes, she has."

"Being away at school has done her worlds of good." Hazen came back and seated himself in the chair by the fireplace. "It's given her confidence in herself. The way she talked in the car you had to look and see with your own eyes that it was the little shy girl that went away to Arizona. I must say, she doesn't hesitate to speak her mind. She says the track coach is a slave driver and she detests him." Hazen smiled. "The cry heard from all athletes. She also said she hates running. She knows it does her good, but it bores her. The way she put it is she runs fifty miles a week and goes nowhere. And she says she doesn't like beating the other girls and getting special treatment for it. I don't think we have an Olympic champion here, Allen."

"So much the better," Strand said.

"Well, at least she's getting a free education and she's the most popular girl on campus."

"So much the worse."

Hazen laughed. "As Leslie would say, 'You're being old-fashioned again, dear.' "

Strand didn't join in the laughter. If Hazen had read the letter of the biology teacher's wife, Strand thought, he wouldn't congratulate Caroline's father on her newfound popularity.

"Well," Hazen said, "at least Leslie seems to be in terrific form. You ought to give a big vote of thanks to Linda for taking her on the trip to Paris."

"It did turn out well," Strand said, without enthusiasm. "Maybe a little too well."

"What do you mean by that?" Hazen scowled at him.

"She wants to go back."

"What's wrong with that?"

"She wants to go back right now if she can."

"Oh." Hazen stared thoughtfully into his glass.

"She seems to think that the man whose studio she worked in can show her the way to becoming some sort of genius."

"Did she say that?"

"Not in so many words," Strand admitted. "She wants to make a career of painting and she thinks Paris is the place where she can get it to happen."

"What's wrong with that? You're not the sort of man who believes his wife should remain eternally chained to the kitchen stove, are you?"

"No, I don't think I am."

"You know I thought she had talent, right from the first night in your apartment when I saw her landscapes. Not a big talent, perhaps, but a true one. And now Linda says the people in Paris are very excited about her work and her possibilities. Sometimes it takes strangers to recognize the virtues of things that we've been looking at for years."

"I know all that, Russell, but . . ."

"But what? What's the hitch?"

"The hitch is that she wants me to go to Paris with her." Hazen didn't say anything, but whistled softly.

"I didn't whistle when she said it," Strand said. "She wants me to ask you if you know anybody connected with the American School in Paris who might be induced to give me a job there. For at least a year. I'd ask Babcock if he'd give me an unpaid leave of absence for the year. Listen, Russell, you've done enough for this family. If it's the slightest bit of trouble for you, just tell me so, and Leslie and I will work something out on our own."

"Let me see, let me see . . ." Hazen put his head back in the chair and squinted up at the ceiling. He didn't seem to have heard what Strand had just said. "Let me see, whom do I know? Of course. Our head man in the Paris office has two kids who go to the American School and he's on the board. I'll drop him a note tomorrow. I'd call him, but it's Christmastime in France, too, and I know he takes ten days off to ski someplace. I'm sure something can be arranged."

"I hate to use you as an employment agency," Strand said.

"A lot of other people use me for a lot worse things. Don't fuss about it."

Mr. Ketley came in and said, "There's a telephone call for you, sir."

Carrying his drink, Hazen went into the library. Strand noticed that he closed the door after him, so that his conversation could not be overheard.

When he came back to the living room, he looked grave. "Allen," he said, "you'll have to make my excuses to everybody. I have to go back to New York. Immediately. That call was from my wife. She arrived in New York from Paris this afternoon. She was on Air France. If she'd picked TWA Leslie and Linda would've had the pleasure of her company for three thousand miles. She's drunk and she says that if I don't get right back into New York tonight she'll drive out in a limousine and show us one and all that she's not to be trifled with. One scene like that a year is more than enough. I have to see what I can do. I'm sorry to be a damper on the party. Tell the others it's business. Tell everybody to eat, drink and be merry."

"When will you be back?"

"I don't know. I'll keep in touch." Hazen took a long lingering look around the room, shook his head wearily. "God, I hate to leave this place," and he was gone.

Strand finished his drink, then walked slowly upstairs to tell Leslie their host had been called back to New York on business.

They had eaten and drunk, but had not been particularly merry. Eleanor and Leslie had talked themselves out in the car and Linda was drooping from jet lag and went up to bed early. Caroline was restless and suggested to Eleanor that they drive into Bridgehampton and see if Bobby happened to be playing the piano that night in his bar. "After Georgia and Dunberry I can use a little night life. Like ten brass bands," Eleanor said and the girls kissed their parents good night and went off.

"Well," Leslie said, "it looks like it's old folks by the fireside night, doesn't it?" She came over to where Strand was sitting and bent and kissed his forehead and ran her hand along the back of his head. He reached and held her around the waist.

"I don't feel so old," he said. "And as for you, if you'd gone into the bar with the girls, the bartender would've asked to see your I.D. card. This is more like the times we used to wait in the parlor until your folks had gone to bed so we could begin to pet."

"Oh, God." Leslie laughed. "I haven't heard that word in thirty years. Pet. Do you think people still do it?"

"From what I hear they just rush into bed," Strand said. He let the hand that was around her waist slide down and he caressed her thigh. "A sensible, time-saving custom. We ought to try it sometime. Like right now."

Leslie leaned back so that she could focus on his face. "Do you mean that?"

"Fervently," he said.

"Is it all right? I mean . . ."

"Prinz gave me the green light. Slightly blurred. But green."

"What did he say, exactly?"

"He said, moderation in all things, but . . . He also said it might kill me or it might make me feel like a twenty-year-old fullback."

Leslie kissed him hard, on the lips, then took his hands and pulled him from the chair.

It didn't kill him and he didn't feel like a a twenty-year-old fullback when he gave her a last kiss and rolled over on his back in the soft, wide bed, but it did make him feel enormously happy.

"We're back home," she said softly. "It's somebody else's house and somebody else's bed, but we're finally home."

"You sleepy?"

"No. Floating."

"I have an elegant idea."

"What's that?"

"I'm going to go down to the kitchen and steal a bottle of champagne from the refrigerator and two glasses and come back here and we'll have a pre-Christmas, post coitum private party."

"The party of the other part votes yes," she said.

When he came back upstairs with the bottle and glasses, Leslie was sitting in front of the fire that she had lit and had drawn up another chair in front of it for him. He popped the cork out of the bottle and poured the cold champagne into the two glasses that Leslie held for him. He took one of the glasses and held it up in a toast. "To Paris," he said.

She didn't drink, but looked at him questioningly. "What does that mean?"

"It means that I talked to Russell before he was called away and of course as usual he knows a man and he's going to get in touch with him and I'm buying a French dictionary tomorrow."

"Oh, Allen . . ." She seemed about to cry.

"Drink," he said and they both drank.

"Allen," she said, "you don't have to do this for me."

"I'm doing it for myself," he said. "I had a chance to think about it in the car and the more I thought about it the more I liked the idea."

"You're sure? You're not making it up just for me? You seemed aghast when I spoke about it at the airport."

"I wasn't aghast. I was surprised. It took a little time to get used to the idea, that's all. My, this is good champagne."

"May we never drink worse." She giggled and held out her glass for more. "The way I feel now," she said as he poured the wine, "I want to say, And then they lived happily ever after."

Hazen called the next afternoon and told Leslie he would try to make it back for Christmas, but he wasn't sure. He hoped they were having a good time, he said, and Leslie told him they all missed him and to hurry back.

They spent the day lazily. It was too cold to paint outside so Leslie started a pencil sketch of Caroline for a later portrait in oil. Strand was content merely to sit and watch and occasionally to go over to the other side of the room where Linda and Eleanor played backgammon.

But when Hazen called the next day to say that he couldn't make it for Christmas, it was Linda who took the call and she came away from the phone with a worried look on her face. "He sounded very strange," she said to Leslie and Strand, who were in the living room. "Not at all like himself. Very disconnected, he rambled on and on, he kept talking about momentous decisions, I could hardly make sense out of him. I asked him if he was drunk and he blew up and shouted 'None of your goddamned business, Linda!' and hung up. Allen, do you know what it's all about?"

"No." He hoped he sounded convincing. "Some sort of business, he said."

"Thank God, Allen, that you're not a businessman," Linda said.

"I do just that every night when I say my prayers," Strand said.

The Christmas dinner, although delicious, was gloomy. Hazen's absence weighed on them all. They had all put their presents under the tree but decided not to open any of them until Hazen's return. The gap at the end of the table made all of them, even Linda, glum. The conversation around the table was sporadic and they were glad when the meal was over.

The weather had turned gray and foggy by the time they finished dinner with a Calvados apiece at three in the afternoon, but Leslie and Linda and Eleanor bundled up and went for a walk along the beach, as though something was drawing them out of the house. Caroline settled herself in front of the television set and Strand went up and lay down to take a nap. In his sleep he dreamt that he was locked in a room with Conroy and Mrs. Hazen and had to watch while they tore their clothes off and jumped obscenely upon one another. He woke up sweating, not remembering the dream clearly, but with a sickly sensation of horror at the grotesque turmoil of his sleeping hours.

He went downstairs and saw that the women had not returned. Caroline was on the phone in the library, but when she saw Strand through the door in the living room, she said hastily, "I can't talk anymore. Good-bye." She put the phone down and with a quick glance at her father turned and sat down again in front of the television set.

Curious, he went into the library. "Caroline, whom were you talking to?"

"Nobody in particular," she said, without looking at him.

"Nobody talks to nobody in particular," he said.

She sighed and pushed the remote-control button to turn the set off. "If you must know," she said defiantly, "it was Jesus. Jesus Romero. He called me. I sent him a Christmas card from Arizona and the school forwarded it to him. He tried to call us at Dunberry and the cleaning lady told him we were here and he wanted to wish me a Merry Christmas. Is there anything criminal in that?"

Strand sat down on the couch next to her and took her hands gently. "Caroline," he said, "we have to have a little talk, you and I."

"We certainly do," Caroline said. She was angry now or was trying to seem angry. "Why didn't anybody tell me Jesus was in jail and is out on bail and has been expelled from the school and is going to have to stand trial?"

"We didn't know you were that interested in the boy. Until very recently."

"Well I am. Very interested."

"I gathered that when I heard about the letters you were exchanging."

Caroline pulled her hands away from his loose grasp. "What do you know about any letters?"

"Quite a lot, at least about the nature of them, although I never read them. Don't worry, they've been destroyed."

"I'm not worried." Her tone was harsh.

"Here are two letters that haven't been destroyed." He took Romero's letter and the one from the biology teacher's wife from his inside jacket pocket, where he carried them to make sure Leslie wouldn't happen on them by chance. He stood up and kept his back to Caroline. He looked out to sea while she read the letters. Then he heard the ripping of paper and saw her throwing the tattered remnants into the small fire that was spreading a cozy warmth into the small library.

Caroline was sobbing now and she threw her arms around Strand as he came over to her. "Oh, Daddy, Daddy," she wept, "what's the matter with me? How can people write such awful things about me?"

"Because you've been cruel and hurt them," Strand said, still holding her, shocked by the violence of her sobs.

"I was just having fun," she wailed. "Most of the letters I sent to Jesus I copied from love letters the girls in my dormitory got from their boyfriends or I took from *Lady Chatterley's Lover* or Henry Miller. I wanted to sound sophisticated and daring, but I thought he'd laugh, too, because when *we* read those letters, *we* laughed. Then when he wrote he was coming out for Thanksgiving, he scared me, he was so serious. And old Assistant Professor Swanson just kept following me around like a sick dog and kept saying he and his wife never touched each other and she was leaving him anyway and I took pity on him. And I told him to spend Thanksgiving with his family. I had to get away from him *and* Romero and I went to Tucson the day after Thanksgiving with a football player who gave me a play-by-play account of every game he played since his sophomore year in high school and I never spent a drearier weekend. That's the kind of screw I am." She had stopped sobbing now and she put an angry vehemence into the "drearier," as though by emphasizing her boredom she was minimizing her guilt. Strand let go of her and gave her his handkerchief to dry her tears. He was relieved that the two letters were finally burned. She looked at him fearfully. "You think I'm awful, don't you? And you're going to bawl me out."

"If I thought it would help I would bawl you out. And I don't think you're awful. I think you've been thoughtless and sometimes that's worse than awful. Why did you hang up when you were talking to Romero and you saw me?"

"Does Mummy know about the letters?" She was stalling for time and Strand knew it.

"No. And she never will, if you keep quiet about them. Now—why did you hang up?"

"I was apologizing for not being there when he came to Arizona. And"—she lifted her head and stared challengingly into his eyes—"I invited him to come out here."

Strand sat down. He feared that it was going to be a long and painful conversation. "This isn't your house, you know, Caroline," he said, trying to keep his voice calm.

"I'm not inviting him to stay. I said I'd meet him in the village."

"When?"

"He'll call and let me know."

"*Why* do you want to see him?"

"Because he fascinates me." She drew out the word as though its sound delighted her. "He did, right from the beginning, when I met him at dinner after he made that fantastic run. I told Mom so, didn't she tell you?"

"Perhaps not exactly in those words. Have you seen him since that night?"

"No. Only the letters. He's so fierce and intelligent . . ."

"He certainly is. Especially fierce," Strand said dryly. "You said he scared you."

"That's part of his attraction. The other boys I know . . . Professor Swanson." She wrinkled her nose in derision. "All made out of the same cold, unbaked dough. If Jesus wants to keep on seeing me, I'm going to keep on seeing him."

"You'll most probably be seeing him in jail."

"Then I'll see him in jail. I'm not going back to that gruesome college, where they say such nasty things about me."

"We'll discuss that later," Strand said. "How much of what they say is true?"

"Some. Not much. Oh, Daddy, boys and girls aren't like what they were when you and Mummy were young. You know that."

"I know it. And I hate it."

"Mummy knows it. She doesn't keep her nose in a book day in and day out," Caroline said harshly. "Who do you think gave me the pill on my sixteenth birthday?"

"I suppose you're going to say your mother," Strand said.

"And you're shocked." Strand saw, with pain, that there was malice and pleasure on his daughter's face as she said this.

"I'm not shocked. Your mother is a sensible woman," Strand said, "and knows what she's doing. I'm merely surprised that she neglected to tell me."

"You know why she didn't tell you? Because she's in the conspiracy."

"What conspiracy?" Strand asked, puzzled.

"We all love you and we want you to be happy." There was a hint of childish whimper as she spoke. "You have an impossible picture in your head of what we're like—including Mummy. Because we're yours you think we're some sort of perfect angels. Well, we're not, but for your sake, we've been pretending, since we were all babies, that we are. We're a family of actors—including Mummy, if you want to know the truth. With an audience of one—you. As for Eleanor and Jimmy—I won't even go into it. Nobody could be as good as you thought we could be and I've told Mummy we shouldn't try, that you'd finally find out and you'd be hurt more than ever. But you know Mummy—she's made of iron—if she decides to do something, there's no bending her. Well, now you know. I'm not saying we're *bad*. We're just human. *Today* human."

"There're all sorts of ways to be human," Strand said. "Even today. Anyway, I owe you—the whole family—an apology. But no matter how blind I've been, or how human *you* are, or how the world is today, I can't approve of your playing so lightly with people's lives—that poor woman at the college—Jesus Romero—"

"Daddy—*I* didn't change the world," Caroline cried. "I just came into it the way it was. Don't blame me for it." She was crying again, wiping at her eyes with his handkerchief. "And I wasn't the one who went looking for Jesus Romero. You dragged him into our lives. Do you admit it?"

"I admit it," Strand said wearily. "And I made a mistake. I admit that, too. But I don't want you to compound the mistake. If you had seen him, as your mother and I have, going after that other boy with a knife, with murder in his eye, you'd think twice about seeing him."

"Daddy, if you're going to sound like a father in a Victorian novel, there's no sense in my standing here and telling you anything."

"No, there isn't." He stood up. "I'm going out and I'm taking a walk."

"Here's your handkerchief back," Caroline said. "I've finished with crying."

He had to get out of the house. He did not want to see his daughter, her eyes swollen, her mouth a hard line, her fury frozen, staring at the milky blind tube of the television set. The darting reflections of the fire on the Christmas tree ornaments annoyed him and the piny smell in the warm room cloyed in his nostrils. He threw on his coat and wrapped the shabby old woolen muffler that Leslie had been trying to get him to throw away for years around his neck. He went out of the house. It was dark now and the light streaming from the windows made swirling pools in the fog that drifted steadily in from the ocean. The rumble of the ocean was muted by mist and sounded like a dirge. He walked away from the beach, down the long straight road, bordered with cedars, that ran through Hazen's property toward the distant road. The women had gone to walk on the beach and he did not want to meet them or anybody at the moment. There were questions to be put and answers to be made and he had to try to arrange them clearly and without emotion in his mind before voicing them.

When he had gone fifty yards he turned and looked back. The lights of the house had disappeared. The cedars made a sighing sound in the varying, wet wind. He was alone, floating somewhere between the sea and nothingness, surrounded by a dripping, dark, unpeopled wilderness.

9

He didn't know how long he'd walked because his watch was useless in the dark, when he decided to turn and head back. He had come to no decisions, had just known he wanted to escape the house. Now, alone in the gray vaporous world, the steady movement of his limbs through the soft, engulfing mist had soothed him, hypnotized him into a state where nothing else mattered but the next step, nothing claimed his attention but the changing ghostly shadow of one tree for another as he passed. But as he started to retrace his way in the darkness, he realized he was lost. He had gone aimlessly down lanes, skirted dunes, seen blurred shapes looming to one side or another that he knew must be houses deserted for the winter. He had heard no voices nor seen a bird.

Even in bright sunlight he wouldn't have been familiar with the countryside. When he had gone for walks it had been along the beach. On the trips into town they had been in a car with someone else driving and he had not learned the geography of the neighborhood. He wasn't disturbed himself because he was lost but knew that Leslie must be back in the house by now and worried about where he had gone. He quickened his pace, arrived at a dead end with a shuttered house sitting across the driveway and forest all around it.

He took crossroads at random, couldn't figure out whether he was moving north, south, east or west. Now he was beginning to tire and his face was wet with sweat and mist. He tore off his muffler and stuffed it into a pocket. He had never felt more like a city man. Accustomed to the logical, neat, marked rectangles of the gridwork of Manhattan, he had atrophied the American talent for the wilderness. He walked on the sandy roads, full of holes, on macadam, gravel. He realized that he hadn't seen a light since he had left Hazen's house. Twice cars had passed him, one from behind him, lights looming in the fog. The last time the lights had appeared suddenly, from around a curve, and had come right at him and he had saved himself only by throwing himself headlong onto the side of the road. He had pushed himself up, trembling, after the car had disappeared, the red gleam of its taillights suddenly extinguished, as though a curtain had dropped behind them. He had fallen into an icy puddle and he could feel the water freezing on his trousers at the knees and around his ankles.

Finally, convinced that he was going in circles, he stood still. For a moment he heard nothing but his own labored breathing. Then, far away, there was a low rumble. The ocean. Cautiously, moving slowly, stopping every few steps to listen, he walked in the direction of the sea's steady music. Slowly it grew louder. At last he reached the beach. He sat down for a few moments to rest. There were no lights anywhere and he had to gamble on going either to his left or right. He cursed his lifelong lack of a reliable sense of direction, stood up and struck out to his left, walking along the waterline, where the hiss of waves sliding in and ebbing out guided him. His feet froze as he plodded painfully in the wet sand that sucked at his soaked shoes at every step.

He was just about to turn around and go in the other direction, had decided to give it one hundred more paces then go the other way, when he saw a glimmer of light through the fog high up to his left. He knew there was a path leading over the dunes to the house from the beach, but he couldn't find it. Now he could feel that his whole body was drenched with sweat and there was an enormous pulse pounding in one temple. He clambered up the side of a giant dune, pulling at the coarse grass to help himself climb, crawling over obstacles on his hands and knees. But the light grew brighter and brighter, dancing in the shifting mist, as though from a ship bobbing on waves.

Finally, staggering, he made it to the terrace steps and went up. Through the French doors, now hazed over, he could see shadowy shapes moving within. He tried to open one of the doors, but it was locked. He pounded on the door, shouted. His voice rasped hoarsely in his throat. The shapes behind the glass panes wavered from side to side, but did not approach. They're playing a foolish children's game with me, he thought insanely, pretending not to hear. He shouted again, the effort making him feel that he was tearing blood vessels and tendons inside his throat.

The door was thrown open.

Leslie was standing there. "Oh, my God," she cried.

"Do I look that bad?" Strand said. He tried to smile. Then he began to sneeze. Again and again and again, mixed with a coughing fit, with his eyes streaming, as he bent over, racked by the coughs. Leslie pulled him into the room and slammed the door behind him. Eleanor came running over and pulled at the buttons of his coat to get them open. "He's soaking wet," she said.

"I got . . . 1 . . . lost," Strand said, between sneezes and coughs. "What time is it?"

"After ten," Leslie said. "We were just about to call the police."

"I think the doctor would be a better idea." Eleanor had managed to get the coat off him. Strand saw that it was matted with mud and ice and clumps of grass.

"I'm all ri—" The next sneeze kept him from finishing the word. "I just took a lit—"

"Let's get him to bed," Leslie said.

With the two women supporting him by the elbows, needlessly, Strand thought, they went upstairs. Eleanor got a big warm towel from the bathroom and Leslie undressed him, clucking distractedly each time he sneezed. Strand noticed, with interest, that his feet were dead white and were numb and that he had cut his knee and a frozen rivulet of blood ran down his shin from the wound.

When he was naked and Leslie had rubbed him roughly with the towel, he felt the circulation starting to reach his feet, which began to sting. Leslie wrapped him in the towel and put him under the bedcovers like a puppy after a

bath. Then the shivering began and he wondered, somehow without concern, if he was in the first throes of pneumonia.

"I'm sorry," he said to Leslie, who was standing at the
side of the bed looking worriedly down at him. "I didn't
realize the fog . . ." Suddenly he was overpoweringly
weary and he closed his eyes. "I think I have to sleep a
little now," he murmured. He opened his eyes and smiled
wanly up at Leslie. "I hope somebody got me a compass
for Christmas," he said and fell into a deep sleep.

He slept all through the night, only dimly conscious at
moments of the warmth of Leslie's body next to his. The
sleep was so delicious that after eating breakfast in bed
he slept most of the next day and night, content to dream,
not to think or speak. When he woke up early on the second morning after Christmas, with Leslie breathing softly
in her sleep beside him, he got silently out of bed, feeling
fresh and rested and hungry. He dressed quickly and went
downstairs and had the Ketleys serve him a huge breakfast, which he ate alone in front of the window facing the
ocean, which glittered in long blue swells under a wintry
sun.

Frightening as the wandering in the dark fog over lost
roads had been and even though he could have been killed
by the car that had sped around the curve at him, he was
glad that it had happened as it had. It had given him a
precious breathing spell, had erased the anguish of the
confrontation with Caroline, had eased his sense of shame
and betrayal. In the clean early morning light, problems
were diminished and soluble. What the family had done to
him or what Caroline had suggested it had done he now
accepted on Caroline's terms. They had acted, however
wrongly, out of love for him and in his heart he embraced
them all. It would never be the same again, he swore to
himself. His eyes would now be open and they would all
be the better for it.

When Caroline came down for breakfast and saw him a
wary look came over her face. But he stood and hugged
her and kissed her forehead. "Oh, Daddy," she murmured

into his shoulder, "I'm so glad you're okay. I was so scared. And it was my fault . . ."

"Nothing is your fault, baby," he said. "Now sit down and eat your breakfast with me."

He noted with disapproval that Caroline told Mr. Ketley that she only wanted some black coffee. "Is that all you have usually for breakfast?" Strand asked.

"I'm not hungry today," Caroline said. "Daddy, there's something peculiar going on and I don't know what it is and Mummy won't tell me. Do you know that Linda and Eleanor left yesterday?"

"No." He put his cup down slowly. "Where did they go?"

"Linda went to New York."

"She said something about that. She's worried about Mr. Hazen." He took a deep breath. "Do you know where Eleanor went?"

"I'm not sure. She and Mummy had a big argument and they sent me out of the house. Eleanor was getting into the car with Linda when I came back and Mummy looked as though she'd been crying and I heard her say to Eleanor, 'At least you ought to say good-bye to your father,' and Eleanor said, 'I've thought it all out and I've had enough arguing and I don't want to have him try to talk me out of it. Just tell him I love him and I'm doing what I have to do.' Then they drove off. I think she's going back to Georgia. Is there something wrong about that?"

Strand sighed. "Very wrong," he said.

"I'm not a baby," Caroline said. "Don't you think it's about time I was told what's happening with this family?"

He looked at his daughter consideringly. "You're right," he said. "It is about time you knew what's happening with this family. It's about time we all knew. Eleanor left Georgia because some people who didn't like what Giuseppe put in the paper bombed their house and threatened to kill Giuseppe and maybe Eleanor, too, if they stayed on."

"Oh, Christ," Caroline said. He had never heard her say Christ before. "And Giuseppe wouldn't leave?"

"The last Eleanor knew he was sitting up at night in the dark with a shotgun in his lap."

Caroline put her hand to her mouth and began to bite at a nail. She hadn't done that since they had broken her of the habit when she was seven. "She's right to go back," Caroline said. "Her place is with her husband. She shouldn't ever have left."

"How will you feel if something happens to your sister?" He tried to keep his voice from sounding harsh.

"I'll feel terrible," Caroline said. "But I'll still think she was right to go back. Daddy . . ." She reached out and touched his hand. "This is an unlucky house. We ought to get away from it. Right away. Before it's too late. Look what's happened here—you nearly got drowned and you nearly died. I got hurt in the car accident with George . . ."

"Honey," Strand said, "you're lying. It wasn't any accident. He hit you and broke your nose. You were lucky you weren't raped."

"How do you know all this?"

"I have my secrets, too. Like everybody else, honey. Actually, you didn't fool the doctor."

"I had to tell him. I asked him not to tell you. I was afraid of what you'd do."

"The doctor told Mr. Hazen. Mr. Hazen beat your handsome young friend to a pulp."

"He deserved it. He said I was a tease. Only what he said was worse. These days, you go out once with a boy, if you don't put out, they think they can call you anything they want. Daddy . . ." She appealed to him. "Nobody teaches you the rules."

"Well, you know them now."

"I sure do. Does Mummy know, too?"

"No. But she will. Because I'll tell her."

"All right." She sounded hostile. "But tell me something. When you started going out with her, what did *you* do?"

Strand laughed. "Fair question, honey," he said. "I tried."

"What did she do?"

"She said stop. And I stopped."

"Times've changed," Caroline said sadly. "Nowadays

boys like George with their cars and fancy clubs and rich
fathers think they have the droit du seigneur or something.
A sandwich, a drink, a movie and then if you don't open
your legs you're a peasant. If I'd had my tennis racquet
with me, Mr. Hazen wouldn't've had to beat him up. At least
Professor Swanson *begged*. Daddy, you don't know how
hard it is to know what to do. I know you didn't like that
boy. Why didn't you say something?"

"There're things that one generation learns that another
generation never dreams of," Strand said. "All charts get
quickly outdated. Consider yourself lucky. You learned
your lesson and it only cost you a broken nose. Be more
careful with Romero. His blood is a lot hotter than your
friend George's."

"Daddy," Caroline said levelly, "you disappoint me.
You're a racist."

"On that happy judgment I must leave you." Strand
stood up. "I have to go have a word with your mother,"
he said. He left Caroline holding back tears, pouring herself a second cup of black coffee.

Leslie was sitting in a robe at the window seat, staring
out at the ocean, when Strand came into the room. He
went over and kissed the top of her head gently. She
looked up and smiled. "I guess you're feeling better," she
said.

"Much better," he said. He sat down beside her and
took her hand. "I just had breakfast with Caroline. She
told me about Eleanor."

Leslie nodded. "I did everything I could to stop her. I
asked her to talk to you. She wouldn't."

"I know. Caroline knew that much. Did Eleanor speak
to Giuseppe?"

Leslie shook her head. "She said she didn't want to
argue with him, either. What're we going to do, Allen?"

"I know what I'm going to do. I'm going to call Giuseppe." He went over to the telephone next to the bed.
There was a small console with buttons on it to call other
rooms in the house and outside lines. He pressed an out-
side-line button and dialed Giuseppe's number. By now he

had memorized it. When Giuseppe said "Hello," Strand spoke quickly. "Giuseppe," he said quickly, "this is important. Don't hang up until you hear what I have to say. Eleanor's on her way back to Georgia."

There was silence on the other end for a moment. Then Giuseppe said, "That's good news." His voice was toneless, exhausted.

"Has anything happened there?"

"Not yet."

"Giuseppe," Strand said, "I want you to tell her that she can't stay, she's got to turn around and come right back."

"You want," Giuseppe said. "What's that got to do with it?"

"Listen, Giuseppe, she got her job back, she's due to start on January second, she's been promoted, she has a big career ahead of her in a job she likes, in a city she loves. You can't let her throw it all away. Giuseppe, I can't let you kill my daughter."

"That's not how I think of her, Allen," Giuseppe said. "I think of her as my wife. It's about time she realized that. And the wife's place is at the husband's side. It's an old Italian custom. Maybe you've forgotten that I'm Italian."

"Being Italian doesn't mean that you have to be a martyr. And for what? A miserable little country newspaper that even Eleanor says a parcel of high school kids could do a better job on than you two."

"I'm sorry that she thinks we're so inept," Giuseppe said. "But that doesn't change anything. When I married her I didn't promise I was going to win the Pulitzer prize for journalism. All I did was promise to love and cherish her, forsaking all others until death did us part. I'm happy to see that she remembers she signed the same contract."

"You're acting like a maniac," Strand said.

"I'm afraid I have to hang up now, Mr. Strand," Giuseppe said politely. "I have to clean up the house and get some flowers and some stuff for dinner and a bottle of wine to celebrate the reunion. Thanks for letting me know she's on her way home."

"Giuseppe . . ." Strand said helplessly, but Giuseppe had already hung up.

Leslie was still sitting in the window seat, staring once more out at the ocean, her face emotionless. "Did you know there was a chance she was going back?" she asked.

"Yes. She told me she was going to try to forget him. If she couldn't, she said, she would go back. She didn't try hard enough, I guess."

"Sex," Leslie said tonelessly. "I suppose she'd call it passion. Love. What damage those big words can do. I did everything I could to try to stop her. I asked her how she could go off like that knowing that every time the telephone rang from now on we'd be terrified it would be a message that she was dead."

"What did she say to that?"

"That she knew the feeling—she'd had it ever since she left Georgia. That we'd have to learn to live with it. I tried to keep it from Caroline, but I'm sure she guessed. How much does she know?"

"Just about everything. I felt I had to tell her. There've been too many secrets up to now."

"It's natural to try to protect the young . . ."

"And the old," Strand said. "Christmas, before I got lost in the fog, I had a talk with Caroline. She said there was a conspiracy in the family to protect me, too, keep things from me. You were in it, too, she said."

"So I was," Leslie said calmly.

"She intimated that there were things you hid from me."

"What things?"

"That you put Caroline on the pill on her sixteenth birthday."

Surprisingly, Leslie laughed. "How dreadful," she said. "In this day and age."

"But you didn't tell me."

"I guess I didn't think you were in this day and age," Leslie said. "Are you so anxious to join your contemporaries, dear?"

"Yes."

"Let me see . . ." Leslie squinted, as though searching

the distance for further revelations. "What other sins have I committed that I've hidden from you to keep you happy in your illusions? Oh, yes. Of course. I arranged for Eleanor to have an abortion when she was seventeen. Would you like the details?"

"Not really."

"Wise old husband and father," Leslie said. "I also knew that she had a lover twice her age, a married man with three children, when she was in college. And she didn't work to save the money for that car she drove in. He gave it to her. Transportation, too, can be a sin, can't it? And while we're at it, I conspired with our dear Jimmy to hide it from you that he was stoned out of his mind on marijuana almost every night and rather than have him leave our apartment once and for all I let him keep the stuff under my brassieres in my bureau. Would you have been happier if I had let him wander the streets?"

"No, I wouldn't."

"More news from the front," Leslie said. "Russell called yesterday with some happy information. He asked me not to tell you. But you'll probably hear soon enough and it's better if you find out from me than if you read it in the papers. If he can't shut her up somehow—and soon—his wife is going to name me, among quite a few other ladies, as a corespondent in her action for divorce."

"That bitch."

"She says she has proof. Conroy swears he saw me go into Russell's apartment one day when I was in New York for my weekly lessons. He says I stayed two hours."

"Russell said he'd seen you. I wondered why you didn't tell me." Strand spoke calmly, waiting for the explanation.

"They're both right. I went to his apartment and Russell did see me and the lunch took two hours. The reason I went was that I was worried about you. I don't think you can stand another year of living in the same house with all those boys and I asked Russell if he could persuade Babcock to let us live off the campus by ourselves. I didn't say anything about it because I didn't want you to think I was fighting your battles for you. Do you think I'm lying?"

"You're not in the habit of lying."

"Thank you," Leslie said. "But Conroy wasn't wrong by much. It was the first time I'd been alone with Russell and suddenly I remembered certain dreams I'd had about him and I realized that I thought about him a great deal of the time and that I wanted him." She spoke flatly, as though going through a speech she had memorized. "And I'm still enough of a woman to know when a man wants me. And I knew Russell wanted me. But he didn't say anything and neither did I and we ate our lunch and he said he'd talk to Babcock and I went back across town for my three o'clock lesson. Are you disgusted with me?"

"Of course not," Strand said gently. "If you must know, I've come closer than that. Considerably closer. If a certain lady had been at home when I telephoned her from Grand Central Station . . ." He left the sentence unfinished.

"Secret sinners all," Leslie said. "It's about time we unburdened ourselves. Our imperfections are the bonds that hold us together. We might as well recognize them. While we're at it," Leslie said, intoning, rocking gently back and forth, like a child crooning to itself, with the oceanic sunlight streaming through the window making her long blond hair glitter, "did you know about Caroline's biology teacher?"

"I got a letter from the biology teacher's wife."

"I heard from a more accurate source. Caroline. She told me she was crazy about him but he was so awful in bed she dropped him. Girl talk. The sexes mingle, but they're short on communication. Do you love Caroline— or me—or Eleanor—any the less for all this?"

"No," he said. "Maybe I'll love you in a different way. But no less."

"While on the subject of sex," Leslie went on, "there's Nellie Solomon. Did you know she's having an affair with Jimmy?"

"Who told you?" For the first time since he had come into the room Strand was shocked.

"She did."

"I had lunch with Solomon. He didn't say anything about it."

"For a very good reason," Leslie said. "He doesn't know. Yet. But he will soon. She's going to follow Jimmy to California. They're going to get married. That's why she told me the whole story. I guess she wanted my blessing. If she did I'm afraid she's in for a disappointment."

"When did she tell you all this?"

"When I was staying with Linda, right before we left for Paris. I tried to get hold of Jimmy, but he wasn't in town."

"What about that dreadful Dyer woman?"

"Oh, you know about her, too?" Leslie wrinkled her nose in distaste.

"I met her."

"Jimmy seems to be able to handle them both." Leslie smiled ironically. "Do you think we ought to be proud?"

"I think he's acting disgracefully all around."

"He is. And in the long run he'll suffer for it. But in a case like this, a young boy and a woman maybe fifteen years older than he, you have to put most of the blame on her."

"She's not a member of my family."

"She will be. Unless they come to their senses before it's too late. Oh, dearest, dearest Allen, please don't take it so hard. They're grown-up people, our children, and they have to lead their own lives."

"They're doing it damn badly."

"Forget them for a few years. Let's concentrate on leading our own lives—well." She stood up and put her arms around him and kissed him. "As long as I know you're all right, I can be happy, no matter what else happens. If we make their lives miserable with our disapproval, we'll be miserable too and they'll fly from us. Permanently. Let's be gentle with them. And most of all, let's be gentle with ourselves. Let's hold our peace and wait for them to come back. As Eleanor said, we'll have to learn to live with it. Whatever *it* is. Now I think the confessional box is closed for the day and it's time for breakfast. Will you join me in a second cup of coffee?"

He kissed her, then followed her downstairs, a wiser

although not necessarily a happier man than he had been a few minutes before when he had climbed the same stairs.

It was snowing the next morning. Strand was sitting in the living room looking out over the dunes as the snow drifted down, powdering the spikes of grass, drifting into the gray sea. It was nearly noon and he was alone. Leslie had gone into the village with Mr. Ketley in the pickup truck to do some shopping. Caroline had come down late for her black coffee and had gone back to her room saying that she had some letters to write. There was a slight hum of machinery off in the servants' wing which meant that Mrs. Ketley was working there. Strand had a book in his hands but he allowed himself to be lulled by the slow rhythm of the falling snow outside the window. The front doorbell rang and he knew Mrs. Ketley couldn't hear it over the noise in the laundry room, so he heaved himself to his feet and went to the door. He opened it and Romero was standing there. A taxi from the village stood in the driveway, its motor going.

Romero was dressed in a bright green oversized parka, faded jeans and a red wool ski cap and pointed scuffed boots. He had started to grow a moustache, a thin black line over his lip that made him look like a child made up for Halloween. At Dunberry he had always dressed carefully in his Brooks Brothers clothes.

"Romero," Strand said, "what are you doing here?" He knew there was no welcome in his voice.

"I told Caroline I would come," Romero said, unsmiling. "Is she here?"

"She's upstairs. I'll call her. Come in." Strand held the door open.

"Will you tell her I'm waiting for her?"

"Come in and get warm."

"I'm warm enough. I'd rather not come in. I'll wait here."

"I'd rather you didn't see her, Romero," Strand said.

"She invited me."

"I still would prefer that you didn't see her."

Romero put his head back and shouted, loudly, "Caroline! Caroline!"

Strand closed the door. He heard Romero still shouting over and over again, "Caroline!" Strand went slowly up the stairs and knocked on Caroline's door. It opened immediately. Caroline had her coat on and a scarf tied around her head.

"Please, Caroline," Strand said, "stay where you are."

"I'm sorry, Daddy." Caroline brushed past him and ran swiftly down the stairs. From an upstairs window in the hallway Strand looked down. Romero was holding the door of the taxi open and Caroline was getting in. Romero followed her. The door slammed shut and the taxi drove off, making wet tire marks in the new snow.

Strand went downstairs and sat down again in front of the window that gave onto the dunes and the sea and watched the snow falling from the gray skies into the gray Atlantic. He remembered what Caroline had said over breakfast the day before. "This is an unlucky house. We ought to get away before it's too late."

When Leslie got back he told her about Romero. Her face was pale and strained. She was having her period, always a painful time for her. "Did she take a bag with her?" Leslie asked.

"No."

"What time will she be back?"

"She didn't say."

"Do you know where they've gone?"

"No."

"It's not much of a day for sightseeing," she said. "I'm sorry, Allen, do you mind having lunch by yourself? I've got to go up and lie down."

"Is there anything I can do for you?"

"Shoot Romero. Forgive me."

He watched her slowly mount the stairs, gripping the banister.

It was already dark, although it was just past four o'clock, when he heard the car drive up. He went to the door and threw it open. The snow was coming down more thickly than ever. He saw the taxi door swing open and Romero get out. Then Caroline jumped out and ran through the snow toward the door. She pushed past Strand without saying anything, her head bent so that he couldn't see her face, and ran up the stairs. Romero stood near the taxi looking at Strand. He started to get back into the cab, then stopped, slowly closed the door and came toward Strand.

"I delivered her safely, Mr. Strand," he said. "In case you were worried." His tone was polite, but his dark eyes were sardonic under the bright red wool ski cap.

"I wasn't worried."

"You should have been," Romero said. "She wanted to go back to Waterbury with me. Tonight. I hope you're happy that I said no."

"I'm very happy."

"I don't take charity from people like you," Romero said. "Any kind of charity. And I don't hire myself out to be a stud to flighty little rich white girls."

Strand laughed mirthlessly. "Rich," he said. "There's a description of the Strand family."

"From where I stand," Romero said, "that's exactly the word. I took one look at this house this morning and I decided I wouldn't touch anybody who even spent one night of her life in a house like this. You've got a problem on your hands with that little girl of yours, but it ain't my problem. I won't bother you anymore. If you ever hear of me again it will be because my name's in the papers." He started to turn away.

"Romero," Strand said, "you're a lost soul."

"I was born a lost soul," Romero said, stopping. "At least I didn't go out and lose mine on purpose. I'll tell you the truth, Mr. Strand—I like you. Only we got nothing to say to each other that makes any sense anymore. Not one word. You better go in now. I wouldn't want you to stand out here and catch a cold on my account, Professor." He wheeled and jumped into the cab.

Strand watched as the lights of the cab disappeared in the flurries of snow. Then he went in and closed the door behind him, shivering a little and grateful for the warmth of the house. He thought of going up and knocking on Caroline's door, but decided against it. This was a night, he was sure, that his daughter would want to be alone.

"Is there anything more you'll be wanting tonight, Mr. Strand?" Mr. Ketley was saying.

"No, thank you." He was sitting alone in the living room. He had had an early dinner by himself. Before dinner he had gone upstairs to see how Leslie was. She had taken some pills and was drowsing and didn't want to move. She had asked if Caroline was in yet and then didn't ask any more questions when Strand had said that Caroline had come in shortly after four o'clock. He had tried Caroline's door, but it was locked. When he knocked Caroline had called, "Please leave me alone, Daddy."

He wished he was someplace else. A wave of homesickness overtook him. Not for Dunberry, never for Dunberry. For the apartment in New York, with Leslie's paintings on the walls, the sound of Leslie's piano, Jimmy's guitar, Eleanor's bright voice as she talked to one of her beaux over the telephone, Caroline murmuring as she tried to memorize a speech from *A Winter's Tale* for an English course the next day. He missed sitting in the kitchen watching Leslie prepare a meal, missed the quiet dinners on the kitchen table when the children were out, missed the Friday nights when they were all together, missed Alexander Curtis, in his old combat jacket, glaring at the city from his post next to the front door of the building, missed walking down to Lincoln Center, missed Central Park. What changes a year, not even a year, had made, what uprootings, blows, sad discoveries, defections.

The rumble of the ocean oppressed him, the waves rolling in implacably, eroding beaches, undermining foundations, menacing, changing the contours of the land with each new season. Old harbors silted over, once thriving seaports lay deserted, the cries of gulls over the shifting waters plaintive, melancholy, complaining harshly of hunger and flight and the wreckage of time.

An unlucky house. Tomorrow he would tell Leslie and

Caroline to pack, the holiday which had been no holiday was over, it was time to leave.

He tried to read, but the words on the page made no sense to him. He went into the library and tried to choose another book, but none of the titles on the shelves appealed to him. He sat down in front of the television set and turned it on. He pushed button after button at random. As the screen brightened he saw Russell Hazen's image on the tube and heard a voice saying, "We regret that Senator Blackstone, who was to be on this panel tonight, was unable to leave Washington. We have been fortunate in finding Mr. Russell Hazen, the distinguished lawyer, well known for his expertise on tonight's subject, international law, who has graciously agreed to take the senator's place on our program."

Hazen, impeccably dressed and imperially grave, bowed his head slightly in the direction of the camera. Then the camera switched to a full shot of the table, with three other middle-aged, professorial-looking men and the gray-haired moderator seated in a circle.

Strand wondered if Hazen's story about having to go to New York to see his wife had been a lie and if the call he had answered in the library had actually been from the broadcasting studio. Maybe he hadn't wanted to let Strand know that he was abandoning his guests for what Strand might think was a frivolous reason.

Strand listened without interest as the other three participants gave their intelligent, well modulated, reasonable views on foreign affairs and international law. There was nothing in what they said that Strand hadn't heard a hundred times before. If he hadn't been waiting to hear what Hazen was going to say he would have gone back into the living room and tried his book again.

But Hazen's first words made him listen very carefully. "Gentlemen," Hazen said, his voice strong and confident, "I'm afraid we're confusing two entirely separate things —foreign affairs and international law. True, whether we like it or not, we do have foreign affairs. But international law has become a fiction. We have international piracy, international assassination, international terrorism, international bribery and bartering, international drama, international anarchy. Our *national* law perhaps is not quite fiction, but the most generous description of it that we can accept is that it is at best semi-fiction. With our legal codes, under our adversary system, in any important matter, he who can afford to hire the most expensive counsel is the one who walks out of the courtroom with the decision. Of course, there are occasional exceptions which only go to prove the rule.

"When I first went into the practice of law I believed that at least generally, justice was served. Unhappily, after many years of service, I can no longer cling to this belief . . ."

Good Lord, Strand thought, what does he think he's doing?

"The corruption of the judiciary, the regional and racial prejudices of the men who sit on the bench have too often been exposed on the front pages of our newspapers to warrant further comment here; the buying of posts through political contributions is a time-honored custom; the suborning of testimony, the coaching of witnesses, the concealment of evidence has even reached into the highest office in the land; the venality of the police has entered our folklore and legal evasion by men in my own profession who have sworn to act as officers of the law is taught in all our universities."

The moderator of the program, who had been shifting uncomfortably in his chair, tried to break in. "Mr. Hazen . . ." he said, "I don't think that . . ."

Hazen stopped him with a magisterial wave of the hand and went on. "To get back to the international conception of law . . . on certain small matters, like fishing rights and overflights by airlines, agreements can be reached and observed. But on crucial concerns, such as human rights, the inviolability of the frontiers of sovereign states, the safeguarding or destruction of nations, we have progressed no farther than in the period of warring and nomadic tribes. We have instituted theft and calumny in the United Nations, where on the territory of the United States, in a forum supported in great part by our own taxes, a cabal

of all but a few of our so-called and infinitely fickle
friends daily mocks and insults us and with impunity does
all it can to damage us. I am a so-called expert on international law, but I tell you, gentlemen, there is no such
thing and the sooner we realize that and remove ourselves
from that parliament of enemies on the bank of the East
River, the healthier it will be for us in years to come.
Thank you for listening to me and forgive me for not
being able to stay for the end of this interesting discussion. I have an appointment elsewhere."

Hazen nodded, almost genially, to the other men at the
table, who were sitting there woodenly, and stood up and
left.

Strand reached over and turned the set off. He sat,
staring at the blank screen, feeling dazed, as though he
had just witnessed a grotesque accident.

Then he stood up and went over to the little desk in
front of the window. He had not brought along the copy
book in which he made the occasional entries in his jour-
nal and so he took some notepaper out of the drawer and
began to write.

*I am alone downstairs in the East Hampton house and
I have just seen a man destroy himself on television. The
man is Russell Hazen. In what can only have been a vale-
dictory speech, he was saying good-bye to his career. What
his reasons were I do not know, but he has denounced
himself, his profession, the rules we all live by and which
have enriched him and brought him honor. I can only
consider it an aberration, but an aberration for which he
will not be forgiven. Since I met him I knew there was a
dark side to his character, an all-pervading cynicism about
men's motives and behavior, a melancholy streak that was
present even in his lightest moments, but I never suspected
that he was tormented enough by it to allow himself to be
overwhelmed by it. Where he will go from here it is impossible to foresee . . .*

Suddenly he felt terribly tired and even the effort of
writing was too much for him. He put his arm across the

sheet of paper and leaned over, his head resting on his wrist, and fell instantly asleep.

He awoke with a start. He had no idea of how long he had slept. There was the sound of a key in a lock and a door opening, then closing. He stood up and went into the living room just as Hazen came in.

Strand stared at him wordlessly as Hazen smiled at him and stamped his feet vigorously to shake the snow off his shoes. He looked the same as always, calm, robust. The expression on Strand's face made Hazen scowl.

"You look peculiar, Allen," he said. "Is anything wrong?"

"I saw the television program."

"Oh, that," Hazen said lightly. "I thought those dreary men needed a little excitement. I thoroughly enjoyed myself. And I got a few things off my chest that I've been thinking for a long time."

"Do you know what you've done to yourself tonight, Russell?"

"Don't worry about me. Nobody takes television seriously, anyway. Let's not talk about it, please. The whole thing bores me." He came over to Strand and put an arm around him and gave him a brief hug. "I was hoping you'd still be up. I wanted to talk to someone who was not a lawyer." He took off his coat and threw it, with his hat, over a chair. "What a miserable night. The drive out in this snow was grim."

Strand shook his head as if to clear it. He felt confused, uncertain of himself. If Hazen was so debonair about the evening, perhaps he had overreacted to the television program. He watched television so rarely that it was possible he misjudged its capacity to make or break a man. Maybe, he thought, he had been wrong in despairing for his friend. If Hazen had no fears of the consequences of his speech, he wouldn't disturb him by voicing his own. "You drove yourself?" he asked.

Hazen nodded. "I let the chauffeur go for the night. His fiancée came into town and I did my share for young love. Where're the ladies?"

"They're up in their rooms. They're making an early night of it."

Hazen looked at him keenly. "They're all right, aren't they?"

"Fine," Strand said.

"Leslie told me about Eleanor's going back to Georgia. That's quite a mess down there, isn't it?"

"Ugly," Strand said. "Gianelli's acting like a fool."

"He's got guts. I admire that."

"I admire it a little less than you do," Strand said dryly.

"I called the police chief down there and told him he had to put a man on to guard their house. I made it plain to him that if anything happened to those kids I'd have his hide."

"I hope it helps."

"It better," Hazen said grimly. "Now, what I need is a drink. How about you?"

"I'll join you." Strand went over to the bar and watched while Hazen poured them two large Scotch and sodas. They carried their drinks back to the fireplace and sat facing each other in the big leather wing-back chairs. Hazen took a long gulp of his drink and sighed contentedly. "Man, I needed this," he said.

"The last time we had a drink like this," Strand said, "the telephone rang and you were gone like a streak. I hope you'll at least be able to finish your drink before you have to go again."

Hazen laughed, a pleasant low rumble. "I'm not going to answer the telephone for a week. I don't care who's calling, the Pope, the President of the United States, any one of a dozen assorted lawyers, they'll have to struggle along without me."

"I'm glad to hear that. How're things going?"

"So-so." Hazen stared into his glass. "Nobody's declared war—yet."

"Leslie told me about your wife's threatening to name her as corespondent."

"She's threatening every woman I've said hello to for the last thirty years. She's digging up graves from Boston to Marseilles. I felt I had to tell Leslie that there was a possibility it would leak. But I told her I didn't want you to know about it."

"We're on a new policy here," Strand said. "Full disclosure."

"A dangerous experiment." Hazen peered intently at him. "You don't believe for one instant . . . ?"

"Not for one instant," Strand said. Looking at the powerful, fleshily handsome man in his immaculate clothing Strand could understand why any woman, even his wife, would be attracted to him. Nixon's Secretary of State Kissinger, in one of his less diplomatic messages, had said when asked about his success with women that power was an aphrodisiac. By any standards Hazen was powerful and certainly by comparison with an ailing, obscure, disabused schoolteacher he must be overwhelming. Love finally could withstand only so much temptation. He wondered just what Hazen had said or done or looked that had made Leslie understand that Hazen had wanted her. Better not to know, he thought.

"I've kept my wife at bay, at least for the moment. The sticking point is this house," Hazen said. "I've agreed to let her strip me of just about everything else, but I have other plans for the house. We'll see." Hazen drank thirstily, emptying his glass. He got up and went to the bar and poured himself a second drink. "Oh, by the way," he said as he came back, "our man in Paris happened to call and I spoke to him about you. He says he thinks it can be easily arranged for next September, when the new school term starts. They have a big turnover in the faculty, people drifting in and out, like the wandering teachers of the Middle Ages. He'll be getting in touch with you. Do you think you can stand Dunberry for another five months?"

"I can. I'm not sure Leslie can."

"Ummm." Hazen frowned. "I suppose she could go alone. It would just be a few months."

"That's a possibility. Don't worry about it. We'll work something out."

"Allen, there's only one thing wrong, as far as I'm concerned, with you and Leslie," Hazen said. His tone was earnest and Strand feared what he was going to say.

"What's that?" he asked.

"When I look at you two, it makes me realize what I've missed in my life." Hazen spoke reflectively, sorrowfully. "The love, spoken, unspoken, intimated, that passes between you. The dependence upon each other, the unwavering support of one for the other. I've known many women in my life and I've enjoyed most of them and maybe they've enjoyed me. I've had money, success, a kind of fame, even that very rare thing—occasional gratitude. But I've never had anything like that. It's like a big hole in me that the wind goes howling through—endlessly. If you're lucky, you'll both die the same minute. Oh, hell . . ." He rattled the ice in his glass angrily. "What's come over me tonight? Talking about dying. It's the weather. Snow on a seacoast. Maybe people are wise to close down their houses, put the shutters up, when the leaves begin to turn." He finished his drink, put his glass down deliberately, with a gesture of finality. "I'm tired." He ran his big hand over his eyes, stood up. "I'm going to treat myself to a long, long sleep. Don't bother to put out the lights. I don't want the house to be dark tonight." He looked around him. "This room could stand a new coat of paint. A lighter color. Well, good night, friend. Sleep well."

"Good night, Russell. You, too." Strand watched him walk heavily out of the room. He stumbled a little as he crossed the threshold and Strand thought, He must have had a lot to drink in New York before he started out, it's lucky a cop didn't stop him on the road or he'd have spent the night in jail instead of in his big warm bed. Then he climbed the stairs to the room where Leslie was sleeping, breathing gently, her bright hair spread out on the pillow, shining in the light of the bedside lamp. He undressed silently, put out the lamp and slipped into bed beside his wife.

Sometime during the night he awoke because in his sleep there had been a noise of an automobile engine starting up, then dwindling in the distance. He wasn't sure whether he had heard it or if he had been dreaming. He turned over, put his arm around his wife's bare shoulders, heard her sigh contentedly. Then he slept.

He awoke early, just as the dawn started to show through the windows. It was still snowing. Leslie slept on. He got out of bed, dressed quickly and started out of the room. He stopped at the door. An envelope was lying on the floor, half under the door. He opened the door silently, picked up the envelope. It was too dark in the hallway to read something that was scrawled on the envelope. He closed the door softly and went downstairs quickly to the living room where the lights still burned and the last ashes were glowing on the hearth. The envelope was a long, fat one and on it was writen one word—Allen. He tore it open. *Dear Allen,* he read in Hazen's bold, steady script.

By the time you read this I will be dead. I came here last night to say good-bye to you and wish you happiness. Everything has piled up on me—my wife, the investigation in Washington, Conroy threatening me with blackmail. I've been subpoenaed to appear before the Committee on January second. I can't appear without committing perjury or implicating, criminally, old friends and associates of mine. One way or another I would have no shred of reputation left at the end of it. I've figured this out carefully and I am taking the only possible way out. When my will is read it will be discovered that I have left the beach house to Caroline. For good and sufficient reason. To pay for its upkeep, she can sell off several acres of the property. There's plenty of it—forty acres—and it's very valuable. All my liquid assets I've left to my wife, with the proviso that if she contests any clause in the will she will be completely cut off. My daughters have substantial trust funds my father set up for them when they were born and there's nothing they can do to break the will. I'm a good lawyer and the will is ironclad. All my pictures have long since been donated to museums with the understanding that they were to remain in my possession during my lifetime. The tax laws make death something of a morbid game, a game at which I was expert. As I look back at it now I knew how to play too many games— legal, corporate, legislative, philanthropic—the sleazy, profitable American gamut. One of the things that endeared you and Leslie to me most was that you were not entrants in the competition. It wasn't that you were above it all. It was as though you didn't realize its existence. It undoubtedly made you a worse historian, but a better man.

Thoughtlessly and without malice, I involved you and your family in my world. Lonely and bereft of family myself, I believed I could insert myself into a happy family. What I thought was generosity turned out to be disaster. Jimmy learned all too quickly how to succeed. Caroline is on the competitive American merry-go-round, whether she likes it or not. Eleanor and her husband have learned failure and live in fear. I hate to say this, dear Allen, but Leslie's new career can only push you further apart and uproot you once again. Opportunity is a two-edged weapon. It might have turned out well, but it didn't. The same might be said in the case of Romero.

The Renoir drawing in your bedroom was bought after I made the arrangement with the government, and I am happy to be able to leave it to you in the will which is now in my partner's safe.

Strand stopped reading for a moment. The enormity of the document in his hand left him numb and the fact that it had been written so carefully, so neatly, by a man preparing to take his life by his own hand made him marvel at the almost inhuman rigor of his friend's self-control. Along with reading law, Strand thought, Hazen must have read Plato on the death of Socrates. "Crito, I owe a cock to Asclepius: will you remember to pay the debt?" A cock for Asclepius. A Renoir for Strand. An antique grace in dying. Famous last words.

Dry-eyed, Strand continued reading.

In the smaller envelope, which is enclosed with this letter, there is ten thousand dollars in five hundred dollar bills to help make the Paris adventure more pleasant for you and Leslie. I suggest you do not mention this to anyone.

You and your family have made this last year of my life an important one for me and I have learned too late what it should have taught me.

Since these will be my last words and we are now, as you said, on a course of full disclosure, I will make one more confession. It sounds absurd for a man my age to say this, but I fell in love with Leslie the very first time I saw her. If ever a woman could make me happy it was she. When it looked as though you were going to die in the hospital in Southampton, I wished for your death. Not consciously or willfully, but for a fraction of a second the thought was there. Then I would not be only the friend of a family I loved, but *of* the family, not merely the guest at the table, but at its head. The fact that I was happy that you survived could never make me forget that dark and evil moment.

Please burn this letter as soon as you have read it and don't let anyone but Leslie know that it was written. I have written another note, which I will leave in the car, explaining merely that I have decided to commit suicide. In it I've written that I am on the verge of a nervous breakdown and fear for my sanity. I have a gun in my pocket and it will be quickly over. They will find me at the end of some lane beside the car.

Don't grieve for me. I don't deserve your grief.

I embrace you all,
Russell

PART FOUR

1

It is a few days before Thanksgiving again, and the first snow is whirling in the darkness outside my window, flurries of white specks flickering through the beams thrown by the lamp on my desk. I am in Dunberry, but not in the apartment in the Malson Residence. I am alone, since Leslie is in Paris.

I did not permit either Leslie or Caroline to accompany me to the funeral of Russell Hazen. There would be no telling what sort of scene Hazen's widow might have made and neither my wife nor my daughter were in any condition to confront that mad and vengeful woman at such a moment. I sat in one of the back pews and she did not see me. Beside her sat two tall young women whom I took to be Hazen's daughters. They were all three dressed elegantly in black and behaved with sorrowful decorum.

I got a glimpse of the daughters' faces as they passed up the aisle at the end of the service. They were not unbeautiful, but they were at the same time hard and self-indulgent and suspicious. Of course, when we finally see people about whom we have previously formed opinions, we are likely to see what we have imagined, rather than what is actually there. Be that as it may, they were two women I would prefer to avoid.

Both the minister in his eulogy and the Times in its obituary spoke of Hazen's great civic contributions, his probity and his many useful services to the City of New York. I could imagine Hazen's bitter laughter if he had been alive to hear and read the tributes to his memory.

Hazen's death and especially the manner of it left Leslie prostrate. For days after it, she would suddenly burst into tears. It was as though all the complex emotions she had kept for the most part under control for my sake and the sake of her children at last had been too much for her and had burst through some psychic dam. It was impossible to comfort her. The depression that had assailed her before our Thanksgiving trip to the Hamptons last year was like a mere passing shadow compared to what she was going through now. She gave up all pretense of teaching classes, had me cancel all lessons in the city, didn't touch the piano or a paintbrush and sat all day, stone-faced when she wasn't in tears, in the repainted kitchen of our apartment in the Residence. She blamed herself and me for what had happened. Somehow, she felt, if we had been the friends that we believed we were, we should have sensed what Hazen was going through and where it was leading and stopped him. There was nothing I could say to convince her otherwise.

When Linda suggested to me that it was dangerous for her to continue in her mourning and that perhaps Paris and work would heal her, I agreed. Leslie listened like an automaton as both Linda and I urged her to take off immediately for France. Finally she said, "Anything is better than this."

So, ten days after Hazen's body, partially covered with drifting snow, had been found on a sandy road leading to the ocean, I put Leslie on the plane to Paris. We didn't speak of how long she might stay or when she would return.

Before leaving, she burned all her old paintings.

Babcock, that saintly man, tactfully suggested that since I was a bachelor, at least for the time being, it might be better for me not to have the responsibility of running a house with nine boys by myself. When the term was over, I moved. As there was no longer any need for me to be on the campus, I rented a small furnished apartment in town over the shop that sells tobacco and newspapers. The smell drifting up the stairs is comforting. The Renoir drawing looks incongruously voluptuous hanging over the cracked old leather couch on which I take my naps. I commute to the school by bicycle, which has improved my *health. I cook my own meals and eat them in peace. I sometimes dine with the Schillers, where Mr. Schiller allows his wife to do the cooking. Mrs. Schiller serves, as her speciality, potato pancakes.*

I spent the summer in France with Leslie. A small portion of the ten thousand dollars took care of the airfare. The summer was not a great success. Leslie had developed quite a large circle of friends, mostly artists, and with her ear for music had become quite fluent in French, the language in which almost all the conversations were carried on, usually about her work and the work of others. My schoolboy French was of little value to me and while everyone, and of course especially Leslie, tried to include me in the give and take of opinions, it was impossible for me not to feel like a rather backward intruder.

Although after her initial surprising success Leslie has not had any of her paintings exhibited or sold, she goes to the studio of the artist she is studying with three mornings a week. He is a small, lively, round old man named Leblanc who swears Leslie will be famous one day. Her paintings have a curious overcast of melancholy, as though there were touches of twilight purple hidden in her palette, even in her noonday pictures. She works with single-minded devotion to her art, and when she is not at her easel, she is tirelessly making the rounds of the galleries and museums. After a few days in the city, I was surfeited and spent most of my time sitting at café tables reading.

We lived in a rather bare one-room studio on the Left Bank, where the atmosphere was pervaded by the smell of paint and turpentine, an odor that gives continual pleasure to Leslie but which finally brought on an allergy in me which made me sniffle and blow my nose constantly. Leslie, who at other times was quick to notice my slightest indisposition, never even remarked that I was red-eyed almost all the time and ran through a box of Kleenex every two days.

Her period of sorrow was definitely over and her energy and enthusiasm, like that of an eager and avid young student, made me feel much older than my fifty years.

The people at the American School in Paris did indeed

offer me a job there, but I decided that I did not want to live in a city in which I could not speak the language and where I would be considered an awkward appendage to my wife by her friends. I remembered the words of an author of a story about another American in Paris, "This continent is not for me." I declined, with regrets. The president of the school could hardly hide his relief. I could understand why. The staff of the school were wanderers and all between twenty-two and thirty and my gray hair must have been a sign of decrepitude and disconcerting permanence to a president who could not have been more than thirty-five.

Leslie took my decision calmly. Art, I have discovered, leads inevitably to the same self-absorption as disease. When one is sick one thinks only of one's illness and the cares or aspirations of others are of no importance.

We spent two weeks down south with Linda in her delightful house in Mougins. I sat in the garden and tried to read in the hot sunlight and swatted mosquitoes, as Hazen had predicted. Leslie suggested that I sell the Renoir and with the proceeds buy a small house next to Linda's property. "You don't have to work anymore," she said, "and this is a wonderful place to sit and do nothing."

She was right about that, but I didn't want to sit and do nothing. Idleness, I found, bored me. I am a teacher. That defines who I am. I am a teacher or nothing. Given just one bright and questing child in a class of thirty who argues with me or whose horizons I feel I am widening and I know that I am doing what I was put on earth to do. Romero, exasperating as he was, was just such a boy. When I told Leslie about my sense of belonging in the front of a classroom, she said that was exactly how she felt in front of a blank piece of canvas. I hope for her sake, if not for mine, that her canvases turn out better for her than Romero did for me.

Nothing I could say or do could make Caroline return to Arizona. Instead, she transferred to Hunter College in New York, intent on majoring in child psychology. She refused to use any of the money that came from selling two acres of the land that Hazen had left her in his will, a deal that had been handled, and handled very well, by one of Hazen's partners. She took a part-time job as a waitress to support herself through college and never yet, to my knowledge, has visited the house on the beach that is now hers. Instead, with the help of one of her teachers, she threw open the house last summer as a vacation home for what the newspapers call disadvantaged ghetto children, of all races, up to the age of fifteen, complete with volunteer counselors from various social worker agencies. "Jesus Romero taught me something about children," she told me when I remonstrated with her. "That is, get to them before they become a Romero." Whether the experiment will succeed or not remains to be seen. In another age and if she had been born a Catholic I believe she would have become a nun. Self-sacrifice in the service of a high-minded ideal may be noble, but a father cannot help but feel that it is a petrification of his child's humanity. Naturally, there has been grumbling among the neighbors in East Hampton and there is a rumor on foot that a petition is being circulated for the Town Council's attention to have the house condemned as a public nuisance.

Caroline hired Conroy to oversee the physical management of the house. She has not forgotten the day he swam out to save me from the Atlantic Ocean. From what she tells me he is efficient and dedicated. There has not as yet been any accusation of homosexual attempts on the young boys collected in the house. The poor Ketleys resigned their jobs in the middle of the summer. They said they had not been hired to work in a madhouse.

I must confess that I haven't had the heart to go down to see for myself what was happening in the place where I had a glimpse of an easeful and generous life such as I had never had before and in which I nearly died.

Hollingsbee called me triumphantly on the day set for Romero's trial and told me that the boy had gotten off with a year's probation. But he is in jail as I write this. In a raid on what was suspected to be a hideout of the F.A.L.N., the terrorist organization working for the independence of Puerto Rico, Romero was picked up, along with a store of homemade bombs, machine pistols and revolutionary literature. I remembered his last words to me in the snow outside Hazen's front door—"The next time you see my name it will be in the newspapers." It might be termed a self-fulfilling prophecy.

With Hazen dead, the power of his protection was gone in Georgia and while Eleanor and Gianelli were not bombed in their home, the newspaper plant was burned to the ground and a night watchman perished in the fire. In our day it has become habitual for victims to be picked at random.

The building was adequately insured and with the money Gianelli received from it he bought into a newspaper in a small town on the west coast of Florida where the lure of year-round sunshine has brought a great increase in population and local prosperity. Eleanor writes that they are finally learning how to run a newspaper and they are doing well. She is also pregnant, and I face the prospect of becoming a grandfather. By the time he or she is grown I suppose my grandson or granddaughter will be walking through abandoned and burnt-out cities where automobiles will be strewn around everywhere, without fuel and immobilized on their last voyages. That is, if he or she is lucky and the men over whom we have no control have not yet decided on starting a nuclear war.

Like most people of my generation I feel powerless and regard the future with cynical resignation.

Rollins, I am happy to say, was taken off probation and played last season on the teams and has been given an athletic scholarship to Penn State. He never did make it below the Mason-Dixon Line.

Jimmy has married Mrs. Solomon, née Nellie Ferguson. In Las Vegas. It seems to have become a dreadful habit in our family. I was not invited to the wedding. The company he runs with Joan Dyer has come out with what is called a Golden Record or Golden Disc, which means that it has sold over a million copies. Have not yet heard it.

I look forward to my classes these days. There is an extraordinary boy called Willoughby who is in two of my courses. He is sixteen years old, a Virginian, with courtly Virginia manners, and seems to have critically read every-

thing from Thucydides to Toynbee, with Caesar, Josephus, Carlyle, Prescott, Hegel, Marx, and Freeman along the way, and of course Gibbon. He is as keen and intelligent as Romero, but with a sense of order and proportion that may come from his Virginian inheritance or some lucky twist of genes that permits him to grasp abstract ideas and the sweep of history without effort. I remember what Crowell, Leslie's gag-writer piano pupil, said about Mozart. I am astonished and delighted with the boy's papers and his arguments in class and the maturity and judgment he shows in the walks we take together in the autumn afternoons. When I read what he has written or listen to him recite, I feel once again the ardor I had when I faced my first classes with the almost religious belief that history, with its investigation of science, philosophy, the rise and fall of empires, the arts and the passions of the past, is indeed the queen of disciplines and the great teacher of mankind.

He says he intends to go into politics and I envision him as a senator by the time he is thirty-five. If there are ten such boys scattered through the country perhaps our troubled and magnificent country, built on courage, faith, savagery, looting, greed, compromise and hope, will at the last gasp be saved from catastrophe.

I had a letter from Leslie today. In it, as in every letter, she thanks me for my forbearance in permitting what she calls her middle-aged apprenticeship. She promises to come back for the summer and suggests that I travel with her through the West, which she wants to try to paint. Her letters are full of love and I have no doubt, although she is far away, that she loves me. As for me, I loved her when she was a young girl in the first row of my classroom, when we stood before the altar, when she first played the piano in our home in New York, when she was big with child, when she bound Hazen's wounds and slapped Hazen's wife in the dining room in Tours, when I put her on the plane to France. Whether it was fate or accident that put her in my classroom and threw her into my arms for life, I do not know or care. I know I love her and always will and the reasons are unimportant. We have done

*what we were fated to do or had to do. She says she will
return. We shall see.*

He stopped and reread the page he had just written. He
shook his head, dissatisfied. He kept thinking of Romero.
Romero haunted this place and Strand knew he was not
through with him. "They graze in peace on grass," he remembered. "You hunt on cement." And, "You won't be
here much longer, either."

Remembering, Strand shook his head again. The gall of
the boy. Or was it the wisdom?

He stared at the opened copy book on the desk in front
of him, reflecting the light of the lamp off the page. Then
he started writing again.

*Do I want to end my life here? Do I want to finish as
an animal who grazes in peace on grass? Where is the
place where I am needed, where I fit the task and the task
fits me? Does a boy like Willoughby need me? The answer
must be no. He will blossom as he must and a man like
me can only be flattering himself to feel that the final result would be his accomplishment. I am merely on the
sidelines cheering on a boy who needs no cheers.*

Cement.

*There are as many Romeros on cement as there are
Willoughbys on grass, maybe more. I have failed with one,
but perhaps it has taught me how not to fail with others.
The men and women here are one kind of teacher. I am
another. I did not enter the profession merely to be comfortable and events have led me to forget that. For a time.
For a time. That time is now over. I will not be shamed
by my youngest child. "When you are ready to come
back," the principal of my school said when he visited me
after I got out of the hospital in the Hamptons, "when you
are ready, just give me a call on the telephone. Your place
will be open." I am ready now and I will call in the
morning.*

Call in the morning. I know the matter is not as simple
as that, and he knew it too. It is the sort of thing a visitor
to a hospital says to a friend agonizing on what may be

his deathbed to pretend that all will be well, that recovery is certain and that he will not die and that his colleagues will be waiting for him to regain his place in the world. Well, I did not die. I will call in the morning, but I will not embarrass that good man by believing him. My place will not be open for me. There will be applications to fill out, suspicious boards to question me, public doctors to be satisfied that I am capable of working, pensions to be altered, positions to be considered, openings closed, transfers to be juggled, long, weary months of waiting, the possibility of eventual denial strong.

Still, I will call in the morning. The effort is necessary for my soul.

It is late now. I have to sleep. I must be fresh for Willoughby in the morning.

He put down his pen, closed the exercise book and rose from his chair and switched off the lamp in the cold, nighttime room.